Dan raced for the door, not even feeling his feet. He wrenched the door open and—God, yes. Oh Jesus, yes.

Claire. *Claire.*

"My God," he breathed, hanging on to the door frame. "You're alive."

There she was. Much thinner, very pale, with short-cropped hair and deep purple bruises under her eyes. Looking sad and lost and lonely. But definitely Claire.

In two strides he was with. He pulled her up by her elbows and put his arms around her. At the last minute, he realized she was trembling badly, so he kept his embrace loose, when what he really wanted to do was pull her tightly against him, using all his strength, and never let her go.

It's okay, he mouthed, then bent his head back to Claire's. They stood there, clinging to each other. Claire to keep upright and Dan to make sure she wasn't a mirage and wouldn't disappear from his life again.

"Sensual and absorbing . . . Dangerously compelling."
—Shannon McKenna,
New York Times bestselling author

Shadows AT MIDNIGHT

ELIZABETH JENNINGS

BERKLEY SENSATION, NEW YORK

THE BERKLEY PUBLISHING GROUP
Published by the Penguin Group
Penguin Group (USA) Inc.
375 Hudson Street, New York, New York 10014, USA
Penguin Group (Canada), 90 Eglinton Avenue East, Suite 700, Toronto, Ontario M4P 2Y3, Canada
(a division of Pearson Penguin Canada Inc.)
Penguin Books Ltd., 80 Strand, London WC2R 0RL, England
Penguin Group Ireland, 25 St. Stephen's Green, Dublin 2, Ireland (a division of Penguin Books Ltd.)
Penguin Group (Australia), 250 Camberwell Road, Camberwell, Victoria 3124, Australia
(a division of Pearson Australia Group Pty. Ltd.)
Penguin Books India Pvt. Ltd., 11 Community Centre, Panchsheel Park, New Delhi—110 017, India
Penguin Group (NZ), 67 Apollo Drive, Rosedale, North Shore 0632, New Zealand
(a division of Pearson New Zealand Ltd.)
Penguin Books (South Africa) (Pty.) Ltd., 24 Sturdee Avenue, Rosebank, Johannesburg 2196,
South Africa

Penguin Books Ltd., Registered Offices: 80 Strand, London WC2R 0RL, England

This is a work of fiction. Names, characters, places, and incidents either are the product of the author's imagination or are used fictitiously, and any resemblance to actual persons, living or dead, business establishments, events, or locales is entirely coincidental. The publisher does not have any control over and does not assume any responsibility for author or third-party websites or their content.

SHADOWS AT MIDNIGHT

A Berkley Sensation Book / published by arrangement with the author

PRINTING HISTORY
Berkley Sensation mass-market edition / August 2010

ISBN: 978-0-425-23599-7

BERKLEY® SENSATION
Berkley Sensation Books are published by The Berkley Publishing Group,
a division of Penguin Group (USA) Inc.,
375 Hudson Street, New York, New York 10014.
BERKLEY® SENSATION and the "B" design are trademarks of Penguin Group (USA) Inc.

PRINTED IN THE UNITED STATES OF AMERICA

10 9 8 7 6 5 4 3 2 1

*This book is dedicated to the two men in my life,
my husband, Alfredo, and my son, David.*

ACKNOWLEDGMENTS

I'd like to thank my wonderful editor, Kate Seaver, and my fantastic agent, Ethan Ellenberg, for this great opportunity. Without you, Gunny and Blondie's story would never have been told! And thanks to my beloved friend Ellen Cosgrove for giving me such great insights into Claire's character.

NE

"DO you think we're going to die?" Claire Day asked quietly.

From a distance, there was the distinctive ripping sound of AK-47s opening up, then the loud crump of an RPG. Another. She flinched instinctively. "AK-47s and RPGs," she murmured. "Full blast. Sounds like they're not running out of ammo any time soon."

She should know. She was a spook for the Defense Intelligence Agency.

Gunnery Sergeant Daniel Weston, Detachment Commander of the Marine Security Guard of the US Embassy looked down at the beautiful woman sitting up against the wall of Post One, right next to him. They'd been sitting hip to hip against this wall behind bulletproof glass for almost an hour.

He'd moved heaven and earth to be in the same place as her and now here he was. Except he'd never expected for them to meet in Post One, under siege, in mortal danger.

He couldn't guarantee they weren't going to die. There was a fucking army outside the embassy gates and if they came pouring in . . . But there was one thing he could guarantee. "I won't let them get you."

Claire's lips turned up. "It's a nice thought," she murmured, glancing up at him briefly, then back down at the floor.

It wasn't a nice thought. Dan would go down fighting, but he would save one bullet for Claire. If the rebels caught her and took her to one of their camps, there wouldn't be much left to bury. They were continuously hopped up on ganja weed and palm wine and ferociously, insanely cruel.

He'd kill her himself before he let that happen.

The rebels had starting pouring into Laka right after 1600 hours, like water from a dam that had burst. Everyone was taken utterly by surprise. If there had been any signs at all that the rebels were close to the capital, Daniel wouldn't have let his Marines stay in Marine House, a mile away, for Thanksgiving.

Let them have their Thanksgiving meal, he'd thought. He didn't celebrate it. More often than not, holidays had been excuses for his old man to get high and stay high.

Thanksgiving was just another day for Dan, so he'd offered to stay on duty while his men celebrated with freeze-dried turkey and canned stuffing, taking turns Skypeing home.

The rest of the embassy staff wasn't doing much better over at the ambassador's residence a block away. Ambassador Thurston Crocker pulled out all the stops for his fellow ambassadors and for visiting bigwigs, but for the embassy staff, he and his wife would have made a minimal effort to please. Soggy canapés, half-thawed turkey and cheap, sulphite-laden sparkling wine, providing a guaranteed killer headache the next morning. And not much of it, either.

Crock-of-Shit was not known for his generosity.

So the choice to stand guard alone at the embassy hadn't been hard. And when he'd seen Claire Day suddenly appear, his choice looked even better. Claire, universally known as Blondie, the resident embassy DIA analyst, was smart and beautiful and dedicated. She was the only other person on post who would work on Thanksgiving.

She'd walked down the corridor toward him, immersed in thought, and he'd had to stiffen his neck muscles, make them a cage, so his head wouldn't swivel to follow her progress down the corridor. Though he'd started his duties as detachment commander a full week ago, it was only the second time he'd seen her at the Laka Embassy. She seemed to work day and night down there in the basement secure room.

Just as she had pulled even with him, nodding at him, lips curving in an absentminded smile, gunfire had erupted in the street outside. Massive gunfire, rifles and machine guns going off in an almost constant clatter. The deafening noise of war.

Dan had sprung into action, rushing her into Post One, the default retreat station, behind bulletproof glass. Once she was safe, he'd left her there to go on recon, fully aware of the fact that bulletproof was a name, not a description. Nothing was completely bulletproof.

It was a real Murphy's Law moment, because the monitors of the security cameras that ringed the embassy chose that moment to flicker and die, another ode to the lunacy of always hiring the cheapest subcontractor.

He'd had no choice but to run to the side door of the embassy, the public entrance. Normally, one of his men would be stationed there but it was a holiday and closed to the public. He hunkered down, slipped out and, using what little cover there was, made it to the huge wrought-iron gates that fronted onto the Avenue de la Liberté.

Shit.

It was a Quentin-Tarantino-on-crack scene.

Hundreds of screaming soldiers, firing their weapons crazily in all directions, pouring into the city. As Dan watched, the entire street shut down, shutters banging closed, windows slamming shut, street vendors pulling up the sheets they displayed their wares on and running away. Some so terrified they just left everything on the ground.

In a few minutes, the big avenue was devoid of civilians and all that was left were crazy, drunken soldiers, shooting in the air, taking potshots at the street lamps and the tires of cars parked on the street.

They were all dressed in tattered red shirts, which was not good. God knew the military junta's soldiers were no prize, but the Red Army was terrifying. They'd been in the bush for years, stealing young boys from their homes and bringing them up brutally, keeping them drunk and drugged and hyped up on violence.

Deserters, if caught, had their limbs hacked off, one by one, day by day for four days. It was known as the Four Day Punishment. The only possible question was "short sleeves" or "long sleeves." Above or below the elbow or the knee.

The red shirts were a symbol of how brainwashed they were. They were convinced that wearing the color red made them bulletproof.

Everyone thought that the Red Army was a thousand miles inland, terrorizing local tribes, but everyone was wrong, because the Red Army was right here, right now.

At least three hundred soldiers careened down the street in the three minutes Dan watched. At this rate, several thousand would be in the city in an hour. Ten thousand by nightfall.

They weren't paying the embassy any attention. Both the Red Army thugs and the government thugs were apolitical. They weren't anti- or pro-American. They were pro-blood diamonds, pro-sex slaves, pro-smuggled guns. Anti-civil society.

If they attacked the embassy it would be because they were looking to wreck all standing buildings in the city center of Laka, not because they wanted to make a political statement. It didn't make them any less dangerous though.

Dan was the detachment commander of a small force of Marines—there were just five of them—and he had to protect both Ambassador Crocker and his vicious wife, Danielle, who hated anyone who wasn't rich or famous. The Crock-of-Shits were horrible people. However, much as Dan and his men despised the Crockers, he knew that he and the men of the Marine security detachment would lay down their lives for the nasty couple. And of course for the rest of the staff.

"Did you call Marine House?" Claire asked.

Dan looked down at her. "Yes, ma'am. They're on full alert. There's not much they can do at the moment. Called the ambassador's residence, too. Everyone's just sitting tight."

With her head bowed, all he could see was absurdly long lashes and the curve of a high cheekbone. But he didn't need to see her features, they were burned into his brain. He'd been thinking of her for a year now, since his last posting in Jakarta.

She'd come to Jakarta for a regional conference on security, one of hundreds of experts called in for a four-day screening of security threats. Mostly men, mostly ugly, so she'd stood out like a beacon. An amazingly beautiful woman, with a reputation for being wicked smart. He'd been nearly poleaxed when he saw her walking down the corridor of the Jakarta Embassy.

That evening, he'd been on guard duty at the embassy reception for all the experts and politicians called in for the conference.

He'd been stationed at the door and knew that he was nothing more than a piece of furniture for the bigwigs in the room.

She'd arrived late and left early, drinking half a glass of champagne and eating nothing. Dan had followed her with his eyes as she made the rounds, spoke politely, laughed once or twice, then took her leave.

Anyone not paying attention would have seen her as a party animal. Well, why not? She was stunningly beautiful— easily the loveliest woman in the room by a factor of ten. Elegant, too, in a black silk suit. Long, pale blond hair caught back in a gleaming bun, which sounded like something Aunt Mabel would sport.

Except Dan knew that it was called a chignon—a long-ago date had nearly snapped his head off for calling the hair gathered at the back of her neck a bun. He never made that mistake again.

The chignon set off Claire's long white neck and made her look like a young Grace Kelly.

He hadn't seen her come and he hadn't seen her go. It was the damndest thing. He could have sworn he hadn't taken his eyes off her, but suddenly she was gone.

He saw her only a few times after that, brief glimpses, then nothing. She was known as Blondie and by the rueful smiles, every man with a pulse had tried to approach her. They'd all struck out.

The embassy website said she was posted to Makongo, a hardship post in West Africa.

Makongo. Okay, he could do Makongo.

He was being promoted to detachment commander and had one more posting to go before he rejoined the normal Marine ranks. He was a good Marine, kept his nose clean and hadn't shot anyone he wasn't supposed to, so his bid for a posting to Makongo was accepted.

Took him almost a fucking year, though. A year in Jakarta in which he went out with a Wall Street Journal analyst, an investment banker and the owner of a school for teaching English. Nice women all of them, but . . .

The analyst had a screechy voice, the banker scared him when she talked of "wiping out" her opposition in the bank and the teacher bored him. They didn't last more than a night or two in his bed. He felt like an asshole, but what can you do? He had Claire Day fixed in his head and she was the only one who could get herself out of there.

So here he was, hip to hip and shoulder to shoulder with her. Piece of cake, getting close to Blondie. All you needed was a vicious rebel army invading the city.

Though it was steamy hot inside Post One—the embassy air-conditioning system was another system installed by the lowest bidder—and he was sweating like a pig, Claire simply glowed. He could smell individual bits of her and they all smelled wonderful. Freshly shampooed hair, some lemony lotion on her hands and something fresh and springlike that he imagined was the smell of her skin.

Jesus, he'd like to smell all that up close. Just put his nose next to her neck and inhale, even though he doubted she'd like him pulling a dog imitation on her.

A loud crump followed by the sound of falling masonry made her jump.

"Another RPG," she said, shaking her head. A thick lock of pale gold hair fell out of her French braid and curled on her shoulder. Dan tightened his hand on his Remington 870 because the temptation to smooth it back was so strong. "They're well-armed."

Dan waited until another burst from a passing vehicle full of soldiers died down. "And evidently have plenty of ammo to burn."

She looked up at him, silvery blue eyes serious, a little frown between ash brown eyebrows. "You know, that doesn't sound right."

Dan took in a deep breath. She was right, it didn't.

Claire shook her head. "I just sent off a report detailing how ragtag the Red Army actually is. We're funding the general way too much on the basis of the minimal threat the RA represents. They stay alive by preying on the tribesmen in the bush, but they have almost zero resources now that they've lost the diamond mines."

He looked down at her, wishing he could read her reports. He bet they were smart and incisive. He would never read them, though, because they were Eyes Only and he was just a jarhead. "You actually called them a ragtag army in your report? I'll bet that went over big."

She pursed her lips, eyes dancing. "Actually, in DIA-speak it's called 'arms procurement deficiencies' and I said that the RA had lots of them. I guess I was wrong." She closed her eyes. "I really, really hate being wrong."

They were silent a second as another burst of machine-gun fire sounded, long and fierce. He'd watched the soldiers briefly from a window. Most of the shots were into the air. Any Marine would be put in the brig for such a breach of firing discipline.

Another jeep full of Red Army thugs roared by, all guns firing. Dan estimated about five hundred rounds shot in a couple of minutes.

"Wow, was I wrong. These guys don't have arms procurement deficiencies." She shook her head again, small fists clenching. "You know, Gunnery Sergeant, I didn't see this coming at all."

"Dan, please," he answered.

A quicksilver smile. "Sure, Dan. I guess there's nothing like an old-fashioned siege to cut through the formalities." She offered a slender hand. "And I'm Claire."

I know, he wanted to say. Her name was burned into his mind. He took her hand in his, wishing his hand wasn't so rough. He loved tinkering, spending most of his downtime in the motor pool, and his hands showed it. Not to mention the shooting calluses.

He had to force himself to let go of her hand, though he wanted to keep holding on to that incredibly smooth skin. His head gave the order to his hand—*let go of her*—but there was a breakdown in communications up there.

He looked down. Their hands were such contrasts. Her hands were long-fingered, slender, with fine bones under pale, smooth skin. His hands were almost double the size of hers, a workingman's hands, big and rough.

Suddenly, at the sight of their hands together, dark and light, large and small, heat bloomed under his skin, a small sun of it. It was the most erotic thing he'd ever seen. Just holding this woman's hand was sexier than being with a naked woman.

His vision narrowed in on their hands, fixing the image in his mind.

Whoa.

His entire nature and every ounce of relentless Marine training made him intensely mission-oriented. They were as close as dammit to a combat situation right now and he was obsessed with a woman's *hands*?

What the fuck?

Dan lifted his eyes and nearly lost himself in hers. They were the most extraordinary color—the pale color of the noonday summer sky, a brilliant silver blue with a tiny rim of darker blue around the rim. He'd never seen eyes that color before and he couldn't tear his own eyes away from them.

He stopped breathing for a second, then came back to himself when he felt her slipping her hand out of his.

Dan looked away for a moment, trying to get back into his own head. He definitely needed to go out and get laid, asap, if holding a woman's hand briefly while looking in her eyes nearly overwhelmed him.

He turned his head back only to find her eyes still on him. Wide, gorgeous, silvery blue eyes. Solemn, serious. She shook her head slowly. "If something serious happens, my head will roll for not seeing this coming."

His teeth ground together. "I didn't see it coming, either, and it's *my* job to keep the embassy safe." Another RPG went off, close to the embassy. "I hate the thought that I allowed us to get caught with our pants down." He slanted her a glance. "Sorry."

She smiled slightly. "No problem. We *are* caught with our pants down, no question."

Oh, shit. Now he had another image in his head he couldn't shake out.

"What?" She'd just said something that he hadn't heard because a vision of a naked Claire Day had blossomed in his head.

"I said," she repeated patiently, "we can wait them out, can't we? We should have food supplies for the entire staff for a month and you should have at least three thousand rounds in the armory."

He raised his eyebrows. The extent of any embassy's food and ammo supplies was top secret. Not even the ambassador was given the information unless it was an emergency and he or she needed briefing. So how the hell did Claire peg it so exactly? She wasn't giving anything away, her face bland and guileless. "I'm just guessing, of course," she said primly.

Well, she'd nailed it. So either she was really, really good at her job or security wasn't airtight.

It didn't make that much difference. Claire wasn't the enemy.

The enemy right now was outside the embassy gates, shooting up a storm. Dan hoped he wouldn't need the three thousand rounds in the armory because there was no backup. If the rebel army broke into the embassy, his five Marines a mile away wouldn't have the firepower to shoot their way to him. Dan didn't want to order his men on a suicide mission.

Right now their best bet was to lie low, be prepared and hope that whatever drama the Makongan Army and the Red Army had going would work itself out without involving the US.

Claire drew up her legs, clasping them and laying her cheek against her knees. She heaved a huge sigh.

"I just hope to God this all blows over soon before it hits the international news. My father will have a heart attack if he hears that there's a revolution on the streets of Laka. He'll be making arrangements to come over the instant he hears there's trouble, which is not good. He's almost eighty and has a heart condition. I just hope to reassure him I'm okay before he gets the news that he should be worrying. All the cell phone towers are down, otherwise I'd have called him already." She looked up at him. "How about you? Who's going to be worrying about you?"

Worry about *him*? Jesus. No one. His job was to worry about the safety of the ambassador and his family, the embassy staff and his men. In that order.

The idea of anyone worrying about *him* was crazy. Even as a kid, he'd learned the hard way to be tough and self-reliant. Dan couldn't remember anyone worrying about him, ever.

"No one. But that's okay. I can handle myself."

"No one?" she persisted, her eyes searching his face. "Not a mom or a girlfriend?"

Dan nearly snorted. The women he bedded were way more concerned about their own pleasure than his well-being. "Mom disappeared when I was two. I don't remember her. And no—" He looked down at her, at the smooth, high cheekbones, long lashes, beautiful mouth. It was impossible to remember any other woman he'd ever been with while looking at her. "Don't have a girlfriend. Being a Marine embassy security guard isn't conducive to relationships."

Dan was brave. He knew he was brave. He'd been tested under fire and had held. After this posting, he was going to be reintegrated into his unit and would probably be sent either to Iraq or Afghanistan and he was fine with that, fine. So nobody could say he was a coward.

But right now, his palms were sweating and he felt like a blowtorch had been applied to his throat at the thought of what he was about to ask. Had to ask. Because he simply had to know.

"And—" His voice came out a croak. He coughed to loosen his throat. "And what about you? Is there, um—" Jesus. What to call the bastard she might be with? *Boyfriend* sounded lame, like high school. *Significant other?* Nah. "Someone?" he ended lamely.

This was a question he'd asked a thousand times in bars, because he had some hard and fast rules for his sex life, written in stone.

No bareback sex, ever. No married women, ever. Or engaged women. Not even women who were going out with someone else.

He didn't need the hassle of fighting with another male over a woman. And most of all, anyone who cheated once with him would cheat again on him.

So at around the third or fourth drink, if they'd got to the point where he knew they'd be heading out together, he made sure she was a free agent.

Bars around military bases are full of chicks who want

to party even when their men are away, and who aren't too particular who they party with. It sickened him, to think of some man off defending his country while his woman was out trolling for sex. If he got even a whiff of that, he was history.

It was really hard to think of Claire not being with someone or engaged. Or hell, even married. What the fuck were men thinking? How could any man be around her for even a minute and not want her for his own?

And yet scuttlebutt—and Dan kept his ear very close to the ground—had it she was single.

God, he hoped so.

If she was with someone, he'd just had himself posted to Laka for nothing, and was going to waste a year of his life in West Africa when where he'd really wanted to be was in the new Baghdad Embassy. If she was with someone, all these . . . things roiling around in his chest, all this obsessive thinking about her this past year was bad news. Really bad news.

Showdown time.

But she only blinked and looked blank. "Someone?" she asked. "Me?" She gave a half laugh. "What you said was absolutely true, Gunnery Sergeant—"

"Dan." His heart had taken a leap in his chest at her blank look and he had to breathe carefully to get it to steady out.

"Dan. Okay, right. Well, Dan, I've lived in Durban, Singapore and now Laka over the past six years. No man would put up with that."

I would, he thought.

Her eyes seemed to glow in the room when she looked at him. "I guess it's a little like being a Marine security guard."

Dan looked at her hands, long-fingered, fragile, soft, with small wrists. Her shoulders and torso were narrow, the line of her collarbones delicate. The long, pale blond hair completely unlike his own dark brown high-and-tight.

She spent her days—and more hours in those days than she was supposed to—in a windowless secure room doing

God knows what on computers. Everything she did, she did with her head. And pretty as it was, he knew she was smarter than she was beautiful, which was saying a lot.

He thought of his men. Ward, Martinez, Buchan, Harvey and Lopez. Tough bastards, hell with a rifle, hard drinkers, good to have at your back but light-years away from being like Claire Day.

No, she wasn't anything like a Marine security guard.

He scrolled back in his head to what she'd said earlier. "Tell me about your father."

"Dad?" The thought of her father made her smile. Good. Dan sure couldn't smile at the thought of his own father, the bastard. He still had the scars.

"Yeah. You smile when you mention him. That's nice."

"He's a great dad," she mused, picking at a thread of her tan cotton pants. In the rush to hustle her into the safe quarters of Post One, her pants had caught on a protruding nail from one of the billion unfinished or botched restructuring projects going on in the embassy. There was a big rip just above the knee.

Underneath, Dan could see smooth white skin. He closed his eyes for a moment. He was here to protect her, not to get all hot and bothered because he saw several square inches of skin. No matter how soft and beautiful.

"Yeah?" he prodded. Get the conversation back to something that would cool him down, like her father. "What's he do?"

"He's a—he *was* a professor of French literature. At University of Massachusetts Boston. He's retired. Has been for a long time."

"I thought I heard some Boston in there." Dan frowned. He had a pretty good ear for accents and could usually pick out where new recruits came from. "Not much, though. A Boston accent is usually a pretty strong regional accent, but yours isn't very heavy."

She nodded. "You're good. Got a good ear. We lived in Boston until I was thirteen, but we spent all our summers in France, where Dad did his research. Well"—she wrinkled her nose—"research coupled with eating our way through the country while he was doing it." She smiled, obviously thinking of happy memories, then her face clouded over. "We had a pretty good time until my . . . my mom was killed. In a mugging. Just one of those wrong time, wrong place things that makes no sense whatsoever and rips your heart out. It was really . . . hard. I think my dad went a little crazy for a few years afterward. He took early retirement when I was fifteen and we moved down to Florida, to a town called Safety Harbor." The smile was back, only sadder. "I think he chose the town for its name, but it's a pretty place and it *is* quite safe, which was exactly what Dad was looking for. A place where nothing bad would ever happen again. My dad, he's—he's overprotective. He couldn't stand the thought of losing me after Mom was killed and I understood what he was trying to do, so I just went along with him. I was studious anyway, so basically I went to school and then came straight home and did extra homework. I took a correspondence course from a French Lycée and got my baccalaureate at the same time I graduated from high school. Then I buried myself in my studies at college, with a double major in French and political science. When I graduated, I sort of took a deep breath, looked up from my books and realized that I hadn't done much else but study since I was fifteen years old. And I realized I wanted more out of life. I wanted to travel. I wanted to stretch myself. I wanted to do something exciting, something adventurous, you know?"

She looked up at him and he nodded. He knew, though that wasn't why he'd joined the Marines. He'd joined because it had been either military service or juvie or an early, violent death. Still, joining up was the best thing that had ever happened to him.

A lot of his men, however, had joined out of boredom and a sense of adventure. Which made them smart because you never got bored in the Marines and if you could stay alive, it was a hell of an adventure.

Another long burst of gunfire, louder and longer. They

were bringing out the heavy artillery. Dan could hear the deep, sharp sounds of a .50 caliber machine gun, probably mounted onto the back of a jeep.

"Fifty cal," he said, just as she said, "Sounds like a fifty caliber machine gun."

Fifty cals were bad news.

She clasped her hands around her knees again, bringing her legs up closer to her torso in an unconscious move to protect herself. It was the animal in her wanting to present a smaller target, but however great her instincts were, they was absolutely useless against a .50 cal bullet.

Everything in the building was useless against a .50 cal, including the thick stucco walls of the embassy and the bullet resistant walls of Post One. They'd crumple in a heartbeat. If the machine gun was close enough, a .50 cal could go right through the building, front to back, smashing through everything in its way. One 120 pound female would be no barrier at all. She'd simply explode.

Claire blew out the breath she'd been holding while the burst lasted. "Yeah, well, this is kind of Dad's nightmare. If we make it, I'll never hear the end of it."

That he could help her with. "You'll make it," he said quietly. "As long as I'm alive, you'll make it. That's a promise." Certainly he wouldn't let her fall into the rebel army's hands. That was a promise, too, though he made it to himself, not her.

She swiveled her head toward him so fast a little cloud of her perfume puffed out from her skin. Another long, thick lock of pale blond hair fell out of the French braid, curling along her shoulder.

Without thinking about it, because if he had let what he was about to do rise up to the thinking part of his brain, he would never have had the nerve, Dan lifted his hand to curl the lock around her ear. The back of his knuckles brushed against the soft skin of her neck and he wanted to close his eyes to savor the feeling. But if he closed them, he'd miss what was flaring in her eyes.

Clear, crystalline, the silvery color of sun on sea. And

startled, as if seeing something she'd never noticed before. In that second, Dan knew, she saw him as a man, not a Marine.

He'd been in uniform all his adult life and was used to people seeing the uniform and not the man underneath.

If you were a civilian, he was a faceless, generic soldier—a useful tool to keep you safe. Tucked away in the shitholes of the world so things could go smoothly at home.

And if you were a bad guy, well, hell—with the full force of the Corps behind him, he represented a world of hurt behind a rifle.

Women came in two types. Military groupies, who got off on the uniform and the weapons—*How many men have you killed?* was a question he got all the time from the groupies—and women who thought soldiers were loud-mouthed roughnecks, totally unsuitable as dates.

Women like Claire—beautiful, sophisticated, smart— well, women like that just steered around him as if he was invisible, like a glorified servant. Women like Claire rarely saw *him*, the man inside.

She was seeing him now, no doubt about it. They were in a situation that could turn desperate in a heartbeat. They were holed up inside a building that was breachable, while what sounded like an army of thousands was shooting up the streets outside.

So far, no one appeared to be targeting Americans but the Red Army soldiers could turn on a dime and decide to storm the embassy and then . . . well, then they'd be lost. He'd go down fighting because that was what Marines did, but he couldn't stand alone against an army.

His men were a mile away and might just as well have been on the dark side of the moon. He couldn't get to them and they couldn't get to him. And even if he had his men with him, six soldiers, however well-trained, however well-armed, couldn't beat an army, even the drugged-up, ill-disciplined and badly trained Red Army.

All of that she knew. She was a defense analyst, after all.

But right now, it looked like she was seeing him and not

the uniform. Or, rather, the Delta pants and a green tee, since he'd taken his jacket off.

He was still holding a lock of her hair, his hand against the warmth of her neck. And she wasn't moving her head away. Which meant . . .

He ran the back of his hand lightly against her neck. God, she felt so friggin' soft. She didn't move, was hardly breathing, watching him carefully with no expression on her face. But some more of her scent billowed up from her, which meant that her skin was warming.

Slowly, wondering if he was going to be slapped down, Dan uncurled his hand, sliding it around until he was cupping her neck.

She wasn't saying no. She wasn't saying yes, but she wasn't saying no. Actually, she wasn't saying anything at all, but whatever she was feeling, it looked like *no* wasn't part of it.

O-kay.

Watching her eyes, ready to back off at any second, Dan bent his head. He watched her until she filled his entire field of vision, until there wasn't anything at all in the world but Claire and then he closed his eyes because his mouth was on hers and he wanted to just concentrate on the kiss.

He didn't know what he was thinking. Man, he wasn't thinking at all. The instant his hand touched her, every neuron in his head shorted because being under siege with a rebel army not a hundred yards away firing live rounds— well, that wasn't the time or the place to get all hot and bothered over a woman.

That had never happened before. An op was an op and though usually being a Marine security guard was a softer duty than most and served mainly to see the world and get a stronger grip on geopolitics, every single Marine who had ever been stationed in an embassy was fully equipped and fully prepared to engage in the case of a threat.

On duty, Dan was a walking, talking mission, as focused as a laser beam. Once, during a firefight, he was so adrenalized he hadn't even felt a bullet crease his forearm.

It was the medic afterward who pointed to the blood on his sleeve. He'd ceased to exist as a man and had turned himself into a weapon.

Not now. Now he wasn't focused on the danger outside, he was totally swamped with sensations, all of them good. Amazingly good. Nothing whatsoever to do with the dangers outside the embassy walls.

God, just the feel of her, warm and soft against him. He'd never felt anything like it. It was like plunging into a warm sea. He let himself float, drifting lazily, her lips moving lightly under his. Everything was suspended. They were in a world without time, no past and no future, just an endless now.

Every sense he had was focused on where he was touching Claire. He couldn't hear anything but her breathing, now slightly sped up. Couldn't see anything when he cracked his eyes open but her—now-rosy skin, long lashes on her cheekbone, another coil of pale blond hair curving around to fall between her breasts. Couldn't feel anything but her—soft and smooth.

He didn't even feel the gravity anchoring him to earth. Couldn't smell anything but Claire. And her taste—ah God. She tasted fresh and slightly minty and absolutely wonderful.

Then she shifted slightly, opening her mouth more for him and the warmth turned into electric heat, sharp and shocking. His hand on her neck tightened, mouth open against hers, as the kiss turned hot, demanding.

Dan tried to follow the woman's lead during sex—and though this was just a kiss, it was sex, too. And way hotter than most of the sex he'd ever had. If the woman liked it slow, he took it slow. If she liked it hard, then he gave it to her hard. But no matter what, he was always in control.

Control had just been whipped out of his hands. His heart raced and his hands shook as he turned to deepen the kiss, fisting one hand in her hair, the other, still holding his weapon, braced on the floor, caging her.

He was coming on too strong, he knew it. He'd taken it

from zero to a hundred in a second, there was no way she could keep up, but he was helpless to stop himself as he leaned forward, backing her against the wall.

He'd been here a thousand times before, in his dreams. During the day, he kept his mind focused on the job and on the fact that she didn't even know he existed. But during the night, with all restraints hemming in, his conscious mind blasted off—ah, his nights were full of her.

Every time he saw her he greedily sucked up impressions, so that his dreams were utterly realistic. He knew she rarely exercised—she spent twelve hours a day underground, after all—but still moved with an incredible lithe grace. He knew that she didn't take the sun well and just stayed out of it, so she had the faintest of tans over mother-of-pearl skin.

The rest he extrapolated.

He knew how she kissed because he kissed her endlessly in his dreams, waking up in a sweaty tangle of sheets and blankets in his small, spare room, aching and hard with a boner that took a cold shower to get rid of.

Well, he *thought* he knew how she kissed and what he would feel kissing her, but he'd been wildly off the mark. The real thing was ten thousand times better. Off-the-scale better.

Fuck, there was nothing like this. He'd never had this reaction before, utterly helpless to stop himself or to moderate the kiss. If he could have crawled inside her, he would have. His mouth pressed against hers, his whole torso crushing her against the wall behind them, his entire heavy weight leaning into her while he ate at her mouth.

Shit, this wasn't good.

She was whispering to him, trying to say something . . . God, how could she be talking while his mouth was on hers? Fuck, he shouldn't be expected to have to think while he was on sensory overload, every sense he had completely taken up with her.

He moved even more heavily against her but came up against a barrier. Her hand. For a second, his mind balked.

She didn't want this? But her mouth was open beneath his, her tongue stroking his.

So what . . . ?

The sound finally penetrated, at the exact instant Claire's hand pushed hard against his shoulder.

Someone was talking. Whispering, actually. A loud, hissing whisper. It wasn't him and it wasn't Claire.

None of that computed. They were alone in the building.

With what remained of his brain cells, Dan realized that something was wrong. He lifted his head and nearly moaned at what he saw. Claire's normally pale skin was deep pink, overheated. Big silvery blue eyes wide and unfocused. Mouth wet and puffy from his. The very picture of a beautiful, aroused woman. The most gorgeous thing he'd ever seen in his life. For a second, he couldn't imagine why on earth he'd lifted his mouth from hers. He could have stayed there for a million years.

"Claire! Qu'est-ce que tu fais? Viens ici! Vite!"

Dan was normally on top of everything but this stumped him for almost a second. He wasn't talking and she wasn't talking. So someone else was talking. In French, yet.

It was as if he'd been on another world, transported far away. But now *this* world, with its vicious dangers, with a rebel army right outside his doorstep, with the safety of an embassy in his hands, came rushing right back in. For a second, Dan was deeply ashamed that he had allowed himself to be distracted even for the space of a kiss.

Then he looked at Claire, so beautiful, softness and light and grace, and he forgave himself. A man would have to be dead not to give in to that temptation. Even a soldier. Even a *Marine,* though Marines had duty flowing in their veins instead of blood.

"Claire!" the voice hissed again and Dan swiveled his head toward the door at the same time Claire did.

Another beautiful woman.

Christ, it was raining beautiful dames today. Narrow face, fine features, skin so black it was almost blue, long narrow hand holding open the door. A foreign national, one of the ten Makongans working in the embassy, the core staff that remained to keep the embassy going while the Americans rotated in and out.

Dan did a quick search inside his head and came up with a name. Marie. Marie Diur. Claire's best friend, or so scuttlebutt had it.

Marie was ignoring him, beckoning to Claire. Claire leaned forward, away from his hand, and stood up lithely.

Whatever this was about, Dan wanted to be part of it. He stood, too, rifle in one hand, the other on the butt of his Browning.

A burst of French from Marie and Claire turned to him, eyes troubled. "She says for you to stay here."

Dan balked. Both of them should be staying here, in Post One, the safest place in the embassy. If there was to be a shoot-out, this was the best place to hole up.

And how the hell had Marie Diur gotten in anyway, with the embassy surrounded by crazed, drunken rebel troops? He opened his mouth but before he could say anything, Claire placed a finger against his lips.

"Please, Dan," she said softly. "I know Marie. She wants to tell me something and she wants just me. Please, stay here and I'll be right back."

Dan's back teeth ground so hard it was a miracle enamel didn't shoot out his ears. "Listen, Claire. The situation's volatile and dangerous. I don't need to tell you that. I don't want you out of my sight. And now that your friend's here, I don't want her going back outside, either."

She looked at him and back at Marie, who was impatiently signaling for Claire to come immediately. "She needs to talk to me. I won't be long." She patted his chest. "Please," she said softly, soberly. "Just a few minutes."

He didn't say anything and she took it as consent.

Claire crossed the room to Marie. They put their heads together, two beautiful women at the two ends of the color spectrum, speaking quietly and quickly in French. The soft liquid sounds carried, though he couldn't understand a word of it. Claire finally nodded and turned to him, holding up her index finger in a universal sign—*one minute*.

Dan watched grimly as the two women disappeared, the huge wooden door of the room Post One was in closing gently behind them. This wasn't right. It didn't feel right. Goddammit, he was giving them one minute and then he was going out to get them.

The radio crackled.

"Gunny, you there?" Marine House. Ward. He was using encryption that scrambled his voice at one end, to be reconstituted on Dan's end. Ward's normal bass sounded like Daffy Duck on helium.

Dan switched on the mike. "Yeah. Give me a sitrep. You've got eyes on the ground." Marine House stood flush with the street and they'd have a better view of what was going on than from what he could see from inside the embassy.

The crackle of static, then Ward's voice came back on, high-pitched and distorted. Dan could hear faint shots outside echoing through the Marine House radio four blocks away.

"—not much of anything. It's like they're just happy to be riding around, shooting at random. We're observing the same jeeps of soldiers circling around and around, so there might be fewer of them than we thought." Ward conferred briefly with Buchan. "Yeah, we're thinking maybe not more than five hundred troops. Maybe less, even. So far they haven't paid us any attention at all. It's hard to know what plans they have, if any. But a hundred to one—those aren't bad odds."

Ward was right. Dan knew that the Red Army numbered in the tens of thousands. If the entire army was flooding into Laka, they were goners. But they could handle five hundred. Five hundred illiterate, superstitious troops, boys who'd been kidnapped from their villages so young they were sometimes shorter than the rifles they carried. Kept drunk or drugged and brainwashed into thinking that their red shirts made them magically invulnerable to bullets.

No match at all. Dan would bet on the odds of a hundred to one, no question. He and his men were elite troops, well-trained and well-armed.

"Okay. Keep watch and let me know if you think new troops are arriving."

"Roger that."

Dan thumbed the off button, then looked at his watch, frowning. Almost five minutes had gone by. Claire had promised to come back in a minute. Five minutes was not one. A lot of very bad things could happen in five minutes.

Protocol dictated that he remain at Post One during an emergency but the hell with it. An emergency hadn't been officially declared. Not yet, anyway. Wherever Claire was, he wanted her back with him, right by his side where she'd be safe. As safe as he could make her, anyway. Marie Diur, too

Cracking the door open, Dan looked both ways. As always near the equator, night was falling fast. No one had bothered to turn on the hallway lights, so the big hallway was cloaked in shadows.

Dan slipped through the door, and walked quietly through the rooms. The waiting room, the consular section, the back offices. He made the rounds of the ground floor perimeter. He knew how to move with stealth and he knew how to clear rooms. Ten minutes later, he'd checked the entire ground floor and had seen . . . nothing. No other consular officers, no rebel army troops. No Marie Diur. Above all, no Claire Day.

He stopped and listened. Like most Marines, his senses were keen. His hearing was especially sharp. He held his breath in his lungs so it wouldn't interfere and sent his senses outward.

The embassy was an old building, built by a French timber baron in the late nineteenth century. It had been built like a Paris townhouse, but in the equator wood and stucco aren't as eternal as in the City of Lights. It required constant upkeep and on the best of days the entire building moaned and groaned and squeaked.

Right now, though, it was utterly and completely silent. The only sounds were those filtering in from the rebel soldiers carousing outside along the Avenue de la Liberté, shouts of drunken male jubilation, crazed machine gun bursts, revving engines.

Inside the embassy, silence.

Dan raced up to the second floor, cleared the rooms, then checked the third floor, essentially storage space.

Only the basement was left, with the locked armory only he and his second-in-command Ward had the code for, the secure room, which was locked and the supplies room, ditto.

No sign of Claire.

The embassy building was charming, an architectural jewel, but it was also small. Everyone worked in close proximity, everyone knew everyone else's business. You could hear phone conversations in the room next door. As long as there were people in the building, the only places that were silent were Post One, the soundproofed situation room, the secure room where Claire worked and the armory, deep underground.

Even if Claire knew the codes, she wouldn't have taken Marie into rooms off-limits to Foreign Service Nationals staff. It was a rule no one ever broke.

If Claire and Marie were anywhere in the building, he should be hearing them. Even whispers carried.

There were no whispers, no footfalls, no sounds at all.

Dan had spent most of his adult life training to sharpen his senses. He took a moment to put himself in hunting mode—attuning his eyes to the semi-darkness, sharpening his hearing even more, Browning out, safety off. Remington on a sling against his back. Ready for trouble.

By the time he'd finished casing the embassy, top to bottom, he was sweating.

Claire had disappeared.

Christ.

Dan didn't know Marie Diur at all. Suppose she was secretly a supporter of the Red Army? Suppose she'd lured Claire into their hands?

The Red Army was made up of crazed scumbags, but the government army wasn't much better. The Makongan Army had plenty of enemies. If the Diur family had suffered at the government's hands, they might well have thrown in with the rebels.

Claire in RA hands was something he couldn't even think about without going crazy. They were brutal beyond belief. God, how could he have let Claire go? He'd lost his head for just a second and it might have cost her her life.

She and Marie hadn't been insane enough to go outside, had they? Or even outside the embassy compound? Did Marie know of some secret entrance? Dan glanced outside the windows at the swiftly gathering dusk. This was the moment when the duty officer switched on the powerful outside lights, illuminating every inch of ground between the walls of the embassy and the gate. Now there was only darkness.

Listening carefully, Dan cracked open the door that led from the back office used by the consular staff to the motor pool. A huge modern garage housing embassy cars had been added to the big back garden, with a concrete shed attached to the back. The garage was modular and had been recently extended to house shipments of AIDS drugs donated by one of those rich-guy foundations.

There was a big truck there now, full of drugs.

The heat was still intense, the coming of night was bringing no freshness at all. If anything, the heat became more oppressive. He took a moment to wipe the sweat out of his eyes.

Dan unslung his rifle and brought it up to his shoulder, starting to slow his breathing and his heartbeat in case he needed to shoot. He kicked the door of the shed open and quartered the room. Nothing. After a minute, he lowered the rifle, frowning, and closed the door of the shed.

A whisper! Definitely the sound of a woman's voice. Soldiers are taught not to whisper in the field. A whisper carries much farther than a low murmur. A woman's voice, with its higher pitch, carried even farther than a man's.

And now . . . another woman answering.

Claire. That was Claire's voice. He'd recognize it anywhere. She was outside when she should be back in the embassy where he could protect her.

He moved forward and . . . never completed the step toward Claire because a giant fist raised him ten feet off the ground and slammed him back against the concrete wall of the shed at a hundred miles an hour.

In the split second before he lost consciousness, while a fireball of light and heat filled the universe, he thought— *Claire*.

Claire was in the middle of the conflagration and was already dead.

He'd lost her the moment he'd found her.

And then the world went black.

TWO

SAFETY HARBOR, FLORIDA
ONE YEAR LATER

CLAIRE Day opened the front door of her father's home and walked in slowly, wearily.

Actually, it wasn't her father's home anymore, it was *her* home now. Her father was gone, dead of a heart attack. Dead, some said, of a broken heart.

Because of her.

She'd just spent a long couple of hours at the cemetery, bringing him flowers. It was her closest human contact since her father had died three months ago—talking to his headstone.

She told him of her grief, how much she missed him, how sorry she was that the fact she'd nearly died in the embassy bombing in Laka had broken his heart.

He listened, she was sure of that. Wherever he was, he was listening to her. He always had. He'd been a strong, loving presence in her life while her mother was alive and he'd been a frightened, loving presence afterward.

Maybe he even forgave her.

It had been cold and windy in the cemetery and she was

chilled to the bone. Luckily she kept the heat on in the house, day and night, unusual in these sunny parts.

Her heating bills were atrocious, but it was the only way she could stay warm. She was always cold these days, her hands and feet pale and bloodless.

She blew into her hands and rubbed them. It was what her mother had done when she was a child, coming in from playing in the snow in Boston. A motherly ritual that she'd taken for granted as a well-loved little girl—a sweater kept warm on the radiator, hot chocolate ready for the microwave and a brisk rub of her hands. Her mother had been a gifted amateur pianist and her hands had been beautiful—long and delicate.

If Claire closed her eyes, she could still see her chubby child's hands being chafed by her mother's warm, elegant, womanly ones.

There was no one to rub Claire's hands now. No one in the entire world. No one to rub her hands, put an arm around her shoulders, give her a hug.

She couldn't remember the last human being who had touched her. Maybe the Gramercys at her father's funeral. They'd hugged her, briefly. But then Mr. Gramercy had managed to insinuate that she'd killed her father by willfully going off on her adventures.

Her knees had nearly buckled at the venom in his voice and at the stab of guilt that had penetrated straight to her heart.

He might be right. If she hadn't wanted to spread her wings and fly, she would probably be somewhere teaching French literature, perhaps translating novels from French in her spare time, an intact human being.

No memory loss, no dizzy spells, no screaming nightmares.

No dead father.

Wiped out, Claire sat down on the couch, hugging herself for warmth, too tired to make it up to her bedroom on the second floor and change into warm, comfortable house clothes.

She was always exhausted after she went out. The outside world was simply too much for her. She planned her outings carefully, going out only when necessary to do some shopping or to take care of some errand or to visit her father's grave. Inevitably she'd come home shaking and spent.

That was her life now, and had been since she'd come out of her coma nine months ago. Physical and mental weakness, a constant feeling of sliding into a deep, black hole, a huge wall of glass between her and the rest of humanity. Those were her daily companions.

The nightmares were her nightly companions.

Claire rested her head against the back of the couch, suddenly overwhelmed with sadness and weakness. Making it upstairs to change felt like a huge challenge, Hilary conquering Mt. Everest.

The big ormolu clock on the hearth mantelpiece struck seven. Way too early to go to bed.

She knew, from bitter experience, that if she gave in to her desire for oblivion too early, she'd just wake up in a nest of sweaty sheets and blankets around midnight, unable to sleep until morning, when she'd get up exhausted and dizzy and unready to face the day. And she also knew from bitter experience that sleeping pills weren't the way to go. They only made the situation worse, befogging her mind without letting her rest.

No, better to stay awake until, say, ten and then hope for sleep. *Sleep.*

She nearly laughed at the longing coursing through her body. God, a full night's sleep. Once, she'd longed for travel and adventure, intellectual excitement. Meeting new people from different cultures. A sense of successfully making her way in this world.

Now she longed for one night's sleep. Without nightmares.

The horrors visited her almost nightly. The nightmares all had the same flavor, which as far as she knew was highly unusual. Claire had read more or less every book Amazon could deliver to her doorstep on sleep disorders and had started thinking of ordering the ones on mental disorders to see if she could find her particular one.

Her nightmares were constant. Sticky heat, the sound of gunshots, evil men coming after her. She'd try to run but find herself unable to move her limbs, which was a classic. There would be whispers, just out of hearing range. Whispers she couldn't understand, whispers of something terrible. A sense of heart-pounding danger, imminent menace.

A shot, a woman on the ground in a pool of her own blood.

Sometimes, though, rarely, in the middle of the nightmares, when she felt her entire body encased in an iron maiden of fear about an unstoppable evil, there would be someone else.

A man. His face was sometimes nebulous, sometimes clear, but only for a second. Not too tall but with immensely broad shoulders, brown hair, vigilant and tough.

She could never make out the color of his eyes, though that didn't matter. What mattered was that when he was in her head during the nightmare, the sharp-edged terror she felt abated a little. In the midst of monsters, he provided a sense of safety.

He wasn't always there, though. It was a sign of her lunacy that she longed for a nonexistent man to save her from her nonexistent enemies in her dreams.

To add to her horror, lately her dreams came to her in the middle of the day, in the form of delusions. She would suddenly zone out and hear voices. Men's voices, indistinct, yet filled with menace. Gunshots and bombs going off. Oppressive heat and fear.

She would suddenly find herself standing stock-still, heart pounding with terror, her mind completely taken over by jolting, horrifying images that were always just at the edge of comprehension.

It was somehow worse than the nightmares, because she could be anywhere. In a supermarket, walking to the library, pottering around the house. There would be no warning. She would simply plunge into a deep hole of horror and have to climb out on her own, shaking and sweaty and terrified.

Claire rubbed her forehead. The Headache was starting. Headache One, thank God. She had a whole classification system of headaches, from One to Five. One was a throbbing pain behind her eyes that at times made her dizzy. Dizzier. She always felt dizzy.

But Headache One was something she could live with, even function with, after a fashion. She'd done her shopping, cleaned the house and even worked on a translation with a One. Twos, Threes and Fours were headaches in increasing scales of pain and by the time a Four came around, her life stopped.

A Five . . . she shuddered. She hadn't had a Five in months and hoped desperately her Five days were behind her. A Five made her long for the peace of death.

Don't think of it. Her little mantra. *Ommm–don't-think-of-it–ommm.* A refrain that ran through her days. Don't think of the headaches, don't think of the months lost to a coma, don't think of her beloved friend Marie, not even a heap of mildewed bones buried in the jungle because they'd never found her body. Not even her DNA. She'd just gone missing and had never been found again.

Above all, don't think of her father. Dead of heartbreak.

One of the many horrifying things about her situation was that she couldn't remember a thing about the blast that had taken her life away.

Her last clear memory was of a reception at the French Embassy where she'd had a lot of fun fending off the French Chargé d'Affaires's amorous advances. He'd been charming and erudite and handsome, though of course married. He'd taken his defeat with immense good grace and she felt she might even have made a friend.

After that, nothing. The reception had been on the eighteenth of November. The blast had been on the twenty-fifth, Thanksgiving.

She had read all about it, when she could read again.

The first time she could read without getting dizzy, however, had been in late March.

Way before that, in December, had been the phone call from Marie's sister, Aba. Her father had taken the call while she was in a coma, but he hadn't told her about it. She'd found out on her own, while checking and eliminating phone messages. Her father had been hopeless about electronics and the message tape had been full.

Claire could remember it exactly as if it had happened yesterday. A sunny day in March, sunny enough to make her want to get up out of the wheelchair and walk into the garden, just for a moment. She hadn't though, because the recorded message had knocked the breath right out of her.

She could remember the light falling onto her father's desk in a bright elongated yellow rectangle. Her finger pressing the replay button over and over, listening to the messages then deleting them. Straightening up as she recognized Aba's voice.

She'd liked Aba, Marie's sister, a well-known physician, almost as much as she'd liked Marie and she'd been invited several times to the home Aba shared with her journalist husband.

She'd never heard that tone from Aba before, though. Low and hostile, filled with anger.

Claire, I'm sure you're now safe and sound after your father came to take you back home to the States. Marie didn't make it, though. We buried her last week. Or rather, we held a funeral ceremony, because we never found the body. I lost my sister because of you and I will never forgive and never forget. She insisted on going back for you. I tried to talk her out of it—why risk her life for yours? But I couldn't stop her and now her blood is on your head. I hope you choke on it.

Claire had never heard such venom, such hatred directed her way. What made it so awful was that she had no idea what Aba was talking about. She didn't remember anything about that day, nothing at all. How had she put Marie in danger? How had she got her killed?

Claire had tracked down Aba's home number. She must have left a hundred messages, but Aba never called back.

Claire knew the bare facts. The rebel Red Army had invaded Laka on Thanksgiving Day and had blown the embassy up, causing immense damage, but taking no lives except, perhaps, for Foreign National Marie Diur's.

And, of course, leaving her with only a shell of a life.

The embassy staff had been at the ambassador's residence and the Marines at Marine House. Claire had no idea at all why she hadn't been celebrating Thanksgiving at the ambassador's residence, though she intensely disliked him and his vicious wife.

She'd probably had a report to write, though it was now lost in the blast and in the traumatized corridors of her brain.

Blowing up the US Embassy had been a really stupid thing for the Red Army to do, because the US government then poured billions into shoring up the Makongan government—which in her opinion wasn't much better than the Red Army itself—turning it into both a US protectorate and an enormous marshaling yard for military and medical aid funneled into West Africa.

Claire had read about the bombing and the aftermath as if reading any other mission report of a colleague's posting. She remembered nothing. That day and the week before the bombing was a complete blank. Not to mention the three months of coma afterward.

There was a huge, gaping hole in her life and sometimes she felt it was going to suck her right down into it until she fell to the bottom and disappeared into the dark, dank depths.

Restless, Claire stood and paced the living room. It took her a while to cross it, it was so big. The entire house was big, much too big for a single woman.

Not for the first time, she thought of selling it, buying a condo somewhere . . . but where? It would be stupid to sell in Safety Harbor just to buy again here. Boston? She hadn't lived there since she was fifteen years old. There was nothing there for her. Washington DC? It might make some sense. Most of her translation clients lived in Washington, though being close to her employers wouldn't make much difference. She did all her work by email.

Living in Washington would remind her of all that she'd lost in the blast. Her father, her friend, her job, her *life*. She'd loved her job as a DIA analyst. She'd delighted in her analytical skills, meeting the challenges head-on, knowing that every time she solved a puzzle, however minor, it was one more brick in the wall keeping her country safe. She'd felt part of something big and important. Hard and necessary.

Those days were gone, forever. Who wanted an analyst who sometimes couldn't tell up from down? Who got dizzy spells and was visited nightly in her sleep by monsters?

She was lucky she had a knack for translating and was slowly building up a clientele. She worked from home. Her clients didn't have to know that dizzy spells rendered her useless several hours a day, or that sometimes she had to go lie down with a headache that made her nauseous.

All they cared about was that she deliver accurate translations by deadline, and she did. They didn't see her and they didn't have to know that she was a barely functioning being.

Oh God, she was so *sick* of this. Sick of herself. Sick of her weaknesses and uncertainties. Maybe if she had somebody to talk to, she could have an hour of peace in her head. But who?

She had nobody in Safety Harbor. She'd left when she was seventeen for college and had come back only for brief visits.

Her entire career had been spent traveling, living for a year or two at a posting, then moving on. The best friend she'd made at work had been Marie, and she was dead. By Claire's own hand, according to Marie's sister.

She'd spent the past year here, it was true, but three months of that year had simply disappeared into the maw of a coma. And when she'd finally surfaced, just learning to walk again and function at the most basic level had eaten up everything she had. No time or energy for making friends. Simply surviving had robbed every ounce of energy in her. So no, there wasn't anyone to talk to.

The house was empty, and completely silent. It was on a street closed to nonresidential traffic and there weren't even sounds of cars driving by outside.

The silence was oppressive, like a living, heavy weight pressing in on her chest. The large house was so still, it was the equivalent of an aboveground tomb. Exactly like her father's coffin, only bigger.

The large band around her chest that had dogged her days since waking up from the coma tightened, making it hard to breathe.

It was so damned *quiet*. As if she were the last human on earth.

All of a sudden, Claire knew she needed to hear human voices the way she needed air. The silence was like a dark hole, waiting to gobble her up, pull her down into an endless, airless cavern. She couldn't stand the silence for one more second. Even canned noise would be better than this emptiness.

With a shaking hand, she picked up the remote and cycled through the channels. Weather, rerun, a romantic comedy she'd already seen and which reminded her of how solitary and unfunny her life was, reality show, weather, reality show, cooking show, sports, weather, reality show . . . God, a reality show in a *convent*?

She shuddered and kept on flipping through the channels. Talk show, sports, weather . . . her thumb was growing tired. Finally, she found CNN. The music and logo for the news hour came up and she settled in, hoping to distract herself. It was no good. Israel, Palestine, bombing in Paris, possible serial killer in Portland, Oregon. This wasn't distracting her, it was pulling her deeper into her slippery black hole.

She picked up the remote again. *Thank God for remotes*, she thought, not for the first time, because she didn't have the energy to get up and switch the TV off.

A young woman came on, pretty, dark-haired. *Breaking News* glowed red at the top of the screen. On the chyron was written *Katie Maroney, Washington DC*, identifying the reporter.

An American Hero tracked along the bottom in bright red letters.

Claire stayed her hand. Okay, a hero. That was good. Right now, she needed to hear about a hero.

It was snowing in DC, tiny flakes spinning in the wind. Claire shivered in sympathy. It must have been freezing in Washington but the reporter was wearing a low-cut jacket and, when the camera pulled back to reveal the smoky ruins of a townhouse behind her, a miniskirt.

Claire winced. She'd have frozen to death with that outfit on in the snow. How could the woman not be turning blue from the cold?

The camera followed as Katie Maroney walked over to a broad-shouldered man, back to the camera, a dun-colored blanket covering his head and pooling around his shoulders.

To one side, a fire truck was the center of activity for at least ten firefighters in gear and protective helmets. An enormous hose spewed a streaming silver arc of water into the townhouse, causing huge clouds of smoke to billow up.

"This is Katie Maroney for CNN. We're reporting to you live from near Dupont Circle in Washington DC," she announced breathlessly. "This afternoon an electrical fire broke out in a townhouse where Mr. and Mrs. Everett Hines and their children, Sally, three, and Michael, five, live. Mr. Hines had gone out for milk when a fire broke out on the ground floor, burning out the electricity and telephone lines. Mrs. Hines's cell phone was broken and there was no way to call 911. Mrs. Hines leaned out of the third-story window and screamed for help. And help, miraculously, came. We have some video footage of the rescue filmed by an onlooker and we're cutting to that right now."

Claire leaned forward. A woman and two small children. *Oh God*, she prayed, *let this have a happy ending.*

The camera cut to shaky, grainy footage, like something out of *Cloverfield* or *Paranormal Activity*, probably taken from a cell. A woman leaned out of a third-story balcony, screaming for help, smoke billowing out from all the windows.

There were excited noises as onlookers shouted for help. Claire could hear one man calling 911. But nobody made a move until a broad-shouldered, dark-haired man dressed in jeans and a leather bomber jacket too light for the weather rounded the corner.

The phone camera somehow knew to follow him. The man in the bomber jacket took in the situation and in a flash ripped off his jacket, wrapped it around his head and plunged into the burning building.

Claire watched, riveted, breath caught in her chest.

Screams and cries of *Oh my God!* and *Will you look at that?* What felt like a million years later, but must have been only a minute, the man burst out of the front door with two screaming children in his arms. Live, red-gold flames were visible through the open door and the cell phone recorded the crackling sounds of the flames and the loud thump as part of a wall crumpled in a billow of fire and smoke.

The cell phone followed the man as he thrust the children into waiting hands and ran back into the building, ignoring the cries of *Are you crazy?* and *It's too late!* and *It's going to collapse, man!*

Sirens wailed as the fire truck and several police cars finally arrived. A dozen people clustered around the fire chief, screaming that there were two people trapped inside the collapsing building. The jerky tape was catching the chief directing his men when someone screamed and the cell phone was whipped back to the building so fast it made Claire nauseous.

She watched the grainy, shaky footage, feeling time stop. It was as if everything were happening in slow motion. The broad-shouldered man appeared in the doorway, limned by the hellish fire behind him, holding a woman wrapped in a blanket in his arms. Fire licked greedily at his feet, climbed his trousers, but he didn't seem to notice. He carried the woman forward until eager arms took her and she was placed on a stretcher, and only then did he fall to his knees.

The grainy footage cut off and the pretty face of Katie Maroney filled the screen once more. Her voice overrode all of the other voices, and a microphone was thrust into the man's face. "That was an amazing rescue! What a hero!" she gushed. "What's your name, sir?"

The man's voice was deep, but weak with pain and exhaustion. His head was hanging down as he gasped in air. He was covered in black soot.

"Gunnery Sergeant Weston. USMC." He frowned, shaking his head, wheezing for breath. "Not . . . Gunnery Sergeant. Not . . . in the Marines anymore. Daniel Weston."

Claire frowned. That name . . .

"Well, Daniel Weston, what do you do for a living?" The reporter seemed to be totally unaware that the heroic man was in pain. Claire would have batted away the microphone and told the woman to go to hell, but apparently the man had better manners than she did.

"Have . . . security consulting business."

"Well," Maroney purred, smiling flirtatiously at the burned, exhausted man, "your wife is going to be very proud of you today, Mr. Weston."

He shook his head again. Two paramedics lifted him up onto a stretcher. He took in a big gasp of air. Maroney's microphone followed him for a moment. "Not . . . married," he said as the paramedics put an oxygen mask on him then carried him away.

With a catlike smile, Katie Maroney turned to the camera. "Well, ladies and gentlemen, there you have it. Former Marine Gunnery Sergeant Daniel Weston, man of the hour. A hero who ran into a burning building twice to save a mother and her two children. And ladies . . ." She leaned closer to the lens with a conspiratorial smile and a wink.

"He's built, he's a hero, he owns his own company and he's single. What on earth are you waiting for?"

Marine . . . Daniel Weston. Claire blinked, the fog in her head parting for a moment. The name was somehow familiar. How could it be familiar?

A thumbnail photo in the upper left-hand corner, clearly taken from footage during the rescue, expanded until it filled the TV screen. *Daniel Weston*, the chyron said along the bottom. *Security consultant.*

Claire gasped, moving closer to the big TV screen, heart pounding. The dark hair was longer, the cheeks more hollowed, as if he'd lost weight. But she knew this man. Somehow she knew him.

And suddenly, she remembered how she knew him.

Frantic, Claire rushed into the library, feverishly pulling open drawers, pawing through paperwork until she found what she was looking for.

A big red folder with press clippings about the embassy bombing. She leafed through clipping after clipping, not caring that some fell to the floor. Finally, she found what she was looking for—a printout of the Laka Embassy staff as of November of last year. And on the second page, there he was.

Gunnery Sergeant Daniel Weston. Detachment Commander of the Marine Security Guard. He'd arrived a week before the bombing. The day of the French Embassy reception.

Claire had no memory of him at the Laka Embassy, none whatsoever. Somehow, the clouds in her mind had parted enough so that she'd known where to look for him. Was her memory returning? Had she had dealings with him in her lost week?

Ordinarily, the Marine Security Guards were just . . . there. In all her postings, the Marines had lived their own, separate lives. They lived in Marine House and though they were at all official functions as guards, they never socialized.

But somehow this Daniel Weston's path had crossed hers.

The printout shook in her hand. She studied the photograph the way ancient seers studied runes. He looked much younger in the official photo than on TV, though of course during the interview he'd just rushed into a raging fire twice and doubtless had been suffering from smoke inhalation.

In the staff photo, he had the high-and-tight Marine haircut—they didn't call them whitewalls for nothing—and a chest full of medals on his dress uniform jacket. She could read the medals as easily as she could read the newspapers. They weren't medals handed out for showing up on time or having polished brightwork on his uniform. They were serious medals for serious acts of heroism. This Daniel Weston had been a good Marine, one of the best.

Brown. His eyes were brown.

Claire could hardly breathe as she held the paper with his bio. He had been there, in Laka at the time of the bombing, though she didn't remember him.

In the past year, Claire had had no curiosity about the bombing itself. She'd barely survived it. Her life had been neatly divided into Before Bombing and After Bombing. And the After Bombing part of her life had left her broken and weak, half a person, almost a ghost.

A woman haunted by nightmares, horrible dreams so vivid she often woke up reaching for a nonexistent knife to defend herself.

Claire was as certain as she could be that this Daniel Weston, who'd been posted to Laka with her, held a key to something. Maybe he held the key to . . . herself.

And surely . . . surely her nightmares were trying to tell her something? Surely there was a *reason* she couldn't sleep, and heard voices and gunshots? Surely there was some element she could understand and, by understanding, eliminate it?

It would simply be too cruel if this was to be her life for the rest of her days—reduced to rubble, a wreck of a woman whose greatest hope was to sleep through the night.

No.

No, she refused even the thought of it.

She was lost in a labyrinth, unable to find her way out. Maybe this man could help her. It was the first ray of hope since the bombing. Perhaps in some way he could help her help herself. Find a way out of the swamp of her nightmares.

Suddenly galvanized, Claire sat down at her laptop, logged on to Expedia and booked the first flight out from Tampa the next morning. Destination: Washington DC. When she finished, she sat back, folding her shaking hands in her lap.

Even the thought of getting onto a plane, flying a couple of hours, taking a taxi, confronting a man who would barely remember her if he remembered her at all, who would probably think she was crazy—it was all too much. She couldn't do it.

What on earth could she say to him? *Can you help me? I think I'm going crazy. I hear voices and see men in my sleep.*

Oh God. Maybe he'd call the cops, have the crazy woman escorted to the door. She sounded crazy even to herself.

Claire sat trembling in her chair, heart beating fast. Maybe she could get her money back if she canceled right away. She reached out a shaking hand to the mouse, then stopped.

However terrified she was at leaving her home, leaving Safety Harbor, contacting a stranger, the alternative was worse. If she didn't make an effort to understand why she had the nightmares, to understand what she was so afraid of, to make some kind of effort to get her life back, she could spend the rest of her days in this condition.

The thought was unbearable. She'd rather die.

She had to know. *Had* to.

Gunnery Sergeant Daniel Weston might have some answers to the Laka bombing. He might be able to provide some information that would fill the terrifying gaps in her memory.

But that wasn't the reason why she was venturing out from her home for the first time in a year. There was another, far more urgent reason. A reason she didn't dare tell him, because then he really would think she was crazy.

Because Daniel Weston was the man in her dreams who kept her safe.

THREE

CLAIRE looked at the address on a sheet of paper in her hand, then back up again at the number on the brass plate. When she swung her head up to check the plate bearing the number 2215, she had a moment's dizziness and clenched her teeth.

Sometimes the dizziness morphed into nausea before she could stop it. *Please God, not now. Don't let me upchuck all over Barron Street.*

The goddess of hurting women listened and the dizziness subsided, leaving her shaken and still disoriented. What on earth was she doing here, so far from home?

Oh yes. Coming to Weston Consulting at 2215 Barron Street in Alexandria because maybe, just maybe, Daniel Weston could help dispel some of the shadows in her mind.

And, though she could hardly let herself think of it, because he haunted her dreams.

So here she was, at— The paper with the address on it shook in her hand as her mind suddenly went blank. She had to check the number, then the brass plaque again.

What a simple thing—to check an address, something any person on earth had to do but once. And yet so hard for her. She *hated* it that she needed to check even simple things twice, three times.

She turned to the taxi driver who had been patiently waiting, probably thinking she was a moron to take so long, and nodded. *Yes, this is the right place.*

He touched his baseball cap with his index finger in a salute, then took off with a squeal of tires, leaving her completely alone on the deserted street.

The trip had been such a nightmare. She'd regretted it the moment she'd left the house in the pouring rain. The taxi had got caught in a jam due to the sudden downpour, tipping her out at departures barely in time to make it to the gate. Two huge Airbuses were boarding and the gates were crowded with far more passengers than the relatively small Tampa airport was equipped to handle.

By the time Claire had fought her way to the gate through enormous pink tourists smelling of suntan lotion, tripped over baby bags and tried to shove her way past a group of basketball players so tall they looked alien, she was sweating and frightened, heart pounding, head so light she prayed she wouldn't faint.

The plane ride had been the most turbulent flight she'd ever experienced. She thanked her wretched stomach that it had refused any food that morning, because she wasn't forced to spew her breakfast into a paper bag like the lady sitting next to her in 26C.

Even finding a taxi at National had been a horror story, since apparently there was a huge snarl-up downtown.

But finally she was here. Shaking, wondering whether she'd lost her mind, almost certain that this Daniel Weston would call 911 to have her carted away—but here.

She'd made it this far, in her first foray out of Safety Harbor since the bombing, which surely should earn her points somewhere.

Now all she had to do was ring the bell, go inside and

ask a man she didn't know if he knew her, and try to figure out why he was haunting her dreams.

Piece of cake.

She drew in a deep breath, pressed the bell and waited. And waited. Nothing happened. Oh God, had she made this nightmare journey for someone who wasn't in? She forced her brain into rewind mode, consulted her muscle memory and realized that she hadn't pressed the bell hard enough.

She pressed the bell again, harder. Almost immediately a female voice with a strong New York accent answered.

"Weston Consulting."

"I'd like—" What would she like? Well, her life back, for starters. To have this perpetual fog in her head lifted. To understand her nightmares. All of that would be nice.

She cleared her throat.

"I'd like to speak to Daniel Weston, please."

The sigh was audible over the intercom. "You and a million other women," the disembodied, nasal voice said. "Do you have an appointment?"

Oh God. Claire was appalled. Not that she hadn't picked up the phone to make an appointment, but that the thought hadn't even *occurred* to her.

This was awful. She was much worse off than she'd thought.

She'd been a successful professional in a hard job that wasn't top-heavy with women. Apart from being good at it, she'd risen through the ranks because she also knew how to play the game, because she knew the rules and abided by them.

Right up there in the rules on how to get by in this life was making an appointment with a busy man whose help you needed.

She knew that, knew it intimately, down to her toes. And yet, when she'd seen the video footage, all she could think of was *This man might help me* as she'd set about feverishly making her travel arrangements with no thought other than how hard it was going to be to trek up to Washington.

And even during the exhausting journey, she'd been so busy surviving her first trip since the bombing it had never once crossed her mind to call ahead and make an appointment.

Claire hardly recognized herself. She was a shell of a woman, more than halfway to going mad. Certainly incapable of living in the modern world.

"No, sorry." She swallowed. "I don't have an appointment. I'm sorry to take up your time."

Another sigh over the intercom. "Well, since you're here, you might as well come up. I'll see what I can do to fit you in. Fourth floor." And with a loud snick the big, solid door unlatched.

Claire placed the flat of her hand against the big polished wooden door, hesitating.

She felt as if she were on a raft somewhere far out to sea, rudderless, completely adrift. There was one island in all the vastness of the sea and it was waiting upstairs. If the island was empty, merely a sandbar, she was dead. Her life was over.

Her fingers caressed the grain of the wood as she tried to steel herself to push the door open.

Opening an unlatched door. How hard could it be? And yet her heart pounded and she felt dizzy, unable to draw breath.

She stiffened her knees and spine. *Just do it.* After all, the worst thing that could happen would be that he'd think her a loon. He couldn't say anything worse to her than what she told herself a dozen times a day.

Claire pushed the door all the way open and entered the building's foyer. It was nice without being obnoxiously upscale. The kind of building small, personal, successful businesses would choose. Clean, with lots of thriving plants.

According to her research, former Gunnery Sergeant Daniel Weston had been out of the Marines for nine months, had started up his company just six months ago and here he was already in a nice building, with a receptionist.

Whoever and whatever Daniel Weston was, he seemed to be good at his job.

Claire forced herself to walk across the lobby to the bank of elevators at the back. When one arrived, she punched the button for the fourth floor and felt her stomach sink as the car rose.

How much of a wild-goose chase was she on? She was going to bother a perfect stranger, whose only connection to her was that they'd been posted to Laka at the same time, though she didn't remember him and presumably he wouldn't remember her.

And, well, of course, she dreamed about him. There was that. Maybe the latest Manual of Mental Disorders would create a new category—women who dream of men they didn't know.

The elevator came to a smooth stop, the doors opening with a muted whoosh onto a pleasant landing with inset ceiling lights, more potted plants and a series of doors with shiny brass plaques.

Right across from her was the door to Weston Consulting. All she had to do was step out and ring the bell.

Without any warning, Claire had a sudden panic attack, the bottom dropping out of her stomach. It wasn't that she was frightened of Daniel Weston. She was frightened of *herself*. At what she had become. This fearful creature incapable of dealing with the world in any way, on any terms.

She was frightened at what might come of this meeting. Or rather, what might not.

She recognized that something wild inside her, something that felt perilously close to hope, had propelled her a thousand miles north, on a trip she wasn't yet ready to take. Only now could she recognize the crazy hope that somehow this man held some answers to the darkness inside her for what it was.

Madness.

She wasn't terrified at what he would say to her. She was terrified that he would have nothing to say to her. That this would be a dead end, and that she was condemned to the shadows in her mind forever.

Trembling, she crossed the corridor and rang the bell. When the door clicked open she stood quaking on the threshold, then drew in a sharp breath and stepped forward.

Inside was a pleasant waiting room decorated in neutral tones, with comfortable-looking couches and some tasteful art. Well, if you had to go to a security consultant, you probably needed reassurance. The calm neutral surroundings actually worked, because she felt her anxiety go down a notch.

"Can I help you?" A good-looking, middle-aged African American woman looked up from her computer monitor. She looked competent, intelligent and kind. She also looked a little like Marie and Aba's mother, who'd basically adopted Claire as the third Diur girl while she'd been in Laka. Claire's anxiety dropped another degree.

"Yes," she said, hating the breathlessness in her voice. Her heart was pounding so hard she wondered whether the silk blouse over her left breast was moving. Thank God she had her coat on. "I've come to see Gunnery—Mr. Daniel Weston. I'm sorry I don't have an appointment. We served together at the Laka Embassy in Makongo. Our tours of duty overlapped briefly. He—he might remember me."

The woman already had a handset to her ear. "Dan, the lady has arrived. Uh-huh." Her eyes rolled skyward. "Yeah, I know. But she said to say that the two of you worked together in Makongo. Her name is—" She looked over her reading glasses at Claire, dark eyebrows up in silent query.

Claire Day, she wanted to say, but somehow the words never came out. To her utter astonishment, her Foreign Service nickname came spilling out of her mouth before she could censor herself.

"Blondie. Tell him Blondie is here."

FOUR

"ANOTHER lady to see you," Roxanne announced on the intercom. "She's on her way up. Jesus, Dan, they're coming out of the woodwork."

"Tell her no." Dan thrust a hand through his hair, nostrils flaring in disgust. Though he must have washed his hair twenty times, it still held the acrid smell of smoke. "Tell her I've gone. Tell her I'm not available until the next millennium. Tell her I'm dead."

"Too late," Roxanne trilled in a singsong voice and hung up.

Jesus Christ. Ever since that reporter put him on the news as some sort of male meat up for grabs, his life hadn't been worth living. He'd had no idea of the impact the news item had made until he walked out of the hospital into the glare of feeder lights and overhead boom mikes, with a hundred screaming reporters and a thousand screaming women.

He'd had to make his way through the crowd by sheer force, hoping he wasn't hurting anyone, but desperate to just get out of there, batting mikes away from his mouth and fending off women who were old enough to know better. Women who wanted a souvenir of him and weren't prepared to take no for an answer.

He'd lost his bomber jacket to a particularly sinewy redhead who threw him a body block and started stripping him. The only way out was to ditch the jacket, like throwing a minnow into the water for the sharks so you could get away.

He'd made his escape in the ensuing scrimmage, accompanied by squeals he could hear a block away.

Home was no sanctuary since he'd crazily allowed his home number to be listed in the phone book. Man, that had been a big mistake, one he wasn't making again. The answering machine tape had run out of room one hour after the show aired. He walked into his home to the sound of the ringing phone and simply pulled the plug. His office email box was full, which he would have thought impossible since he had tons of memory. But it looked like every female loon in America and even some in Canada had come out of the woodwork to send him photos. Lots of them. Not all of them with clothes on.

Just glancing at the subject lines—most of which were propositions for sex—made him shudder as he quickly ran down the list of literally thousands and thousands of emails, deleting everything that wasn't work-related.

It took him hours.

The instant he emptied his inbox, it started filling up again. At this rate, he was going to have to change his email address, which was a real pain. It meant contacting all his clients and buddies, changing the web page and notifying his bank, accountant, lawyer and doctor.

Gah.

What the fuck was the matter with these women anyway? It was like he'd flipped some kind of switch he never even knew was there. Or had emitted some kind of whistle on a high-pitched frequency only women heard.

He'd done exactly what any other man would have done. Certainly one as well-trained as he had been. Any cop, any firefighter, any pilot, certainly any soldier, would have done exactly the same. You'd think he'd morphed into Superman and the entire female population into Lois Lane.

And his secretary Roxanne hadn't been any help at all. She found the whole thing hilarious. When he'd walked in this morning, she'd simply saluted him and pushed several sheets of paper across her desk at him.

"Messages. My hero." She'd actually fluttered her eyelashes, the minx. She smiled at his snarl and when he'd slammed the door behind him, he could hear her laughing.

Shit, shit, *shit*. He wasn't going to get any work done today, and he had the World Bank security assessment report and a Homeland Security contract to get through, not to mention preparing for a big meeting in Baltimore this afternoon with the CEO of an enormous hedge fund. But how could he concentrate on work through a solid wall of women?

His old Marine buddy Andy Crossley had called, sniggering. "Maybe they'll do a made-for-TV movie. Man, you are going to get *so* laid for the next year, you lucky dog. All you'll have to do is snap your fingers."

Fuck that. He didn't want to get laid. Well, of course he did, he had a Y chromosome after all, but not to any of the women so frantic to get in touch with him.

There was only one woman he wanted, and she'd been in the cold, cold ground for a year now.

Shit. He tried, he really did, to keep Claire Day out of his head, but it wasn't working. It hadn't been working for a whole fucking year. It was like she was stuck in there.

He hadn't even been able to go to bed with someone—a full year of chastity, completely self-imposed. He told himself it was because the women he dated all had fatal flaws. They were too this or not enough that.

Bullshit.

He realized it was bullshit when he accompanied a very pretty and nice enough brunette home after dinner last month without even a good-night kiss, thinking he liked her but she wasn't blond.

The instant that thought struck him, he knew he was in the deepest, deepest shit, because the problem with all of these women was that none of them were Claire and Claire would never walk this earth again.

So he told himself he was too busy building his business to have time for sex and tried to forget about it. Which was okay during the day, sometimes, but his wayward head betrayed him at night, when as likely as not he'd fall asleep thinking of her, wake up thinking of her and suspected that the dreams he could never remember were of her.

It was insane. He remembered every second he'd spent with her that last day. He remembered the sound of her voice, the curve of her cheek, that lock of shiny, pale blond hair curling over her shoulder.

He remembered the hot kiss, the taste of her mouth, the shape of her tongue, the feel of her skin, the smell of her.

He remembered the affection in her voice as she spoke of her father. Above all, he remembered how strong and brave she'd been alone with him in an embassy and a city under siege, with no guarantees that it would end well. And it hadn't, not for her, anyway.

It hadn't ended well for him, either. He'd blown out a knee and an eardrum, didn't have a spleen anymore and had spent three months in physical rehab. Worst of all, he'd never be an active duty Marine again, which was like a kind of death.

Not Claire's kind of death, though. She was gone forever. Nothing he could do and nothing he could say would change that.

Dan hardly recognized himself. He didn't do mooning. He never wanted what he couldn't have. He was a hardheaded, practical man. He was a fucking *Marine*, for God's sake. Even with a busted knee, no spleen and one eardrum blown out, he was a Marine. Once a Marine, always a Marine, forever. And Marines took life exactly as it was and didn't wish for the impossible.

So what was with the wanting a dead woman? What was that about?

Claire Day was never coming back and he had to recognize that before he blew a gasket or his dick shriveled from lack of use. Maybe he should just . . . what? Accept the advances of a couple of the less loony-sounding women? Only how could he tell? It's not as if they had an *I'm only temporarily deranged due to the news report but am actually very sane* sign hung around their necks.

Maybe he should have them vetted by Roxanne. Yeah, that would work. Roxanne would have made a great Marine. She cut straight through any BS and was as tough as any drill instructor he'd ever had.

So let her sift through all the phone calls and letters and emails to see if there was anyone viable he could date. Maybe go to bed with, just to get Claire Day out of his head.

Jesus.

He rested his forehead on his hand a minute, tired and frustrated that the thought of just going out and bedding a woman didn't hold any appeal at all.

The intercom crackled to life. "Dan, the lady has arrived."

"Damn it, Roxanne, I don't have time for this," he growled.

"Uh-huh. Yeah I know. But she said to say that the two of you worked together in Makongo. Her name is—"

She conferred with someone and as Dan heard the soft voice replying he sat up straight, electrified. Christ, it sounded like . . . But that was crazy.

"Blondie," Roxanne said. "She said her name is Blondie."

He raced for the door, not even feeling his feet. He wrenched the door open and—God, yes. Oh Jesus, yes.

Claire. *Claire.*

"My God," he breathed, hanging on to the door frame, hoping his metal knee wouldn't collapse. "You're alive."

There she was. Much thinner, very pale, with short-cropped hair and deep purple bruises under her eyes. Looking sad and lost and lonely. But definitely Claire.

In two strides he was with her. He pulled her up by her

elbows and put his arms around her. At the last minute, he realized she was trembling badly, so he kept his embrace loose, when what he really wanted to do was pull her tightly against him, using all his strength, and never let her go.

She felt so . . . fragile. As if her bones would bend under his hands. Dan was about to let her go when he suddenly felt her hands clench around his back and her forehead bury itself in his shoulder.

An enormous shudder worked its way through her body. She sobbed once, a harsh sound coming from deep in her chest, then she pulled in a sharp breath to stop another one coming out.

She was trembling so hard Dan was scared she might hurt herself, so he wrapped himself around her, keeping his hold gentle. His eyes rose to meet Roxanne's kind, chocolate brown eyes. She looked troubled.

It's okay, he mouthed, then bent his head back to Claire's. They stood there, clinging to each other. Claire to keep upright and Dan to make sure she wasn't a mirage and wouldn't disappear from his life again.

"I thought you were dead," he said finally into her hair. That glorious, pale, shiny hair, now cut boy-short. It was still as soft as he remembered, though. Like goose down.

He kept his voice low and had to swallow against a tight throat.

It was as if he hadn't spoken. Claire pulled away slightly and though it cost him, he let go of her. He kept his hands loose, ready to catch her if she fell. She looked as if a strong wind would blow her away.

Claire watched his eyes carefully, as if there might be something very important in them. "You know me," she whispered. "You remember me. Oh God, it's not all in my head."

She swayed and Dan gripped her elbows. He wasn't going to force her to have this conversation on her feet. She looked close to collapse.

"Yes, I know you." Dan kept his voice gentle. "But I

thought you were dead. I thought you died in the blast. Listen, why don't we go into my office and . . ." *Stay with me. I'll never let you go again.* "And we can catch up."

"Oh yes," she breathed, sounding relieved. She turned and with shaking hands gathered her purse and umbrella. Dan ushered her into his office then stuck his head back out. "Roxanne, how about—"

"Coffee," Roxanne said promptly. "Lots of it, black and strong. Milk and sugar. Croissants from the French pastry shop across the street."

Bless her. At that moment, Dan loved her. "You be sure to tell that husband of yours he's a lucky man."

"I do, constantly." Their eyes met and Dan could read infinite kindness there. "Go on in, I'll bring the coffee soon."

He nodded and placed a hand at Claire's back. Because it was the gentlemanly thing to do, but also because she looked like she needed it.

Once inside his office, he took her coat and showed her to the most comfortable armchair, the one he sometimes took a short snooze in. He didn't sit behind his desk. He sat on the couch, at right angles to her.

She sat down gingerly, at the edge of the seat, and folded her hands in her lap. Her hands were trembling. Dan looked at them, wanting to hold them so badly he hurt with it.

What the hell.

He reached over and encased her hands in his. They were ice-cold. He didn't say anything, just sat there until her hands warmed up a little and stopped trembling.

She watched his eyes carefully, unmoving.

She opened her mouth, then closed it.

"What?" Dan kept his voice low and gentle.

"I—you're going to think I'm crazy."

He tightened his grip on her hands. "I'm pretty tolerant. Why don't you try me?"

She drew in a deep breath, like someone about to dive, then stopped.

He simply waited, hands over hers.

"Were we—were we lovers?" she finally whispered, then gasped at her own words.

SHE really was crazy. Completely blitzed, off her rocker.

Claire waited, trembling.

Of all the things she could have asked—*Do you remember me? You were there the day of the bombing. What happened?*—that was the one that burst forth out of her mouth. It was a massively embarrassing question. Insane, actually. But it had welled up out of her with an unstoppable force, the words out before she even knew she was going to say them.

The thing was, there'd been some . . . image, some aura of her having been intimate with him.

It wouldn't have been such an awful question if he'd been a less attractive man. But the fact of the matter was that he was almost insanely attractive, in a very rough way.

When she'd had her meltdown out in the reception area, her arms had been unable to encompass his immensely broad back. His muscles had been like steel and she'd clung to him the way you'd cling to a girder in a storm. Hard, unyielding, safe.

She didn't date much, but the men she did date—had dated, when she still had a life—were metrosexuals. Soft and funny and even a little flighty. Daniel Weston was the exact opposite of her usual date. He was hard and serious and right now she wanted to cling to him and never let him go.

And he was letting her cling to his hands, letting the crazy lady work out whatever nuttiness was in her head. Which was obviously filled with fluff because the first thing she'd talked about was . . . being his lover.

Where had that come from?

Obviously it had come from her deep loneliness and sorrow. A year completely alone, she falls into the arms of a dangerously attractive man—a very *male* man—and crazy Claire goes right off the deep end. It was totally humiliating and if she had any backbone at all, she'd stand up, apologize for bothering him and fly straight back to Safety Harbor.

Except . . . her cold hands were encased in his large, brown, warm ones, and they felt so *good* there. She looked down at them, suddenly ashamed of herself. Of her weakness. Her inability to remember anything, the constant feeling of standing over an abyss.

"No, we weren't lovers. Why do you ask that?" Daniel Weston was watching her carefully, eyes dark and intelligent.

She told the truth. "I don't know. I have no idea why I said that. It wasn't what I was going to ask at all."

His gaze was so steady. "What were you going to ask?"

"If you were with me," she answered simply, watching him. "That day. The day of the bombing." The day her world died.

He didn't answer, simply bowed his head, eyes fixed on hers.

Yes!

There'd been no one she could talk to, no one at all. The entire staff had been at Crock-of-Shit's reception, all the Marines at Marine House. Marie was dead.

By the time she'd woken up from the coma, Crocker had retired and most of the staff had been reassigned. There was no one to ask that she knew of. She'd been alone with her nightmares and the black hole in her head instead of memories.

"You were there, on guard," she whispered. He had to have been. An embassy was never left without a Marine guard.

She hadn't even thought of that.

Claire Day, able to write a report on threat levels based on scanty intel and still be right, had been totally unable to think her way through this. "You weren't at Marine House?"

"No. I was at the embassy," he answered soberly.

"Because I can't remember anything," Claire whispered,

searching his dark eyes for answers. "Nothing at all. The last thing I remember was the reception at the French Embassy."

"November eighteenth." He nodded. "A whole week before. My first official day of duty was November seventeenth, but I spent that day and the next being briefed. You don't remember anything? Anything at all?"

"No." She didn't tell him of her nightmares, the incessant heat, the whispers and gunfire. "Nothing. It's like this huge hole in my head. And I'm sorry about the question about being lovers. I have no idea where that came from." She gave a little half laugh that came out sad and unfunny, and decided to tell the unpleasant truth. "I sustained massive head injuries. I've had . . . problems since the bombing."

A swift knock, and the voice of the receptionist through the door. "Dan? Can I come in?"

He released her hands, stood and walked swiftly to the door, opening it. Her hands immediately felt cold again.

The receptionist stood on the threshold with a big tray holding a pot of coffee, two big mugs, a sugar bowl, a milk pitcher and two plates, each with a huge croissant on it. She set the tray on the coffee table and stood back, eyeing him, then eyeing Claire with a worried expression on her face.

Claire was ashamed of the way she'd behaved earlier, falling apart in this man's lobby, making this very nice lady worry about her. She drummed up a smile. "Thank you so much. The coffee smells delicious."

The woman's worried expression lightened slightly. "You're welcome. You two eat every bite now, you hear me?"

Daniel Westin snorted. "Yes, ma'am." He rolled his eyes at Claire after snapping off a military salute. "You'd better obey Roxanne here because her revenge is swift and brutal if her orders are ignored."

The receptionist smiled, showing dazzling white teeth, and swatted him on the arm. The air of affection between them was palpable. "Go on now. You just make sure that girl eats something. She looks like she's about ready to fall down." She turned and met Claire's eyes. "Did you have breakfast this morning?"

Claire was taken aback by the first personal question anyone had asked her in over a year.

"Um, no." She sketched a shaky smile. "Lucky thing, too. I flew up from Florida and it was one of the most turbulent flights I've ever been on. The lady sitting next to me tossed her breakfast right into the barf bag."

Roxanne shook her finger. "And I'll bet you anything you didn't eat much yesterday, either."

Actually, Claire hadn't eaten *anything* the day before except for some milk and honey. She'd come back from the cemetery so depressed her appetite, never strong since she'd woken up from the coma, had deserted her completely. The hot milk and honey had been to warm her up.

"Uh-huh," Roxanne replied nodding, as if Claire had spoken. "I thought so." She pointed a slender brown finger at the tray, looking first at Daniel, then at Claire. "I don't want to find even crumbs on that plate."

Daniel grinned. "Yes, ma'am." And he gave another ironic salute.

The door closed quietly behind her and Daniel bent to the tray, giving Claire a sharp-eyed glance. "Roxanne's right," he said quietly. "Try to eat something. You do look like you're about ready to fall down."

In her previous life, Claire would have bristled at those words. She'd never taken orders well and was lucky that she often worked alone. Few embassies could afford two DIA analysts and so she was always at the top of her own pecking order. No bosses and no colleagues, just as she liked it.

But right now, what he said was so palpably true her indignation lobe just switched off.

"How do you take your coffee?" he asked.

"Black," she replied.

He looked at her, a long, penetrating look out of those intelligent dark eyes. "Are you sure you don't want to try the coffee with some milk and sugar? Might be a bit easier on an empty stomach."

Claire shrugged. "Okay." She watched as he made the coffee almost white and refrained from wincing as he proceeded to dump half the sugar bowl into the mug.

"Here." He put a plate with a huge croissant in front of her, followed by a mug of pale coffee. "Those come from a French pastry shop across the way and they're not half bad."

Claire leaned forward carefully, checking her stomach. To her astonishment, it wasn't closing up like a fist, it wasn't lurching back in horror. It was . . . quiet. Calm, peaceful. Not noticing that she was about to eat something. Maybe thinking of something else.

She pulled off a corner and smiled. The exact same buttery smell of the croissants she used to eat in Paris wafted up, except this croissant was about three times the size. A croissant on steroids, but excellent just the same, she found as she put the soft puff of pastry in her mouth. Heaven.

Dan was watching her carefully, nudging the mug closer to her. "The coffee now."

Okay. It didn't taste of coffee, it tasted of milk and a mountain of sugar, but it was warm and went down and stayed down.

He nodded as she sipped. "So . . . you don't remember anything?" His jaw muscles rippled. "Nothing at all?"

Claire shook her head, tearing off another small bite. "No." Her voice came out almost a whisper. She cleared her throat and pushed her diaphragm to make her voice stronger. "Nothing. I read some of the after action reports, but it was like . . . like reading about the Beirut bombing of the Marine barracks back in 1983, which we did in my poli sci classes at Georgetown. It felt sort of long ago and far away, you know what I mean?"

He nodded soberly.

"But—" She took another sip of the overly sweet brew and put the mug back down. The room was quiet. The reception area had overlooked Barron Street but this office overlooked a series of back gardens, lushly green in the damp air.

"But?" he prodded quietly and Claire nearly wept with frustration.

There'd been something she wanted to say. A memory had flashed across her mind. Or maybe not a memory—a vision.

It was gone now, like so many things in her life. It had retreated back into the big black hole of her mind.

"Nothing," she whispered. How could she tell him she saw things that came and went? And that she had difficulty distinguishing reality from visions? He'd think she was insane, and he wouldn't be far off the mark.

Change the subject. It was a tactic she'd developed this past year, when she found herself forgetting things that everyone knew, or blurting out something that made people look at her as if she'd just been beamed down from Mars. When that happened, she changed the subject. Comment on something entirely different.

Her mind whirred uselessly as she checked the room for a diversion, but nothing presented itself. The furnishings were bland, not expensive, not cheap. Bookshelves, a couple of framed certificates.

Her eyes alit on the *Washington Post* on the coffee table, open to the Politics section. She'd had zero interest in politics this past year, but something about the article arrested her attention. A photograph. Of a smiling, good-looking man.

Oh, yeah. He'd have landed on his feet.

Bowen McKenzie. She'd overlapped two tours of duty with him, in Durban and Laka. It had been an open secret that he was CIA. He never really tried to hide it. She imagined he felt it gave him a dashing air. Hinting that he knew dark secrets was part of his special seduction technique, which had worked on every available woman he'd come across in the Foreign Service between the ages of twenty and fifty, married or not, with the exception of Claire and Marie Diur.

Claire would rather have put her hand in a thresher than go to bed with Bowen. He'd made her skin crawl. But she'd been a lonely exception, and Bowen had taken her refusal personally and had made it his mission to change her mind.

He hadn't been successful and it had burned.

"Bowen's in Washington? I wonder if I should have gotten in touch with him, too." Her mouth twisted with distaste at the thought.

"Would have been useless," Daniel answered. "Bowen wasn't there that day."

She sighed in relief. Talking to Daniel Weston was infinitely nicer than dealing with Bowen McKenzie.

He was sitting across from her, in Male Mode—knees apart, leaning forward, clasped hands between knees. His shoulders were so broad they blocked her view of the lower edge of the window.

There was nothing polished or elegant about him. He was dressed more for comfort than for style, in corduroy trousers, a heavy brown sweater with a blue shirt collar underneath and boots rather than dress shoes.

She stared out the window. It had started sleeting, needle-like shards of ice pinging against the windowpane. The windows had triple-glazing so there was no noise, not even from the sharp wind bending the branches of a big, old oak in someone's backyard.

There was something about what he said . . .

She turned back to him.

"Bowen wasn't there?" She frowned. "But . . ."

There was something wrong in that. Wasn't there? Bowen McKenzie had been working with a private think tank on some big development project with military implications, some big new unholy alliance the CIA had been forging. She knew he'd staked his reputation on it and that he was incredibly ambitious. He'd rarely left Laka in the previous six months. "Are you sure?"

"Absolutely. He wasn't even in Laka, he was in Algiers, meeting with the deputy premier."

"Are you sure?" Why was she insisting? It was just that . . . for a second there, clouds parted in her head and she thought she had a memory of Bowen in Laka that day. A memory of a memory.

"It was my job to keep track of everyone working at the embassy," Daniel said gently. "I'm sure. McKenzie was on a two-day trip to Algeria, due to come back the twenty-seventh." He shook his head. "Of course, he came right back after the bombing. I heard about that from my second in command, later. By the time he made it back to Laka, I was being operated on in Ramstein."

"You were hurt, too?"

He nodded curtly and said nothing. He didn't want to talk about it. Fair enough. She understood completely.

Close up, she was able to appreciate how incredibly fit he was. He'd been hurt in the bombing, too, but there was absolutely no sign of that. None.

He looked as strong as an ox—broad, without a hint of fat. Large, very strong hands. Huge thigh muscles visible even underneath the thick corduroy material of his trousers.

He no longer had that Marine staple haircut, the white-walled high-and-tight she was so familiar with from embassies. If anything, his hair was a little shaggy. He could use a haircut. A lock of hair had fallen over his forehead and, crazily, her hand itched to brush it back for him, which was nuts, of course.

She should be used to her wayward thoughts by now, but wanting to smooth back the hair of a perfect stranger was pushing it, even for her lunatic self.

And yet, and yet—oh, man. She almost shook with the effort to keep her hands in her lap. Daniel Weston seemed so incredibly . . . solid. So strong and reassuring. This enormous source of strength and . . . heat.

Focus, Claire!

She circled back to what he'd said. That Bowen hadn't been in Laka the day of the bombing. Claire searched his eyes, so dark and certain of what he'd said.

Unlike her, who doubted everything.

She hated that about herself. There was no longer any internal sense of whether something was true or not. A lifetime ago, she'd been an analyst, capable of sifting through contradictory facts to get at the kernels of truth. She'd been very, very good at it, and hadn't realized how much she cherished that ability until it was gone. Until she'd been left with a world that shifted constantly beneath her feet.

She had a feeling Bowen McKenzie had been there in Laka at the time of the bombing, and he hadn't been. Just one more example of not being able to trust herself.

And yet . . . *why* was she so sure Bowen had been there? Did she have a memory that was superimposing itself on her lost week?

Oh God, nothing made any sense. And she was taking up this very nice man's time. She stood up.

Suddenly, visions dredged up from some deep dark place within her came shooting into her mind.

Heat, low vicious whispers, a glance up out of feral eyes, a shot ringing out, a head exploding . . .

"Oh!" She bent forward, eyes closed tight, as a burst of pain exploded in her head. She held her head tightly between her hands, because when this happened, when her head felt like exploding, she had to hold it together or she'd find shards of skull on the floor. At least that's what it felt like.

Spots danced in front of her eyes and she managed by a miracle to keep upright. Once, alone in the house, she'd fainted, waking up on the cold marble floor after night had fallen.

This time there was someone to catch her. Two big, strong hands, pulling her against a broad chest. She couldn't fall to the floor if she wanted to.

For a second, she blanked completely, senses flooded with conflicting input. She was dizzy, despairing. Chilled, scared. There was what was inside her—a cold sort of despair that she would never get her life back, ever again. That she was condemned to live forever in this frozen wasteland where nothing made sense.

And then there was the input of her senses right in this

instant—a feeling of immense safety, in the solid grasp of a man who wouldn't let her fall.

For an instant, for only an instant, Claire allowed herself to lean on someone else. Her arms went around that hugely broad back and she simply held on for dear life, because that's what it felt like. Holding on for her life, before it slipped away entirely, in falls and headaches and the horrifying sense of sliding away into insanity.

All the bad things simply . . . stopped. Her taut muscles loosened, her eyes closed, her nose was buried in a sweater that smelled of fabric softener and man, with a faint tang of smoke.

She was being held tightly, engulfed in strong arms and warmth and her mind simply blanked.

She was so used to the background buzz of anxiety and fear in her head, a constant hiss of static tinged with darkness, that she simply blissed out at its absence.

No bad thoughts or feelings, no dizziness or sudden panic. Just this blissful . . . nothingness. Enveloped in a cocoon of safety and strength where no terrible things could happen. Where if the floor were to open up into an abyss, he'd catch her.

She stood for long moments, forehead dug into the chest of this man she knew only in her dreams.

Claire stepped back when she could feel Daniel checking his wristwatch behind her back. She tested the ground, found it solid again.

He winced. "Listen, I really, *really* hate to do this, but I've got an appointment in Baltimore I can't break. It's an appointment made a month ago, unfortunately, and I simply can't cancel. Much as I'd like to."

Claire flushed, ashamed of herself. "Oh my gosh, of course. I'll get out of your hair—"

"No, no." He looked at her in horror. "I'm canceling everything else on my schedule. This meeting shouldn't take more than a couple of hours and I should be back by six. Certainly I'll be back in time to take you out to dinner. When's your flight back?"

"I haven't actually booked a return flight," she confessed. Staring at the empty *Return Flight* field on the website, she'd pulled a complete blank. Fixing a return had simply been too much for her, so she'd booked a one-way ticket, cost be damned.

His mouth lifted in a smile. "Great. Then that's settled. May I pick you up at seven at your hotel?"

Normally, she didn't like being steamrolled, but it didn't feel like that. It didn't feel like he was taking over her life. It felt like being cared for. She hesitated, then nodded.

He looked pleased. More than pleased, actually. He looked . . . interested.

"Seven is fine."

It had been so *long* since she'd felt anything like this, since she'd been part of that whole man-woman thing. Her only contact with men over the past nine months had been with doctors and physical therapists, then lawyers as she settled her father's estate. She'd nearly forgotten that she was a woman. Daniel Weston made her feel female once again.

She felt a connection to him and even though it was probably a sign of her craziness, because the connection was in her dreams, right at this moment she didn't feel cold and alone and listless, which had been her default emotional setting for more time than she cared to think about.

He smiled down at her and she smiled back, amazed that her cheek muscles didn't crack. Dinner out tonight, at seven. For the first time in a long while, she had something to look forward to.

Dan helped her into her coat, big hands resting on her shoulders after she'd shrugged it on. They stood there, her back to him.

A storm was rising outside and the sleet was pinging hard and fast against the windows, the wind bending the branches of the trees in someone's garden, but no sound penetrated into the office.

They simply stood quietly, Daniel not making a move, until she finally bent to get her purse.

His hands lifted and he crossed to open the door for her. Roxanne was smiling as she said good-bye.

The instant they were outside, he opened up a big black umbrella and cocked his elbow out in a clear invitation.

Just like that, she was walking down a city street arm in arm with a man. When she'd woken up at four a.m. after a restless night's semi-sleep, the last thing she'd have expected to happen today was this. The day had started with the flight from hell and now look.

Life's surprises were sometimes good, not always bad. She had to remember that.

The sky was slate gray, lit by sheet lightning to the north. Thunder growled in the distance. The sleety rain was coming down so hard it started bouncing off the sidewalk. With a quick glance at the sky, Dan hurried his pace, making sure the umbrella covered Claire. He pulled a key fob out of his pocket and thumbed it. Ten feet away, a black BMW's locks opened with a whump.

He settled her in the passenger seat, holding the umbrella over her, then rounded the car.

"So." He turned to her, one big hand on the wheel, the other on the key in the ignition. "Where we headed? Where's your hotel?"

"It's not a hotel, really. More of an upscale bed-and-breakfast. It's on a cul de sac just off Massachussets Avenue. It's called Kensington House. On Warren Street." It was a charming turn-of-the-century townhouse, with a welcoming touch. Claire had found it on the net and had been delighted with the place when she'd checked in this morning.

"I think I know the place." At her raised eyebrows, he shrugged. "I'm a walker, it's how I get to know cities. I walk them until I know them. And I think I've walked by it a couple of times. Now buckle up."

The rain was pelting down, huge drops drumming on the roof, water already gathering at the sides of the roads. Traffic was snarled, the sounds of hooting horns penetrating even the soundproofing of the BMW.

Claire stayed silent as Dan drove because she'd be in a sweat if she had to drive in this bad weather. It didn't seem to faze him, though. He was a superb driver, in complete control of the car, as relaxed as if they were taking a drive down a sunny lane in spring.

She really admired good driving, perhaps because she was a lousy driver herself. She'd never owned a car until she inherited her father's old Ford, and she drove as little as possible.

Dan made his way with ease through the streets, taking shortcuts she'd never known about, though she'd lived in Washington for four years while getting her degree. She didn't know half the streets he was driving down.

It was almost . . . peaceful in the quiet car. Once she realized that Dan was such a good driver, the rain became a soothing background noise instead of a source of stress.

She sat back in the comfortable leather seat and sighed. It felt so *good* to let go, just for a little while. To let someone else take charge. To just . . . be.

Traffic was intense and the drive took almost forty minutes. She leaned her head back and might even have drifted half asleep. Her eyes snapped open when she felt the car brake to a stop.

"Nice," Dan said, pulling up outside the big brass and wood front door of the townhouse.

"Yes, it is," she replied. "Comfortable, too."

He helped her out of the car and walked her into the lobby, which had once been the home's foyer. It was decorated like a sitting room, with only a long teak counter betraying the fact that this was a commercial building. A very pretty Chinese-American girl was standing behind the counter, reading a book. She looked up and smiled at them as they walked in. The brass nameplate on her starched white shirt read *Amy* and she'd checked Claire in.

"There you go, Ms. Day. Room seven." Amy had been reading what looked like a dense textbook. She noticed Claire's interest. "Big exam coming up."

"Good luck." Claire smiled, remembering all that hard work in college. Hard, satisfying work. It had been so simple—work hard, reap rewards.

Life wasn't that simple anymore.

She turned to Dan. He had a face that looked as if it didn't smile much, but he was smiling down at her now. He was so close she could feel his body heat, smell soap and still the faintest overlay of smoke. He'd been through a harrowing experience just—what was it?—yesterday, but you couldn't tell it from looking at him. He looked tough and indomitable.

Oh God, *she* used to be tough, too. Not running-in-a-burning-building tough, necessarily, not shoot-your-opponent-dead tough, but she'd held her own in a man's world. She'd had a reputation as a real no-nonsense pro.

She didn't feel tough or hard or even very professional now.

Dan was watching her so carefully, dark eyes so knowing. Did he know what was going through her mind? Did he read how unsettled and rattled she was at her core?

He picked up her hand and, to her astonishment, brought it to his mouth, brushing his lips over her knuckles. Such a—a chivalrous gesture.

It seemed so out of place coming from a man like him. He was a *Marine* for God's sake! She'd loved the Marines in all her postings. They'd been, to a man, smart and tough and efficient. But she'd have sworn that there wasn't a romantic bone in the entire Corps.

"So, get some rest this afternoon," he said, letting go of her hand, then lifting his to run the back of his forefinger down her cheek. "You look tired, some rest will do you good. You must have gotten up at the crack of dawn."

She smiled. "At four."

"There you go. So get some rest and I'll be here at seven."

He stood there, not too tall but so very broad, smiling down at her. Strong, serious, reliable. Claire suddenly knew, in a flash of insight so strong there was no possible room for doubt, that he would be here at seven. And if he wasn't, it meant he was either dead or in the hospital.

"Okay. I'm—I'm looking forward to it."

She was, she realized suddenly. They weren't just polite words. She really was looking forward to it—the first thing she'd looked forward to in such a long time.

He nodded. "Great, me too. I know a fantastic little place in Georgetown. I'll book for a quarter to eight."

They stood there for a long moment. Amy was openly watching them, gaze shifting from her, to him, then back to her. Clearly, she felt something more was required.

Claire stepped back, because the temptation to step forward, right into Dan's arms, was so strong.

"See you at seven, then," she said and turned down the corridor of rooms. At number seven she stopped and looked back. Dan hadn't moved. He'd watched her, every step of the way.

Her room was very comfortable, with a little parlor area outfitted with a sofa, a desk and a chair. Claire unpacked her bag, taking her time, eyeing the bed. It was a big four-poster with a huge down comforter, and it beckoned to her.

She sat on one of the two chairs and stared out the window at the sleety storm outside and thought of nothing at all, savoring the unusual feeling of relaxation.

Just as she was contemplating lying down, there was a soft knock on the door. She checked the peephole. Amy, the girl from the front desk, stood holding a tray and grinning.

Claire opened the door.

"This just came, Ms. Day." Amy placed the tray carefully on the desk and stepped back.

Claire lifted silver covers and discovered a fragrant, steaming bowl of cream of mushroom soup, a small salad, hot focaccia bread and a slice of dense chocolate cake. There was a half bottle of chardonnay and a large bottle of Evian. A small white envelope leaned against the wine bottle with her name in bold black ink.

She opened it.

Enjoy the lunch, she read. *See you at seven. D.*

She did enjoy the lunch, to her utter surprise. This past year food—the smell of it, at times even the sight of it—made her stomach clamp shut. Just knot right up until she thought she'd never eat again in this lifetime.

But not now. Now she felt . . . open. Almost hungry.

She ate about half of everything. The soup settled, warm and comforting, in her stomach. The hot focaccia made a pleasing contrast with the crisp salad greens and the chocolate cake was simply divine, the platonic ideal of a chocolate cake. It was what chocolate cake would taste like in heaven.

How could she have forgotten how much she loved chocolate?

And the wine. She loved wine. Why had she stopped drinking it? Because it was too much trouble to go to the wine shop and buy it? Because in her knotted-up mode it turned sour in her stomach? Because she'd forgotten about the very concept of pleasure?

This wine went down like a dream, tasting of summer and sunshine, and relaxed her. The bed beckoned even more loudly than before. She changed into her pajamas and slipped under the covers, expecting to lie there for a couple of hours, bleary-eyed and tense as she usually did. Instead, she went out like a light.

It was dark when she woke up again. For an instant's panic, she thought she'd slept through until seven, but the clock showed five thirty. She'd slept a solid four hours. Another first. In the past year, she hadn't managed to sleep for four hours straight through the night, let alone during a nap.

Though packing for a possible date hadn't even occurred to her, she did have a change of clothes. Black pants, black cashmere turtleneck sweater, black boots. And some Body Shop creams. The bath's hot water finished relaxing her and she had fun grooming, lavishly overdoing the White Musk body cream, head to toe, and drying her hair carefully with the hotel dryer and a round brush instead of just letting it air dry.

And makeup! She'd almost forgotten makeup existed and found pleasure in applying the Dark Female Arts. Leaning forward over the sink, she almost didn't recognize the woman in the mirror, with color in her face and on her lips. One natural, the other artificial, but still. She looked . . . normal. Not white-faced and pinched, some alien being from a cold, airless planet.

Welcome back, she told her image in the mirror. *You've been gone for a long time.*

Even drawing out the womanly preparations for a night out—her first in over a year—she still had forty-five minutes left before Dan was stopping by to pick her up.

The novel she'd packed held no appeal. Clearly, it was the brother-in-law who had offed the banker. Money, power, revenge. Important things in the world, but now faraway concerns.

Out of sheer habit, she'd packed her netbook, simply because she'd packed a computer in every suitcase since she was sixteen. She hauled it out and powered it up.

This whole Bowen in Algiers thing was so strange, though she couldn't put her finger on why. At times, everything was strange to her. But still . . .

Bowen was a master of misdirection. He was CIA after all. Suppose he'd spun a story and had actually been in Laka that day?

If he had been, if her memory—or what she thought was a memory, or a memory of a memory—was correct, maybe it might mean she was getting her mind back. Her life back. If not, if he'd been away as Dan insisted, she'd be no worse off than before. Still crazy and out of it.

Hmmm. Why not do a little digging?

Claire logged on to the DIA website, clicking through until she came to the section containing reports, password-protected. She was no longer an active member of the DIA, and her badge and pass had been canceled, but experience told her that they'd probably forgotten to cancel her password.

She knew people who had *123456*, their date of birth, their mother's maiden name, their pet's name as passwords. It was little short of lunacy. Claire had always had complex, randomized passwords she committed to memory.

39*Zan103hzy.

Her pretty pink netbook whirred discreetly.

Bingo. She was in.

A minute later, she was scrolling through reports back to last November. It took a while. DIA had been busy this past year. The world was a huge, dangerous place and DIA kept track of it all. She flipped through the world's hotspots and crises patiently and . . . there it was.

The embassy bombing in Laka, in a pdf file. The report was sixty pages long. No time to read the whole thing. The easiest thing would be to do a search and find. She typed *Bowen McKenzie* into the search field, pressed enter, and discovered that he was only mentioned once in the report. As absent on the twenty-fifth of November, due to a two-day meeting with the deputy prime minister of Algeria in Algiers. He'd arrived in Algiers on the evening of the twenty-fourth and made it back to the Laka Embassy only after the siege and the bombing.

Claire froze, trembling fingers curved over the keyboard. Oh, God. The memory had been wrong. The clouds hadn't parted at all. What she'd seen so clearly for a tempting moment hadn't been a memory—it had been the artifact of a still-sick mind.

She wasn't getting better. If anything, her hallucinations had picked up enough real-world grit to seem true. Maybe this was going to be her reality for the rest of her life—flashes and visions from a sick mind. This was so *scary*.

Over the past year, Claire had gritted her teeth as she lost her father, learned to walk again and slowly brought her body back from near death. There had been endless sleepless nights, days and nights of heart-wrenching panic, nightmares where she woke in a nest of sweaty sheets, heart pounding, curled up against the headboard in defense against the monsters of the night.

That were in her head.

She bore all of that with, if not grace, then stoicism. And she realized now that all this time, in the back of her mind was the conviction that it was all temporary. That sooner or later she'd get her health and then her mind and then her life back.

It had been a given. She was too young for life to be over, she'd barely begun it. Wasn't that what always happened on those made-for-TV movies where the heroine overcomes extreme odds and prevails by sheer dint of willpower?

But . . . what if that wasn't the scenario? What if the scenario for the rest of her life was this bleak and empty reality? What if she was going to be like *this* the rest of her life? Weak and hurting and alone, because who would want a woman on the borderline?

Another forty, fifty years of this. Of waking up from a restless sleep with tears drying on her face. Of having flashes of violence suddenly flood her mind. Of finding herself crouching, terrified, in the post office or the frozen foods section of the supermarket. Of seeing and hearing things that weren't there, but still felt terribly real.

A lifetime of being afraid, nauseous with anxiety.

She powered the netbook down, closed the lid and sat there with her hands on the shiny pink surface, seeing her slightly distorted reflection. Pale, mouth a thin line. She sat for a long time, trying not to think of anything at all.

Finally the hotel phone rang. She glanced at her watch. Seven sharp.

Dan, waiting to take her out to dinner.

She put the laptop in its case and vowed to do her best to enjoy the evening out, her first in a year and maybe her last for a long time to come.

FIVE

HE was careful, cautious, thorough. Always. Those traits had taken him a long way, and would take him to even greater heights. He was halfway there already. Laka had laid the groundwork, been the base. He'd built on that, until now he was rich and powerful and about to get even richer and more powerful. He was damned if he'd let anyone or anything stop him.

So far, it had been smooth sailing, but he knew enough to keep his guard up. Some would call it paranoia, but then he'd been CIA for twenty years. Paranoia was in the CIA songbook. Paranoia was in his DNA. It had kept him alive and prospering in a hell of a lot of dangerous places with dangerous people.

So he kept his ear close to the ground, had trip wires everywhere, letting him know if anyone came prodding at his perimeter. Any unhealthy interest in him and his affairs, well . . . one of the advantages to his time in the CIA was a small army on call. Good men who'd served their country and now served him. And he sure as hell paid a lot better than Uncle Sam.

He'd placed beacons in the pixels of the logos of all the reports on the Laka bombing. CIA, DIA, State, Marine Security Detachment records. Expunging his name had been easy for someone who knew what he was doing. The beacons sent a signal to his computer if anyone searched for his name in the reports. His computer was programmed to buzz him if it received a signal.

A whole year had gone by without any warning signals. He'd started to relax. Even started to think of removing the beacons, which represented a tiny risk, but a risk nonetheless. Maybe some Homeland Security nerd, bored, looking for something to do, would come up with an algorithm to find beacons. So he'd been weighing the pros and cons of removing them.

He hadn't come this far by courting risks.

The buzz had come in the middle of a dinner in his honor in the grand ballroom of the Willard. Throw a rock and you'd hit an ambassador, a minister or a billionaire. All there for him, to honor him for trying to turn a continent around. Good works, writ large, the kind that went into the history books, and you could buy a piece of it. Be counted as among the great and the good.

Black tie, twenty-five thousand dollars a plate. Cheap at the price.

And they vied for tickets, fought over the privilege of being there, because it was the event of the month. People lining up to give him money, to praise him.

At the discreet buzz in his two-thousand-dollar tuxedo pants, he excused himself and found a quiet corner to consult his PDA. Immensely powerful, as small as a cell phone. It gave him access to his home computer.

Fuck! He actually stepped back in surprise, then caught himself gracefully. Someone had done a search on his name! Someone with a DIA password. What the hell was that about?

He emailed an NSA agent who moonlighted by the hacker name of Wizard. Wizard was kept on retainer, a cool two hundred thousand a year, to be useful in exactly this kind of situation. Wizard would find out who was sniffing around his perimeter.

Five minutes later, a message popped up on his Black-Berry. The request had been traced back to the IP address, then triangulated for the street address.

He frowned. The request had come from a hotel, a small one, basically a bed-and-breakfast, in downtown Washington. He scrolled down . . . and froze. The request had come from room seven of the hotel. The guest who was checked into room seven was Claire Day.

Shit!

When he'd first heard that Claire Day had been wounded in the blast, he'd worried that she might have seen something. The embassy was supposed to have been empty except for one lone Marine Guard. And yet Claire Day had been found outside in the compound, very badly injured, and had been immediately whisked away by her father.

He'd kept a close eye on her, ready to give the order to have her taken out at any time. But she'd spent three months in a coma and by all accounts was barely back on her feet. She was down in Florida and no threat to him.

What the fuck was she doing in Washington DC, checking up on him? She was supposed to be down south, still loony from the blast. Barely able to walk and suffering from amnesia. Whatever she was doing, she was a danger to him. She had to go. He should have taken care of this from the start, when he first heard she'd been at the embassy during the bombing and had survived.

It never pays to let loose ends free. They need to be snipped, fast.

The voice of the secretary of state boomed from the ballroom. "And now, let's give a special hand to our guest of honor, a great American and a great philanthropist, a man who single-handedly . . ."

The secretary was going to call him to the podium very soon. He pulled out a throwaway cell phone from an inside pocket, using a handkerchief. He always carried a throw-away cell in case he had to call his team together. The cell phone would go into the drains several miles from here when he was done. The cells were never used twice.

Heston, the head of his team, picked up on the first ring.

"Yes?" No names, ever.

"Clean-up action," he said. "Room seven, Kensington House, Warren Street, off Massachusetts. Booked in the name of Claire Day. Get the computer in the room, then trash the room. Make it scary, like some lunatic broke in. She's messing with me. We want to make sure she stops."

"Yessir. What about the woman herself?"

He thought about Claire Day. What did she know? Had she seen something? Had she been biding her time, waiting to strike him down? Was she planning on fucking with him?

She'd been a looker in her day, though she probably wasn't one now. And a real uppity bitch, too. Turned him down flat, secretly laughing at him while she did it. Well, it was payback time. Whatever she thought she was doing, she had just made a big, big mistake. No one crossed him. No one.

And he wanted no loose ends, not now. Especially not now.

"Terminate. Make it look like she interrupted the burglary," he said, flipping the cell closed. He strode down the carpeted hallway under the enormous chandeliers and entered the ballroom to thunderous applause, the man of the hour, a true American hero.

THERE she was!

Coming down the hallway, as stunning as ever, only now thin and pale. This morning she'd terrified him. As she'd clutched at him, as his arms had gone around her, it had been like holding an injured bird in his hand. The contrast to the Claire Day he'd known in Laka—smart, resilient, tough—had been shocking.

She'd been rendered down to bedrock by the blast, and was barely holding herself together.

At least right now she was looking just a little better than she had in his office, thank God. She must have eaten at least part of the lunch he'd had sent to her and she clearly had gotten some rest. He wouldn't bet on her stability in a stiff wind, though.

But she was still Claire. Heart-stoppingly beautiful, a deep intelligence in those gorgeous silvery blue eyes, even if the expression in them now was sadness and despair.

She was smiling at him faintly as she walked down the corridor, eyes meeting his, and Dan's heart simply turned over in his chest as he watched her.

He was a Marine, always would be, even if he was out of the service. He'd been one of the best.

Marines by nature and by training are tough and unsentimental. Dan was particularly unsentimental, especially about women. His mom had run off when he was two because his dad had been one real mean son of a bitch. Apparently, it had never even occurred to his mom to take her son with her, wherever she went. So she'd left him behind, a small child in the hands of a violent drunk.

Most of the women Dan had had sex with were out for a good time, which he did his damnedest to give them. The few others who wanted more were the women who hung out at military bars hoping for a soldier husband, with a regular paycheck and government benefits.

Women who weren't too good at holding down regular jobs, who often drank a little too much and partied a little too hard and were casting their net for a husband who'd keep them. Most of them expected to divorce eventually, but Uncle Sam would make sure they got those alimony checks, which is what counted. Particularly if they'd popped out a kid or two.

Claire was completely different, in every way, from any other woman he'd ever known.

She simply exuded intelligence. It was like an aura around her. Even now, beaten down by life, wounded inside and out, nothing could quench the sharpness of her gaze. He'd done a little rooting around on her in his days of crazy infatuation back in Jakarta and she was exactly what she looked like. Smart, dedicated, hardworking.

She'd raced through high school—*two* high schools, actually, a French one and an American one, though Dan could hardly fathom how that could be. He'd gotten his GED after joining the Marines. Though, after that, after not worrying about where his next meal was coming from and not having to deal with his father's drunken rages anymore, he'd aced more or less everything.

She'd gotten top marks all the way through college. Info was a little harder to come by after she'd been recruited by DIA. They didn't throw around data on their agents, but the Foreign Service gossip machine was the most potent intel-gathering machine in the world, bar none. And FS scuttlebutt had it that Claire Day had been one of the finest officers in the system, her reports sharp and accurate and cogent. Personally, too, in a business that often beat its agents down into alcoholism or paranoia, she'd stayed right on top of it.

Even now, nearly killed by a blast that had taken out an entire embassy, she was diminished and physically weak, but not once had he heard her complain about her losses. She'd lost a job she loved and a year later was a shadow of her former self, but she hadn't mentioned that once. Dan had heard injured SEALs bitch and moan more than Claire.

Hell, when he'd realized that he had to leave the Marines on a medical disability, even he'd gone on a five-day bender with Frank Colacella, who'd lost an eye in Iraq.

Dan went to meet her.

"Hi." Her mouth was tilted up. She touched his coat sleeve. "Thanks for the lunch. I really appreciated it."

Dan put his hand over hers, feeling the delicate bones and soft skin. He forced himself to smile into her eyes instead of closing his, leaning down to her and sniffing like a dog.

Man, she had something on her that reached into his

head and messed with him there. And then, well, traveled down to his gonads and grabbed him, hard.

He tightened his hand on hers slightly. "Did you eat it all?"

Her eyes rolled in her head and she gave a half laugh, letting her hand drop from his arm. "Yes, Mom. I ate most of it and drank a glass of wine and then slept for four hours. I couldn't believe it."

"Great." He held out his arm to her in an exaggerated gesture of chivalry, Fred Astaire to Ginger Rogers. "Shall we go, madame? Your chariot awaits."

That beautiful smile broadened for just a moment, then her face lapsed into its default somber expression. "I'll just leave the key," she said softly. "Then we can go." She looked up at him. "And you'll tell me what happened that day?"

His own smile disappeared. "Yeah," he said softly. "I'll tell you everything that happened that day."

She approached the small wooden counter that served as a reception desk, in a corner of the cozy room made to look like a living room. Now there was a young guy with a head of thick, black, curly hair behind it, wire-rimmed glasses gleaming, finger on the open page of a thick book.

Dan could read upside down, a skill that had proved useful over the years, but he didn't need it here. Not with all the formulas looking like chicken tracks on the page. No words, just numbers and symbols. Some student, earning money for college by working as a hotel clerk.

The US Marine Corps had paid for Dan's college education and in return he'd given it love and devotion, a thousand rounds a month of practice shooting and 150 push-ups a day.

Claire handed over the key. A real key, not the chip card most hotels had nowadays. Dan frowned.

Cards had their security holes but they were way safer than a brass key, no question. Cracking a card key security required some computer skills, a little savvy. Real hotel keys were security nightmares, since the locks had to accommodate master keys, which were held by the manager, the deputy manager, the front desk staff and every single maid and waiter in the hotel. The manager's dog probably had a copy.

It wasn't even a Yale, just an old-fashioned key that would fit an old-fashioned lock. The kind that was pickable in under a minute.

Dan wouldn't let her back into the room until he checked it first.

Claire turned from the counter and smiled up at him, at the exact second a picture of being with Claire in her room—her *bedroom*—flashed into his mind and oh, fuck. There it was, an image of a naked Claire on the bed, real as life.

He'd been celibate an entire year, like a goddamned monk. Sex had somehow fled his life, departed to some unknown destination. But now it came roaring back. He'd always had a strong sex drive and hormones now flooded his body, a huge tsunami of prickling heat all over, red hot around his groin.

Every single hormone that had deserted him over the past year pinged to life. Full, pulsing life.

He swelled erect, right there in the small, pretty lobby of Claire's hotel.

Oh, *shit*.

A boner—a real blue steeler. At the worst possible time. Thank God he had on a heavy winter coat down to his knees.

Claire dropped the key into the young guy's outstretched hand and turned to Dan, slipping her hand into the crook of his elbow. Through a wool winter coat and a thick cotton shirt, he felt the heat of her small hand like a brand.

She looked up at him. "Shall we go?"

"Gah," he answered. Or something. Some kind of noise issued from his mouth, he had no idea what.

It struck him all over again that this was *Claire*. The woman he'd been mooning over for . . . ever, it felt like. A woman who gripped his imagination even when he thought she was dead.

Smart and beautiful and brave. Claire, right here with him. Claire, pale and shaky, barely on her feet. Claire, who needed him.

So *he* needed to keep his head out of his ass and his shit wired tight. Sure, he wanted her, had for a long time now. Had been blinded by lust since he'd first set eyes on her. But she was traumatized and had been badly wounded and he could just fucking tuck it away now.

He willed his boner down a little and tipped an imaginary hat. "Ma'am?"

That got a smile out of her. A fleeting one, but he felt like he'd made the sun shine all by himself. One thing was for sure. She hadn't spent the past year smiling.

Well, he was going to dedicate himself now to raising a smile on her face more often. Not to mention trying to get her to gain at least fifteen pounds and lose that sad expression.

Step one, feed the woman.

"LET'S go," he said.

Dan pulled out Claire's chair and seated her into it as if she were the Queen of Georgetown.

Such elaborate manners from a Marine made her smile. Marines weren't known for their romanticism or chivalry.

If you needed a rifle or a good man at your back during combat, a Marine was the man for you. If you were looking for hearts and flowers, well, look elsewhere.

He looked every inch a Marine, though—incredibly strong, rough and rugged, face drawn and serious, as if seating her were a mission and he was going to do the best job possible. Just like a Marine.

The restaurant, however, was luxury civilian, all the way.

Located on the second floor of an eighteenth-century townhouse, it was warm and cozy and shrieked money and style. It looked exactly like the kind of place you had to

book weeks in advance to have any hope of finding even a
bad table, let alone the one near the fire that the maitre d'
had steered them to.

Claire opened the huge ecru linen napkin and placed it
on her lap, fingering the fine material with pleasure.

She leaned forward. "I hope I haven't taken you away
from something, Dan. I appreciate your spending time
with me, but if you're busy, I could have ordered something
in my hotel room."

He lifted his head at that, his eyes catching hers. They
were so dark, so impelling. "I guess I need to make something really clear here," he said, voice low and serious.
"Right now, there isn't any place in the world I'd rather be.
Or anyone I'd rather be with."

Oh.

Their eyes met, held. She was the first to look away, a
little astonished at the flutter she felt in her stomach.

He was deadly serious.

Wow. She was used to flirting, had been since puberty.
But the blast had clearly knocked out the flirtation lobe of
her brain because she had no comeback at all.

Flustered, she opened the menu.

The food was Mediterranean fusion with the kind of
loving, elaborate, flowery descriptions that, if you weren't
hungry could be faintly nauseating, and if you were,
made your mouth water. To her surprise, her mouth was
watering.

She ran her eye down the menu. "Have you eaten here
before?"

He hadn't looked down at the menu, simply continued
looking at her.

"Yeah, I eat here a lot. The owner is a Greek-American,
a former Marine and a friend. This place opened about a
year ago, and I try to throw as much business his way as
possible. But I wouldn't have brought you here if the food
wasn't really good," he finished earnestly.

Claire hid a smile. *Semper fraternis*, the second half

of the Marine motto, the one people forgot about, though Marines never did. *Forever brothers*. Marines joined a brotherhood that lasted a lifetime.

She looked around, at what was on other diners' plates and at their happy faces. She couldn't remember the last time she'd seen so many happy people all together. It was like all that happiness and contentment were realigning the molecules in the room.

"Well, everything looks and smells wonderful. I was just wondering if you had any suggestions."

"The tarragon rabbit is good and so's the seafood couscous."

Claire glanced down. Each dish had a seven line description, promising everything but eternal youth and world peace. "How about we have one of each and share?"

"Done. Hector the head waiter'll automatically bring me the house wine, which is really good. A Syrah from Lebanon. Is that okay with you?"

A Syrah from Lebanon sounded wonderful. "Fine."

Somehow the waiter knew that they were ready to order because a second later there he was at the table, greeting Dan quietly as an honored regular.

The waiter uncorked a bottle and poured them both a finger in the red-wine glass. Dan waved for her to go first. Claire narrowed her eyes at the explosion of sun-drenched fruity flavors bursting in her mouth.

He smiled at her expression.

"Tell me," she blurted, "tell me what happened that day in Laka." Then bit her lips.

There was a protocol to this kind of thing, no one knew that better than she did. Her social antennae used to be sharp, finely tuned. If you wanted information from someone, you were supposed to approach the subject subtly, not just blurt out your question, as if that were the purpose of going out and anything else was a waste of time.

He'd taken the trouble to offer her this dinner and she'd tried to cut to the chase instead of enjoying it.

Claire hung her head, examining the tablecloth. Pretty, linen, cream-colored with subtle patterns woven into it. She looked up, wincing, expecting to see him frowning with displeasure at her bluntness, but all she saw was a dark, patient gaze.

"Sure," he said, his deep voice a low rumble. He reached a long, thick arm across the table and took her hand.

Claire was so surprised, she didn't react, just stared down at their joined hands. It was odd, feeling her hand completely encased in his. His skin was rough, lightly callused. The grip light, yet strong. Her hand felt . . . good in his. Warm. Safe. Right.

"What do you want to know?" he asked.

She shifted uncomfortably. Amnesia scared a lot of people. Hell, it scared *her*. The coma was almost better, no one could expect her to have memories of that. But she'd been conscious during the siege, and the week before. She'd lived, presumably interacted with people, gone to work, gone home, probably had a beer with Marie, as she did every Wednesday afternoon when the staff got out early.

There was nothing there of all of that. Just a huge, gaping, black abyss where other people had memories.

"I don't remember anything," she whispered.

Dan's hand tightened briefly. "What's the last thing you remember?" he asked quietly. "And we'll take it from there."

"I told you this morning, the last thing I remember is the reception at the French Embassy on the eighteenth. After that—nothing."

Dan shook his head. "I had just arrived and spent that day and the next being briefed." His mouth lifted in a half smile. "But I heard from impeccable sources that the food at the French Embassy was spectacular and they imported the champagne—the real stuff."

Claire smiled. "I don't usually eat and drink much at these dos, but I had a few canapés and I can report that, yes, the food was delicious and the champagne was the real deal and it was excellent."

"And after that?"

"After that," she said softly, "nothing." The word hung there, stark and cold. "I remember walking home from the French Embassy instead of having the embassy driver accompany me because it was such a pleasant evening. It's about a twenty-minute walk. I had a glass of iced tea on my balcony, went to bed after going over some reports . . . and the next thing I remember is waking up in a hospital room in Clearwater, Florida and it was the twenty-eighth of February. There's nothing in between."

Nothing but darkness and the images and sounds that haunted her nightmares. She leaned forward, hand still in his much-larger one. "I read the reports afterward, when I could read. But I don't have a feel for what happened. There's no resonance there. It's like reading a historical report. Something that happened a hundred years ago. But you were there. What happened?" She watched his eyes. "Tell me everything."

"Okay." Dan took a deep breath, broad chest expanding. "I was on duty, the second shift, noon to eight p.m. The embassy was empty, or so I thought. I'd told my men to stay in Marine House. I thought everyone was at the ambassador's."

Claire shuddered. "I can't even begin to imagine my spending more than fifteen minutes at a reception the Crockers threw, unless a gun was put to my head."

"Amen." He grinned at that. "I was convinced I was the only person left in the entire compound and around sixteen hundred you come walking down the corridor. Surprised the shit out of me." He dipped his head. "Begging your pardon."

Claire felt another smile coming on, unused muscles coming into play, pulling the corners of her mouth upward. "Marines swear, Dan. It's in the job description. Please don't censure yourself for me."

As a matter of fact, the complexity, inventiveness and sometimes sheer poetry of Marine profanity was a secret hobby of hers. She had a little notebook full of beauties she'd heard in her day.

She clutched his hand. "So . . . where was I? Where had I spent the day?" It felt so . . . odd asking someone else, almost a perfect stranger, information about herself. Luckily, Dan didn't make her feel strange at all. Some people treated her as if she were suffering from dementia.

Not Dan. His gaze was direct, and he answered her questions as if they were the most normal thing in the world.

"In the secure room, apparently. I don't know when you got in, but it was before noon, which is when I came on duty. And I still don't know how you got in without Sergeant Ward, who was on duty until noon, seeing you. When he handed me the duty roster, he said the embassy was empty."

Claire pursed her lips, shrugged her shoulders, did her best to look innocent.

It was standard DIA practice. The fewer people who knew their comings and goings, the better. If she hadn't announced herself, it was because she'd been working on something confidential, and she'd have slipped in by a side entrance.

"So you saw me at four and then—"

"All hell broke loose."

She nodded. All the reports said that the rebel army made its move around four p.m., an hour before last light.

But it still made no sense to her.

She remembered clearly the reports she'd written about the Red Army and the Mbutu regime. Her analysis had been that there was no danger of the desultory civil war making it to the capital, knowing full well that the state department would base its decision on whether or not to evacuate family members and civilian staff partly on her analysis.

Claire didn't make mistakes. She must have been appalled at hearing and seeing the Red Army pouring into Laka, contradicting every report, every cable, she'd written over the past year.

The Red Army attacking Laka, bombing the US

Embassy in the first direct attack against American interests on African soil since the Kenya bombings, was *huge*.
History-making. She closed her eyes and pinched the
bridge of her nose. Why couldn't she *remember*?

She lifted her head. "So . . . shooting suddenly breaks
out. What happened then?"

"What happened was I rushed you to Post One, fast.
Made you rip your pants on a nail."

Claire smiled. "Well, you were probably saving my life,
so I guess a pair of ripped trousers is a small price to pay.
Though—they didn't attack the embassy right away, did
they?"

"No. We spent some time together before."

His eyes were so dark she could see tiny orange flames
from the hearth reflected in them, so piercing she felt as if
he were walking around inside her head. He nodded his
head slowly, gaze never leaving hers. And smiled.

It rearranged his features completely, lightening them,
making him look younger. She'd thought he was in his for-
ties, but she saw he must be in his thirties. Early thirties,
even. Marines usually had three postings in the Embassy
Security Detachment, usually early in their careers. She'd
thought he was older because his default expression was
so somber.

At that precise moment the food arrived, the waiter slipping huge platters of steaming, delicious-smelling food in
front of them.

Oh no.

Claire looked at the heaps of food in horror. Her stomach clenched closed painfully, just shut right up. There
was no way she could handle all that food. Just seeing it
nauseated her. Her stomach started a slick, greasy slide
up her esophagus. She sat rigidly, willing the bile rising
in her throat back down. Cold sweat coated her body and
she placed her hands in her lap so he wouldn't see them
trembling.

Saliva filled her mouth, the prelude to vomiting.

Oh God, what to do? Dan was being so kind. She was stuck between the hard place of offending him and the rock that was lodged in her stomach.

A stocky, very dark-skinned man in a floor-length apron and chef's toque appeared and he and Dan went into the male greeting dance, backslapping, high-fiving, fist-bumping.

"Dan the Man!" the chef boomed.

"Stavros!" Dan boomed right back and thumped him on the back hard enough to raise some flour. With his arm still around the chef's back, he steered Stavros to Claire. "Claire, I'd like to introduce you to the guy who cooked your dinner, Stavros Daskalakis. Stavros, Claire Day. She was stationed in Laka, too. DIA."

Stavros's eyebrows rose to meet the lower rim of his toque. "A spook."

"A spook," Claire agreed, rising on shaky legs. She held out her hand, having surreptitiously wiped the sweat off on her pants. She turned her back on the groaning table. "Pleasure to meet you."

He caught her hand in his spotlessly clean one. "The pleasure is all mine." His eyes slid to Dan's. "Prettiest spook I ever saw."

Claire didn't say anything. About 90 percent of DIA analysts were men, most of them trained to be bland and colorless, totally unnoticeable. Saying she was the prettiest wasn't saying much.

Dan smiled easily. "Hey, Stav, why don't you show Claire your pottery collection? I think she'd like to see it."

Stavros looked blank for a mere fraction of a second. "Sure," he said and steered Claire to the far wall, where there were fairly authentic-looking ancient Greek vases, black on red and red on black. Normally, she liked classical art but right now she saw the vases through a gray mist, completely concentrated on not barfing all over Stavros's nice hardwood floor as he recounted the history of each vase.

She heard his voice dimly, like a gnat buzzing in the distance. Yet years in the diplomatic service, as a spook, had trained her well. She could ooh and ahh and make polite conversation in the middle of a firefight, let alone with massive nausea cramping her insides.

Stavros put an ochre and black vase in her hand so she could feel how light it was. Apparently, that was a sign of antiquity, all the water in the clay having completely evaporated over the centuries. She held it for a nanosecond, smiled—*that* was hard, she had to think about every muscle—and handed it back before it slid out of her sweaty hands and two thousand years of Greek history shattered on the floor.

Whatever had possessed her to think she was ready for real life? Her system was so fragile she couldn't even handle *dinner*, for God's sake.

What had she been thinking, to come up here to Washington, to bother a man she didn't remember, simply because she thought she'd seen him in her *dreams*?

There. That, alone, should have been enough for her to understand that she wasn't ready for the world.

Claire wasn't in any way fanciful. Her thoughts had always been prosaic and reality-based and her studies, and then particularly her job, had only honed that. She didn't believe in fairies, or in angels, or in wishing things to be true because you wanted them to be true. She believed in facts.

Her job had been to look facts square in the face, however unpalatable. A wishful thinker in the Defense Intelligence Agency was worse than useless—she was dangerous.

So Claire was used to being brutally clear about the world and as a consequence, brutally clear about herself.

The fact that she'd ignored how much of a human wreck she was in order to fling herself up to Dan's office was so un-Claire-like, it was as if another woman had done it. And she was another woman. The bombing had split her life into two, the Before Claire and the After Claire.

The Before Claire had been decisive and business-like, humming with activity, busy with plans, focused and steady and ambitious. The After Claire . . . well, she was a pathetic husk of a woman, with no past and above all, no future, just an eternal, dark, airless present.

Time to go. This wasn't going to work, not on any level. She couldn't in any way face the food, the evening, the man.

Make your excuses and go, while you still can. Before you're sick all over this nice man's restaurant.

Panic rose while she tried to make polite noises at what Stavros was saying.

She was bathed in cold sweat, her head swam as if she were drunk or drugged. Voices sounded faraway, yet sharp and threatening. Her heart pounded, as if she'd just run a race, so fast and so hard it felt like it was going to pound its way out of her chest.

It was horrible. It was why she so seldom went out. If she had a panic attack in her home she could just stay rooted to the spot until it passed, no matter how long it took. No one to see her, no one to point fingers at the crazy lady.

Outside . . . outside was a different matter. She'd once had a massive panic attack in the bank, feet nailed to the floor, sweat pouring over her, shaking like a leaf, unable to respond to anyone. The manager had called 911. Ever since then, she'd arranged for home banking.

A huge one was coming. A tsunami rolling toward her, as her heart picked up speed and she had to stiffen her knees to stay upright. Panic attack plus nausea, a lethal combination. Oh God, she had to get out of here, fast.

Maybe she could just rush down the stairs, hail a taxi and disappear. Dan knew where she was staying, of course, but who'd chase after a crazy woman?

She'd have to leave behind her expensive down coat, but she could buy another one.

She'd spend another of her sleepless nights, make the long trip back down to Florida, get into her house and lock the door behind her and stay in, maybe for days. Listen to the slow ticktock of the clock on the hearth echoing the thud of her own heart, one of the few signs she was alive.

Claire ran through excuses in her mind as she thanked Stavros and turned back to Dan.

I'm so sorry, I really don't feel well, no, please don't bother, I can catch a cab, there are plenty this time of the evening . . .

Then a hot shower to try to chase away the icy chill in her core, which wouldn't work. Slipping into bed, hoping for sleep, and that wouldn't work, either.

Tomorrow morning, sleepless and exhausted, making her way back south again. Entering her big, silent house that reeked of loneliness, despair and lemon polish.

She clearly wasn't capable of being out in the world. Maybe she never would be. Maybe she was damaged beyond repair.

The thought struck her like a sledgehammer. Coming to Washington had been . . . been like a little test. One she'd failed miserably. She wasn't capable of handling a trip and a perfectly nice dinner with a perfectly nice man.

More than perfectly nice. Attractive, thoroughly male, yet without those creepy macho vibes that made her reject most advances. He hadn't made one suggestive comment, had been the perfect gentleman, taken her to a nice restaurant. And she felt she was about to step into a deep black hole simply because she couldn't deal with the food.

Dan appeared beside her, large hand reaching out to cup her elbow. His hand was warm, strong. He nodded over her head and Claire was stymied for a moment. Incapable of thought. Who was he nodding to?

"Thanks," he said and she turned her head. Behind her Stavros gave a two-fingered salute and smiled at her.

"My pleasure," he said and moved back toward the kitchen.

Dan led her back to their table and she stopped in her tracks. He stopped, too.

The table that had been groaning with food, huge platters of the stuff, enough to feed a family of eight, had been cleared. There were now two small plates—dessert plates from the look of them, as opposed to the enormous platters the size of an Olympic discus—with small tastings of all the dishes.

Small enough so that her system didn't go haywire at the sight. Oh God. That's why he'd sent her off with Stavros. Not to admire the vases but to have the waiter clear away the heavy platters of food and replace them with small plates and small portions. Small enough not to freak out the crazy lady.

"This okay?" Dan asked quietly. He stood so straight, so still, his sharp, almost Aztec features hard, dark eyes glittering. "Better?"

She met his eyes. "Yeah. Better."

He held out her chair and she sat, gingerly, not entirely sure whether she was staying or would suddenly leap up and run out. It was touch and go.

She folded her hands on the table. "How did you know?" she whispered.

Dan shrugged. "I'm a soldier. Was a soldier. I've seen PTSD before."

PTSD. Post-traumatic stress disorder. What some soldiers in the field got after battle. She hadn't gone into battle. She'd just been blown up.

"It's nothing to be ashamed of," he added, his voice low and intimate. "One of my buddies got blown up by an IED and wouldn't leave the house for two years. Takes different people different ways."

Claire could absolutely understand Dan's buddy. Not leaving the house for two years sounded perfectly reasonable. The outside world held horrible dangers, big black pits yawning open, ready to gobble innocent people up.

He reached over and placed his big hand over her folded ones and let it rest there. She looked at it, mesmerized. This past year had not been kind to her. She was as white as skim milk and had lost so much weight the tendons in her wrist and the back of her hand stood out. She was continually cold. Everything about her was pale and weak.

Dan had been wounded in the blast, too, but he had bounced back. His hand over hers was broad and tanned and strong. It felt like a small furnace over her cold skin.

They sat there, not talking, watching each other. And a funny thing happened. The heat from his hand spread, slowly traveling up her arm, warming her skin. She'd been trembling slightly, from the cold, from emotion, but the heat made her muscles relax, melting that inner tension that was with her, always.

She sat back with a sigh, a fierce inner battle having been won. She was going to stay, she wasn't going to run.

Dan slid his hand back across the table. "We okay?" His deep voice was quiet.

She looked into his dark eyes and found not a trace of censure or worry. No hint whatsoever that he'd invited a lunatic to dinner. A woman any other man would have dumped back on her doorstep in an instant.

None of that. If anything, his body language was warm and welcoming. He leaned forward, watching her, a faint smile on his face.

"Yes," she said. "We're okay."

He gave a sharp nod and picked up his fork. "Good. I'm glad."

He started eating, finishing the small plate in an instant. He was a big man, broad and thick. What he'd eaten wasn't even enough to be starters for an active man his size. But he sat back with a sigh and nodded his head at her plate. "It's good stuff. You might want to try it."

Maybe it was the heat that had penetrated the normally icy chill surrounding her, maybe it was his smile, maybe it was the fabulous smells rising off the tiny plate. Whatever it was, she lifted her fork and put a bite in her mouth.

Amazing. Her stomach didn't close up like a fist. Bile didn't tickle up her throat. Her head didn't swim.

Wow. She ate and the world didn't come to an end.

She finished about half of what was on the plate, then

slid it away, not wanting to push her luck. Not wanting to throw up all over the nice linen tablecloth.

"I haven't eaten this much in one go in a year." She patted her mouth with the napkin and sat back.

"You need warm food and company while you eat."

She looked away for a moment. Food had never been a problem before . . . before. She'd enjoyed food as much as anybody else. But after she'd woken up from the coma, she never knew how food would hit her system. Once she'd fainted right out of her kitchen chair and it was only a miracle that she hadn't had anything in her mouth, otherwise she'd have choked to death.

She was really careful after that.

If she needed company, though, she was out of luck.

"Dessert?" he asked.

Claire shook her head. She didn't want more food. She wanted more information.

"You were telling me about that day in Laka. There was shooting in the streets outside the compound and you rushed me to Post One. Then what?"

Something flared in his dark brown eyes, something hot, instantly dampened. "We sat and listened to the fighting outside on Avenue de la Liberté for about an hour."

"They didn't shoot at the embassy, though, correct?"

"No. The Red Army seemed intent on carousing in the streets and shooting up the lampposts, but until the bombing, they didn't scratch the embassy."

"That's odd . . ."

"Yes, it is strange," Dan replied. "I checked in with the ambassador's residence and everyone was safe, and then I checked in with Marine House. It was better for everyone to just stay where they were. So we hunkered down and waited."

He was watching her carefully. Was he checking to see whether any of this jogged her memory?

"And then?"

He cleared his throat. "After a while, your friend Marie popped her head around the door. It was at last light. She wanted you to go with her. I was against it, but you insisted. Said you'd only be a minute."

Claire's heart squeezed at the sound of Marie's name. Whatever had happened afterward had cost Marie her life.

Dan narrowed his eyes. "You don't remember *any* of this?"

Claire shook her head. "Nothing. Absolutely nothing."

She kept quiet about her nightmares. They weren't memories. They were only hell. "So then what happened?"

"After about five minutes I started getting worried. Checked in with the ambassador's residence again and then Marine House and then I went looking for you."

"Were you armed?"

His head reared back. "Damn straight I was armed. My Remington and my Browning."

Dumb question.

"You weren't anywhere in the embassy," he continued. "I checked the building." He frowned at her. "I found it impossible to believe that you'd have willingly left the embassy building, but the fact was, you weren't there."

Why *had* she left the embassy? Dan was right. If she had left, it had been insane of her. They'd had training courses and every course had stressed staying safe.

DIA agents weren't trained warriors. They had information, sensitive information in their head and it was their duty to keep that head on their shoulders. Claire couldn't even begin to imagine what could have convinced her to leave the safety of the embassy and Post One, particularly if she'd had the protection of the detachment commander.

So another mystery had just been added, as if she didn't have enough black holes in her life.

She leaned forward. "So then what?"

"I was going out into the compound grounds." He frowned and she understood. Protocol was that the detachment security guard, and especially their commander, stay inside the embassy building in case of attack. He'd broken protocol for her. He could have been severely punished, could even have been given a dishonorable discharge for desertion. "I heard a woman's whisper and then the bomb blew. I happened to be standing right behind a concrete pillar and that saved my life."

"Oh, Dan," she murmured. She laid her hand on his forearm. "I'm so sorry." She'd put him in danger and she didn't even know why.

He covered her hand with his and again, she felt the warmth creep up her arm. His jaw clenched. "I only wish I'd tried the grounds earlier. Maybe you wouldn't have been blown up by a bomb. Maybe I'd have found you and brought you back inside. Maybe the past year wouldn't have happened."

Claire blinked. He meant it, every word. It was there in every sober line of his dark face. Had he been beating himself up this past year? Blaming himself for what had happened?

"Good Lord, Dan! You can't blame yourself for the crazies in the Red Army! And you certainly can't blame yourself if I was nuts enough to go outside. I had no business leaving the embassy, and I can't imagine why I did."

Dan's face was even more drawn, narrow nostrils white with some strong emotion.

"I thought you'd died," he said starkly. "I thought I hadn't been able to keep you safe and you paid for that with your life. That you were dead, and it was my fault."

Claire drew in a shocked breath. Both hands were on his forearm now and she could feel the steely muscle underneath. Everything about him was strong, grounded, healthy. She hated that he had been carrying this guilt when all he'd done was protect her.

And . . .

Her eyes met his. His head had moved forward, too, until mere inches separated them. This close to him, touching him, inhaling the clean, musky scent of him . . . something lit up inside her head.

The question came welling out from some hidden spot deep inside, completely unstoppable. It was out before she could clamp her mouth closed, another sign, if she needed one, that she was crazy.

"We weren't lovers but—did we kiss?" she asked, shocked at herself as soon as the words left her lips.

$\mathcal{S}$IX

PRIVATE enterprise. There was nothing like it, Carl Heston thought as he parked just off Massachusetts. He'd been in government service and now he was in the private sector and there was no comparison.

Take this mission. In his base of operations, no less. Though when missions were out of town or abroad, the Boss was as generous as they come. Business class to Africa, all the way. Shit, that beat sitting on a bench in the freezing, noisy hold of a C-130, pissing into a bottle.

This op didn't require travel, just a little B and E and a little wetwork.

Uncle Sam had spent over a million dollars training him to do just this. He'd served two tours in Iraq and one in Afghanistan. Breaking into a bed-and-breakfast and taking out some woman—piece of cake.

And tomorrow there'd be 150K more in his account in the Caymans. Added to the cool million already there. Oh yeah, working for the Boss, that beat putting up with crappy XOs and sleeping on the stony ground and eating MREs for months. Not to mention getting shot at. He hadn't yet been shot at once, working for the Boss.

Cushy jobs, superbly well paid. Man, that was the way to go.

And even better. He'd set up a network of operatives for the Boss, all over the country, good men all, and he got 10 percent of their fee.

Heston got out of his Ford Transit and started walking briskly toward Massachusetts Avenue. Just another businessman or lobbyist or lawyer. Washington DC was lousy with them and he was walking right through lawyer spawning grounds. Nobody even spared him a second glance, which was exactly as it should be. He had an excellent dark-haired wig covering his ash blond hair, dark contact lenses covering his light blue eyes, bushy dark moustache, big horn-rimmed glasses he didn't need and shoes that surreptitiously added three inches.

The first things the police ask of witnesses: hair color, eye color, height and distinguishing characteristics.

Dark, dark, six feet, dark glasses, moustache.

All wrong.

Like many Special Forces soldiers, he was of medium height and whippy rather than bulging with muscles. What kind of man he was could be easily hidden underneath the Brioni suit, Izod shirt and Dior tie, carrying a Halliburton briefcase. You could stand in Dupont Circle with your arms out and touch someone just like him every ten seconds.

Ah, but the other men wouldn't be like him at all. They wouldn't have his stamina, for one. Heston could outrun anyone. He could run until his heart gave out. The other men wouldn't be as proficient as he was with a weapon—rifle or pistol, made no difference. Or knife. Or a goddamn rock, if necessary.

He could outgun and outrun more or less any man alive. And *his* briefcase wasn't filled with depositions and briefs. It held a lock gun, four ounces of C-4, his broken-down AR-7 in foam cutouts with the thermal imaging scope, a

Walther P38, ammo for both and a laser light, in case the B and B had security cameras. The thing weighed fifty pounds but he carried it as if it weighed nothing.

And it *was* nothing compared to the hundred and fifty pounds he carried when making HALO jumps in Helmand. For which the fucking US government paid him a grand total of forty thousand fucking dollars a year.

He earned twenty times that with the Boss, and no rules of fucking engagement, either, except for *get the job done*.

Heston walked down Warren Street, right past the pretty, flimsy front gate with a discreet brass plaque. Kensington House. Fancy carved gate on a latch. No lock. No security cameras. No bars on the first-floor windows. He shook his head. Some people had shit for brains.

He pulled out his cell phone and dialed the Kensington House number.

"Kensington House." A brisk male voice.

Heston breathed heavily, turned his voice into a rheumy, phlegmy geezer's voice. "Hello?" he quaked. "Is this—" Heston rustled a piece of paper close to the cell. He breathed heavily in and out, putting a wheeze in it. "Is this K-Kensington House?"

"Yes, sir," the voice on the other end said patiently. "How may I help you?"

"My niece is staying there. Claire. Claire Day. My brother's girl. Can you put me through to her?"

"I'm sorry, sir," the voice said politely. "Ms. Day is out. May I take a message?"

Perfect.

Heston hacked a cough, drawing it out. Old geezer, one foot in the grave. "Yes. Please tell her Uncle Charlie called. I'll call again."

Heston walked quickly back to Massachusetts, to a small sidewalk florist. He spent over a hundred bucks buying every rose the guy had left. Once white things the florist called baby's breath and some big green leaves had been added, the bouquet was as big as a soldier's rucksack.

Fifteen minutes later, he was walking into the quiet,

SHADOWS AT MIDNIGHT   103

elegant lobby of the hotel with a big, friendly smile on his face. Briefcase in one hand, white roses in the other. Lawyer Guy on a romantic mission.

"Hey."

A dark-haired young man with wild hair looked up from a book and smiled faintly.

Heston looked around the lobby, as if in appreciation of the elegant wall sconces and antique armchairs. No security cameras here, either. Not one. Jesus.

"May I help you?" The clerk's voice was very formal.

"Yeah." With a big shit-eating grin, Heston placed the hand holding the big bouquet in its fancy wrapping on the counter. His left hand. "You've got a guest staying here tonight. A Ms. Day. Ms. Claire Day." He winked heavily. "Looker, know what I mean?" Heston had no idea whether Claire Day was a looker or not. She could have seven chins for all he knew, or cared. "We, ah, had a little disagreement." His grin widened. "All my fault, and I want to make up for it." His hand wagged the bouquet a little. Christ, it was big enough to atone for murder.

The clerk looked him in the eyes, not smiling, reaching for the bouquet. "I'll be happy to see that Ms. Day gets this."

Heston pulled the bouquet away from the clerk's hand. "Ah, ah, ah. I was hoping to leave it in her room. Actually, I was hoping you would let me into her room so I could wait for her. She should be back soon."

The young man's face was stiff with disapproval. "I'm afraid that's impossible, sir. If you wish to leave the bouquet and a message I'll be glad to give them to Ms. Day when she returns. Or you're welcome to wait in the lobby for her."

Heston's eyes flicked to the cubbyholes behind the clerk, keys dangling from brass hooks. There was a folded sheet of paper in the cubbyhole of room number seven. A message from good ole Uncle Charlie.

Oh yeah, Uncle Charlie'll call back real soon.

Heston leaned forward again, a hundred-dollar bill folded between his fingers. "She's really, really mad at me," he said, his voice low and coaxing. "It wasn't all my fault, but you know what women are like, there's no reasoning with them. But you know what I think? I think if she opens the door to her room and sees me with a bouquet of roses and, say, a really good bottle of champagne and two flutes, well I think she might start to forgive me, what do you say?"

Leaning down casually, the fingers of his right hand opened the briefcase, out of sight of the clerk, and came out with what he wanted. He palmed it.

The clerk was stiff as a board, features pulled tight in disapproval. "I'm sorry, sir—"

Heston's right hand snaked out from the open briefcase, KA-BAR knife gripped in his fist while with his left he dropped the flowers and grabbed the clerk's jacket lapels, jerking him halfway across the counter. A second later, Heston gently slipped the KA-BAR between the third and fourth rib and punctured the fuckhead's heart.

The clerk opened his mouth, but only a gurgle came out, eyes wide and shocked, as his mind tried to grapple with the unthinkable. His olive skin turned pale as the blood drained from his face. They stood there, face to face, so close Heston could kiss him, while Heston watched the clerk's face cycle through shock, despair, hopelessness. Waiting for death.

Heston knew precisely what was happening inside the man's chest. He'd punctured the aorta and the blood was pumping out at three feet per second, straight into the chest cavity. Heston had knowingly sliced sharply down, severing the aorta. If a heart surgeon were here right this second, he could do nothing to save him. The damage was irreparable and death came fast. After a minute and a half, the clerk stopped breathing, the light fading from his eyes.

Always a good moment.

Heston let go, letting the clerk slide back down behind the counter. He worked quickly, but carefully. Good soldiering was all in the details.

Pulling on a pair of latex gloves, he pulled a bleach-soaked rag from a Ziploc bag and wiped the doorknob, the counter, all the surfaces he'd touched. The cleaned knife went back into the briefcase. He circled the counter, stepping over the dead man, and gently lifted the key to room number seven from its hook, together with the slip of paper. He pulled the body into the back office, turned off the light and quietly closed the door.

There was a Dumpster across the street. He threw the bouquet in, then jogged back up the front steps, opened the door to room seven, then back down the hall to put the key back on the hook. The key board was on the left-hand wall. When the clerk didn't come out, she'd just reach up to get the key herself. The hotel was small, guests probably did that all the time.

Inside Claire Day's room, Heston stopped and took stock. The Boss wanted the computer, first and foremost. Okay. The netbook was small—and *pink*, for fuck's sake!—and fit easily into his briefcase. He stuck in the cloth carrier and the charger and carefully put the usual hotel crap—stationery, a pen, a brochure on Washington inside a big folder—at the center of the small desk. There was nothing there now to even hint that she'd been carrying a computer with her.

He checked the closet and the chest of drawers. Wow, the chick traveled light. There was nothing in the closet except one pair of wool pants, a pair of shoes and a roll-on trolley suitcase. The chest of drawers held a nightgown, a change of underwear and a sweater.

Heston picked the bra and panties up in his gloved hand. Ms. Day might not be a clothes hound, but she sure had sexy underwear. Silk and lace, pale lilac. He brought the silky under things to his nose and sniffed. Some fancy perfume. Pure woman.

Man, that would usually be enough to give him a hard-on, but not now. Not on an op. When he was on an op, he forgot thirst and hunger and horniness.

He became a tool, like a hammer or a gun. Hard and cold and unfeeling.

He'd learned that lesson the hard way. It had cost him a dishonorable discharge.

And anyway, he wasn't here to moon over underwear, he was here to take away evidence that might hurt the Boss, and to get rid of the woman.

He brought out his folder. The KA-BAR was too unwieldy for this kind of work—he needed a tool, not a weapon, for this.

Inside of twenty minutes, all Claire Day's clothes and underwear were slashed into small pieces of fabric that floated around the room, the curtains were slashed, as were the pillows and the mattress and the cushions of the two chairs.

Heston looked around, pleased. The effect was of rage, of intimate threat. Guaranteed to send the cops on the lookout for a violent killer, probably one who knew Claire Day.

He eyed the curtains. Part of one panel was still relatively intact. That wouldn't do. When he finished, he'd switch off the lights and sit on the wrecked mattress, rifle in hand, ready and waiting.

Phase one of the mission was almost complete.

DID we kiss?

The question hung in the air. Claire's pretty mouth was a shocked *O*. She hadn't wanted to ask the question, that was clear. And the strong, controlled woman he'd kissed a year ago would never have asked the question, she'd have finagled the info out of him, cleverly and casually.

But that Claire was gone.

In her place was this pale, shaking ghost. Man, she was in bad shape. So thin he could feel bone when he touched her, bruised-looking eyes with a lost look in them, the very light tan she'd had in Laka gone without a trace, though she now lived in Florida.

This new Claire had had a panic attack when Stavros's waiter started piling food on the table. Dan could have kicked himself in the ass. It hadn't even occurred to him that her system simply wouldn't be able to deal with it. And yet he'd seen how thin she'd become, held her briefly in his arms and felt the fragility. Duh. It meant her system couldn't handle food.

He'd seen that before. He'd seen every manifestation of PTSD there was. His gunner in Afghanistan, who'd had both legs blown off, had simply turned his face to the wall, unwilling to live. He'd had to be fed parenterally for a couple of months to keep him alive.

Dan hadn't thought of that. He'd simply wanted to take Claire to a place that was warm and welcoming, where the food was good and where she could relax. And Stavros's place fit the bill. Except Stavros overdid the portions, always had. Marines had hearty appetites. And shit-for-brains Dan hadn't thought of that.

Man, Claire had nearly fainted. She'd been pale before, but as the waiter slid the dishes in front of her, she'd turned the color of ice. He was lucky she hadn't fainted, or thrown up.

But she'd had a panic attack. And in her panic, she'd blurted out her question and now looked as if she'd accidentally tripped a land mine.

This was going to be hard. But Dan was a Marine. He knew how to do hard.

He picked up her cold, trembling hand.

"I don't know why I said that." Claire's shaking voice was high, breathless. "It's crazy. I am so sorry. I don't know where that came from, it just—"

Dan laid a finger across her lips. "Sh." He couldn't stand to see that lost look on her beautiful face. "Hush. It's not crazy. You're not crazy." Reluctantly, he lifted his finger from her mouth. She had amazingly soft lips. He remembered that, nightly. "And for your information, we did kiss. Just before you left with Marie."

"We did? We kissed?" Claire's huge, silver blue eyes never left his face, watching him as carefully as if he were a grenade that could blow up at any moment. Or as if he would kiss her again.

Which, well, he wanted to do. Badly. So badly he held his right fist under the table, tightly clenched. It had taken all his willpower—and he had a lot of willpower—to take his finger away from her. He didn't just want his finger against her mouth. He wanted his own mouth there, too. He wanted to be mouth to mouth, chest to chest, groin to groin, with Claire Day. So close he could breathe for her. So close he could feel her heartbeat.

"Yeah." His voice was hoarse. He cleared it. "And then you went out and got yourself blown up."

Her face lightened a little. It wasn't a smile, but it was the ghost of one. "I'm sure the two events were unrelated," she said. The big chandelier in the middle of the room reflected off her eyes as she searched his, bright lances of silver. "How did we—how did we get to that point? Had we been . . . dating? That past week? Because I don't remember you at all."

"We didn't date." Dan pushed a small plate of baklava a little closer. "Eat some of that. You don't have to finish it, stop when you don't want any more. But I want you to eat a little. One. Just a bite or two of one, if you can't finish it. Please."

Because now Dan knew what his new mission in life was. Dan had been intensely mission oriented ever since he joined the Marines. He focused on his goal and he achieved it.

And now his goal was to take care of this incredible woman. She was magic. Smart and beautiful and strong, brought low by thugs. He'd lost her and by some miracle had found her. He wasn't losing her again. No way.

"Yessir." A corner of her beautiful mouth lifted. For a second, Dan had a flash of the woman that was, hidden somewhere inside this frail, wounded creature. She wanted out and he wanted to help her get out. "Nobody disobeys the detachment commander."

That was true. In times of danger, the detachment commander was commander in chief. He was to be obeyed instantly. He was God.

"Damn straight." Dan cut a corner of a piece of Stavros's superb baklava. "Now put that in your mouth."

"Yessir," she said again. He watched the forkful disappear in her mouth, and envied it. "So." She tilted her head to one side, considering him. He knew what he was. A battered thirty-four year old with a metal knee, no spleen, half deaf in one ear, who'd had to start over from scratch. A man who owned his own home and his own business, but who didn't have looks and didn't have charm.

She smiled. "I guess it was that old classic. The moonlight, the exotic locale, the gunfire . . ."

"Exactly." Great. A flash of the old Claire Day. "Now eat."

SHE ate. *Two* pieces of the baklava.

Dan talked to her constantly while she ate. At first, she almost had to choke the food down. Then she started taking small bites with more ease, all to the tune of his deep basso profundo.

He was interesting, but she found herself tuning him out, letting the low rumble of his voice roll over her while she observed him. Though he wasn't overly tall, he had the broadest shoulders she'd ever seen, twice the size of the chair's back. He had on a white dress shirt, but no tie. A tie would look strange on him, she thought. A little too milquetoast and civilized for that strong, tanned throat. Instead, he had the first button of the shirt open and an intriguing swirl of dark hair peeped out.

Her last lover, Maurice, sweet, vain Maurice, had manscaped like crazy. It had itched like the devil growing back. Over dinner Maurice would constantly scratch his chest and she had to pretend nothing was happening. Just like she pretended that she was using her Clinique eye lift cream up faster than usual while the skin around Maurice's eyes grew noticeably softer.

Dan Weston was the furthest thing possible from a metrosexual. Judging by the fine, weather-beaten lines around his eyes, he had never in his life moisturized. She couldn't even begin to imagine him going in for a chest and leg wax. Maurice had had a weekly manicure. Dan's hands were big and rough, callused, the nails clean and cut but not manicured.

They were fascinating hands, though. Dark and broad and sinewy, the forearm muscles visible beneath the shirt-sleeve. They were the strongest hands she'd ever seen.

Everything about him fascinated her. The ultra-strong, fit body. The deep voice. The utterly male vibe coming from him like steam off a grate, mixed in with a gazillion male pheromones.

It wasn't until they were getting ready to go that Claire realized that the fascination he held for her had sucked her right out of herself. For a year now, she'd been like the walking dead. Barely able to function, hardly aware of the world outside, living completely inside her broken self. She'd barely spoken a dozen words to anyone.

And now she'd eaten—if not a full meal, at least food—with another human being, talked to him, sat so close she could feel his body heat.

She felt like a baby that had spent its first year in the dark, but now was walking on shaky feet toward the light. It was wonderful, but she also felt exhausted. What little energy she had had been eaten up in the panic attack.

The huge fire at her back, Dan sitting so close to her, melted the icy core she carried around inside herself. She felt warm, for the first time in a long time. Warm and . . . sleepy. Her eyes drooped.

Dan laughed, jolting her upright. "I guess you're not up for this great jazz club on Wisconsin Avenue right now."

"Guess not," Claire said sheepishly. Then, before she could stop herself, "Maybe tomorrow night."

Well, that was dumb.

She was a *spook*, for heaven's sakes. Or had been. Capable of keeping her country's secrets, more than capable of the security dance, where you doled out just enough intel to get what you wanted, making sure, always, the equation was in your favor.

Claire had gone to endless international meetings and to an infinity of cocktail parties where her brief had been to draw out some shard of intel and she had never, ever blurted anything out. Every word she spoke had been as precisely calibrated as if it had been turned on a lathe.

And now look at her. Just opening her mouth and . . . plop. Whatever was bouncing around in her crazy head at that moment came falling out. Lord.

"Sorry," she muttered.

She had no idea where she would be tomorrow night. Probably back home, in her big, empty house. Why should she be here? She'd come racing up thinking this man could magically erase the clouds in her mind, but he couldn't. He could only make her eat and feel warm.

Whatever had happened in Laka remained essentially a mystery, except for the intriguing detail that she'd kissed him.

But besides the kiss, what claim did she have on his time? None. He was a busy man, ran his own company and successfully, too, if that office was any indication. A successful businessman didn't have time to just drop everything because an old acquaintance showed up. An old acquaintance who didn't even remember him.

"I'm sorry. That was dumb of me. I should be . . ." *Home by this time tomorrow.* The words stuck in her throat.

His mouth turned up as he watched her flounder. Was that—was that a *dimple*? Maybe dimple was too strong a word for what appeared on that rough face. A dent. It was definitely a dent. A smile-induced dent.

Dan picked her hand up and brought it to his mouth, hot breath washing over her palm. He planted a soft kiss in the center of her palm. She caught her breath, pulled her hand away and placed in on her lap, under the table. Curling her fingers around the spot that felt as if a small sun had blossomed there.

"I'd love to take you wherever you want to go. Tomorrow, the next day. Whenever. Today you surprised me. Tomorrow I'm clearing the decks for you. My time is yours."

Claire blinked. She opened her mouth then closed it. There was nothing she could say that wouldn't be wrong. Her mind was blank, utterly void.

He watched her, eyes fixed on her face. "You're tired," he said gently, reaching out a long finger to touch what she knew would be the bruised flesh under her eyes. God knows she'd seen enough of that in the mirror this past year. "Do you want me to take you back to your hotel?"

Such an easy question, with no easy answer.

Yes, please, I am dying to get into my nightgown, crawl into the unfamiliar bed and stare at the ceiling until a shallow, troubled sleep takes me around three in the morning, during which I will probably be woken up by a nightmare. My favorite.

Or—*No, God no. Take me home with you, get me naked and have wild monkey sex with me.*

Whoa. Where had *that* come from? Never over-sexed at the best of times, Claire had spent the past year essentially dead from the neck down, in a sexless, utterly manless place.

She didn't want him to take her home and throw her on the sofa and have his wild way with her. What she wanted was to be a woman who *wanted* that, a woman with a few hormones floating around in her system.

Her head hurt.

"Yes," she whispered. "Back to the hotel, please."

Dan obviously ran a tab because they didn't go through the whole check and tip thing. He simply gave some kind of invisible signal and a waiter appeared with their coats. A minute later they were walking to his car.

It was freezing cold. The stars were like glistening diamonds in the clear black sky overhead. The sidewalk was slippery with ice. Claire wasn't used to cold weather anymore and looked down to watch her feet.

And then she realized she didn't need to. Dan had curled

his arm through hers, his muscular frame warm and solid at her side. Claire knew, with a sure animal instinct, that she would never slip and fall with Dan Weston by her side. She was perfectly okay as long as he was there.

After a minute, she relaxed and enjoyed the cold air against her face after the heat of the restaurant.

The last of her nausea cleared away in the chill night air. With Dan walking beside her, strong, focused and attentive, panic attacks seemed far, far away. Through her clothes and his she could feel strength and heat, the kind of strength and heat that was contagious, that she was able to borrow for a while. The best kind.

They approached the BMW and Dan put his hand in his coat pocket. The vehicle suddenly popped to life, headlights flashing, doors unlocking, like a living thing glad to see its master.

Dan opened the passenger door and helped her inside. She was still arranging her big down coat around her knees when he got into the driver's seat.

He gave her a brief glance then bent to turn the key in the ignition. It was so cold their breaths created white clouds around their heads.

"It'll warm up in a second." He turned to her and pulled her seat belt out and down, clicking it into place.

Then he lifted his head. They were almost nose to nose and the expression on his face took her breath away.

Pure sex. Pure male desire. That's what she saw on his hard features. Their eyes met. Held.

He was utterly still. A muscle twitched over his cheekbone.

He wanted her and she had no idea what to do with that knowledge. Her mind was completely fogged up, more than usual. His desire and hers twining in a complex mix of emotions she had no idea how to untangle.

Her desire.

That was another shocker.

He wanted her and she wanted him right back, but for all the wrong reasons. Because he was so hot he melted the icy chill that surrounded her. Because he had strong hands that wouldn't let her fall. Because he was completely, gloriously sane and she was . . . she was slightly loony on her best day. Because he was a Marine and was guaranteed to make her feel safe when she woke up at three in the morning, alone and terrified, with the echo of danger and voices clamoring in her head.

Those were not good reasons to take a man to your bed.

His dark eyes traveled down her face to her mouth, lingered there, then moved back up to her eyes. She'd felt his gaze like a caress, like a kiss. He was so dense with muscles it was like he exerted his own gravity field. Because she felt its tug so much, and wanted to fall forward into him, she pulled back. Not by much, just a slight shift of balance, but it was enough to trigger a release of the tension. Dan pulled back, too.

A minute later, they were on the road. The night was clear, inky black, frost riming cars and hedges and bare tree branches. Claire turned her head and stared out the window because the urge to stare at him was way too strong.

If she stared at him the way she wanted, she'd be sending him the exact opposite signal she'd sent by pulling back. Yes, no, yes, no . . . just another sign of her lunacy.

But oh, how Dan attracted the eye. Maybe it was because she hadn't been near a man except for her father and doctors for a year, but he seemed to her to encompass everything wonderful about his gender.

Claire had always liked men. She'd missed the company of men this past year, terribly.

And here was the malest man she'd come up against in a long time, making his intentions clear. She could have his company for as long as she wanted it, which was nice, but sex was going to be thrown into the pot, which was *theoretically* nice, but . . .

She simply had no idea whether she was up to it. Whether her weakened body could withstand sweaty sex, whether

her weakened mind would bear up under the stress. Oh, God. She had no idea of anything, except for the fact that she was a mess.

Better to just shut up.

Dan seemed comfortable with silence, though, and found no need to fill the void with guy talk or even seduction talk. He simply drove, easily and well, checking on her from time to time.

Claire remembered a saying an Italian—a very handsome, very drunk young Tuscan cultural attaché—had once told her when trying to wheedle her into bed. *Una parola è poco, due sono troppe.* One word isn't enough, two are too many.

So she held her peace, enjoying the heated cabin as the luxurious car arrowed its way through the dark, cold streets, enjoying the feeling of being taken somewhere without having to arrange it or worry about it.

The soft hum of the powerful engine lulled her into a pleasant lassitude. Dan rolled to a gentle stop and killed the engine.

"We're here," his deep voice announced.

A streetlight cast enough light into the cabin to see him by. In the penumbra, his strong features only half-lit, he looked almost exotic, skin the bronze of an ancient weapon. Deep-set eyes, high cheekbones, firm mouth. Strong sinewy hands still holding the steering wheel. Shoulders so broad they cut off her view of the street as he turned to her, watching her.

Oh, God.

The temptation to ask him inside, to take him into her room, was so strong she had to clench her teeth against it.

This man, she knew beyond a shadow of a doubt, could make her forget her problems. Sex with him would burn away all thoughts of the bombing a year ago and all memories of this past cold, lonely year.

When he opened her door and her feet touched the ground their eyes met in an electric moment of perfect understanding.

He wanted her. What she was going to do about it was up to her.

In about three seconds, Claire was going to have to make a decision, a big one. An important one. One that would have consequences.

She'd been used to making decisions in her job. Big ones. Important ones. Fully aware that they had consequences, and serious ones. A wrong report and all hell could break loose.

Like when she hadn't seen the Red Army coming.

But ordinarily, she felt more than up to the task of deciding, of assessing a situation and coming down on one side or the other, because she had always had a strong feeling for which side was the right one.

Right now, it felt utterly impossible. Her mind was split into two parts. Yes. No. Yes. No.

Yes. Wow. If Dan Weston lived up to his appearance and the vibes he gave out, he'd be amazing in bed. And oh, how she could do with some hot sex, hot enough to take her out of herself, warm her up from the inside out. Make her forget. Drown her in sensuality. Oh, yeah.

No. No, of course not. Was she crazy? Well, yes, she was, that was the whole problem. Dan had the right to make love to a whole woman, a woman whose elevator reached the top floor.

Was her body even, um, up to it? Her hip bone had been shattered in a million pieces and was held together with titanium pins. So many she set off metal detectors at airports. She'd only been walking for five months. He was a heavy, vigorous man. Maybe sex was beyond her, maybe he'd break a bone or something.

Or, worse, maybe she had become shriveled or something, inside. Maybe she'd end up not being able to do it. Or maybe she could manage it and then she'd fall asleep, only to wake up terrified and sweaty from a nightmare.

Man, that would be guaranteed to send him screaming into the night . . .

Claire's head was swirling by the time they made it to the front desk, and she still wasn't any closer to a decision.

She waited a moment for the clerk to show, frowning slightly. He'd struck her as a very conscientious young man who wouldn't desert the front desk, but who knew?

Well, the keys were hanging on a board to the left. As a matter of fact, all ten keys were there. Either there were no other guests or they were all out to dinner.

She stretched out a hand and a second later, Claire was on the floor with a ton of man on top of her. A large, armed man. Somehow, Dan had conjured a big black weapon from out of nowhere. A Glock 19. A gun that meant business.

"Sh," he whispered in her ear and she nodded. She wouldn't have had the breath to talk, anyway. He was amazingly heavy and he covered her completely, head to toe.

So much for the fear that she couldn't have sex because her bones might break. If her bones hadn't broken now that he'd jumped on top of her, they sure wouldn't during sex.

But sex was very far from Dan's mind. She looked up at him, trying to take her cue about what was going on from his face.

Whatever it was, it wasn't good.

He looked grim and hard, narrowed eyes quartering the room, just like a soldier would. One corner, blink to black, another, blink to black and so on. He was fast and thorough. After he'd searched, he lowered his head until his lips touched her ear. "Bloodstains on the floor." His voice was the merest whisper, and carried no farther than her ear.

Claire nodded, understanding completely. Bloodstains and no clerk at the front desk. It could mean anything, but mainly it could mean trouble. They'd both spent a lot of time in places where trouble was always the most likely explanation for any puzzling phenomenon, particularly where blood was involved.

Dan got off her, still crouching, and signaled for her to come around the desk. She scooted as fast and as quietly as she could and crouched behind the desk. She could see it now, clearly. A trail of blood that led to a closed door that probably opened onto a back room.

Big gun at the ready, Dan gave another sweep of the room with his eyes and reached out to open the door to see where the blood trail led. The knob turned but the door would only open an inch or two. Something in the room was blocking the door. Claire's eyes met his. She could feel her heart thudding.

Dan put his shoulder to the door and shoved, opening it enough to stick his head in. Claire saw the sole of a boot. Dan glanced down, then pulled the door quietly closed. His face was grimmer than before.

Claire felt sick to her stomach. The clerk had seemed like such a nice young man. What had happened? Drug dealers? A burglary gone bad?

Dan reached up to grab her key. Still crouching, Glock held as if it were an extension of his hand, he moved forward then stopped, frowning. Claire had him by the coat. She'd simply grabbed a hunk of material and grimly hung on. No way was he going exploring and leaving her here alone. She signaled urgently with her hands. *I'm coming with you!*

Dan's jaws worked, processing that. He shrugged and gestured for her to remain behind him.

Claire scrambled up in a rush, careful not to make any noise. Yes, of course she'd stay right behind him. He was armed and she was not. He was a former soldier and she was a former desk jockey. She was crazy, not stupid.

Dan moved quietly into the lobby, Claire trailing him. A little brass plaque on the right-hand wall of a wide corridor said *Rooms 1-10* with an arrow pointing down to the end. He stopped in front of each room and listened. Claire couldn't hear anything over the thudding of her heart, but he seemed to be satisfied that the rooms were empty. There was a tiny space under the door of each room showing darkness.

He stopped in front of her room, number seven, and

pointed at the bottom of the door. A faint light glimmered. He looked a question at her and she shook her head sharply. She distinctly remembered turning out the light. She believed strongly in energy conservation. Not even in her most crazy periods did she ever forget to turn out lights. It was ingrained behavior.

The faintest sound penetrated the door. As if someone were . . . ripping something?

Someone was definitely in there.

Dan's big arm flattened her against the wall several feet away from the door. He crouched and quietly inserted the key in the lock with his left hand, right hand gripping that big, bad Glock. He twisted the key, pushed open the door and dove into the room.

For the second time in her life, Claire's world exploded.

SEVEN

THERE he was!

The fucker was ripping up the curtains. In his peripheral vision, Dan could see that he'd already trashed the room. The man had a weapon in a shoulder holster and Dan rolled to the side, behind an armchair, before he could pull it.

A second passed, two. A lifetime in combat.

The man wasn't shooting at him. There was only one door and Dan hadn't heard glass shatter so the man hadn't left.

Dan peered around and froze. The intruder had pulled a rifle with a scope to his eyes. A small rifle, an AR-7. Lightweight, small profile, easily concealable. The perfect hit man's weapon. But why a goddamn *scope* in a room? And he wasn't aiming at Dan, he was aiming at the wall.

What the fuck?

Two booms, loud in the small room. Dan flinched and closed his eyes at the shards of brick wall flying by, feeling the burn of small lacerations on his face and hands.

Goddamn!

The man knew Dan was crouching behind the sofa. If

his rounds could penetrate a brick wall they sure as hell could go right through a foot of upholstery. He knew Dan was armed so why the *hell* was this bozo aiming at the wall . . .

It hit Dan like a sledgehammer upside the head. His blood froze. That wasn't a scope fitted on to the rifle, it was a thermal imager. And he was aiming at Claire!

Dan didn't dare stand up. He didn't have body armor on, goddammit, so he couldn't draw the man's fire. Though he'd gladly take a bullet for her, if this guy was gunning for Claire, Dan couldn't do her any good at all if he was dead or if he was gut- or lung-shot.

He had to stay alive. The trick was to distract the man somehow.

Another round went into the wall and Dan gritted his teeth, feeling himself go into firefight slo-mo. Though everything was happening in the space of fractions of seconds, it felt like hours as he set up the geometry of things, aware that he was operating with only half his mind. The other half was mired in bright red waves of panic at the thought of a wounded Claire outside in the hallway. That slender body prone, still, bleeding.

Dan shoved the image back into the deepest corner of his brain. He didn't need this. He didn't need the image of a broken Claire in a hotel hallway flashing bright in his head. It distracted him, slowed him down.

He always kept his cool in a firefight but this was the first time he faced an opponent with split attention.

It was deadly. He had to focus and move fast if Claire was to have a chance of surviving this.

Dan jerked at the leg of a console table that was still upright. The fucker hadn't gone after the furniture. Maybe he hadn't had time yet. The console tipped forward and he caught a big porcelain vase filled with silk flowers. He hefted it, jaws clenching. It was heavy. Good.

If he peeped around the corner, he'd get his head blown off, so he simply lobbed the heavy vase at where he had triangulated the man's head to be and gave up a silent cry of victory as he heard the sounds of china shattering and a man's low curses.

Glass shattered.

Dan rose, grim and ready, Glock up and firing, but a briefcase was sailing through the window and the man was diving after it through the glassless window frame. Dan rushed to the window, peering into the darkness of the hotel's back garden.

There he was! Zigzagging through the bushes, agile and strong. He knew what he was doing. Dan fired at center mass, a savage burst of glee coursing through him as his round hit the intruder in the back. The intruder gave a grunt and stumbled, then shot the padlock on the fence surrounding the hotel on the run and powered his way through it.

Shit! Fucker had body armor on! Dan slapped the window frame in frustration. For half a second, he fought the temptation to go after the intruder. Jump right out that window and go in pursuit and find him and waste him. It's what every cell in his body wanted, he yearned for it, but there was only one thing in the world more important to him than revenge and she was out in the hallway, defenseless, maybe bleeding to death.

Dan raced out into the hall. Horror nearly knocked him off his feet when he saw her, facedown and still. So still. He slid down on his knees next to her, frantically touching her all over.

"Claire! Claire! Goddammit, Blondie, talk to me!"

He turned her over, looking for blood, feeling for broken bones, but she was intact. He shuddered with relief when she opened her eyes and looked up at him. Big, beautiful silvery blue eyes, aware and *alive*.

He pulled her up and into his arms and completely forgot how fragile she was, clutching her close to him with all his strength, simply breathing her in. Finally, when he got himself under control, he gently helped her stand up.

Claire's light blue eyes roamed over his face. "Is he gone?" she whispered.

"Yeah." Dan had an arm around her back, steadying

her, feeling something strange against his hand. "Are you hurt anywhere? Fuckhead had a thermal imager. He could see you through the scope. My heart nearly stopped when he shot through the wall. But he—"

Missed. Dan was about to say the fucker missed when he realized what he was feeling. Her big black down coat was ripped all across the back, stuffing and feathers coming out of the rips.

Claire threw her arms around his neck. She was shaking so hard he tightened his grip to absorb some of that terrible trembling.

"Sh." He rocked her gently, back and forth, holding the miracle that was a live Claire in his arms. He brushed his lips back and forth over that goose-down soft hair, absorbing every detail of her because another few inches and he'd be howling over a dead body.

She snuggled more tightly against him, seeking the comfort of his body and if he could have, he'd have had her crawl right in under his skin.

A miracle. A fucking miracle is what he was holding in his arms.

The big puffy coat, which held her body warmth, had shown up on the thermal imager as heat. The man thought he was shooting at a plump woman, but he was only hitting a down coat. That, and the fact that she'd been lying tight in next to the baseboard and the man had had an awkward shooting angle, had saved her life.

They clutched each other for long minutes, both desperate for comfort. Dan thought he might need it more than she did. Every time he closed his eyes, he could see Claire's lifeless body on the inside of his lids.

Still holding her tightly with one arm, Dan pulled out his cell and called one of his best friends.

"Yo, Gunny. This better be good, I'm just now going off duty and I have a hot date."

"You can get laid another time," Dan growled. Lieutenant Marcus Stone got laid quite enough, he could do without tonight. Abstinence for a change would do him good.

"I'm on Warren Street. In a small hotel called the Kensington House. There's a dead body in the lobby, looks like a knife attack and there's been an attempted murder in room seven. Victim a Ms. Day. Ms. Claire Day. She survived the attack."

"Whoa," Marcus growled. "Day? Claire Day? *Blondie?* She's alive?"

Dan grit his teeth, regretting that he'd once gotten very drunk and spilled the beans to his friend. "Get over here, stat. And bring the CSU."

"Yeah, buddy." Marcus sobered up. "On my way. Don't touch anything."

Dan tightened his hold. No problem. The only thing he wanted to touch was Claire.

FUCK!

Heston got into his car, wincing at the lancing pain in his back. Maybe a rib was broken, maybe not. The important thing was to get word to the Boss that the mission had failed.

No one could have expected an armed man accompanying the woman. The Boss hadn't. There hadn't been any mention of anyone but the woman. The Boss knew that and he wouldn't take it out on Heston.

It was the Boss's gift—leadership. He was always fair and always reasonable and that was why his men would walk into hell for him. Heston would, damn straight. The Boss had always sent him on ops with the best intel and the finest equipment, which was more than he could say for the US government, which had sent him out on patrol in Iraq with canvas-sided vehicles and, for the first few months, inferior body armor.

It was the Boss, actually, who'd got him the best armor possible on the private market and passed it on to him, in exchange for a little job that had cost Heston nothing except some time and effort. And on top of it, the Boss had paid him ten thousand dollars. In cash.

Right now, Heston—whose father had never been able to hold down a job and had never had a bank account—had a million dollars in an account offshore and owned his apartment outright. Thanks to the Boss.

And this was the beginning. The Boss had plans, big ones, and Heston intended to be at his side when he got where he wanted to go.

He ignored the pain as he cruised the streets, checking his six. No one followed, he made sure of that. After a quarter of an hour, he pulled into a dark side street and pulled out his cell. A one-off, prepaid, untraceable.

Problems, he texted. The Boss was at a dinner at the Willard with big shots, people he needed for the next step. Heston hated to interrupt him, but the Boss would want to know. A discreet one-word message. And the Boss would decide whether to interrupt the dinner or not.

Heston's cell phone gave an incoming message trill.

Room 415 in half an hour.

EIGHT

CLAIRE clutched at Dan as he rocked her in his arms. He was whispering something in her ear, something reassuring, but she couldn't hear him over her thundering heartbeat. She thought her heart would beat its way right out of her chest. Oh, God. Oh, God.

She shook. It was like a year ago, only worse, because she could remember this, remember the terror of feeling bullets catch on her coat as she tried to press herself into the ground, make herself invisible. She'd had an instinct that to get up and run would make her more of a target so she'd laid there, still, waiting for a bullet to smash into her.

Dan had simply rushed into the room. It was the bravest thing she'd ever seen. He hadn't hesitated, not one second, in facing an armed man.

Claire tightened her arms around his neck. She was sure she was choking him but until he complained, she wasn't going to let go.

Dan somehow absorbed some of her shock and terror, somehow made her wild trembling slow down. Finally,

finally, she was able to draw in a deep breath. It felt like she hadn't breathed in centuries. She gasped.

"That's right. Breathe in, breathe out, that's a good girl. I know you're scared, but it's okay now. He's gone and he's not coming back." The deep voice was murmuring in her ear, words she could barely understand, though she understood the tone. It represented strength, and safety.

Dan loosened one arm around her and made a call on his cell. Her scattered brain could barely understand what he said, but she clung to his steady voice.

His arm went back around her, mouth close to her ear. "Police are on their way. Do you understand me, honey?"

It took a second to penetrate, but then Claire nodded shakily against his neck.

"We're going to have to make a statement to the police when they arrive. The clearer our statement, the more quickly they can catch him."

He waited and she nodded again, throat too dry to talk.

Her breathing slowed, deepened. She loosened her hold on his neck, drew away.

Claire tilted her face up to his. They stared at each other. Dan was looking grim, mouth tight, nostrils flared and pale.

"Who—" All she produced was air. Claire coughed to loosen her throat and tried again. "Who was he?"

The blind panic was subsiding, she felt steadier.

"I don't know who he was," Dan said, his low rough voice frustrated, "but we'll goddamned find out."

"Did you get a look at him?" To Claire, he was a faceless monster on the other side of a wall. "Could you identify him in a lineup?"

Dan's jaws clenched. "Yeah, I got a look at him, but he was about average everything. Average height, weight, average skin color."

Claire tried a shaky smile. "That's a new one. Average skin color? What's that?"

He shrugged. "White with light tan. Dark hair. Brown eyes. Lighter than mine."

"Half the world's population has brown eyes. I wonder—" She stopped, listened. The faint wail of sirens, coming closer.

Dan dropped his arms. "I'll go out on the front porch. Signal them."

"I'm coming with you," Claire said hastily. No way was he leaving her alone in here.

One piercing look at her, top to bottom, and he held out his hand. Okay, he'd probably seen what a wuss she was, how she'd had a flashback panic attack, but she didn't care. She just knew that being next to him, holding his hand, made her feel better.

Out on the hotel's porch, they watched as two police cars pulled up and killed their sirens. A white van braked right behind them. Three uniformed officers and a tall man in a suit got out of the cars and several techs spilled out of the white van.

The man in civilian clothes attracted the eye. Tall, broad, steel gray eyes, whitewall haircut, ramrod straight. The detective.

And a former Marine, she'd bet money on it.

The detective clapped Dan on the back and they walked back into the lobby. Three young techs rushed by them carrying heavy cases.

"Claire, this is Detective Marcus Stone. Marcus, Claire Day."

"Blondie," the detective said.

"Marcus . . ." Dan growled.

Claire looked at the detective, confused. "Do I know you?"

He bit his jaw, looked at Dan then coughed into his fist. "No, ma'am," he said gently. "But Dan has told me all about that day in Laka. It was a terrible thing."

"It was, yes, Detective." Claire jumped at a sudden flash. It was just the tech taking photos. Of the dead body. "Sorry," she murmured weakly.

"I'm going to have to ask you to look at the body, see if you recognize him. I'm sorry."

Claire breathed in and out. She could do this. She could.

Dan's arm tightened around her waist. Oh God, her legs were back to rubber. It was entirely possible that Dan's arm was the only thing holding her up. Though her head swam and it was hard to breathe, she stiffened her knees. Claire clung fiercely to consciousness. *Don't faint don't faint don't faint . . .*

"Yes, um, all right."

They walked back around the counter and into the back room. The door had been propped open and Claire simply stared. She jolted as another bright white light went off.

"Steady," Dan whispered.

A couple of techs were dusting for prints. A middle-aged man who had been crouching by the body rose. He had obscured her view but now she saw the body clearly. Saw the olive skin now a dusty pale color. Open, staring eyes. Blue lips. And bright blood all along the once snowy white shirt and on the tan carpeting.

A handsome young man, someone's son, maybe someone's husband, and now he was dead.

"Do you recognize him?" The detective's voice was gentle, but he expected an answer. Claire had to help, not hinder. Someone had murdered this young man and she had to do everything in her power to help find that man and bring him to justice.

"Yes." She was pleased to note that her voice was steadier. "He was the clerk on duty. This morning and at lunchtime there was a woman at the front desk. Her name was Amy." She looked down sadly at the blood-flecked brass plaque. "His name was Roger. I have no idea what his last name was."

"Yeah, it's him," Dan confirmed. "He was at the front desk when we left earlier this evening."

"Okay." The detective looked at Dan. "Anywhere we can sit down?"

"Yeah, over here." Dan led them to the little living room suite in the corner of the lobby. The detective sat down heavily in an armchair, pulling out a notebook and clicking a pen. Dan steered Claire to the small sofa across from the coffee table, a mere millisecond before her knees would have given out completely.

The tech was taking so many photos in the back room it looked like strobe lights. A sudden image of the dead boy's face floated right in front of her eyes. Still, white, cold as ice, blue tongue protruding slightly from blue lips. White shirtfront red with blood . . .

Dan's voice came from faraway, as if he were in another country. He was calling her name, but she couldn't turn her head to him. If she turned her head, the world would spin, spin completely away.

A strong hand clasped the back of her neck and pushed her head down to her knees and a distant voice told her to breathe in.

She pulled in a deep breath. *Out*, the voice said after a second or two, and she blew out the breath.

In and out, in and out. She opened her eyes and stared at her knees. No spots. She swallowed. No bile. She lifted her head slightly. No spinning.

Claire sat up again, cautiously. Yes, her stomach stayed where it should be, mid-torso, not sliding up her gullet.

"Sorry," she gasped. "I, um, it, um . . . "

Dan stood up abruptly and disappeared down the corridor. Claire couldn't muster the energy to wonder where he'd gone, she was too busy keeping her stomach where it belonged.

"No problem, ma'am," the detective said.

Claire tried on a smile for size. "I'm sorry about being such a wuss." She drew a deep breath, hoping to shatter the iron band around her chest. "I don't know what's wrong with me."

"Adrenaline dump." A faint smile creased the detective's hard face, crinkling his eyes. Another non-metrosexual who didn't moisturize. "Perfectly normal, ma'am. Blondie. Dan and I have both been real shaky after a firefight."

"Is that true?" Claire turned to watch Dan as he crossed the lobby. He'd shot at someone not half an hour ago and he looked perfectly fine. Grim, but fine. *His* hands certainly weren't shaking as he held a small bottle of ice-cold water out to her.

Claire took it eagerly and downed three-quarters of the icy cold water in a couple of long gulps and that overheated feeling that precedes throwing up started to subside.

Dan nodded. "Yeah. Hands shake, spots in front of your eyes, you want to vomit. Classics." She met his dark eyes. He might not be feeling the symptoms but he knew. He knew and he understood.

The detective coughed, a little *I'm here, too*, reminder. "I've got Dan's vitals, can I have yours?"

Claire pulled a blank. Vitals? Was that, like, internal organs? That queasy feeling came back as a loud rushing sound filled her head.

Dan finally broke the long silence. "Claire Day," he said.

Oh my God. *Get a grip on yourself.* "Oh! Sorry. Claire Lorena Day, born in Boston, September fifteenth, 1982. Currently residing at 427 Laurel Lane, Safety Harbor, Florida." She watched the detective bend his head over the notebook, his crew cut so extreme she could see scalp. It wasn't quite the high and tight of active duty, but it was the closest you could get to a military cut in civilian life.

Luckily, he didn't ask her what someone from Florida was doing in Washington DC, because *On a wild-goose chase* would have had to have been her answer.

"So . . . what went down?"

Dan nodded at her. She should go first. Okay. "We went out to dinner, Dan and I. He drove me back here, where I'm staying. We walked into the lobby together and the lobby was deserted."

"Is that normal?"

Claire shook her head. "I have no idea, I've never stayed here before, I found it on the internet. As I said, the, um, dead man was on duty when we left at seven so I assumed he was the night duty guy. He said he'd see me later, so I imagined that the front desk was always manned. When it isn't, they usually tell guests that they have to be in by a certain hour."

Detective Stone nodded. "So then what?"

"I was reaching to grab my key when Dan pushed me to the floor and jumped on top of me."

Stone's gaze tracked to Dan and he raised his eyebrows.

"Blood," Dan said shortly. "Enough for it not to be a paper cut. Someone had been seriously hurt."

"Yes." Claire nodded. "Dan walked around the desk in a crouch, opened the door to the back office and saw—" *A dead body. A murdered young man.* "Roger. And a lot of blood."

Stone frowned at Dan. "You didn't call it in right then and there?"

"I was going to, but first I had to see if there was any immediate danger. And there was. Fucker was waiting in Claire's room." His jaw muscles worked violently. "We went down the corridor, checking rooms. He had the light on in Claire's room, and he made a slight sound. He was trashing the room, ripping the upholstery and the curtains."

Claire nodded. "Dan had me crouch by the side of the door, then kicked it open. And then all hell broke loose. I fell to the ground."

"Saved your life." The words sounded harsh, bitten out. Dan met Stone's gaze. "He had an AR-7 with a thermal scope and he aimed directly at Claire, through the wall. He had an armed man—me—shooting at him and he didn't shoot back. He wanted Claire. She's alive because he had a bad angle from where he was shooting and because she had on this big down coat, muffled her thermal profile. But he caught the coat. Show him, honey."

Claire tried to turn, but couldn't break Dan's grip. "You'll have to let me go." Dan's arm dropped reluctantly and Claire slid her coat off and held it up for the detective to see. It was the first time she'd seen it, too. Long slashes in the back of her coat, edges singed where the bullet burned. Where a man had thought he was firing into living flesh.

She shuddered, then frowned. "An AR-7. That's a *rifle*. Why on earth would a burglar bring a rifle with him? Besides the question of why a burglar would be armed at all and risk a longer sentence if caught."

"You know your weapons, ma'am." Stone gave a wintry smile. "AR-7s have their uses. For certain . . . purposes."

"Murder," Dan said harshly. "That's its main use. It's a classic hit man's rifle. Lightweight, the barrel and the action fold up into the stock. He had a briefcase, one of those Halliburton deals. An AR-7 would have fit easily into it. The guy came loaded for bear. Actually, he came loaded for Claire." He huffed out a breath of anger and clenched his fists. His eyes met Stone's. "Fucker wanted Claire, no question."

"You worked for DIA," Stone said to her, making it sound odd. Not an accusation, just a possible explanation for a hit man in room seven.

"No, no!" This was crazy. "No one could possibly want to kill me. I am—was an analyst. Analysts write reports, we're not operators, not in any way. No DIA analyst has ever been killed in the line of duty." A number of them had drunk themselves to death, but that was another story. "And any information I might have had is a year out of date. This is a fast-moving world. No one's going to come after a lowly analyst whose intel is old. Trust me on this."

It had the cold, hard ring of truth. Dan and Stone sat there, chewing on it.

"Sir?" A tech in paper overalls, latex gloves and booties came out of the back room. "We're done here. Got a whole mess of fingerprints, take a month to get through them. Coroner's done, too. Proximate cause of death, internal hemorrhaging from sharp instrument penetrating the heart. Coroner says he thinks the autopsy will give us a clue as to the type and length of the blade."

Everyone turned their heads as two techs carried a body bag out on a stretcher. Claire thought of the young man, with his entire life ahead of him, now zipped up in heavy plastic, dead. And soon a mother, a sister, a girlfriend, perhaps a wife and children, would be mourning his loss.

As if by an unspoken signal, they didn't speak until the body had been carried out to the van. A primitive gesture of respect for the dead.

The lead tech walked back in, turning to the detective. He was young, tall, sandy-haired, with one of those mobile, expressive faces comics had. But he didn't have the expression of a stand-up comic. He looked sober, older than his years. Claire imagined he'd seen a lot of the worst of human nature. "We'll go to the hotel room now, sir. Dig out some bullets."

"I want to go with you." Claire surprised herself with the words. They came from the deepest part of her being.

Dan shifted uncomfortably. "Claire, honey, I'm not too sure . . ."

Claire ignored him and turned to Stone. "Detective, I want a look into that room. I never got a chance because the man started shooting immediately. I never got through the door. I want to see. I won't touch anything, I understand full well it's a crime scene, but I want to see." Her voice was firm. She would see it with or without his permission.

The detective hesitated a beat then said, "Let's go."

They trooped down the corridor, Dan by her side, so close she could feel his body heat. He was still on hyper alert. He kept his left arm around her and his Glock in his right hand, eyes vigilant.

They made it to the open doorway. Dan's arm around her waist braced Claire as she stepped back from her room as sharply as if someone had attacked her.

She stared at the room, *her* room. All soft surfaces had been slashed. Couch and chair cushions, the mattress, the pillows. The few clothes she'd had with her, including nightgown and change of underwear, had been slashed to shreds and the knife had destroyed her other pair of shoes

The destruction was . . . cold. And calculated. Things that might have made a noise smashing, such as the pottery body of the lamp, the big bowl of flowers on the desk, a series of decorative plates on the wall, were all intact. The frenzy of destruction mainly affected soft things and her personal effects. Someone had gone out of their way to destroy her personal things. She shivered.

"Okay," Dan said abruptly. "That's it. Marcus, do you need us to be here?"

"She can't take anything from the room," Stone said sharply. "It's all evidence."

"There's nothing to take anyway," Claire said and stepped into the room. She turned her head and saw into the bathroom, then walked in. Her toiletries had been swept to the floor, where they'd shattered. He'd probably closed the bathroom door for that, so the sound wouldn't alert anyone. The sharp smells of creams and shampoo and Miss Dior assailed her nostrils.

They didn't make her nauseous, though. She was too angry for that.

She stepped back into the room. There was nothing of hers that could be carried away. Even her small carry-on had been slashed and was unusable.

"My computer," Claire said suddenly. "It's gone."

Dan stiffened and looked around.

"You sure?" the detective asked. "Maybe he destroyed it."

The closet door was open. The only other place that she hadn't checked was under the bed, so she bent to look, taking care not to touch the bedclothes. A smooth expanse of shiny hardwood floor. No computer.

"It was small, a netbook. But if he smashed it to bits, those bits would be here. And he couldn't have flushed the hard disk down the toilet. So he took it."

"What was on your computer? Anything sensitive?"

Claire knew what the detective was thinking. She was ex-DIA. A spook. Marines instinctively distrusted spooks and they were quite right. She could have had Homeland Security intel on her computer.

"No." Claire shook her head decisively. "I told you. I haven't been with DIA for over a year, and I had to hand in my agency-issue laptop. This computer was new, anyway. There's nothing on it besides a few high-end translation programs and glossaries and some translations. The original text and my translation of it. I have started working part-time as a translator from French."

"Any confidential texts there?"

Claire smiled at the thought. "No. Absolutely not. I translated two children's books recently, an article and a trade-fair website. This was only a netbook, I didn't even have most of my files on it. I brought it along out of habit and to check my email without having to go to an internet café. This hotel had Wi-Fi. I checked before making the reservation."

"Will you be harmed in some way if the laptop—"

"Netbook."

"Netbook," the detective repeated patiently. "If the netbook is destroyed?"

She thought. "No, not really. Everything I need for my new job is on my desktop at home. If the man stole the netbook there's the economic loss. But the text I was working on is also on my thumb drive and on the desktop back in Florida and I use a remote backup service." She frowned. "The netbook was new, but it wasn't wildly expensive. If he decides to fence it, he won't get much. That was probably the most expensive thing of mine in the room. But—" She drew a deep breath. It had to be faced. "He wasn't here to steal."

"No." The detective was writing in his notebook and didn't look up. "He wasn't here to steal. We can leave the techs to do their work. Let's go down to the station house."

Claire watched as one of the young techs used a long tweezers-like instrument to gently extract something oblong and metallic from a baseboard. There would be several bullets embedded in the hardwood floor outside that wall. The ones that had narrowly missed being embedded in her flesh.

Claire swayed, then pulled herself upright.

"Negative." Dan's deep voice was sharp as he narrowed his eyes at his friend. "She's dead on her feet. She got up really early this morning to catch the first flight up. I'm taking her home."

The detective flipped his notebook shut and looked hard at Dan. Dan looked hard at him right back. Claire could almost see the lines of male will surge back and forth.

Dan won.

The detective sighed. "Okay. I want both of you at the M Street station by eleven at the latest and we'll get all this info into the files. Stay within the city precinct." This to Dan. Dan nodded, then looked at her, one eyebrow raised.

The question was clear. Was she willing to come home with him?

The answer to that was clear, too.

Hell, yes.

*N*INE

ROOM 415 of the Willard Hotel was sumptuous. The Boss always had the finest of everything. Heston walked gingerly into the room.

The Boss had a thermos of coffee and some fancy sandwiches waiting. Heston could smell them from the door. The Boss thought of everything.

Heston was coming to report failure, but the Boss knew he'd also been on a mission and if there was one thing soldiers needed after an op, it was fuel. They also needed a woman, stat, but Heston could get his own woman. After.

No alcohol. The op wasn't over. It had just switched gears.

The Boss had been staring out the window at the bright lights of Pennsylvania Avenue below, the White House lit like a birthday cake in the corner of the window. The Boss pulled the drapes shut, in case someone was aiming a laser lens at the window. The room would have been swept twice for electronics.

The Boss never took chances. It was why he was who he was and why no one could stop him.

The Boss turned back to the room and gestured with his hand. "Sit down, Heston," he said, his voice pleasant.

"Yessir." Heston scrambled to sit in one of the plush chairs, sinking right in. The material was super soft, like silk. Hell, at the price of these rooms, it probably *was* silk. The coffee was poured into cups so thin you could see light through them, with little roses curling around the cup. Delicate, fragile.

Fuck.

Heston didn't want to break the frigging cup. His hands were big and hard. Hands meant for shooting and killing, not for holding ultra-delicate china.

But it was one more test. Heston secretly believed that the Boss was watching him, training him . . . *grooming* him. For bigger and better things. And, shit, he wanted to be by the Boss's side, every step of the way.

The Boss waited until Heston had had his coffee and refused refills, then leaned forward in his chair, face open, without a shred of disappointment or censure. "So, tell me what happened. You said there were problems. What were they?"

Heston told him, beginning to end, leaving out nothing.

The Boss sat back and stared at the wall. Face totally expressionless, totally still, except for the slight rise and fall of his chest. Finally he refocused his gaze on Heston. "This was my fault. The mission was to get a computer and eliminate a woman. You couldn't possibly have known there could be an armed man involved. So . . . the man knew what he was doing?"

This was just like the Boss, taking the heat. Heston's heart broke open, just a little. He'd had a brutal father and he'd served with shit officers. He'd never had anyone like the Boss in his life.

"Yessir, he sure did. Had a Glock, knew how to use it, too. He was trying to draw fire away from the woman. Like I said, she was lying on the floor outside the hotel room. I'm almost certain I got her three times. She presented, ah, a large profile."

The Boss's eyes sharpened. "What?"

"Well, I mean she was big. A big woman. The angle wasn't good but I think I got her."

"Big woman, eh?" The Boss stroked his chin. "Well, whatever. We'll see soon enough. I've got my computer expert hacking into the local police stations. As soon as we've got the report, we'll see if it's for one body or two." The Boss looked at him, a flash of something hard, like steel, crossed his face. "You'll be ready, with at least four men, for the next stage. Stay close to here. Use the safe house. Stay there until I call."

"Yessir." Heston dipped his head. "We'll be ready. And next time I won't fail."

"No." The Boss leaned forward and gently touched his knee. He was smiling now. "I know you won't fail. I'm counting on you."

FUCKING idiot, he thought when Heston left. A useful idiot, a loyal one, too, but an idiot nonetheless. He was tempted to give one of his men the order to take him out.

Though . . . Heston was usually efficient, he would say that for him. And this debacle was not entirely his fault. He'd been told his adversary was a lone woman.

Who the *fuck* had been with Claire Day? She'd been a DIA analyst, so she'd know men in the military community. But what had tipped her off that she should come accompanied by a gunman? The response had been so fast, it was as if she'd expected retaliation.

He sat and thought about it, about Claire Day as he'd known her and what he knew of her today.

She'd come prepared. He had to factor that in.

Claire had been super-smart, back in the day, known for the precision of her analyses. A real comer. But he'd been given to believe all that had gone, that she was a shell of a woman now, barely able to function. Had been in a fucking coma, for Christ's sake!

She'd completely quit the DIA. There was, as far as he

knew, no question of her ever coming back to work in any capacity.

That was not the Claire Day who'd escaped an assassination attempt by a bloody good soldier. It didn't matter how she did it, or that an operator had backed her up. The point was, she'd been smart enough to get backup.

Claire Day was after him, he could feel it. He'd always trusted his instincts and they'd always been good. Now every cell in his body told him to make getting rid of her his top priority. Except she'd gone to ground and he had no idea where.

If she wasn't dead—and he had a gut feeling she wasn't— she was plotting his ruin.

How to find her to eliminate her? How to get rid of the bitch, once and for all? He had to know where she went to ground. So . . . how to find out where she was?

He texted Heston, on his way to the safe house.

Do u have men near Safety Harbor, Florida?

The answer came within two minutes.

Yes. A good man, a quarter of an hour away.

OK. Have him burn down Claire Day's House. 427 Laurel Lane. Burn it fast, it can look like arson.

He waited another five minutes then his cell buzzed.

On his way.

He smiled. How to find out where Claire Day was? Why, smoke her out, of course.

DAN'S home was the most secure place he knew of. He had top of the line everything, at cost, courtesy of a Marine buddy who manufactured industrial security systems. He had the level of security of a bank or a defense depart-ment tech company. If a person so much as breathed on his perimeter, he knew about it, whether he was home or not.

And he'd made damned sure, driving back, that he wasn't being tailed.

He disengaged security at the gate, reengaged it and drove into his garage. When he killed the engine, he turned to Claire.

She was the color of ice again, shivering, though she tried to hide it. He'd turned the heat in his BMW on full blast, so much that he was sweating as he drove over the icy streets to Alexandria, but she was still trembling when he killed the engine.

It wasn't the cold, anyway, it was the shock. She'd seen a dead body and been attacked, in one night. It would be almost too much to bear for the strongest woman, let alone a woman who'd been grievously wounded and was barely back on her feet.

Dan watched her in the silence. He had a neon garage light that cast no shadows and was always on, even though the two security cameras had infrared capability. He was a strong believer in overkill. It was the old military slogan—two is one. One is none.

"How you doing?" he asked, keeping his voice quiet. The only sound in the garage was the ticking of the engine cooling.

"F-fine." She tried a shaky smile.

She wasn't fine. She was paler than when she'd had the panic attack.

She looked so lost and alone.

She wasn't alone, goddammit. As far as he was con-cerned, she'd never be alone again. He had her covered now and he was going to do his damnedest to make sure nothing bad ever happened to her again. Or at least nothing bad that he could prevent.

He had no idea why someone tried to kill her, which was truly scary shit because sure as anything that guy was going to come back to finish the job.

Fine. Bring it on. Fucker'd have to go over Dan's dead body, and he was a hard man to kill.

They needed to find out the source of the danger to Claire and neutralize it. But first, he needed to get her safely in the house and some color back in her cheeks.

He put a finger under her chin and turned her face to his, trying not to wince at her expression.

Still, God, she was so fucking beautiful. Shocked and pale and scared, she was still the most beautiful woman he'd ever seen. And by some miracle, she was here with him, where she was going to stay.

She was in his care now and he had to do this right.

First things first. "How about a shower, hot milk with a couple of fingers of whiskey and about ten hours of sleep?"

"Oh, man," she sighed and sketched a smile that nearly broke his heart. "Sounds wonderful. Are we safe here?"

"Yeah, we are. You can let down your guard." He hesitated a second, weighing the appearance of paranoia against putting her mind at rest. Reassuring Claire won. "I believe strongly in home security. I've got motion sensors, cameras around the property and the house, steel-reinforced doors, bullet-resistant windows." And, well, voice recognition software, automatic sensor polling and a steel-toothed strip that would rise from the ground at the gate on command. She didn't have to know all of that. All she had to know was that he was going to keep her safe.

He went around to the passenger side, opened the door, and held out his hands. Claire looked at his hands, then into his eyes.

The world stilled. Everything in Dan stopped—breath, thoughts, heart.

Slowly, Claire leaned forward, placing her hands in his. It was like being in a dream, all in slow motion, just the two of them in all the world. He lifted her out slowly, jaws clenched. She was featherlight between his hands, more like cloud and smoke than a woman.

But her face—that was all woman. Clear, porcelain skin, silver blue eyes, luscious mouth that didn't need lipstick to make a man think of sinking right in to her. She was finally out of the car but Dan didn't move, and neither did she. She stood, her hands still in his, that gorgeous face tilted up to his.

What was a man to do? Dan did the only thing he could do, what he'd been aching to do since eleven thirty this morning when she showed up on his office doorstep, this woman he thought was dead, and was instead alive, a fucking miracle.

He lowered his head, slowly, knowing that this was going to be momentous. It would divide his life into a before and an after. So he took it slow and easy. Just a touch of their lips at first. He felt an electric charge down to his toes.

Both of them drew in a breath that sounded loud in the hush of the garage.

The one thing Dan wanted to do right now, more than anything in the world, was to pull Claire right down to his hard, cold cement floor, slide her pants down those long, slender legs and follow her down, unzipping.

Two seconds later he'd be in her, the place he'd wanted to be—goddamned *yearned* to be—for almost two years now.

She'd let him, oh yeah. Her eyes were soft and warm as they looked at him.

Big Man. He was Big Man here, he'd saved her life, now had her in his home. No, she wouldn't fight him.

He could see it, feel it, taste it. It could happen, right now. Right here.

He'd let her keep her coat on, not even in his feverish state of desire did he want her naked back to be on the chill, rough concrete flooring. No, he'd let her keep the coat, the sweater, even the pants down to her knees. All he needed was a shot at the part of her his dick was weeping to enter.

So down on her back, the puffy coat softening the rough floor, maybe he'd be in time to put his own coat on the floor for her, unzipping as he came down on top of her, pulling himself out of his pants, parting her with his fingers and oh, man, just sliding right in. The image was positively electric.

He hadn't had sex in a year so he'd probably come in the first five seconds but that was okay, no way he'd lose his hard-on. In fact, he might sport his hard-on forever, the way he was feeling right now.

Maybe be buried in a closed casket because they couldn't get it to go down.

Once he got into Claire, there'd be no stopping him, because he was as revved as he'd ever been in his life.

Having been in a firefight didn't help, either. It was a known male reaction to danger—a woodie that lasted until the adrenaline passed through the system, usually through the dick.

Way out in the field, where there were no women to help you get rid of your hard-on, soldiers used their fists. After combat, barracks smelled like goats had died in there.

But he didn't need to use his fist here, oh no. He had the world's most beautiful woman right here, right in front of him, looking at him with soft eyes.

Oh man, once he was in her, he'd hold her hips while he did her hard, or pull her knees up and apart to give him more access. Just let it rip, get rid of all that adrenaline and break a year's abstinence by pounding into her . . .

Christ.

He would hurt her. The way he was feeling right now, he'd hurt her, hurt *Claire*. Fuck, what was he thinking— holding her down with his hands? He had big, strong hands and he could keep her still under him, no question. Though of course he'd probably bruise all that lovely pale skin, hurt her, make her feel trapped under him . . .

He closed his eyes.

This was not good. What he was feeling was not good. He was a man known for his control and he was on the razor's edge of losing that control right now, with a woman he cared about, a lot.

He opened his eyes again and saw Claire. Really *saw* her. Smart and courageous. An amazingly beautiful woman without an ounce of that power-hungry coyness so many beautiful women developed over the course of a lifetime leading poor males around by their dicks. A one-in-a-million woman.

She'd been blown up a year ago, spent three months in a fucking coma. She'd been shot at only an hour ago, her personal effects viciously destroyed—and he was fantasizing holding her down with all his strength while he fucked her? On the cold concrete of his garage floor?

Shame flooded him. He was better than this.

"Come in," he said gently and saw her relax slightly. She was smart. She'd picked up on his almost violent vibes, probably wondering what was in store for her. Relaxing a little as he showed a modicum of self-control.

Oh man, what an asshole he was.

The garage gave onto the kitchen and he walked her in, flipping on lights, taking her coat, moving away, giving her space.

She was looking around curiously. What was she seeing? The kitchen was clean, thank God. He wasn't a slob. Any sloblike tendencies he might have had had been beaten right out of him in the corps. So his spaces were all neat, everything squared away.

On the other hand, he didn't decorate. Everything was functional, with no personal touches at all. The kitchen was top of the line, as was his security system, home entertainment system and computer system. Everything else was chairs and beds and closets, chosen for being well-constructed and bland.

He pulled out a chair, gestured. "I think I promised you some hot milk."

"And whiskey." She turned her head to watch him. "Don't forget that."

No, he wouldn't. They were safe and if he couldn't dump some of his combat stress through immediate sex, whiskey would have to do.

The microwave pinged and he brought out a bottle from under the sink. He poured a finger into her warm milk and splashed four fingers into a tumbler for himself. He downed it in two gulps and placed the milk in front of her.

She cupped the mug in her hands, closing her eyes and bringing it to her nose and sniffing, a slight smile on her lips.

Oh Jesus, he thought. *Just look at her.* That long slender neck tipped back as she drank the mug of milk and he was nearly brought to his knees.

Any makeup she might have had on at the start of the evening had disappeared, her short hair stuck out from her head, her clothes were rumpled, the knees of her pants scuffed from when she'd hugged the ground in an effort to evade bullets.

She'd been through the wringer and she looked it.

He couldn't take his eyes off her.

Claire finished the milk and looked up at him. Like in the garage, it was as if the entire world had hushed. There were no sounds, none at all. His home was tightly built, soundproofed. There weren't even the small creaks and groans most houses had.

Not even the sound of breathing, because he forgot to breathe as Claire met his eyes. After a minute, his chest expanded and he sucked in air.

She was like a pearl in his kitchen—pale, glowing, perfect.

He'd have to be a saint to resist. He wasn't a saint.

Touching Claire was a real no-no right this instant because Dan had no idea if he could control the strength in his hands. So he clutched the table's edge and the back of her chair and bent down slowly to her. She was in his embrace, but . . . not.

Some tiny vestige of sense was jumping up and down inside his head, waving a red flag.

Watch it, or you might hurt her.

How the fuck was this supposed to work?

How was he supposed to slake his lust without scaring her or—God!—hurting her.

His hands were trembling, which was truly scary shit. Dan's hands never trembled, ever. He'd been a sniper. Snipers' hands were steady no matter what. Which made the trembling worse because this was way outside his experience.

Their eyes met, held. Her eyes moved left to right and back, as she watched his eyes. Waiting to see what he was going to do.

He was going to kiss her, slowly.

Keeping in control. He hoped.

His mouth touched hers, a swift electric taste of her that went straight to his dick. Oh God.

He pulled away, watched her eyes, carefully. *Give me a sign, honey.* Was this something she wanted or was he constructing this whole scenario out of his own massive lust?

It was gone almost before he noticed it, but he caught it. A smile. A lightening of her features, lips slightly curved upward.

A smile. In reaction to a kiss.

This was good.

Sex was going to happen.

Mentally punching the air while keeping a prudent grasp on her chair and the table, Dan bent down again.

Longer. Sweeter. Even better than before.

Her eyes fluttered closed.

Again. His mouth on hers, opening hers, that first wild taste of her, tongue meeting tongue. Heat prickled through his body. He lifted his mouth again, tilted his head for a better, deeper fit. She tilted, too, pushing up against him.

There were sounds now. His harsh breathing, the wet succulent sounds of kisses and, deep in her throat, a moan.

Oh man, it was too much. Time for action before he exploded in a million pieces.

Dan bent and lifted her in his arms.

IT was like flying, being carried by him.

Claire had no feeling of strain or gravity or anything at all but his mouth on hers, his strong arms under her and a sensation of weightlessness. Of floating above the world.

When she'd come out of the coma, weak, muscles

atrophied, she felt as if she'd woken up on Jupiter or some other heavy gravity world. Everything was hard, the whole world conspired to pull her down, down. In the beginning, even lifting her feet had been hard.

This was delicious, the world had loosened its ties and she floated above it.

Dan's house was big. They crossed a couple of rooms with large open spaces and very little furniture, which was a good thing because Dan was kissing her with his eyes closed. Clearly, though, he could navigate blind because they made it to his bedroom without tripping and falling.

Another big room, very spare. Only this one with a huge bed against the wall, the largest, most visible thing in the room. There was a big wooden headboard and about an acre of mattress with an enormous navy blue comforter on it.

The bed where they were going to make love. In about two seconds, if she was reading him right.

He was so tense she was afraid his muscles would twang if she touched him. His face was even darker, a dull red riding his cheekbones. He was breathing heavily as he let her slide down him by simply removing the arm under her legs.

She was plastered up against him and could feel everything—the ripped muscles, his chest bellowing in and out and, wow, his arousal. Huge and so hot she felt it through her clothes and his.

He reached for the hem of her sweater, eyes on hers. He stopped, waiting for a sign from her. "Do you want this?" His low deep voice seemed to fill the room.

There was no breath in her lungs to answer so she stood on tiptoe and kissed him.

There. There was no turning back now.

His hands shook. She put her hands over his and they stilled. She watched his eyes in the darkness. "It's okay," she whispered.

Claire had no idea how her body would react to sex, whether she was up to it or not. But she wanted him to know that any problems were hers, not his. If it didn't work out, it would be her fault, not his.

She was naked in seconds, or at least that's what it felt like, her clothes drifting off her as if in a dream. Sweater, bra, pants, panties. It seemed like Dan's large, strong hands just swiped the air and off they flew.

When she was naked, she stood there, so close to him her breasts almost touched him when she breathed in.

He stood, unmoving, for long moments, so still she would have thought him dead if his chest weren't moving. He reached out a hand to her, moving slowly, as if through something denser than air. When he touched her, she shivered, though his hand was like a furnace.

He placed his open palm on her chest, between her breasts.

"You're so beautiful," he whispered.

"Thank you," she whispered back. It was a moment for whispers, as if the whole world were holding its breath to see what would happen next.

His large, warm hand traveled slowly down her front, over her belly. He turned his hand and cupped her, the gentle shifting of his hand an invitation to open her legs.

Heat was coursing through her body, centered on where his hand touched her. Every cell in her body felt so *alive*. Hot and swollen.

Sexual desire. This was desire. It had been so long, she had forgotten the feeling, so long it took her a moment or two to even recognize it.

Claire tipped her head back a little because it felt like her neck muscles weren't strong enough to support her head. Every muscle she had went lax, the heat coursing through her seemingly melting them. She stiffened her knees to keep upright.

And then—oh God—he touched her there, at her most sensitive tissues, a rough finger circling her.

Her vagina clenched in excitement.

He stopped and huffed out a breath. "Oh, Christ," he breathed.

Another slow circle around her, the rough skin of his fingers adding to the intense pleasure.

He swallowed heavily.

Their only connection was his hand on her sex but Claire felt touched all over, skin prickling with heat.

"I haven't had sex in a year," he said, his voice hoarse. "I think I only have one condom and I don't know if it's expired or not. And one condom isn't going to be enough. I don't know how we're going to get around this."

Well, that was easy.

"I haven't had sex in four, maybe five years," she said. It had been either a love life or a professional life and she'd opted for the latter. "But you don't need to worry about condoms. My doctors put me on the pill."

His face changed, muscles pulling as if in pain. He made a sound deep in his chest and a second later, she was lying on the bed while his clothes flew around the room.

She watched him undress jerkily, a touch of unease entering her mind as she saw exactly what his clothes had kept covered up. It was clear that he was a strong, fit man, nothing could hide that. But naked, he was almost frightening in his power.

Deep, solid muscles, the heavy raised veins of an athlete, so little body fat she could see the striations of muscle in his abdomen. And, oh . . . a penis that was almost frightening. She'd felt his arousal in the garage but nothing prepared her for its appearance. It looked like a club, hard and huge, already weeping at the tip.

Her body closed in on itself a little. *I don't know if I can do this,* she thought.

But it was too late because his heavy weight was coming down on top of her, one hard thigh separating her legs, his hand separating the lips of her sex and with one hard thrust he was inside.

It hurt.

They froze, both of them. Claire was almost afraid to breathe. Her entire lower body was scrambling to accommodate him, deal with the tight feeling of intrusion.

"Shit." His voice was ripe with frustration. He lifted himself up on his elbows and looked down at her. "You weren't ready."

His head hung down and he closed his eyes. "I'm sorry, I'm sorry. I should have waited but I just couldn't . . . I'm an idiot. Sorry." He shook his head in sorrow. "And I don't think I can pull out, either. Just . . . can't. What are we going to do?"

"Kiss me," she said softly.

He looked startled, as if he was expecting her to scream and push at his shoulders. Then his face changed, moved in a smile. "Oh yeah," he breathed. "I can do that."

He settled on her completely, forearms bracketing her shoulders, and gave her a series of first-date-at-the-prom kisses. Light, tender. The kind of kisses where you'd never imagine that they could be lying in bed together and he was heavily wedged inside her body.

Kisses lighter than air, kisses with a smile. She smiled back and, for the first time, lifted her arms and embraced him.

Wow. He felt as powerful as he looked. Just to test it, she dug her nails into his shoulders and couldn't make a dent. Like trying to make a dent in steel. She did have one effect, though. His penis swelled inside her, impossibly.

And, impossibly, she contracted around him. He lifted his head at that, staring down at her from an inch away, nose almost touching hers.

"You like that." The deep voice was rough.

"I—I guess I do." She was breathless with the excitement that was starting to rise from her groin, but also with his heavy weight. It felt good, though. Actually, everything was starting to feel good.

She moved, experimentally, embracing him more fully, her arms trying to encompass his wide back, the slabs of muscle flowing under her fingers, thighs widening to welcome him and he slid a little farther inside her, the feeling now electric, on the razor's edge of intense pleasure and pain and he was moving in her more easily, small intense rocking motions that slid her right over onto the pleasure side as she threw her head back and closed her eyes to concentrate on the heat that was exploding between her thighs, pulsing in wild contractions . . .

And Dan stiffened, groaned loudly, swelled even more inside her and started climaxing, shuddering and shaking, large chest bellowing to pull in air.

Claire's body quieted slowly as she felt warm honey drip through her system. She felt like she was floating on a cloud with a very heavy body on top of her keeping her from drifting way out into space.

Crazily, even after the orgasm, he hadn't softened inside her, but he was moving more easily now.

He lifted himself up and smiled down at her, a sweaty lock of dark hair falling down on his forehead.

She had the right to do this now. Smiling herself, she smoothed his hair back.

"Well, that was fast." He looked down at her, eyebrows raised.

"Mmm," she replied. "Rocket man."

"Are you comfortable? Any creases in the sheets under your back?"

"No," she said dreamily. "I'm just fine.

"Great." He settled his heavy weight back down on her. "Because this is the position we're going to be in for a while. A long while."

TEN

CLAIRE stepped out of the shower and wrapped her hair in a big white towel.

A white T-shirt had been placed on the counter next to the sink. It fell to her knees and billowed around her but it was clean and ironed. She sniffed at the material but all she could smell was detergent. She'd been hoping for the smell of Dan. His smell would be embedded in the deepest recesses of her brain to the end of time.

Oh, God. A mixture of soap and musk and man. Intoxicating. Enthralling. She'd had her nose next to his neck while climaxing and it seemed as if her entire body, every sense she had, locked on to him. The smell of him, musk and male, the taste of him, salty and spicy, the feel of him, hot and amazingly hard all over, the sound of him, breath heaving in and out of his lungs toward the end as he slammed into her, that deep moan as he sank on to her after his gazillionth climax, the sight of him, that dark intense face an inch above her own, moving as his body thrust in and out of hers . . .

It had been sex as she'd never had it before. So intense

every cell felt charged with electricity. It was as if Dan had given her an infusion of life, together with the sex. She felt warm, inside and out. Her skin tingled down to her fingertips and toes. She felt wonderful, even . . . hopeful.

The future was not an endless series of dark days and darker nights. It held hope. She felt more clearheaded than she had in a year, as if some heavy boulder had been rolled away.

She had no idea what turns this relationship with Dan would take but, for now, it was simply delicious. This feeling of being wanted. When he turned that dark gaze on her, eyes glowing with desire like coals, it turned her inside out.

He *saw* her.

She'd been so used to being nearly invisible, sliding through other people's lives like a ghost, wanting nothing, asking nothing, receiving nothing. It was as if she barely existed. Dan's desire gave her weight and heft. He listened to her, too, giving her back her identity as someone whose thoughts were of value.

And they *were* of value. A gray heavy fog had suddenly lifted and she could see into the distance. Her mind could embrace yesterday, today and tomorrow, instead of being able to think only in an eternal now.

It felt like she was coming back into herself. Claire welcomed this gingerly, the first hint of dawn's light after a long midnight. The feelings were incredibly good but so very new. Tentative and fragile.

"You okay?" He was there, by her side. He moved so quietly. He was such an immensely strong man, with dense, thick muscles. You'd think he'd make a noise when he moved, but instead he glided silently, like an insubstantial spirit instead of a very substantial man.

"Oh yeah," she breathed.

"I like that T-shirt on you." He grinned, sliding a hand up her thigh.

Claire watched his face and saw the second he realized she wasn't wearing underwear.

"Oh, Christ." His face tightened. A dull red bloomed on his high cheekbones. He closed his eyes, briefly, as if in pain, then opened them again, a fierce light shining in his dark pupils. "You shouldn't do this to me. I have a weak heart." He patted his chest, right over his heart.

That was nonsense.

He most certainly did *not* have a weak heart.

She'd felt it galloping while they'd been making love, then felt the slow, steady, strong beat of it afterward, her ear right over where his hand was now patting. Thump, thump, thump, a steady sixty beats per minute. An athlete's heart.

It had been the most delicious sound, sexy and reassuring at the same time. Simply lying in his arms, ear over his heart, had been almost as wonderful as the lovemaking, though that had been off the charts.

The sheer human connection had been so wonderful.

Nighttime had been reserved for her deepest loneliness. At times, scrambling up in bed, gasping and shaking from her nightmares, Claire had had the panicked feeling that she was all alone in the world. That all of humanity had been erased from the earth, leaving only her to face dragons on her own. Achingly alone, with monsters loose.

So listening to Dan's steady heartbeat, feeling his strong arms around her, touching him from the tips of her toes to the top of her head, well that had been sheer joy.

She'd felt enormously safe in his arms, as if nothing bad could ever happen to her, ever again.

The look he was sending her didn't make her feel safe now, though. Not at all. As his big, callused hand moved up the outside of her thigh, smoothing up over her left buttock, across the small of her back and down again, his eyes narrowed, his thin nostrils flared in that male predatory look that would be frightening if she were his enemy.

She wasn't his enemy and it wasn't a fighting look. It was male desire. Focused like a laser on her.

He'd put on pajama bottoms, leaving that wide, hard chest bare. The bottoms couldn't hide his desire, though.

Underneath, as he touched her, his penis swelled and rose in straining jerks as he caressed her bottom.

Heat flared inside her, every animal instinct she had jolted into awareness. Heat flared from him, too, making a faint musky smell rise from his skin. He inhaled and exhaled sharply, as if his lungs couldn't pull in enough air.

Hers couldn't, either. Her chest felt constricted, as if a big band of something had been wrapped around it. The hard calluses on his fingertips rasped across her skin like a cat's tongue, creating goose pimples. The hair on the nape of her neck and along her forearms rose, as if she were terrified.

She wasn't terrified. This wasn't fear.

She glanced down, at the thick solid shaft that moved with his every caress and felt her own sex contract sharply in answer. Almost a prelude to an orgasm, just from having him touch her.

Amazing.

Dan bent his forehead to hers, hand moving slowly up her back. Claire stepped closer, so close she could feel his penis against her belly through the material of his pajamas and her T-shirt. She angled her head in invitation, eyes on his.

Their mouths met, clung. He licked his tongue into her mouth and Claire pulled away. It was sensory overload. Every inch of her skin tingled. She stared into his eyes, the black pupils almost eating up the dark brown irises.

"Claire," he murmured and bent his head again.

This time their bodies met completely, chest to chest, loins to loins, one hard male thigh between hers. Heat flared, muscles contracted where they touched. Dan cupped the back of her head and she had to let her head rest in his hand because the muscles in her neck went lax.

Everywhere their bodies touched, she . . . glowed. With heat, excitement, arousal. He held her more tightly and she rose to her toes to torture herself, rubbing her hips against the smooth, steely column that was now fully hard, long and thick and full.

She broke contact for a moment, gasping, trying to pull

air into overheated lungs while "Amazing Grace" sounded in her head. Why was the song playing? Had someone switched on a CD player?

It took her almost a full minute to remember that "Amazing Grace" was her cell phone ring tone. No one ever called her. She hadn't heard it ring at all this past year. She kept it with her as a safety precaution.

She blinked, looked around. The sound of the music was muffled. "That's my cell. I think—" Where was it? Ah, in her purse on the coffee table in the living room. "I think I should take this."

Dan nodded, opened his arms, stepped back. He looked so appealing, standing there, strong, broad-shouldered, aroused penis making a tent of his loose pajama bottoms. She nearly flung herself back into his arms.

What did she care about a cell phone call? She couldn't even remember who had the number. The tones of the song rang on and she finally found it and flipped it open.

"Hello?" she asked breathlessly, as if she'd just run in from the garden or something, when actually she was breathless because she'd just been in the arms of the sexiest man alive. Her eye chanced on the wall clock in Dan's living room. Good God. It was past two a.m. Not only was a cell phone call extremely rare, she couldn't begin to imagine who on earth would be calling her at such an unearthly hour.

Claire hadn't recognized the number on the display, though it had a 727 prefix. Safety Harbor. Who could be calling her from Safety Harbor?

"Hello?" she said again.

A woman's voice answered. "Claire? It's Maisie." There was terrible background noise. People shouting, some liquid, whooshing sound. Were those *sirens*? Everything was garbled, the voice sounding as if it came from deep under water.

Claire pulled the cell phone away and frowned at it, trying to piece together the words she'd heard. Had she heard *crazy*? Was someone from home calling her at two in the morning to say she was crazy?

This felt like one of her nightmares, only a new one.

"I'm sorry?" she asked sharply, bringing the phone back to her ear. "Who is this?"

Dan had followed her into the living room. His head turned at the tone of her voice. He took a step toward her.

Another shouted few words, drowned out by the noise. There was a loud crackling noise and the sirens sounded closer. Definitely a new kind of nightmare. *"Who is this?"*

Dan was standing next to her now. Claire pulled the cell phone away so he could hear, too. He frowned when he heard the loud noises.

The roar faded a little. The caller either walked away from the source of the noise or was cupping the receiver with her hand. "Claire. It's Maisie. Maisie Cumberland."

"Maisie! How do you have this number?" Maisie Cumberland was a neighbor, her house a few homes down from Claire's. She'd been a friend of her father's.

Claire suspected that Maisie had wanted to be more than friends with her father, but Dad had been like a wolf. He'd mated for life with her mother. After she died, he no longer wanted a partner.

"Your father gave it to me some time ago." Of course. This cell phone had been her father's. She'd completely forgotten that. "I took a chance that you might be using his phone. Claire . . ." A loud siren, very close, drowned her out.

"Maisie, I lost you!"

". . . completely destroyed. Claire, I'm so sorry."

"What?" Claire met Dan's eyes, which mirrored the worry in her own. "What's destroyed? What are you talking about?"

"Your home, Claire. It's burning up. The fire brigade is here, but they're not having much luck. Oh, honey, I am so sorry. Here, talk to the fire captain."

Heart thudding, Claire could hear the loud crackle of a

fire, men shouting, giving orders. She heard Maisie speak to someone, she heard her name spoken, then—

"Hello?" A deep, strong male voice. "This is Captain Ferguson of the Safety Harbor Fire Brigade. I understand that you are the owner of the house at 427 Laurel Lane."

"Yes, I am, Captain." Claire's knees were trembling. Dan led her over to an armchair and she sank down gratefully. He crouched next to her, listening. "What—what's the situation there?"

"I'm afraid I don't have good news, Ms. Day. Your house is nearly destroyed. We got here right away, but the fire grew very rapidly. We suspect arson. There's a sharp odor of accelerant and the entire house went up at the same time. Usually, when an accident happens, fire breaks out in one room and spreads to the rest of the building. In this case, the entire building caught fire at once."

Claire brought a shaking hand to her mouth. "Oh my God," she whispered.

"There won't be much that can be salvaged, Ms. Day. I'm sorry. Are you insured?"

"Y-yes." But the insurance records were in her house, burning. Right now. She wasn't even certain what company it was, her father had stipulated the policy twenty years ago. The contract was gone. Together with her father's collection of first editions. And her mother's lovely watercolors.

All her own books and clothes. Every stick of furniture she owned. All her mementos of her travels. Her collection of music. All her records and documents. Her small collection of jewelry, her mother's wedding ring, her grandmother's wedding ring, her father's wedding ring. All the family photographs. Everything that was her past, everything that was her present.

Everything. Up in smoke. Her entire life. Gone.

Dan took the cell phone from her shaking hand. "Captain Ferguson," he said in his deep voice, "this is Daniel Weston. Gunnery Sergeant Daniel Weston, USMC. I am a friend of Ms. Day's. Can you repeat the status of the house, please?"

"More or less destroyed, Gunny. We're slowly getting the fire under control, but it will take another hour, at least, before we can put the flames out. After which we won't be able to enter the grounds for another couple of hours. But we'll get the property sealed off with police tape. We're treating it as a crime scene. Where is Ms. Day?"

"We're in Washington DC."

"How fast can Ms. Day get down here?"

Dan looked at his watch and at her. "We'll be down on the first flight tomorrow morning. Save what you can of her home, please."

"We'll do our best. You guys get down here. Someone has pulled something really nasty. We'll have to act fast to nail him." The connection was cut and Dan flipped the phone closed.

It was almost too much to take in. Claire sat, shaking, in the armchair, trying to get her mind around the size of the loss. Her insides, the core of her, felt chilled again, like when she woke up from nightmares.

Only this time, the nightmare continued after she woke up.

Dan was crouching by her side. He pulled her into his arms and with a gasp of breath, Claire went there. He surrounded her with heat and strength. She turned her nose into his neck and breathed in deeply, arms tight around his neck. She was hanging on as if she were drowning and this were her last lifeline.

Bless him, Dan didn't mumble any platitudes about it being all right, and she would rebuild. It wasn't all right, and there was no rebuilding what she'd lost. Her parents were gone, every memento of them was gone and she was spinning out in blackest space. Without a past and without a future. No platitudes would help that, none.

"I'll book our tickets online," he said, finally. Claire had no idea how long she'd spent in his arms, leaning heavily against that broad, strong chest, arms clinging tightly to his neck. A minute, five, thirty. She'd lost all cognition of time.

His words jolted her. My God. She had to get going. Booking tickets. Yes. A lot of things were necessary now. Making plans, making lists. Filing claims. Dealing with the police. Trying to cope with the loss of everything she had in the world.

It all stretched out into an unwanted and unpalatable future. The only thing she felt even remotely capable of doing right now was lying against Dan's chest and holding on.

A rhythmic buzzing sounded. Sort of like a cell phone ring, but sort of not. Dan stiffened and pulled a cell phone out of his pocket. He looked at the display.

"Christ," he breathed and stood up. He had a hand under her elbow so she had to stand, too. He reached a long arm out and switched on the TV. She'd noticed that he had one of those big-screen plasma things men loved so much in the living room. And small flat panel TV screens scattered about the house.

He wanted to watch TV now? At two thirty in the morning?

The screen sprang to life. It was split into four images. At first, Claire didn't understand. What she saw was grainy black-and-white images, with color blobs moving. Like scenes from some science fiction movie.

"What's—" she began and he pulled her to the ground and reached out to something on the wall that doused all the lights.

"Men," he said grimly in the dark. "Coming for us."

$\mathcal{E}$LEVEN

BACK in his office, Bowen McKenzie paced the room, recognizing the behavior as anxiety-driven. He hated that. Someone was going to pay for making him feel this way.

He never worried. He didn't do worry. He laid his plans carefully, chose the right people to implement them and waited for the successful results.

Failure or unplanned eventualities were not allowed.

Having Claire Day on his tail was a big unplanned eventuality, huge, and he needed to put an end to it immediately. He needed to find where she'd gone to ground and who she'd gone to ground with.

Whoever the man was, he was damned good if he'd outwitted Heston. Unless, of course, it had been a fluke. A casual acquaintance who happened to be there with her. But what the fuck was a casual acquaintance doing armed?

He didn't believe in coincidences.

Where the fuck was she? And who was she with?

He switched on his monitor. The processor was always on. He Skyped *offtoseethewizard*, uncaring that it was past midnight. He'd just had word that his man—Heston's man, to be precise—had done what he was supposed to do in Safety Harbor.

Now it was a question of time.

He didn't have long to wait. A small screen popped up with Wizard's odd, triangular face and spiky dyed black hair filling it.

"Dude," Wizard said dreamily, lifting his eyebrow pierced with five small silver rings. Fuck. He was high. Still, Wizard was a genius. Even high, even semi-comatose, he was better than anyone else. But the timing was tight and he needed Wizard sober and clean, goddammit!

"Snap to it." He put some command into his voice, which was usually enough to make Heston and his men snap to attention.

But Wizard came from different stock. His mouth beneath the straggly goatee stretched in a smile. "Hey."

"Concentrate. There is going to be a cell phone call soon. The call will come from a small town in Florida." He gave the coordinates for the area around Claire's house. "It will be made to a cell here in the Washington area. Maybe as far as Baltimore, I don't know. Let's say a radius of a hundred miles. I need for you to track that call and give me the coordinates of the receiving cell."

"Dude." Wizard's voice was sharp as he sat up, suddenly sober. "Oh man. We're talking satellite time. Real time. It's one thing to go over records a week later, it's another to hack into a system in real time. Whoa." Wizard shook his head mournfully. "That's heavy stuff, man."

A direct look into the webcam. He made his voice cold. "An extra hundred K should make it lighter."

A thoughtful look crossed Wizard's face. Wizard was working on some esoteric software he was sure would net him a billion dollars. That was Wizard's dream. To set up a company marketing something he called mind-blowing, sell billions of dollars of his mystery product, take it public the year after and retire on the proceeds. Just chill out and get high for the rest of his natural life. Wizard hated Cubicle Life, as he called his job at the NSA.

But to do that, to set up that hypothetical company that was going to net him billions before he turned thirty, Wizard needed cash. Huge gobs of it.

An extra hundred thousand would definitely get him closer to his goal.

"Okay," Wizard said, frowning. He was in some basement. Probably his parents'. An overhead neon light reflected off the brow rings. "I'll start now."

"You do that," he said sourly as Wizard's image disappeared from the small square on the screen.

He sat, waiting, drumming his fingers on his desk.

Shit. This was not the right time to have Claire Day, or anyone else, nosing around. Everything had been proceeding so well, so smoothly. Long-held plans coming to fruition, right on schedule, as if he were plugged in to some divine clockwork mechanism designed just for him.

And he was. Hadn't he felt the wind of destiny powering him forward time and time again? He worked hard and created his own luck, but there was no doubt that he was moving in the direction fate had planned for him.

He fingered the sheet of paper on his clean desk. Tomorrow's schedule, including a meeting with a reporter for *Vanity Fair* about his work in Africa and a photo shoot by Annie Leibovitz to go with it.

The article was the beginning of the next stage, the stage that had begun in Laka. He'd spent ten years planning this and it might take another ten, but he was going to achieve his goal. Nobody was going to ruin this for him, least of all some coldhearted bitch who should have died twice over.

His monitor came to life, Wizard's odd face popping up in a window. He wasn't smiling. "Here you go. Man, I had to do an in and out, real fast, know what I mean? Anyway, here it is. The outgoing cell is registered to Maisie Cumberland, 429 Laurel Lane, Safety Harbor, Florida. The receiving cell phone was listed in the name of Richard Day and its location was in the DC area." He gave coordinates. "I checked the land registry and it's a house registered to a Daniel Weston. Googled him. Ex-Marine. Detachment commander of the US Embassy in Makongo. Was wounded in the Laka bombing, retired on disability. Runs a security company now. Hey, weren't you stationed in Laka at the time of the bombing?"

He froze, panic blossoming in his chest, cold shards of terror slicing him open. *Oh fuck fuck fuck!*

Wizard was looking at him strangely, head tilted to one side.

He had no time for Wizard now. He had to move fast, block this disaster before the whole thing unraveled. "I have to go. I sent the money, check your account." He disconnected the webcam hastily and stood up, unable to sit still a second longer.

A siren was sounding in his head, in time with his thudding heart. What a clusterfuck. A total disaster. He hadn't really taken the Day woman seriously. He'd done his research, had Wizard hack into her hospital files, had even sent a man down to study her for a few days.

Everything—the medical records, the discreet questioning of neighbors, a weeklong phone tap—everything had pointed to Day as totally harmless. The very picture of a broken woman. Amnesiac. Needed extensive physiotherapy to walk, to maintain balance. Rarely left the house. Had no social life. Barely on the grid.

He'd decided to let her live, though she'd been a loose end. And now look at how she repaid his generosity! The bitch was coming after him. She'd recruited the Marine detachment commander at Laka and she was coming after him!

He remembered Gunnery Sergeant Weston, too. A highly decorated soldier. A fucking Marine. Marines don't quit.

Whatever else you could say about the bitch, Day had been on the ball. If she'd got her marbles back, if she and Weston were on his trail, he was up shit creek. Immediate damage control was essential.

He needed Heston.
He needed his army for this.

IT'S a goddamned army, Dan thought.

He counted three on the perimeter, two more in forward positions. And they were good, too. They'd disarmed his outer perimeter. But two is one and one is none, his mantra. So he had two alarm systems, the second sounding when the first was deactivated.

They wouldn't know that. They wouldn't be expecting him to be at DEFCON 1 now.

Dan watched as they fanned out, finding cover. He watched the lead guy pull something out of his knapsack. It looked like heavy binoculars as he brought it up to his eyes. A thermal imager to let them know where the warm bodies were.

Good luck with that. Dan had had his house clad in a plastic that was opaque to infrared. The only thing a thermal imager would see was a blank wall. The windows had been coated with polycarbonate, which made them bullet resistant and resistant to laser listeners.

The invaders were blind and deaf. No soldier liked to go into battle blind and deaf. They would stop, regroup. There would be a hierarchy, a leader. The leader would have a contingency plan and would have to communicate it to his men. It would take a little time.

The time Dan needed to get Claire out of here, get her to safety.

"Keep low," he whispered. "Get in the kitchen." She moved quickly toward the kitchen.

Good girl, smart girl. She didn't protest or ask questions. She simply took her cue from him and did what he asked.

Dan ghosted his way to the bedroom, grabbed Claire's pants off the floor, her boots, two other T-shirts, two black watch caps and two warm down jackets of his. With his booty, he moved back to the kitchen, watching the monitors along the way.

The men were still in position, having taken what cover they could. But they'd take steps soon. He had to hurry.

The kitchen was dark, but Dan knew exactly where to go. He'd actually practiced this in the dark, blindfolded. He had the safe hidden under the sink open in five seconds and was pulling out what they would need and handing it back to Claire.

Two guns, a Springfield .45 and a Desert Eagle, three clips each, a grenade, a flashbang, a thousand dollars in cash, his KA-BAR, a set of keys to a vehicle he kept in a garage across town and two untraceable, pay-as-you-go cell phones.

Alternative identity for himself, including a passport, but nothing for Claire.

Lastly, a duffel bag to keep the kit in.

He held out the clothes. Claire nodded, slipping into her pants and boots and putting on his black down jacket. She swam in it, but at least she'd be warm.

Dan looked critically at her hair. It was beautiful, like golden sunshine, but a dead giveaway in the dark. He held a watch cap out and she covered that glorious hair with it, tucking in stray golden curls.

Blondie. His Blondie. Looking at him gravely, ready to follow his every lead. He'd lost her once, he wasn't going to lose her again.

They went through the side door of the kitchen that opened onto the garage. He led her to his Yukon, glad that he'd sprung the extra ten thousand to have it armored.

It was, as always, parked with the rear to the rear wall, ready to shoot out of the garage.

He put his lips close to her ear, nose touching her neck, and closed his eyes at the smell of her, the feel of her. He placed a grenade in one hand and a flashbang in her right.

"Get in and crouch down in the footwell. I'll open the doors to the garage and the gates at the same time. Keep your window open. When we're past the garage gates, lob the grenade and the flashbang out the window. Just throw them as far as you can. You know how to pull the pin on a grenade?"

She nodded solemnly, silvery blue eyes serious and focused. "Good girl. The flash grenade has a pin, too." He showed her. "Pull them both at the same time and throw them out together."

The flashbang would blind the intruders for crucial minutes, the sound would deafen them for longer. And with any luck, the grenade would take at least two or three of them down.

He had a monitor in the garage. Oh, shit. The bright body-shaped flames were on the move again. They were surrounding the house. The leader would send at least one, maybe two men to the garage. They all had night vision goggles.

Dan examined their outlines carefully. They were carrying carbines, probably MP-5s.

His SUV was armored, but an MP-5 at close range could do some damage and certainly shoot out his tires. They had to move fast now.

He'd installed two speeds into the garage doors and gates. He used the slow gear for everyday use, but the fast gear had been installed just in case he needed to make a super-fast getaway. At the time, it had added five thousand dollars to the price of the system and he remembered thinking that maybe he should pass. Now he was grateful he'd sprung for the extra gear. It was going to save their lives.

Two is one. One is none.

The monitor showed the men about twenty meters from the house.

Their leader was waiting for everyone to be in place. The leader wasn't a big guy, probably around five ten—it was hard to tell with the wavering outline of the thermal image. He was definitely in control, though. He'd move forward a few meters, wait for the others to catch up then hold up his fist in the universal stop signal.

The leader stood, arm raised, ready for the final rush.

Dan had run out of time.

He lifted Claire up into the footwell, ran around the side and ignited the engine. He kept all his vehicles fully serviced and with full gas tanks at all times. It was almost freezing outside, but the engine came to life with a powerful purr.

On the monitors, the men rose, all together as a unit, carbines to shoulders. Claire peeped over the windowsill, saw what was on the monitor and drew in a shocked breath. She understood the maneuvers. Understood the men were ready to attack.

As he thought, two were stationed outside the garage doors.

With a remote, Dan turned all the lights in the garage on to maximum power.

The glare from the light inside the garage through the open door would blind them with their night vision on.

He looked down at Claire. "When I give the signal, pull the pins. There's a delay time of between one point five to two seconds on both but you calculate one second. Throw them both as far from us as possible."

She nodded, right hand white-knuckled around the grenade, the left around the flashbang.

Neither needed telling that if she made a mistake, fumbled, dropped it, the grenade would detonate inside the SUV cabin, turning them into pulp instantly. And then the flashbang would illuminate their messy remains with a million lumen, so the invaders would have a real good look at their blood and guts spilled all over the vehicle once they recovered from the stun effect.

And if it was the flashbang that went off inside the vehicle—well, he didn't know what the effect of a flashbang, designed to stun and blind soldiers within a radius of a hundred meters, going off inside an enclosed space would be, but he suspected it wouldn't be pretty.

Claire look up at him and met his eyes. Hers were so beautiful, and rock steady. So were her hands. She'd been shaken to the core at hearing of the destruction of her home, but now she seemed calm and solid.

She was afraid. She would be stupid not to be afraid, and the one thing everyone in the Foreign Service agreed on was that Claire Day was as smart as she was beautiful. Smarter.

But she was in charge of her fear. Or at least Dan hoped so.

He was putting his life in her hands.

"Okay?" he whispered to Claire, putting the key in the ignition, while checking the monitors. The men were gathering, combat ready. It was about to go down.

Dan didn't dare take the time to repeat the plan, go over it, step by step, as he'd liked to do. As a soldier, he'd always been a meticulous planner, making sure his men understood the op perfectly. But there was no time. They were down to the second now. They had no margin at all if they wanted to survive.

Dan switched on the ignition.

"Ready," she whispered back and buzzed down the passenger side window.

On the monitors, the leader suddenly stood straight, pointing to the house. The signal to charge. The red and green ghost men on the monitors suddenly stood, too, all together as a team, carbines to the shoulder. On the attack.

"Go!" Dan pressed the remotes for the garage doors and the gates. They sprang open in an instant and he gunned the powerful engine, pedal to the floor racing through the doors. The outside gates were already completely open. He sped down the driveway, shouts sounding through Claire's open window, wincing as bullets glanced off the chassis.

Please don't let them shoot the tires, he prayed. He'd caught them by surprise, but they were already reacting.

The invaders were dressed in black tactical suits with ski masks. One near the garage let loose a burst that pinged off the passenger door and with a roar of outrage, Dan swerved and clipped him.

One down, he thought savagely, feeling the jolt through the vehicle as the body bounced off the fender.

"Claire," he shouted, but she had already pulled the pins, coolly waited a second, then peeped over the sill to aim at the center of his lawn. She threw the grenade first, then the flashbang.

"Get down," Dan roared, pushing her head down with his hand, and then all hell broke loose.

Dan pressed the accelerator to the floor racing out of the gate, wrenching the wheel hard to the right the instant he could. As the back of his vehicle cleared the gate, then fishtailed to make the curve, they heard a loud explosion, followed by a high-pitched scream. A second later, the front of the SUV was pelted with clumps of grass-covered sod, torn-off tree branches and, horribly, a human hand.

Right then, the night lit up like daylight at the same time the shock wave of noise hit them. The flashbang had exploded.

Even if the invaders had their vehicles within close range, they weren't going anywhere right now. They'd have their wounded to tend to, and they would be blind and deaf from the flashbang for at least several minutes.

But even though he was mathematically certain that the men who had tried to invade his home were wounded or temporarily incapacitated, he took strong evasive measures, speeding at ninety miles per hour through red lights, twice making a viciously tight U-turn on an empty street, tires squealing and smoking.

All the while he analyzed the tactical situation.

There had been at least five men that he could count, which was massive overkill in his book. It was either a snatch and grab or it was a hit. Either way, sending five men for a man and a woman meant that they had no margin for failure and that they had huge resources.

At that point, if they had manpower to spare, they could easily have had a backup team waiting outside his house, in case they made it out. Dan raced down streets he knew like the back of his hand, at twice the legal speed limit, checking his rearview mirrors constantly.

It was only by the miracle of his top-of-the-line security that they were alive.

As they sped through the streets, Dan could see Claire in his peripheral vision, still crouching in the footwell. She braced herself against his violent twists and turns between the seat and the door. She had to stay down. The combat driving took every ounce of attention he had. He couldn't slow down, stop taking tight corners, for the time it would take her to get up in the seat and pull the seat belt over.

So she stayed down while he shot down streets, braked suddenly, took turns without signaling, gunned through red stoplights, all the time tracking westward.

After half an hour, when he was absolutely certain he wasn't being tailed, he pulled into a driveway on a dark, residential street. The bushes lining the driveway were overgrown and brushed against the sides of the vehicle as he drove up.

There was a garage out back. He parked his Yukon behind the house. Dan killed the engine and pressed back against his seat for a second, to relieve some of the stress. The house shielded them from the streetlights. It was dark, utterly silent after the engine's full blast roar.

He told Claire he'd be right back, and entered the garage with his key.

If they'd come to his house, they knew who he was. They'd look up the vehicles he owned. The Cherokee he would drive out of this garage was registered in a different name, a Marine buddy who'd died in Iraq.

Dan opened the passenger door of the Yukon and met Claire's eyes, the pale blue seeming almost white in the gloomy confines of the vehicle's cab.

She was safe. Against all the odds, against an army coming after them, she was safe. But he had to make sure.

"Are you hurt anywhere? Are you okay?" His voice sounded harsh because his throat was so dry.

She coughed and whispered, "Yeah." The voice was low but not shaky. "I'm fine. Thanks to you."

"Come here." Dan could barely get the words out from his tight throat. "Now."

"Oh, yes." She moved with the grace of water, simply floating down from the vehicle and into his arms, the black watch cap falling off as she buried her face in his neck. Oh man, she was alive. Visions of a dead Claire had been right there in the back of his mind, in nightmarish detail. He knew what bodies that had died a violent death looked like.

There was another possibility, too, a nightmarish one, right up there with Dead Claire on a scale of horrible. There was the possibility that whoever was after her wanted her alive, to torture her for something that might be in that beautiful head of hers. She was a former spook. She said she knew nothing, but who the hell knew what was what in the shadowy world of intelligence?

It was a cruel and cold world, with plenty of men and countries willing to kill and maim for anything that might give them an edge.

To lose her horribly just after he'd found her . . . Dan shuddered and hung on for dear life, heart pounding, palms sweating, tightening his arms around her slender body hidden beneath his huge down jacket.

He was sweating all over, drops falling down his temples and his hands were shaking, suddenly totally incapable of thinking of anything but a dead Claire.

Seeing her, lifeless on the hotel carpet, her life's blood flowing out to create a macabre red frame, or on his kitchen floor, a bullet through the head, shards of bone and brain on his walls or—a charming scene in the little trifecta of horrors running through his head—Claire's body, charred and smoking, caught in the fire in her home.

Dan hung on for dear life, sweating and shaking, completely undone. Later, when he could think straight, it would astonish him.

He was known for his cool under fire. In Afghanistan, he'd held off fifteen insurgents single-handedly while the

medics worked on the wounded at his back, a cold killing machine, keeping the terrorists back until the medevac
helicopters came. He'd moved from rock to outcropping to
dip in the ground, making every shot count. The insurgents
thought they were facing a full team of snipers and had
finally slithered back into their holes when the *whup whup*
of the Chinooks' rotors filled the air.

He'd held them off for six hours, had slept well that
night and had gone back into the field the next day.

Part of the job. Part of the mission. No sweat.

But now he was shaken to the core, the adrenaline of
the escape coursing through his system like poison and the
only antidote was Claire, safe in his arms.

He lowered his cheek to rest it on the top of Claire's
head, shuddering. For a few moments, he lost all tactical
awareness, another thing that would astonish him when he
could think rationally later.

In danger, a soldier is aware of everything, always.
Tunnel-visioning, fear that narrows the world down to what
is immediately in front of you, like seeing through a straw,
is one of the best ways to get killed.

Dan was always aware of everything, his senses moving
outward, even under fire. *Especially* under fire.

But right now, his senses, everything that made him the
man he was, focused narrowly and tightly on the woman in
his arms, on her softness and vulnerability. He was aware
of her hair tickling his nose, the soft puffs of her breath
against his neck, her arms around his back, her slight
weight pressed against him.

And, oh God, pressed right against his hard-on.

She moved slightly and he was instantly hard as a rock.
It was uncomfortable, inconvenient, totally uncontrollable.
Post-op horniness, all that adrenaline sloshing around with
nowhere to go except straight to his dick. She shifted again
and, damn, felt it.

It would be hard not to. He was hard as a hammer. And
when she moved against him, he lengthened and thickened
even more. She couldn't help but feel it. Oh, Christ.

Claire pulled away, arms still around his neck, nose an inch from his.

"What do we do now?" she asked softly.

Go to bed. Have sex until we pass out.

Oh man, for just a second there he was so tempted. He'd never been this tempted before, to have sex no matter what the consequences. He'd never felt this horny before, either. Whenever he needed a woman, there'd always been one handy. No big sweat. This past year of celibacy had been totally self-enforced. Hardly a week had gone by when he hadn't had an offer to break it.

So he wasn't used to this level of desire, as if he would die if he didn't have sex *right now*.

And he could picture it, too. Right now and right here. Both the Yukon and the Cherokee were plenty roomy, though he hadn't been tempted by car sex since the age of seventeen. The seats were large, comfortable and could be let back. Just recline them. Claire on top. His own personal fantasy, one that had kept him awake more nights than he cared to count this past year.

All he'd have to do was unzip, and there he was. All ready. More than ready. Claire's clothes would need a little more work, but hell. He was a Marine, he didn't sweat the small stuff. He'd just slide her pants and panties down those long, slender legs, right off her feet. He'd let her keep the boots. And well, her sweater . . .

And then, oh Christ, her breasts with those small pink nipples would be right there . . .

Wait. What the *hell* was he doing?

They'd just escaped twice with their lives and his head was in his *dick*? He was responsible for Claire's safety while she was in the red zone and he was thinking about *sex*?

He was appalled at himself, ashamed. He willed his hard-on back down and met Claire's eyes. This beautiful woman's life was in his hands. He had to think with his big head.

He stepped back and helped Claire up into the Cherokee then got behind the wheel.

"Where are we?" she asked.

"We're safe, if that's what you want to know." Dan blew out a breath. "This is the house of a friend of mine. He's away for the week."

"How'd they find us before? At your house? Were we followed?"

"Good question. And it needs an answer because we weren't followed." He was going to kill the guy responsible.

Dan reached into the duffel bag and pulled out one of his two throwaway cell phones. He fit a receiver to his ear and punched in the number.

"Stone." There was a loud background noise, like a diesel engine. Dan could barely hear him.

"Marcus? Dan here. You've got a leak on your team. It nearly got us killed." He could barely suppress the anger in his voice. His vocal cords were as clenched as his jaws.

A leak out of the fucking cop shop. It was the only explanation. Someone on Marcus's team was in the pocket of whoever was after Claire. And whoever the fucker after her was, he was powerful and connected. That was becoming very clear. The officer who leaked info might not even be aware of the consequences of what he did.

But he'd nearly got them fucking killed.

"What the hell are you talking about?" The background noise, like a loud throb, grew louder. "A leak? What kind of leak?"

"Get to someplace quieter," Dan growled. "I can barely hear you."

Half a minute later, Dan could hear a door shut and the noise level dropped. "Better?"

"Yeah."

"So what's this talk of a leak? My men and I don't do leaks."

No, they didn't. Marcus ran a tight ship. But goddammit. *Someone* had talked.

"I took Claire home. We weren't there an hour—" Dan's eyes met Claire's. He felt a surge of heat in his body as he remembered exactly how they'd spent that hour. Though he could barely see her, he could almost feel her blush. "About an hour after we arrived, the house came under attack."

"What?"

"Yeah. Real pros, too. Five of them, wearing tactical suits. Night vision goggles, carrying MP-5s. They knew what they were doing. We got out by a miracle. So you tell me, Marcus. You and your men were the only ones who knew that I was with Claire and that I was taking her home with me. Someone talked. Someone wrote a report back at HQ and emailed a copy to the wrong guy. Or blabbed to a reporter. Or called it in to someone outside the force. I don't know how the hell it happened and I don't care. All I know is that we nearly died because someone on your team dropped a dime on us."

Dan was ready to expect a blast from Marcus, but instead he got a thoughtful tone. "I don't know, Dan. The thing is—we haven't filed a report yet."

"What? What do you mean?"

"I mean that the entire team that was at the hotel—except for the techs who took the body away and didn't know who you were—has been called to another crime scene. A double homicide on a boat moored at the New Town Marina. The murderer chopped a hole in the hull and we're sucking out the water now. You heard the diesel engine of the bilge pump. The team's been with me. We came directly here and no one's talked on the phone except for me. And I didn't tell anyone about you. I will, in the report, but I haven't yet."

Dan tried to think it through and stiffened. "Goddamn," he breathed. "From Florida. They traced the call from Florida."

"What?"

Christ, time was tight. He signaled to Claire to buckle up. They had to move fast.

Dan pulled out into the street, still heading west. "While we were at my house, Claire got a phone call to her cell from her neighbor in Safety Harbor, Florida. The neighbor said that Claire's house was burning down. Claire spoke briefly with the fire chief there and they suspect arson. Said the house went up all at once. So someone traced that call to her cell and triangulated her location and sent five men to my crib. All in the space of less than an hour. You need to send your men to my house fast. Go in silent without sirens. They had at least one wounded, maybe more. Get some prints, some DNA, get something. And for Christ's sake find out who these fuckers are because they're still out there."

Dan could practically hear the gears grinding in Marcus's head. The same gears that were grinding in his own. There were conclusions to be drawn, none of them good.

One—whoever was after Claire was ruthless and wanted her dead, badly. There had been two attempts on her life and they'd burned down a home to smoke her out.

Two—whoever wanted her dead was either very powerful or very rich or both. Probably both, which wasn't good. Someone who commanded huge manpower, too, spread out over the country.

His blood chilled. Just about the only entity he could think of that could field men on an instant's notice almost anywhere was . . . a government entity.

Christ. Was the CIA after her? NSA? Some shadowy agency even he didn't know about? If that was the case, their lives as they knew them were over.

"Do my best, Gunny," Marcus said and rang off.

Dan stretched out his hand. "Let me have your cell phone, honey."

Without a word, Claire handed it over, blue eyes huge as she watched him. She nodded. "They tracked the phone," she said. "They can follow our movements."

"Uh-huh. But not anymore." Dan buzzed down his window and threw her cell phone out. He watched in his rearview mirror as it bounced once, twice, on the paved surface, and come to rest in the middle of the lane, where the next car would crush it.

Whoever was following the signals put out by her SIM

card would expect them to keep tracking west. Instead, on a deserted stretch of residential road, Dan pulled a neat 180 and backtracked.

"Where are we going now?" Claire asked quietly.

Dan reached over, picked up her hand and kissed the palm. "Where no one will ever find you."

$\mathscr{T}$WELVE

CLAIRE listened as Dan talked to his friend, the detective. Marcus.

Dan looked grim, face drawn, nostrils pinched. Completely different from the man she'd made love to. The face above hers, nose to nose, as they made love, had been tight and focused, smiling into her eyes.

It seemed like a lifetime ago.

She'd forgotten everything while in his arms—the dead man, her trashed hotel room, the past year. All set aside while her body exploded into a bazillion powerful orgasms.

She hadn't been *Poor Claire* then, a shell of a woman alive by the skin of her teeth, barely together, barely *there*. No, in Dan's bed she'd been *Hot Claire*. Hot in every sense of the term. The way Dan looked at her, touched her, made her feel like the most desirable woman in the world. Having this strong, uber-male man completely focused on her . . . it had been so wonderful. Even the notion of cold had been banished in the bed, as he warmed her inside and out.

It was all gone now. The heat and the desire and the

sheer joy of *life* tingling throughout her body, from finger-tips to toes. Gone as if it had never been.

They'd taken it away from her. Her world had been barren and cold and empty but at least it had been safe. And now even safety had been snatched away by unknown forces. Someone or something that wished her harm had come ravening up from some dark hellacious pit to take away what little had remained of her life.

Someone or something that had killed a man, tried to kill her, torched her home, come swarming at Dan's home like a multi-headed monstrous beast.

She'd gotten a good look at the men as she lobbed the grenade and flashbangs out the window. In their black tactical suits and night vision goggles, they'd looked like aliens. And maybe they were. Because surely nothing human would come so suddenly, so ferociously.

The instant she had that thought, she put it aside. If there was one thing her time in the DIA had taught her, it was that there was no end to the wickedness of man. Humans were violent and avaricious. There were men who would literally stop at nothing to get what they wanted.

She'd seen it so often, especially in the third-world posts where she'd been stationed. Tyrannical dictators, who ruled by the sword and crushed anyone who threatened them. Somehow these men were always able to lift rocks and unleash the crawling monsters who lived beneath them.

She'd seen cruelty and monstrous evil, but it had never touched her personally. She'd been protected by her job, by the fact that she was an emissary of the most powerful country on earth.

And now the monsters were after her. Personally.

Claire had seen cruelty and violence in her postings, but she'd also seen amazing courage.

NGO workers who refused to be intimidated and con-tinued dispensing medicine, vaccines, food, books despite death threats, sometimes from the very people they were trying to help. Women who banded together to fight for their rights, even though they knew that some of them would be tortured or stoned to death. Men and women who marched for freedom and democracy at the cost of their lives.

They'd done it.

So could she.

Whoever "they" were, they'd made a mistake in torching her house. Everything Claire had, everything she owned, everything that was a souvenir of her parents or her past, had been destroyed.

There was nothing left of her old life. She'd been stripped bare. But by the same token, she had nothing left to lose.

Claire glanced over at Dan. "That was a remarkable piece of driving back there. Did you take a defensive driving course?"

He shot a glance at her. A faint smile lifted his mouth. "Actually, I'm a combat driving instructor."

Oh. Well that explained a lot. "You saved our lives."

"Actually, you saved our lives. If you hadn't kept your cool and thrown the grenade and flashbang exactly right, at exactly the right moment, at exactly the right spot, they'd have gunned us down. You kicked ass. I'd say we're about even in the Saving Lives Superbowl."

Claire sat up straighter, smiling a little. "You're right. I did kick ass."

"Damn straight." He was grinning now. "I wouldn't want to meet you in a dark alley."

Claire looked at him. Immensely broad-shouldered, immensely strong, good with weapons, combat driver, ex-Marine. All-around tough guy. "Oh yeah. Watch your step around me, mister. I take no prisoners." And she laughed.

She *laughed*.

It sounded so odd, coming from her throat. Odd and dry, a sound she wasn't used to making. She hadn't heard herself laugh in . . . what felt like forever.

"Sounds good," Dan murmured. His eyes were scanning the road ahead and the rearview mirrors constantly. "You laughing."

"Particularly when there's nothing to laugh about."

Claire shook her head, still smiling. "Do you know where we're going?"

"Oh yeah." He pulled out his cell and punched in a number on speed dial.

"Hey," he said suddenly. Someone must have picked up at the other end. "No names. I need to meet you at that place where you tried to pick up that Swedish girl. Uh-huh." He listened for a couple of seconds. "Well, I can't help it if you didn't score. Can't stay on the line very long. I'll be there in ten." He flipped the cell closed. "Good buddy of mine. He'll help us out. We need to go to ground and he has a place that's off the grid."

"Former Marine?"

"Yeah. Like a brother."

They all were. It was something Claire admired enormously in the Marines. They belonged to a vast brotherhood for the rest of their lives.

Unlike DIA analysts.

Spooks were unsociable by nature, by training and by command. There was nothing sadder than a DIA or NSA party. Secretiveness was so ingrained in them, they had no social skills at all. They just sat around not talking, getting morosely drunk, and no one ever drove anyone home afterward.

She hadn't gotten one call from a colleague this past year. She was out of the service and therefore untouchable.

"Are you sure that's an untraceable phone?" she asked Dan. No one knew better than Claire what cell phones really were—huge transmitters emitting one giant *here I am, come get me* signal, like an enormous arrow in the sky, pointing straight at you.

"Yeah. My name doesn't figure on any paperwork in connection with this phone. But just in case, I was traveling east while talking and now we're going north and I only stayed on the line for a second or two." He buzzed down the window, tossed the cell out. "And now it's gone."

"Theoretically, we can be traced," Claire mused. "If they have your voice on file, they could be trolling the airwaves and trying to come up with a voiceprint match, then put out a watch for that signal."

"Yeah, they could." Dan's mouth tightened. "But only the NSA has those types of resources. And if the NSA is after us, we're fucked. Pardon my French."

It was true. If the NSA was after them, they were royally fucked. She shook herself. There was no reason on earth for NSA to be on their tail. She'd never broken security, and she'd been out of commission for a year. Dan was a former Marine, for God's sake.

As a matter of fact, it would be hard to find two citizens who were less of a security risk to their country than her and Dan.

Claire felt a bolt of heat run through her body, electric and fierce. It wasn't sexual heat. It was—it was *rage*. She was so *angry* at whoever was after them—or after her. They'd burned her house down, so the efforts of this shadowy "they" were directed against her. Dan was collateral damage.

Never mind that he was a hero, had put himself in harm's way for his country, had saved two children and a mother only a few days ago. He was with her and this phantom someone was willing to kill him the way you swat down a troublesome insect.

The shock of losing all her worldly possessions was starting to wear off, and in its place was a white-hot anger at the devastation they were willing to wreak, and to no purpose she could understand.

Claire had no enemies. She was sure of that. She'd been a loyal team player. She'd been a good, smart analyst and had been on good terms with all her co-workers and superiors.

Furthermore, she'd been at the beginning of her career. She'd barely begun to climb the ranks. Even if she'd been the type to do so, which she wasn't, she hadn't walked over anyone to be promoted because she hadn't been promoted yet.

For a second, she mourned what might have been. Claire had worked hard because she was ambitious. She wanted to advance in her career, maybe even go all the way to the top.

The bomb in Laka had done more than shatter her life, it had brought an end to her career. All her hopes and dreams had been cut off, forever. There was no way she could ever hope to join DIA again. The job was too important to be put in the hands of someone who was damaged goods.

Her life had been ruined in more ways than one. And why?

There was no way in hell she'd offended someone, or done something wrong that could have brought this level of revenge raining down on her head. She simply hadn't been powerful enough.

And as for doing something this past year—it was impossible. She'd spent three months in a coma and then nine months basically in the house, with music and her books for company, seeing no one but her doctors.

And yet, and yet. A monster was on her tail, wanting her devastated, wanting her dead.

The only way out of this was to find out who was behind all this violence and why.

The only good thing to come out of this whole mess was that electric jolt of white-hot anger coursing through her body. She had no tools and no help outside gallant former Gunnery Sergeant Dan Weston. But they had his courage and tactical ability and she had her mind back again. Anger was already firing her synapses, like a supercomputer, powering up. Whoever the hell this guy was, he'd raised the stakes so high that she had to get to the bottom of this or die. Because otherwise he'd kill her first.

"There he is," Dan murmured. Claire hadn't recognized any of the streets they traveled down. When Dan pulled into a side street along a small park, she had no idea where they were. The park had streetlights ringing it. One streetlight was broken. Under it, a pickup was parked.

Dan parked behind the pickup and got out. A man was leaning against the front fender of the pickup, straightening up when Dan got out of his SUV. Claire followed.

"Hey man." The gave each other those hard manly thumps on the back that would have staggered her. Dan looked up at the dark streetlight. Claire could see that the big halogen bulb was broken. "Good thinking, bro."

Dan reached for Claire, grasping her hand. Then he put his arm around her shoulders and gathered her to him as he turned to the other man. The body language was very clear. *This is my woman.* The other man acknowledged that with a sober nod of his head.

He was as physically unlike Dan as it was possible to be. Tall, whip-thin, with eyes so pale blue they looked white and a light blond crew cut so severe he looked bald. And yet the two of them shared a look—tough and competent and hard. Not men to be messed with in any way. Good men to have at your back.

"Claire I want you to meet Jesse Conn. Jesse, Claire Day."

"Ma'am." Jesse took her hand in his big, rawboned one and squeezed gently. "Pleased to meet you." He came from somewhere in the deepest south. The "ma'am" had at least eight syllables in it.

"Jesse." Claire smiled. She looked swiftly up at Dan then back at Jesse. "I think we're going to be needing your help."

"Yes, ma'am. Dan's like a brother to me. I'll help you bury the bodies."

She laughed. "That won't be necessary. To tell you the truth, we came very close to *being* the bodies, but we're here, thanks to Dan."

"Roger that." The pale eyes flicked over to his friend. "Nothing will happen to you, ma'am, as long as Dan is alive."

It was a nice thought. But Dan was one man, made of flesh and blood. One man, however good, was not going to stop an army. They had to get to the origin of the monstrous shadowy force. They couldn't win this blind.

"So, man," Jesse said to Dan, "what's up?"

Dan told him, concisely and clearly. He was obviously

used to giving field sitreps. As he talked, a furrow etched itself between Jesse's brows.

"Bad juju, bro."

Dan nodded. "Yeah. We don't know who's after us and we don't know why. We just know he's got major resources and we're going to have to regroup until we can get ourselves more intel. So we're going to need the cabin for a while. I don't know for how long."

Jesse was already digging into his jeans pocket and pulling out a set of keys, together with a wad of bills. All hundreds from what Claire could see. "I thought you might. Cabin's a good place to go to ground. Stay as long as you need it. There's some basic foodstuffs there, but there's a small grocery store about ten miles down the road. Bill's a good guy. If someone comes sniffing around asking for you, he won't talk."

Dan took the keys and the money. "Thanks, man. Appreciate it. I'll get the money back to you. I've got some with me but I don't know what we'll be needing and they could trace a credit card."

Jesse shrugged. "Anything else?"

"Yeah. Call—no, stop by Roxanne's and tell her to go visit her mother in New York for a few days. Tell her to buy a ticket on the company account and not come back until I send word. Her husband'll understand. He'd be the first not to want her in the line of fire."

Oh God, Claire thought. Roxanne. Gentle, kind Roxanne, possibly in danger because of her. And Dan's business. It hadn't even occurred to her what the cost to Dan would be. He was involved in her mess now. For the duration, until they figured this out, his company had to grind to a halt. She knew enough about the business world to understand what that meant. Angry customers who would never come back, advances that would have to be repaid, new customers finding an empty office.

Dan glanced at her quickly, then did a double take as if reading her mind. He frowned and shook his head slightly. *Don't worry about it.*

Jesse nodded. "Count on it. That it?"

"Yeah, we're good to—"

"No," Claire said crisply.

Going to ground wasn't going to help them uncover what was behind all this. Until they knew, they were vulnerable. Prey. She turned to Jesse.

"I'm going to need a laptop, mine was stolen. It doesn't have to be expensive, a netbook will do, but it needs to have at least a 160 giga hard drive and 1.6 gigahertz speed. I don't need encryption, I can download an app for that, but it'll have to be preloaded with a good spreadsheet program. I don't need Word, Google docs will do. Then I need a Thuraya satellite phone. Buy it anonymously. Or put down a false name as the purchaser." Thuraya phones were run by a company headquartered in Saudi Arabia and their phone records were sealed until the end of time. Not even the NSA could penetrate them. It was the phone drug lords and terrorists used. And now Claire Day.

She opened her purse and had a sharp pang of pain. The breath simply whooshed out of her lungs as she looked inside. Wallet with a little cash and credit cards and ATM card, cosmetics case, keys to a burned husk of a home, flash drive, passport, day planner with a year of blank pages.

It was everything she owned. The only personal possessions she had left in the world. There was nothing else.

It would all have to be reconstituted, together with her broken-down self.

Claire Day 2.0.

She slid out her ATM card and held it out to Jesse. "Here. The PIN is 21539. I have a special arrangement with my bank and I can take out up to a thousand dollars a day. Put on a baseball cap with the longest bill you can find, the thickest coat you own to disguise your silhouette and wear sunglasses. I'd like for you to drive as far as you can away from where we're going and take the money out in two hundred dollar increments from five different machines. Space the ATMs as far as possible. Don't choose them on a vector, but mix up the locations. And tomorrow morning do the same. Take out another thousand in two hundred dollar amounts. Dan, give me your ATM, too."

He already had his out. Jesse took it. "PIN's 73105," Dan said before Claire asked.

"Do the same with Dan's ATM card, only in different places."

"You won't have far to go," Dan said wryly. "Unlike Claire, I can't take out more than three hundred a day."

"Well then, Jesse should at least split it into two withdrawals of 150 dollars each. Don't let the security cameras catch your face, Jesse. They usually have a forty-five degree angle, so from seven feet out, make sure your face is as covered as possible. Come to think of it, do you have a laser light?"

Jesse nodded, looking confused.

"Good. Use ATMs that are deserted. Shine the laser light in the security camera as soon as you get close enough, it'll wipe the camera out, drive them crazy. And wear gloves. They're going to be checking the security cameras of the ATMs and if there's one where there is very little traffic, they'll try to pick up some prints. Meet us the day after tomorrow in a place only the two of you know about with my computer and Thuraya phone and make sure you're not followed."

Jesse was staring at her, slack-jawed, then closed his mouth with a snap. "Yes, ma'am." He blinked at Dan.

Dan shrugged. "DIA," he said, as if that explained everything.

"Ah, a spook." Jesse looked at Dan and Claire. "Okay. There's a diner twenty miles east of the cabin on the county road. It doesn't have security cameras and the owner's a former Marine. Buddy of mine. Let's meet there at noon the day after tomorrow. I'll bring the money and the computer and the satphone." He addressed Claire directly. "Anything else?"

"Yes." Claire looked down at herself. "Go to one of the big box stores and get us a change of clothes. Several changes. Go for warmth because we don't know what's going to happen and where we'll be going. Get me a couple of short-sleeved and long-sleeved T-shirts and two wool turtleneck sweaters and two fleece hoodies. Track suit pants, that way you don't need to worry about sizes. Just get a small everything. Warm boots, size six and a half. And buy me a parka." She narrowed her eyes at him. "Can you buy women's underwear?"

His eyes rounded and he took a step back as if she'd asked him to French-kiss a rattlesnake. "No, ma'am."

Claire sighed. Pity. Though God knew what he'd choose. She was a fanatic about nice underwear, but sending Jesse into a La Perla store would probably give him a heart attack. She'd just have to wash her undies until they got to a clothes shop without security cameras. If such a thing even existed. "Can you buy clothes for Dan, too?"

He nodded his head energetically. "Yes, ma'am. That I can do. From the skin out."

Well, at least Dan would have new underwear.

"You need weapons?" Jesse asked Dan.

Dan shook his head. "No, I'm good. I've got my Springfield and my Desert Eagle in the Cherokee. And a long gun in the back. Plenty of ammo, too."

Jesse looked more settled now that he was back on familiar terrain. "Check the gun locker in the cabin. There's plenty of firepower there if you find you need it, plus a couple of KA-BARs, just in case. I'd like to bring in Frank Rizzo and Dave Sawyer. We might be needing some manpower here. They're good men to have at your back."

Claire was alarmed. Any new element could be dangerous, a way for their unseen enemy to hone in on them. "Is there some institutional tie there? Between you and Dan and Frank and Dave? Something someone can trace? Anything linking you guys up?"

Jesse looked uneasy. "Well, yeah. We were all in the same battalion. Dan and I were stationed in Okinawa together and Frank and Dave and I were in Guatemala."

"Can someone trace that connection?" Claire glanced at Dan, then Jesse. "Whoever is after us can probably access military records. How many former Marines do you think are in the greater Washington area?"

"Well, that's easy," Jesse said. "I'm head of the Jarhead Club. There are about five hundred former Marines in a radius of about a hundred miles. I think that should muddy the waters a little."

It would. She hoped. "Can you contact them in a secure way? Untraceable? I don't think they'd be able to follow every retired Marine, but maybe they could follow every retired Marine who was in Dan's battalion."

Jesse nodded, face grim. "I'll make sure the contacts are secure. Good point."

"Claire." Dan put his arm around her waist. She leaned back for just a second, just long enough to feel that solid chest against her back. The rage that had welled up had fired her with energy, but the adrenaline was depleting and she felt exhausted. "We should be going," Dan said gently. He looked at Jesse. "Thanks for everything."

Jesse waved at him as he got back into his own vehicle. "See you the day after tomorrow at the diner. I'll bring your gear and the money." He drove off and silence settled over the little park.

It would soon be first light, the sky would turn pewter in the east. The residential area was dark and quiet. Claire simply stood for a moment, her back resting against Dan, trying to gather the energy to do the next thing, whatever that was.

Dan turned her around, dropped a quick kiss on her mouth, then steered her to his vehicle. "We need to get going," he said, his deep voice low. "Jesse's cabin is about six hours away."

"Where is it? Can someone track it down?"

He answered while switching on the engine.

"The cabin's about forty miles from New Hope, Pennsylvania. It's in real rugged country, the last two miles to get to the cabin are hardly more than a rutted track. You need four-wheel drive when it rains. And no, nobody can find it. Jesse's stepfather left it to him, but the title never changed. No one would ever contest it, so Jesse just left it. And Jesse's mom and stepfather had a common law marriage, so even if someone knew about Jesse, they couldn't trace the property to him. The cabin was never declared, so on paper it's just a piece of swampland. And Jesse's father was a Vietnam vet and paranoid as hell, so he went into the deed office in New Hope and when no one was looking, he changed the coordinates."

Paranoid, huh? As opposed to Dan, who kept CIA-level security in his home, together with a small arsenal.

Still, Dan's paranoia was the reason she was alive. She wasn't going to quibble.

They were driving down deserted streets, starting to exit the city limits. There was something hypnotic about watching Dan drive. He obviously felt no one was following them, because he wasn't doing the incredible stunt-driving gyrations he'd gone into on the way to meet Jesse. His driving now was smooth and steady, movements precise, like clockwork.

The sound of the powerful engine was muted by the bodywork, which she now knew was armored. And no doubt the windows were bullet-resistant. It gave the SUV the feel of an airplane. She loved flying and right now, it was like being utterly safe in a plane, in the hands of a pro at thirty-five thousand feet.

Safe. Warm. Watching the buildings become spaced farther and farther apart, with long stretches of woodland in between.

Her eyes drooped.

A slight whir and the back of her seat went down. Dan reached behind him and a soft blanket fell over her.

"What's this?"

"You should rest."

"*I* should rest? What about you? You've still got a lot of driving ahead of you." She should keep him company, keep him awake.

"Uh-huh. Close your eyes."

"What?"

"Humor me. Close your eyes for just a minute."

Claire rolled her eyes, then closed them, just to humor him. She had no intention of sleeping.

Two seconds later, she was out like a light.

*T*HIRTEEN

RICHMOND, VIRGINIA

BACK home, Bowen couldn't believe it when Heston called in failure. *Bastard!* Heston had been a decent soldier but civilian life had made him soft.

One ex-Marine and one loony bitch had gotten the better of him *and* his men. *Twice.* One more failure and Heston was going to find himself at the bottom of the Tidal Basin with a couple of holes in his chest to make him stay down.

He texted Wizard. Find Daniel Weston and Claire Day. Check names of friends. Find Weston's employees. I want to know if they buy anything or travel. Top priority.

A minute later a text came from Wizard. $$$$$????

He sighed. Goddamned mercenary son of a bitch.

100 K was the response. There. That should keep Wizard happy.

Okay. He was doing all he could on that front. Keeping his finger in the hole in the dike. But in the meantime, there was progress to be made on the other front.

He had hired a publicist, one of the best. Ostensibly to highlight his charity work in Africa, but actually to promote him. The publicist had understood that perfectly.

Each month, the publicist sent an update of articles on his work, mentions he got on blogs, videos of his interviews. This month there was the write-up in *Vanity Fair* and a *WaPo* interview. He'd made a list of HuffPo's movers and shakers and *Time* did a special on development and did a sidebar about drugs for Africa with a nice photo where he had his face tilted upward into the sun, a man who was seeing the future and making it happen.

And, best of all, the top political blog discussed possible successors to the senior senator from Virginia, Jeffrey Neff, now mired in a corruption scandal.

The usual suspects and a few outsiders were mentioned as possible successors. The last of the outsiders, a man known for his philanthropy. There was a little profile of each possible candidate. His read:

A possible dark horse is former Homeland Security officer Bowen McKenzie, a man who quit his job after the bombing of the US Embassy in Laka, Makongo, last year to dedicate himself to eradicating disease in West Africa. McKenzie is widely respected for his fundraising for the New Day Foundation, which operates out of Laka, Makongo, and distributes antiretroviral drugs, antimalarial drugs and antibiotics throughout West Africa. McKenzie would be a breath of fresh air among the tired old pols whose names are being pulled out of the usual hat.

That was thanks to his publicist.

Neff was like an old bull elephant wounded by the corruption scandal. There was also word that Neff frequented prostitutes and his men and Wizard had a standing order to find them.

Bowen was going to bring the son of a bitch Neff to his knees.

Senator, he thought, *you're a dead man walking.*

He sat back in his chair, pleased, contemplating his future. He had big, big plans. One loopy former DIA analyst and one former jarhead were not going to stand in his way.

NEAR NEW HOPE, PENNSYLVANIA
NOVEMBER 27

Dan sat by the side of the bed in Jesse's cabin and watched Claire sleep. She'd slept through the six-hour drive as if in a coma. Her eyes had flickered under the closed lids when he drove up to the cabin and killed the engine, but she hadn't woken up.

Dan had simply carried her in, blanket and all, and put her under the covers after taking her boots off. She didn't have a nightgown anyway. He wanted to slip under the covers, too, and put his arms around her, but he ended up sitting on a chair, holding her hand, watching her face.

Asleep, the lines of fatigue and ill health smoothed themselves out and the beautiful Blondie that had set the Foreign Service males into a testosterone-fueled frenzy came back.

Jesus Christ, she was beautiful. The short, pale blond hair formed a halo around that perfect face. Every line of her was perfect, or would be perfect if she could manage to put on a few pounds.

He'd fantasized about her, even dreamed about her. More nights than he cared to count, before Laka, he'd jacked off to her. When he thought she was dead, he couldn't jerk off to the thought of a dead woman. He simply spent the nights with a sad boner and nowhere to go with it.

And now here she was. More beautiful than in his memory. More . . . everything. Smarter, braver, sharper. Even recovering from near-death, even on the run from killers, even with amnesia, Claire was an extraordinary woman. He'd never met anyone even remotely like her.

He was under no illusions that the sex last night had been anything more than comfort sex for her. She'd been scared and stressed and he'd been handy.

What the hell. It didn't matter. He'd take whatever he could get. Probably she hadn't quite realized it yet, but she was his. He'd just stick around until it sank in.

And while she was in danger, he had no intention of ever being more than a hand's span from her until he figured out who was after her and he could kill the fuckers.

Well . . . until *they'd* figured out who was after her. Claire was scary smart. Smarter than he was, that was for sure. If anyone could get to the bottom of this shadowy business, she could. She had a spook's convoluted mind.

That was okay. Dan was fine with being the muscle in the relationship. All he wanted was to keep her safe.

He was astonished at the rush of protective feelings she aroused in him. He'd never felt that for a woman before.

His sex partners were kept at a distance. He liked sex and except for the past two years when the idea of Claire messed with his head and his dick, he had as much of it as he could.

He'd had no idea at all what sex with emotions was.

Scary, that's what it was. Things running wild in his chest, feeling ten feet tall, then shit scared he'd lose her. Both emotions at once. This protectiveness was brand new and terrifying.

What blew him away was the wild *possessiveness* that reared up and grabbed him by the throat. Something he'd never felt before, ever, about anyone.

Touch Claire, and you were a dead man.

Claire was *his*. He'd seen the flare of interest in Jesse's eyes and he'd immediately put his arm around Claire. Jesse was a good friend. He'd got the message immediately. What scared Dan was what he'd have done if Jesse hadn't got the message.

Ripped Jesse's fucking head off his fucking shoulders, that's what he would have done.

Whoa.

He and Jesse went back a long way. They'd gone through basic training together, a major bonding experience. He'd saved Jesse's life in Afghanistan.

Dan would give all his money, his help with anything, an arm, a kidney, to Jesse. Just not Claire.

Claire was his.

He sat in the dark cabin, while the day went by and the woodstove warmed the simple cabin, holding Claire's soft hand in his and watching over her sleep. Letting these raw emotions run through him, helpless to stop them.

He'd rarely thought about having a woman of his own. What the hell did he know about relationships? Fuck all, that's what he knew. The couples he'd seen growing up had been like how-not-to manuals. Some had even tried to kill each other.

But when he did think about it seriously, he imagined it could be sort of nice. In some vague future. Maybe.

It hadn't occurred to him that it would *hurt*. That he'd barely be able to deal with the terrifying rush of feelings he couldn't control slicing through him.

Control. It was what had made him the man he was. As a teenager he'd acted out his rage and had been in and out of juvie for stealing, getting into fights, just about everything except drugs and booze. His father had immunized him against drugs and alcohol. Dan had seen up close and personal what getting high and staying high meant.

But everything else—man, he'd been up for it. You name it, he'd done it. He'd been on a fast track to nowhere, a candidate for dying young with a big splatter, when he'd joined the Corps.

The Corps had saved his life and taught him discipline. That's what the Corps was all about—discipline and control. He'd taken to it like he'd been born to it. He was in control even in combat, cool and calm and precise.

This—this was scary as hell. He'd been completely self-sufficient up until now, completely his own man. But now his happiness, his whole fucking *being* was tied up in a slender woman who had big trouble on her tail.

Jesus.

He sat, holding her hand, trying hard not to think about

this massive curveball life had thrown at him. His head was a jumble but one thing was very clear. Watching over her, touching her, knowing she was safe, that was what made him happy.

An hour passed, two, three. The clock in his head told him it was late afternoon. Tomorrow was going to be busy. He needed to be sharp. Fast reflexes had got them out of two ambushes. God knew what tomorrow would bring. But somehow he couldn't bring himself to let go of her hand and lie down in the bed.

In some crazy way, it was as if staying awake could keep the monsters after her at bay. It was nuts, of course, but he was getting used to the idea by now of Claire messing with his head.

As if his thoughts had reached out and touched her, Claire suddenly opened her eyes. There hadn't been any coming up out of sleep.

She woke up like a soldier, instantly alert. One minute she was deeply asleep, the next she was watching him out of those gorgeous silver blue eyes. Each time her gaze shifted, it was like lightning flashing in a summer sky.

She looked around, as if orienting herself. She hadn't seen the cabin yet and he could tell she was having trouble placing herself.

The cabin was simple, a one-room structure with rough, handmade furniture. A bed in the corner, a long hand-hewn table in the center with three chairs—Dan was sitting on the fourth—a stone counter with wood-fired range and oven. A big stone bowl under a hand pump. A wood-stove for heat. A huge stone hearth that was black with use, but swept clean of ash.

She'd fallen asleep in twenty-first century Washington and woken up in nineteenth-century Pennsylvania.

He saw the exact second she realized what she was doing here. The two attempts on their lives, the close escapes.

"Dan?" she said softly. Something in her voice raised the hair on the nape of his neck. He could feel the hairs of his forearms brushing against his shirtsleeve.

So lost. She sounded so lost and so lonely. A unicorn in the forest, in the gunsights of cruel hunters.

Well, she wasn't lost and lonely. She was right here, with him. He was by her side and, by God, would stay there forever, if she let him.

He'd been thinking the thing through, planning tomorrow, putting together a tentative strategy while holding Claire's hand. All thoughts fled from his head, though, when her eyes met his.

She didn't say anything. She simply lifted the covers in an unspoken invitation.

Hell, yeah.

He forced himself to take his clothes off normally, not in a frenzy like last time. Sweater off, placed on the chair he'd been sitting in. He didn't fold it. There were limits to what a man could do, but at least he didn't rip it off and toss it over his shoulder. His shirt seemed to have a million buttons, all tiny. He was never going to buy a shirt ever again, not with Claire around. Maybe he'd just wear one of those Arab *thoubs*, go commando underneath, pull it up and off and there you were.

Instead, he struggled with the buttons, the cuffs, had to bend down to unlace his boots, take off his socks, winced as he unzipped over his blue steeler. It took what felt like forever but finally he was naked. He looked down at himself and winced. Oh man. Every single drop of blood in his body seemed to have pooled in his dick.

He checked Claire, hoping she wasn't looking uneasy. She wasn't. She wasn't even looking at his hard-on, she was looking at his face, arms up, an expression on hers that nearly unmanned him.

Trust, affection . . . love?

Dan had no idea, all he knew was that no woman had ever looked at him that way before.

For a second, it made him uneasy. It would almost be better if what he saw on her face were lust, because that was something he was familiar with, something he could handle. This—it was truly scary shit.

"Dan?" She reached out and touched his arm.

A shudder ran through him at her touch. It was as if something immense had suddenly slotted into place, something in the universe aligned. Her hand on his arm felt *right*. Something that simply had to be.

"Yeah, I'm here," he answered huskily. He placed a knee on the mattress and bent down to her. "Raise your arms over your head."

Instantly, without even thinking of it, she obeyed, her long slender arms rising above her head. He pulled her T-shirt off, undid her bra, slid her pants down her legs and simply looked.

Was there any woman in the world who looked like that? Pale as moonlight, graceful, small perfect breasts rising and falling with her breaths. Her left breast pulsed with her heartbeat.

This was magic. Everything about her was magic.

"Come to me," she whispered, and he did, rolling on to her and in her in one smooth movement and he felt an immense peace come over him.

Home. He was a man who had never had a home before, but now he did.

Claire was home.

FOURTEEN

THE diner was exactly where Jesse said it would be and Jesse was already there, waiting for them.

Dan entered the way Doc Holliday must have entered the OK Corral. Watchful, face grim, ready for anything. He'd been super-vigilant on the drive from the cabin to the diner, too, but they had encountered exactly one vehicle. A farmer carrying bushels of rosy apples in the back of his pickup.

Dan was also armed to the teeth. Claire had watched him strap on two guns, a .45 and a scary Desert Eagle, both fully loaded, and put three clips in each pocket. He had a knife in a sheath hanging down his back—a big black one that looked ready for business, down to a big groove for the blood.

His Cherokee also held a Remington rifle with a scope that looked a yard long, ammo, night vision goggles, several grenades and something that looked suspiciously like C-4.

That old military saying—there wasn't any problem that couldn't be solved by judicious use of C-4.

He'd looked at her as he armed up. Did he think she'd

mind? She was only sorry that they didn't have an RPG and a fifty cal machine gun.

She'd kissed him to reassure him and the kiss had lasted ten breathless minutes.

He'd been aroused and so had she. Breaking off the kiss had been incredibly hard. The heat that flared up between them simply blew away all her anxiety and fear.

Claire shot straight into another land and another time when Dan kissed her. A place where the bombing hadn't happened and no one was after her. Her father was still alive, her home was intact and so was she.

It was sunny and hot in that other place. Roses bloomed and robins sang. She could stay in that other place forever, kissing Dan, feeling his strong arms around her, gasping for air with each surge of his penis against her belly, feeling an accompanying tug in her groin.

He'd finally held her at arm's length and growled, "Later." And then he'd given her a look that would have incinerated rock.

But that one word had been enough to shut it down. The roses withered, the birds grew silent, dark clouds covered the sun. They were catapulted back into the Land of Bad Things.

Jesse stood when they walked into the diner and didn't sit back down until Claire was seated. The two men sat with their backs to the wall and she sat perpendicular to Dan, looking out the window over the dark parking lot.

Jesse looked grim. He nudged a huge shopping bag with his foot over to Claire. "First off, here's your stuff. It should keep you guys going for a while."

He slid the satphone over to her. She picked it up, liking the feel of it. Thuraya satphones were heavier than cell phones. But then they did a heavier job. Jesse slid across a USB modem and she put both in her purse. Then he pulled out a netbook and opened it, facing her.

"It belonged to a friend of mine. He emptied the hard disk. It's got everything you need, plus Wi-Fi capability."

That was good. And if they were in places where there were no hot spots, the Thuraya would take care of it

Claire powered it up. It came to life crisply, a good sign. She checked the computer resources, hard disk properties, ran a few tests. "Perfect," she said.

Jesse nodded. A zippered bag followed. "There's the cash in there. If you need more, I can front you." His eyes slid to Claire's. "I went to eight different ATMs, and I blinded all the security cameras. And streetlights all around tended to malfunction." His mouth lifted in a half smile. "I hope it drives them nuts. Here are your cards back."

Claire put her hand over Jesse's. "No, keep pulling out money in small increments. If you can, give one of the cards to a friend who lives out of town and have him drive around. That *will* drive them nuts."

He nodded and put the two cards back in his jeans pocket.

"Did you talk to Marcus?" Dan asked.

Jesse nodded. "Oh yeah. They don't have any clues at all on the hotel knifing and about a ton of bleach was poured over your front lawn, so there's no DNA there. I know you said the bad guys took some hits, but Marcus didn't find any trace evidence. These guys know what they're doing."

Dan nodded. "Marcus get anything off my security cameras?"

Jesse shook his head. "Nah. They all wore ski masks, so facial recognition software won't work. I saw some footage, though. You did some great driving. And Claire, you should be in major league baseball. You threw the grenade and the flashbang right where they would do the most good." He brought two fingers to his forehead in a salute. "You're a dangerous woman."

It would be nice to think so. She turned to Dan. "When this is all over, I want you to teach me how to shoot."

He smiled ironically.

She was—had been—a military analyst. She had a deep knowledge of military hardware, including drones, tanks, gunships and aircraft carriers and their tactical and strategic uses. She knew every gun ever manufactured from the 1950s on. But she'd never shot a gun in her life. It was all book knowledge.

Now she wanted a hands-on knowledge of guns. Have the feel and the heft of them in her hands. So she could shoot any son of a bitch who came after her.

"Count on it." He closed his eyes briefly and sighed. "Okay, Jesse, tell Marcus to keep his eyes peeled."

Claire leaned forward. "Tell him I'm going to set up a bulletin board only he and I can access. I'll text him the BB info and our passwords. We need to know anything he comes up with that can help us. We need to know who we're up against." She looked at Dan. "I want to do some sniffing around on the internet and the sooner we get going the better. Can we order some takeout and eat back at the cabin?"

He nodded. "Good idea. What do you want?"

Claire consulted her stomach and it gave her an enthusiastic internal organ equivalent of two thumbs up.

She took stock of herself. She'd been a human wreck when she'd come rushing up to Washington on the flimsiest of excuses. Seeing a man she'd dreamed about.

But then she found out Dan existed. He was real. She'd known him in her previous life! He was real and warm and solid. He'd saved her life twice yesterday and the good news was . . . the danger was real, too.

Someone *real*—a flesh and blood human, not the monsters in her head—was after her. He was real and he was dangerous, but being *real* meant he could be destroyed.

The next step was figuring out what was behind all of this, and now that she was facing real world problems, she could bring her real world skills to bear and—modesty aside—her real world skills were formidable.

The old Claire, the Claire from before, was rising up in her, stretching, looking around. *Well well well, what have we here? You thought I was gone, but here I am. And someone's after you? Oh, that won't do. That won't do at all.*

She'd been beaten almost into oblivion, but now she was back and out for blood.

Most of it was thanks to Dan. His solidity, courage, steadfastness. Oh, and the sex, too, which was off the charts. Blinding sexual pleasure as a reality stimulant. Hmmm.

He made her feel like a giantess, bigger than life. A woman who could make a man like Dan literally pant with desire.

Heady stuff. He'd awoken Old Claire, Strong Claire. She was back in the game and she was . . . hungry.

"Double cheeseburger with all the trimmings, a double order of fries, big portion of coleslaw and two—no make that three slices of apple pie. A la mode." She turned to Dan. "And what will you be having?"

WATCHING Claire Day concentrate was amazing, Dan thought. She had plugged in her flash drive and downloaded her files, plugged in the modem and was ferociously surfing the net. Eyes tracking left to right, speed reading, while her fingers were a blur on the keyboard. It was a miracle the keys didn't simply go up in smoke.

She'd been on a tear since they'd made it back to the cabin.

First, she'd eaten like a sailor who'd been shipwrecked at sea for a week. She'd attacked the food they'd brought home from the diner, finished off the second of his roast beef sandwiches and downed a can of peaches Dan had found among Jesse's supplies.

It was like some spirit had come down and infused her with the life force. Her skin had lost that sickly milk color and was now slightly rosy, her eyes glowed with an unearthly silvery light and . . . well, she was just unbearably beautiful.

Dan's heart gave a huge thump every time he looked at her.

It was more than just perfect features, beautiful skin,

glossy hair, straight white teeth. Lots of women had them, though none in such stupefying abundance as Claire.

No, it was the sense of being in the presence of some supernatural being, smarter and fiercer and more powerful than any normal human.

Claire was almost ferociously intelligent. Scuttlebutt in the Foreign Service had been that she was headed for great things before the bombing. Now, of course, her career was gone, but her intelligence wasn't. Nor was her will.

The Claire who'd come to his office the day before yesterday—Jesus, it felt like a year ago—had been a beaten woman, shaken and trembling and unsure of herself. By some insane twist, the attempts on her life had galvanized her. Far from cowering, she was determined to find out who was out to ruin her life. Again.

Whoa.

There was a thought there. Something that might be important, a glimmer of something that was gone as soon as he tried to grasp it.

It was important, or was it? He couldn't tell anything anymore. Dan was operating on no sleep. He should have rested last night, caught up on his sleep. On ops, he never allowed himself to get exhausted if he could help it. Whenever there was half a chance to grab a few winks, he took it.

Combat sleep, soldiers called it. An ability to drop into REM sleep almost instantly, wherever, whenever. You never knew when you'd next have the chance.

He'd given up his sleep to hold Claire's hand and watch her face as she rested.

He'd do it again, in a heartbeat. He couldn't have slept, not even if you'd pumped him full of Thorazine. All he knew was that Claire was absolutely safe as long as he was watching her and touching her.

It was the only thing that reassured him.

The sex they'd had hadn't even begun to get her out of his system. If anything, she messed with his head more than before and she'd been fucking up his love life for a while now.

Now it was worse. Much worse.

Now he knew exactly how satiny her skin was, how soft her hair felt between his fingers. How warm and tight she was between her legs, her sheath silky and welcoming after that first initial discomfort he'd give his right arm to avoid.

It was incredibly politically incorrect, but, man, he loved it that no one but him had entered her in the last few years. And no one ever would again except him.

She was his, every square inch of her.

Oh shit. At the thought of sex with her, his dick went ballistic. Major Wood Alert. It was like his dick wanted to make up for his Claire-induced celibacy by getting inside her and staying inside her for as long as was humanly possible.

And then as soon as the sex was over, it wanted right back in again.

He was sitting at right angles to her, watching her pound that keyboard while staring narrow-eyed at the screen. Wonder Woman would look like that at an enemy just before grabbing her lasso and attacking.

Man, who would have thought intensity on a nuclear scale would be such a turn-on?

He didn't want to bother her. She was gazing into the screen the way a seer would gaze into her crystal ball. Breaking that intensity would be a real shame.

His dick, however, felt very strongly otherwise. His dick didn't care what the hell she was doing, it wanted to be inside her, *now*.

His boner moved in his jeans and Dan would have sworn that it listed to the right, to get closer to her.

Keep it zipped, he thought, but couldn't help the sigh that escaped.

"Not now, Dan," she said absently, and pounded some more on the keys. She flicked a look up at him, no doubt reading his arousal on his face. Her gaze honed back in on the monitor. "But hold that thought."

Dan wanted to help but didn't know how. He'd cleaned and oiled his weapons, had spoken on the satphone with Marcus to see what progress had been made in the investigation—zip—and Marcus had spoken to the chief of police and fire inspector in Safety Harbor to find out the state of progress there—zip—and now he didn't know what to do. Finally, he couldn't contain his curiosity. "What are you looking for?"

She sighed and sat back, shaking her fingers and rolling her shoulders.

Well, that was something he could help with. He stood behind her and massaged her shoulder muscles, frowning. Christ, she was stiff as a board. And now that she wasn't Wonder Woman pounding at the keyboard, he could feel under his hands how fragile she was, how delicate.

Smart and beautiful, but vulnerable.

"Oh God, that feels good," she moaned. "Don't ever stop."

They both turned their heads at the sound of the windowpane rattling. Tiny needles of sleet pinged against the glass. Dan went to add a couple of logs to the fire then returned to Claire.

He nudged her. "So . . . what were you doing?"

She sighed. "It was a long shot. I was wondering if I'd done anything this past year that in some way pissed someone off." She craned her head to look at him and gave a wistful smile. "Seems impossible though. This past year I've just mostly stayed in the house. I went food shopping, and not much of that because my appetite was gone, and I went twice a week to a rehab center to strengthen my muscles and I went every four and then six weeks to the hospital for a checkup. That's about it. However, I have started doing some translations from French to earn some money and I was checking them to see if someone inadvertently sent me a nuclear code or something."

That was promising. Dan peered down at the screen. "And?"

Her slender shoulders lifted in a shrug. "Nothing. I'd only just started. Among other things, I've translated a children's book, the minutes of the World Congress of Wallpaper Glue Manufacturers, if you can believe that, an analysis of the French stock market that was published in *Le Monde,* a fair-trade website, and, a brochure from the Lyon Tourism Board, things like that. I've studied those files inside out. They're exactly the length they should be, not a byte more or less. There is absolutely nothing confidential in them. In fact, except for the children's book which was cute, there isn't even anything interesting in them." She blew out a breath of frustration. "I don't know what to do next."

Dan did.

He lifted her out of the chair and carried her to the bed.

FIFTEEN

PENNSYLVANIA
NOVEMBER 29, EARLY MORNING

THE heat was a damp, scorching blanket that penetrated to the bones and sapped strength. The kind of heat that gave you permission to kill because hell couldn't possibly be worse than this. It had to be hell itself here, with no mercy and no respite anywhere. Just an endless, violent heat that echoed the violence all around.

The noise was deafening. Bullets flew past, so many you couldn't tell the shots apart. The rifles' reports and the thwacking of bullets as they hit concrete and bark and human flesh were so close together that at times it seemed as if the bullets hit their targets before being shot from the guns.

There was evil here, close behind her. You could sense it, you could almost smell it—a hot, mechanical smell that had nothing human about it. Just as there was nothing human about the bloodred walls, close and narrow, that suddenly appeared to define this hot, feral world.

She was running, stumbling, crawling, then picking herself up and running again, heart pounding, breath rough in her lungs, slicing like shards of glass. The walls narrowed as she ran, closing out the light that offered a small hope of salvation.

There was no salvation. She knew that, even as she struggled to escape. The violence was too powerful, there were too many of them, the evil was too strong.

Something terrible was happening, the knowledge was there, in her bones, though she couldn't quite grasp it. She'd need time for that and time had run out.

Feet pounding, she looked back and stumbled in horror. He was close and edging closer.

Not faceless, as she first thought, not faceless at all. The horror chasing her had a face and a name, though she was too terrified to remember. Whoever he was, whatever his name, he was out for her blood. He wanted her dead.

She ran and ran and yet every time she glanced back over her shoulder, he was closer. He glided effortlessly in the glistening darkness. Now she could see he was dressed in black and had dark, gleaming eyes. He wasn't running, he wasn't winded. He just slithered forward, somehow keeping pace with her without effort.

Oh God, the walls were sliding closer, bloodred, shifting with each step she took. Her knuckles brushed against the wall as she ran, then her elbows and then her shoulders.

The walls were sticky and smelled horrible—they reeked of death and decay. Something fetid from the bowels of the earth. She stumbled and put out a hand to break her fall. Her hand came away from the wall dripping red. She stumbled again in horror and she saw now why the walls were red—they were covered with blood.

The walls narrowed, closed, became a dead end. She slammed into the end wall and shuddered as she felt the dark, viscous liquid covering her, dripping onto the ground. She slid on the slippery floor as she turned with her back pressed to the wall to face the menace coming after her.

Panic rose in her, opening its dark wings in a sibilant flutter.

He was there, right in front of her. Huge, eyes red with

bloodlust, carrying something in a large, leathery hand. He slowly brought it to his shoulder as if he had all the time in the world. A rifle. Aimed at her.

"Claire," he said and she shuddered. His voice echoed, the bass tones reverberating through her stomach. He smiled, horribly, and the inside of his mouth was red. "Gotcha."

She braced herself, crazy as that sounded. You can't brace yourself against a bullet. Watching as he lazily took aim, still smiling. A long claw of a finger hooked in the trigger guard tightened . . .

"Claire!" he boomed. "Look at me!" And she stared into her own death . . .

She broke free, gulping, desperate for air. The sound of her gasping was loud in the night. Someone was holding her down as she beat desperately against strong arms, trying hopelessly to escape the monster.

"Claire, honey, it's just a dream. Calm down."

The low deep voice sounded in her ear. A universe away from the horrible booming voice she'd just heard.

She was exhausted, sweaty from trying vainly to escape, and she finally quieted. There was nothing she could do to escape from this kind of strength.

"That's right, honey," the low voice said in her ear. There was no trace of violence or madness in the voice. "Relax. I'm going to turn on the light, you okay with that?"

She wasn't okay with anything, but she nodded wearily. Whoever owned that strength could do what he wanted.

Claire blinked when a lamp turned on, eyes narrowing against the sudden light. She looked around, panicky and dizzy, and couldn't understand where she was.

Wooden walls, a few faint embers glowing in a hearth, rustic furniture . . .

Dan.

Reality came rushing in, one great cold wave of it.

Dan. Dan and Jesse's cabin and someone or something who was after her, just like in her nightmare. That hadn't changed. Whoever was after her might not be able to float instead of walk, and might not have a blood-filled mouth, but he was more real than her nightmare.

"Oh God, Dan!" Claire threw her arms around Dan's neck and clung, trembling. "It was so horrible! He was after me and there was so much blood, oh God!"

His hold, already tight, tightened some more. One big hand covered her head as he murmured, "It's all right," over and over again.

It wasn't all right, and they both knew it.

Contact with Dan's skin, feeling his strong, steady heartbeat and hearing the sound of his even breathing calmed her a little. Her heart stopped that thudding, panicky stutter and slowed down. She was able to breathe again, first in great big gulps of air, and then finally in the kind of yoga breathing the rehab instructor had taught her to use when she confessed she was subject to panic attacks.

In. Hold for five beats. Out. In. Hold for five beats. Out.

It worked. She finally loosened her arms and eased back.

"I'm going to get you some water," he said and crossed the room.

Naked, he was an extraordinary sight. Broad, heavy shoulders tapering down to a narrow waist, smooth buttocks, hard hairy thighs with the muscles very visible as he walked.

If I can admire his ass, I'm feeling better, she thought.

Walking back, he was even more admirable.

"Open up," he said, holding the glass to her mouth. She drank, long and deep, feeling the cool rush down her throat, damping down the last vestiges of panic. She tipped his hand away. "Thanks. I feel much better."

"I know." He leaned over to kiss her forehead. "You were checking my butt out. Then my package."

That earned him an elbow in the ribs, which he took like a man.

"Come here." A few minutes later, Claire was sitting up in bed in the *V* of Dan's legs, her back against his chest, his arms around her.

It was wonderful. She felt warm and safe, with as much

of her as possible touching as much of him as possible. His body was like a bulwark around her.

They were in as untraceable a spot as could be found. He was by her side, literally forming a human carapace of protection around her. Her problems hadn't gone away, but he was creating a safe space for her and had made it clear he would stand by her for the duration.

The last of the nightmare dissipated like black smoke and her muscles relaxed. His didn't. As a matter of fact, she could feel his penis rising in urgent surges against the small of her back.

His arms tightened. "Ignore that," he ordered. "It's just sort of this automatic mechanism around you. What was the nightmare about?"

Claire shuddered and leaned her head back wearily against his strong shoulder. "Classic nightmare. A chase one. I've had a hundred variations on that one this past year, though this one was particularly vicious."

"Because you actually are being chased."

She sighed. "Yeah, I guess so. There's this . . . recurring dream—nightmare, actually—I have of someone coming after me, only usually I never see the face, I just know he's there. This one was a little more . . . colorful. Detailed."

"Tell me," he urged. "Talk it out. It'll make you feel better."

Oh God, yes. She felt better already. All this past year, she'd woken up alone from her nightmares, heart pounding, breath wheezing in her lungs.

It had gotten so bad that she had to leave a night-light on, like a child. She was ashamed of herself when she switched it on before going to bed at night, but the shame fled when she woke up at three a.m., sweating and terrified, and was at least able to see that she wasn't in a dark pit with monsters after her, but safe in her own bedroom in Safety Harbor.

This nightmare had definitely been the worst ever. She thought her heart might have given out if Dan hadn't been there.

She closed her eyes briefly. Remembering dreams, or nightmares, wasn't easy. For a while, she'd tried to write them down immediately upon waking, but very little came. She couldn't remember details, all she could remember was the overwhelming feeling of imminent danger and deep terror.

But this one stayed with her. Perhaps because it had been more terrifying than usual or because she'd actually seen the face of her nemesis. For whatever reason, she could still call up some of the details.

"I'm running. Escaping something, something horrible. Bullets are flying. I can hear them thwacking things all around me."

Dan had curved around her in a completely protective embrace, arms crossed over her breasts, head bent close to hers. Against her back, she could feel the vibration of his voice in his chest when he spoke in her ear. "You were shot at. It would be a miracle if you didn't have nightmares about that."

She twisted her head to look at him, suddenly curious. "Do soldiers have nightmares after a firefight?" She found it hard to think of Dan having nightmares. He seemed so solid, so strong.

"Yes. They do." His face was grim.

"Then you know that horrible, out of control feeling. That heavy weight of overwhelming menace."

He nodded, head so close to hers she could feel his beard stubble against her cheek. "Yeah. So—you were being shot at?"

"Mm-mm." Though the room was fairly chilly, she felt warm all along her back. Dan was like a furnace. His heat distracted her and she was finding her memories of the nightmare fading quickly. The sound of the gunfire in her head was faint now, though there was something about the quality of it . . .

She shook her head. "I couldn't see who was shooting at me. It was wild gunfire." She stopped. She had the craziest feeling that the memory of the nightmare was edging into a real memory, like a tectonic plate suddenly slipping sideways.

Dan sensed her sudden preoccupation and nudged her shoulder with his. "And?"

She took a deep breath, unable to shake this intense feeling of something . . . *underneath* the nightmare, fighting its way through.

"And I was running desperately down this corridor, just running as fast as I could. The walls were red and sticky and gave off this horrible smell."

"Blood on the walls."

"Uh-huh." She shivered. Dan's heat was amazing but not even he could dissipate the chill of the memory of blood-covered walls. "And then—oh God, it was horrible—and then the walls started closing in on me. Just getting narrower and narrower. And I started sliding and slipping in the blood."

"Sounds awful," he murmured in her ear, kissing her jaw.

Claire tilted her head so he could have better access. He had a heavy beard and hadn't shaved. His jaw rasped against hers. She loved it. All those tiny bites of reality—the raspy skin, the calluses on the hands that were stroking her ribs, the heavy pelt of chest hair tickling her back—they grounded her. Pushed the nightmare even further away.

"And there was someone after me."

Dan suddenly went very still. "Who was he? Do you remember?"

Claire closed her eyes. In her nightmare it had been dark, as if even light itself had been suffocated. The man's skin had reflected the dark red of the walls and his eyes had had a violent red gleam in them. And yet . . . and yet there had been something familiar about him. Something about the cast of his face, the shape of his head. The way he had tilted his head, studying her coldly. The way he'd said her name in a low whisper. *Claire.*

"Um. No. I didn't recognize him. There were bits and pieces that seemed familiar, but isn't that how nightmares are? I guess you just cobble together flotsam and jetsam from daily life and they roil around in your subconscious and come shooting up at night as dreams. Or nightmares, in this case."

"So, he was chasing you?"

Claire nodded. "It was—it was so horrible. He didn't run after me, he just . . . *glided*. And he called my name, Claire. He had lifted his rifle and was sighting through it. You woke me up just as he was pulling the trigger."

He gave her another little kiss on her jaw. "You know, they say you can never die in a dream. You wake up before-hand. Always."

She'd read that, too, but . . . "I don't know, Dan. It seemed so, so *real*. Big chunks of it felt more like a memory than a dream. And there was something about the gunfire . . ."

Claire fell quiet. Dan let her be, letting her think it through. She turned it over in her mind, trying to pin down the sensation. It was one of the still-clear memories of the nightmare, the wild shots, coming rat-a-tat-tat, without rhyme or reason.

So totally unlike the way well-trained soldiers shot.

That was it!

"The gunfire bursts were indiscriminate, just someone pulling the trigger of an automatic and letting go. In the hotel and at your house, whoever those men were, they were observing fire discipline. There were no wasted bul-lets, they fired in controlled bursts. Instead, in my dream, in the nightmare, they just let go. There was no fire disci-pline at all."

She wasn't a DIA analyst anymore but she had been. She'd been paid to notice things like that.

"That was what it was like in Laka, wasn't it?" she suddenly asked Dan. "It must have been, even if I don't remember it. Third-world soldiers on a rampage don't respect fire discipline, I know that. I read in the after report of the siege in Laka that something like a million rounds were expended in a couple of hours."

"Yeah. They were firing like crazy."

Claire opened her mouth, then closed it.

"What?" Dan asked.

"I—" She huffed out a breath. "Nothing. It's nothing."

"If it's nothing, then there's no reason you can't say it."

"You'll think I'm stupid."

As an answer, he picked up her hand and brought it to his mouth. "I don't know how I could do that, when I think you're the smartest person I've ever met." His breath was hot over the palm of her hand. He pressed a kiss there, then brought her hand back to the covers. "You want to tell me?"

It was hard to tell him something she barely understood herself. "Um. OK. There was something—something about the dream that reminded me of Laka. The day of the bombing. Only that's crazy, because I don't remember that day. Anything about it. And yet the two things are—" She pinched the bridge of her nose, eyes closed, concentrating fiercely.

Her shoulders lifted on a big sigh and dropped. This was so *hard*. Just putting things into words made them dissipate, like trying to catch smoke in your fist. "Somehow they're connected. It's like my memory of that day in Laka is coming back, but it's not. It's like a memory of a memory. I told you it sounded stupid."

"Actually," Dan mused, "it doesn't. It sounds like real memories are pushing up into your conscious mind, only there was trauma there. It's like your mind is sounding you out to see if you can take it, so the info starts out as dreams."

"Nightmares."

"Yeah. Nightmares. Anything else?"

"No, I—" This was going to sound really crazy. "Well, yes. At times, I get a flash of *Bowen*, of all people, connected with these nightmares. And come to think of it, there was something . . . almost Bowenesque about this monster trying to kill me. Which is, of course, crazy, because Bowen would have no reason to kill me. Unless he gets homicidal whenever a woman turns him down." Which didn't make sense. Bowen was certainly not sex deprived. He'd been screwing everything not nailed down all over the world. "And of course you have to factor in that all CIA personnel are nuts to begin with, by definition."

"Except McKenzie wasn't there that day."

Bells jangled in her head, and made it hurt.

"Well . . . that's the thing. Whenever I hear that, whenever I read that, it just sets off all my alarms. I don't know why." She gave a half laugh. "You know what? Yesterday afternoon, when you repeated that Bowen wasn't at the embassy the day of the bombing, I just—well, it just sounded wrong. So I logged on to the internet in my hotel room and I checked the DIA report. And, sure enough, Bowen was in Algiers and I'm officially crazy."

"You checked a DIA report? How'd you do that? Wouldn't you need a password?"

"Yes, of course. All reports are accessible by password only. But the thing is, though they took my badge and I'm no longer on the employee rolls, they forgot to cancel my password, so I was able to get in."

Dan got out of bed, slid into a pair of jeans, went to the hearth and laid two logs in the fire. He came back to her and sat down on the edge of the bed, thigh to thigh, frowning. "Let me get this straight. You checked on the DIA report on the Laka bombing?"

Claire nodded. She missed his warmth at her back.

"Did you just read it through or did you check for Bowen's name?"

"The report was sixty pages long and I was tired so I went to the document search function and looked specifically for Bowen McKenzie. Why?"

Dan's frown deepened. He turned his head toward the stone hearth. There was a whoosh and then a loud crackle as the dry wood caught fire. The resin in the bark popped loudly, a friendlier echo of the gunshots she'd heard in her nightmare.

He shrugged, the hard muscles in his shoulders bunching and releasing. "I don't know. You check for Bowen McKenzie's name and, what? Four hours later someone breaks into your room. Coincidence, you might say, but I don't believe in coincidence." He pinned her with his dark gaze. "I was told McKenzie was in Algiers but I never really checked it. Can someone fake or alter a report?"

"Absolutely not, that's—" Claire began huffily, then stopped.

"What?"

She picked at the lint of the wool coverlet. It was government issue and had probably covered the strong young body of a US soldier somewhere in some desert or jungle. Her hand clenched in the rough wool, then unclenched.

Dan put his hand on her shoulder and shook it a little. "Claire, what?"

She frowned. "It was a pdf file, and unchangeable. But . . . I guess if someone really knew what they were doing they could make some changes. Delete a name, for example. Change the wording."

"Could you do it?"

Well, what the hell. If she were still in government service, admitting that she could change an official report would have gotten her into immediate trouble. But she wasn't in government service anymore. The US government had divorced her. She was a free agent. "Um, yes. If I had a strong enough incentive," she added primly.

"And how could you know if someone had messed with the report?"

As if pulled by a string, Claire rose to her feet, snatching up a T-shirt from a chair to cover her nakedness. There was a grunt of disappointment behind her and she turned to smile at Dan. It had been a long time since anyone cared whether she was naked or dressed.

Claire crossed to the netbook and fired it up. "Hmm. You couldn't tell from the report itself if it's been altered. But nothing is ever lost on hard drives. Everything is still there. You just have to go deep into the system and find the cache file on the hard drive. A little like mining for gold underwater."

"Can you do it?"

She was already pounding the keyboard, sitting down just as Dan shoved a hard wooden chair under her.

"Oh yeah," she said softly. "I can do it."

And she did. It took her half an hour, during which she kept blowing out her breath in frustration and slapping the table in anger. She nearly took Dan's .45 and shot the net-book through its treacherously slow heart.

But finally, finally, drifting deeper and deeper into the DIA's system, so deep she was half expecting demersal fish to drift across the screen, she found it. The original report, written in haste by Harold Stella, the guy who took her place in Laka. He'd obviously used secondary sources and the byline was November 27, two days after the blast, which meant he'd been flown in and conducted hasty inter-views on the fly in a bombed-out building.

It was a fleeting mention, a backhanded one, actually, coming right after the listing of those who had been at the ambassador's house. The only mention of Bowen also included her name. *Bowen McKenzie and Claire Day were not present at Ambassador Crocker's Thanksgiving reception.*

The line had been amended in the official report to read—*Claire Day was not present at Ambassador Crock-er's Thanksgiving reception and Bowen McKenzie was in Algiers in secret talks with Deputy Premier Abdul Azziz.*

Claire studied that sentence. The original didn't state *where* Bowen had been, just that he hadn't been at the reception. Someone had changed the report to specifically state that Bowen had been somewhere else.

But . . .

He'd *been there.* She was sure of it. How could she be sure of it? Claire sat back and blew out a frustrated breath. "So—was Bowen there or not? And does this have any importance or not?"

Dan nodded. "Oh yeah, I'd say it's important. The bomb-ing was an attack of a foreign entity on US soil." It was true. The embassy compound had extraterritorial jurisdic-tion and was considered American soil. It was exactly as if an attack had been carried out in New York or Boston or Chicago. "It was the first successful bombing of a US embassy since 1998. Something like ten million dollars' worth of food aid and medicine was destroyed. A lot of things changed, overnight, after the attack. The Red Army was wiped out and Mbutu consolidated his power. Mbutu has a stranglehold on the country and its resources now, and his strength is backed by us. Bowen's made his reputation becoming Our Man in Africa and they say he's eyeing a political career."

Claire blinked. "That's right, you told me. It sounds so very weird. So un-Bowen."

Dan leaned over and wrote *Bowen McKenzie* in the Google search field and pressed enter. Two hundred thousand hits came up. Claire quickly read the top twenty while Dan talked.

"Our guy's been very busy this past year. He helped put the embassy back in shape and he acted as Mbutu's right-hand man for a while—with presumably the blessing of State and CIA—in shutting down the Red Army. Money and munitions simply poured into the hands of the central government. The Red Army didn't stand a chance. I think there might be a few stragglers somewhere in the bush, but they're not in any position to do anyone any harm."

"Money and munitions," Claire mused. "That could be a lot of corruption right there."

"Well, whatever you're thinking, that's not it. McKenzie didn't set himself up as some power behind the throne or anything, though I imagine he could have. Mbutu's brutal but he's not the sharpest knife in the drawer. McKenzie could run rings around him. Instead, McKenzie quit the CIA and got some rich guys to set up this huge foundation focused on West Africa, which he manages. They distribute free medicine to the Makongans. Antiretroviral drugs, antimalarial drugs, you name it. And now they've extended the scope of the Foundation and Laka is a marshaling point where they funnel in medicine to West African countries."

Claire gaped. "So, Bowen became, like, a *philanthropist*?" Oh man, this did not square with the Bowen McKenzie she knew. The Bowen she knew was shallow and self-centered and, well, horny. The Bowen she knew didn't even care for the wife he apparently had squared away in Virginia, let alone poor, sick Africans.

"Yeah," Dan said wryly. "I know." He lifted his shoulders in a shrug. "What can I say? Maybe the bombing made him see the light."

"Maybe." But she didn't believe it. Not for one second. People didn't change that much. "Though he wasn't there, remember? The report said he was in Algiers."

Dan nodded. "Secret talks with the Algerian Deputy Premier." He jerked his thumb at the netbook. "Said so, right in that file."

"What was the deputy premier's name again?"

Dan shrugged and shook his head. "Don't remember."

Claire was already back at the keyboard. "Never mind. Saint Google will come to the rescue. Deputy Premier, Algeria. His name is Abdul Azziz . . ." She suddenly pulled in a shocked breath. "Oh my God."

"What? What is it?"

Claire turned the screen so Dan could see better.

Abdul Azziz tué par assassin mystérieux.

He was frowning. "I don't read French, but I do recognize assassin. What happened?"

"Abdul Azziz killed by mysterious assassin." Claire read the article all the way through. She started at the top and translated for Dan. "This is an article from *Le Temps*, the largest French-language newspaper in Algeria. Dated November 27 last year." Claire's eyes met Dan's. November 27 was two days after the bombing. She translated the rest. "Deputy Premier Abdul Azziz was killed today by a sniper as he was entering the Ministry of Agriculture. Deputy Premier Azziz was supposed to address representatives of farmers' organizations to discuss new rules for exporting agricultural produce to the European Union. As he was walking up the steps of the Ministry, he was felled by a 7.62 bullet from a sniper rifle. No organization has come forward claiming responsibility for the assassination. Abdul Azziz was born in Oran on September 28, 1968 ... blah blah blah. The rest is his life. My God, Dan. He was killed two days after meeting with Bowen—"

"After supposedly meeting with Bowen," Dan said grimly. "At this point, we don't have any corroboration at all that Bowen was there and not in Laka."

"And Azziz was killed by a Nato bullet."

"Yeah, it was definitely a bullet Bowen would have had access to."

Claire couldn't see Bowen getting his hands dirty but she could see him ordering someone else to get his hands dirty. "Not to mention he'd have access to a sniper, too."

It was an open secret. In danger zones like Laka, the local CIA agent would have several operatives on call. Not intelligence types like Bowen but real hard-asses. SpecOp types who could get any kind of wetwork done for you.

But ... much as she would love to have Bowen be the villain, it didn't make sense. The pieces didn't fit together at all.

Claire's satphone buzzed and she looked at Dan. Only Jesse had the number.

"I'll get it," Dan said, while Claire read through the article in *Le Temps* once more, on the off chance that a second reading would prove more enlightening than the first.

Dan was grunting now and again into the satphone, listening to Jesse's report. He finally closed the connection and sat for a moment, head down.

Dan's default expression was grim. Now he looked like he'd just been told the world really was going to end soon after all.

"What?"

He shook his head. "Nothing. A big fat nothing, still. No trace of the guy from the hotel, no trace of the guys who attacked my house, no trace of the guy or guys who torched your house. Nada. They could have been beamed down from outer space to do the job, then beamed back up, for all we know. And we've got Marcus on our side, who's no slouch, and Jesse said that Marcus said that the fire inspector down in Florida knows his stuff, too. This is bad shit."

It was. Claire knew full well that, in police work, if nothing was found in the first twenty-four hours, it was a very bad sign. Cases went cold very fast.

Marcus was a DC cop, a homicide detective in one of the murder capitals of the country. Very soon he'd be knee-deep in new homicides and would have to relegate her case to the back burner.

"We can just hole up here," Dan said, jaw muscles clenching. "Wait it out. No one can find us. I hate the thought of just sitting here, but at least you'd be safe." He was wound so tight every muscle of his torso showed, the tendons in his neck standing out. "One thing is for sure. No one's going to hurt you, ever again. Not while I'm alive."

She looked at him. Bare-chested, he looked like a force of nature. Dressed, you just saw that he had very broad shoulders and looked very fit, but take those clothes away and he was breathtakingly ripped. She'd felt him all over, and all over he was like warm steel.

His muscles were the real deal, the kind of muscles you developed from a hard life, not in a gym. He wasn't handsome, not by a long shot, but the billion pheromones of sheer utter maleness more than made up for that.

He was smart and capable, he'd been a good soldier, he was apparently a successful businessman now.

This magnificent man had just placed his life in her hands.

He'd just stated his willingness to put his entire existence on hold until they could eliminate the danger to her.

He wasn't like her. He hadn't spent the past year completely cut off from the world, doing nothing. No, he'd spent the past year building a new life and a new company from the ground up. And he was making a success out of it, too.

Claire knew perfectly well what being a one-man show

meant. She'd barely begun dipping her toes into becoming a professional translator, and it was daunting working alone. Your company was as strong as the energy you put into it.

He didn't have partners. If he didn't do a job, it didn't get done. Running a company like his entailed not just doing the job, but running the business aspects as well, pricing your services so you'd turn a profit, keeping books, client relations, getting out quotes . . . this was all stuff he had to do and if he was gone, no one else was going to do it for him. Not even his wonderful secretary, Roxanne.

Claire felt a sharp pang to her heart every time she thought about Roxanne going home to her mother. For the duration.

For what duration?

There was no end point at all, no deadline. They could stay in this limbo forever, while Dan's business self-destructed and his life's work went up in smoke.

Claire simply couldn't allow that, couldn't let Dan's life be ruined because of her. They had to turn the tables somehow, go on the attack. It would be dangerous but she simply didn't see an alternative.

A half-formed plan was starting to coalesce in her mind, but first she needed to communicate to Dan how much his offer meant to her.

She leaned forward and kissed him, a quick buss on the mouth, a little thank-you kiss you could give your favorite uncle.

She could feel him jolt in surprise—he wasn't expecting it. He was still all wound up, having thrown the gauntlet down at their shadowy enemy, and his warrior's blood was up.

But his warrior's blood was able to turn on a dime.

What she'd meant as a gesture of affection, a sign of gratitude, turned almost immediately into pure sex. She was already pulling back when Dan fisted his hand in her hair, bent down to her and opened his mouth over hers.

Oh God. Instant heat, rising up from her toes throughout

her body, as if she'd walked right into an oven. Her muscles instantly let go, so that it almost felt like he was keeping her upright by his fist in her hair. Then his other arm went around her waist and she was plastered against him, chest to chest and groin to groin.

Oh wow. It wasn't just his blood that was up. He picked her up and settled her on his lap without breaking the kiss and just like that, they zipped right to Stage Ten Foreplay, the stage just before sex.

And Claire was up for it, no question. She felt every body part loosen and melt, including her brain. He had placed her so that the *V* of her legs was right over his penis and with each strong pulse of blood, making him longer and thicker, there was an answering tug in her own groin. Both their bodies were rushing blood to where, very soon, something important was about to happen.

This was so . . . strange. Claire had never been sex-obsessed, not even in college when hormones were at their peak. She'd had lovers, of course. A few, a very select few, because she was incredibly picky.

The candidate had to be smart and not embarrass her when he opened his mouth and above all, not be a creep or a jerk. And after she joined the DIA, it had been clear to her that she should keep her nose clean, otherwise her career would suffer.

So all in all, sex hadn't figured too much in her life, other than as a pleasant distraction, a fun activity, to be enjoyed preferably after an elegant meal and a movie or a concert.

So this flash of white-hot heat in a crude cabin in the woods after a meal of canned baked beans and canned peaches . . . whoa. Nothing like this had ever happened before.

Dan held her so tightly she couldn't move, could barely breathe, had to breathe through his mouth. Which must be a powerful narcotic because her head began swimming, while her body began this luscious spiral toward a climax . . .

Dan pressed upward with his hips and her vagina contracted, hard, readying to have him inside her, preparing for his penetration.

She had to pull back, right now, or she'd forget everything she wanted to say, but oh, heavens, it was hard. She couldn't move her head back because he was holding it in his big hand and she couldn't wiggle out of his embrace. Those steely muscles were too strong. So she did the only thing she could.

She bit him, hard.

"Ow!" he complained and pulled his head back. But he was smiling. And he was aroused. Massively. If she hadn't felt it between her thighs, just looking at his face would have been enough.

That dark face was tight, eyes narrowed, nostrils flaring, lips almost blue with blood and slightly swollen from her own mouth. God only knew what she looked like. Sex on a stick, if he was anything to go by.

"I need your attention for a moment," she said softly, as he bent his head again, only to stop when she lay a finger across his mouth.

For just a second, Claire wavered. He was staring at her, those dark eyes circling her face, lingering at her mouth. A lock of his dark brown hair had fallen across his forehead and she reached out to brush it back. His head followed the curve of her palm, like a big cat asking to be stroked.

He was temptation incarnated.

She bent forward until her forehead touched his. "Dan," she whispered, "I need you to pay attention."

He nodded without breaking the connection between them. Though he wasn't thrusting up at her, his penis was still huge and hard between her legs, big hand against the small of her back holding her against him. It was almost impossible to concentrate.

But they needed to take proactive steps or they would either die or have to live their lives cooped up in a rustic cabin.

"Okay. I'm listening."

"I've been thinking." Claire pulled her head up and back and watched his eyes. He didn't even try a joke about how dangerous a thinking woman was. He simply watched her soberly, ready to listen to what she wanted to say.

"Shoot," he said quietly.

Claire tried to gather her thoughts together, though *thoughts* was perhaps too strong a word, implying rationality and reason. She was going to use reason to sway Dan into doing something he probably didn't want to, but reason had nothing to do with it.

Her idea sprang from a feeling, growing ever stronger in ways she couldn't explain even to herself, that the answer to everything lay in Laka.

"I—I know you think this might be crazy," she began slowly—

He immediately put a finger over her mouth. "Nothing you say can possibly sound crazy. Don't even go there."

Claire let out a long breath and felt the muscles in her chest relax a little. "Okay. I'm not entirely sure why I think this, but I am convinced that these . . . problems I'm— we're having originated back in Laka. The thing is, I can't tell you why, but it's a gut feeling I have. I think we need to go there, as soon as possible."

There was more but she just shut up and bit her lip, to see what his reaction would be.

He didn't say anything for a moment, mulling it over.

He spoke slowly, reasonably. "These days, Makongo's more of a military dictatorship than anything else. And the embassy is shut up real tight. No one in Mbutu's government is going to talk to us and no one in the embassy will talk. Neither of us work for the government anymore and I think we'd simply be kicked out on our asses. Not to mention the fact that the embassy staff has almost completely changed."

"The FNs would still be there," Claire said. "And the Marines. You'd know some of the Marine contingent, even though most of the ones who were in Laka last year would have rotated out. You're still plugged into the Marine network."

Dan nodded soberly. "Yeah, I am."

"So . . . there'd be someone there who'd be willing to talk, at least unofficially."

"Claire . . ." Dan sighed. "Even if there are Marines from last year's posting, they were all in Marine House. I know you don't remember what happened the day of the bombing, but you do remember that I told you I was the only one on guard duty that day. So there isn't anything anyone can tell you."

She shrugged, uncomfortable.

Claire was an analyst and she'd been a damned good one. Except for the huge howlers regarding the Red Army in her last report as an analyst, she'd always been absolutely correct in her reading of situations. She had never put in a report an unsubstantiated rumor or conclusion that she couldn't back up with facts she had checked herself.

She was a careful, rational thinker. Every time she wrote something down in a report, it came from her head and was based on her reading and knowledge and experience.

But it was her body that was talking now, almost violently.

Whenever she thought of Bowen, her whole body reacted with revulsion. Granted, Bowen was a creep, always had been, always would be, and his recent incarnation as philanthropist filled with the milk of human kindness didn't convince her one bit. But the mild distaste with which she had thought of him before was now an almost violent, nauseating disgust. It was impossible to describe.

She looked Dan straight in the eyes and spoke soberly. "I don't know if you're going to enjoy hearing this, but . . . it's as if the violence these past twenty-four hours has sort of . . . shaken something loose in my head, Dan. I have this feeling deep in my bones that there is something in Laka we need to know. I wish I could be more specific than that, but I can't. It's just—just a gut feeling. But it's getting stronger. And my feeling is that we need to move fast. I mean like right now." She looked outside the window at the utter blackness of the night. It was four a.m. "Or rather at first light. I have my passport with me. I always carry it with me, an old habit."

She bit her lip and watched him. There wasn't much more she could say, because she couldn't reason her way through her feelings. She had no facts to parade before him to convince him. All she could do was baldly state what she felt and see what happened. See whether Dan would take her feelings seriously.

Dan didn't say anything, just looked at her intently for a minute, two. Finally, he lifted her off him, reached for the satphone and dialed a number without looking at the keypad.

Someone answered. She recognized Jesse's voice with its soft Southern inflection at the other end.

Dan spoke without taking his eyes off her. "Jess? Who's your go-to guy for docs?" He stopped and listened to Jesse's tinny voice reading out a number that Dan didn't write down. "It looks like we're going to have to leave the country, and we have to do it soon. I'm going to need a passport card for Claire, we'll go up into Canada and exit from there. I'll keep you posted. And Jess—we might need you and Frank and Dave in Laka, Makongo. Do you think you could manage that? Front the tickets and just keep pulling money from the ATMs. Great."

Dan closed the connection and punched in another number. He spoke while the phone rang. "If we have to leave as soon as possible, we can't get you a fake passport. They take about at least a week to produce. But we can—hello? Jesse gave me this number. Sorry to call at this hour. Uh-huh." Dan smiled, his first smile in a while. "You brother was in the Second Battalion? Uh-huh. Those guys saw some real action in the 'Stan. Listen, a friend needs to get out of the country fast, to Canada. Tomorrow if possible. I know you can't make a passport that quick but could you manage a passport card? Yeah, I can get you a digital photo." Dan quirked a brow at Claire. She nodded. She had several photos on her flash drive. "I'll get it to you by secure email. A woman. Uh-huh. Yeah, Jesse can get them to me. Yeah? Great. Thanks, man. Tell your brother Semper Fi."

"Okay." Dan took her hands in his. His hands were warm, tough. Her hands felt so *safe* in his. "If we leave the country from here we're going to light up someone's map, we need to create a little diversion. Tomorrow afternoon Jesse'll bring your card, and we'll leave immediately. We'll cross the border into Canada with your passport card and my fake passport and find somewhere to sleep once we're across the border. The next day, we go to the airport in Montreal and buy two tickets to Paris with cash. That should slow them down some. They'll be checking for credit card payments. From Paris we'll buy tickets to Lungi with cash, then take a puddle-jumper to Laka. It's the closest to a shot we've got. They won't know I'm with you. I'm hoping it'll give us at least a head start. Jess and Dave and Frank will be coming on another flight, maybe from Cairo. No one could link their names to ours. No one will know we've got backup." He looked down at their joined hands. "And honey? You're going to have to do some quick work in Laka because I don't think we'll have much more than twenty-four hours before they figure out where we are and they come after us."

Claire nodded. She had no idea if twenty-four hours would be enough. She also had no idea what to do once she was in Laka. All she had was this crazy compulsion to be there.

She hoped with all her heart she wasn't dragging Dan and his friends into a wild-goose chase. In Laka they'd be exposed—way out there. If their enemy or enemies came from there, she was dragging them straight into the heart of danger.

She might have signed their death warrant.

"Dan," she said, her voice trembling. "Thank you so much. I hope—"

"Sh." He grinned wickedly and ran his hand up over her hip. Her panty-less hip. And unleashed a firestorm of feelings.

"So, then," he said, pulling her to him, "we have to wait for your card. What are we going to do in the meantime?"

"You'll think of something," she murmured, before his mouth came down on hers.

Heat flared in her, sudden and total, infusing her whole body with an incandescent glow. He held her tightly against him, kissing her deeply while she lit up from within.

She held him hard, loving the solid, steady feel of him. He was so strong, so *unshakeable*. The world could come crashing down around her, *was* crashing down around her, but he would still be there, solid, even in the rubble.

She could count on him in every way.

Count on him for blinding pleasure, too. All the background noise of danger and terror buzzing in her head, the black fog of imminent peril, dissipated. Just drifted away, like fog under the morning sun.

She wanted more, she wanted it all, and she wanted it *now*.

Claire stepped back out of his arms and pushed him a little, in the direction of the bed. He was so surprised, he actually took a step back.

She watched his eyes as she pointed behind him. "On the bed, right now," she whispered, because the excitement had caught in her throat. Everything inside her was thrumming with desire, so intense she could hardly breathe.

Dan's eyes flared, and he grinned. "Yes, *ma'am!*" he growled, and moved toward the bed. He put his knee on the mattress and she squeezed his arm, pulling him back.

"Don't even think of getting on that bed unless you're naked." He looked at her, saw she meant it and let out his breath in one, excited gust. Making a noise low in his throat which she took to mean assent, he pulled his clothes off, his eyes never leaving hers.

Inside her was a driving drumbeat, unlike anything she'd ever felt in her life. Almost panicky in its urgency. She felt swollen, as if her skin were too small to contain her, tight bands gripped her chest, her hands shook.

Out of nowhere, this enormous tsunami of desire

washed over her. The times they'd made love, Claire had realized that Dan's desire was greater than her own. She'd been happy to make love with him, particularly once they got going, but she recognized that she would have been just as happy to cuddle up and feel him holding her. Reassurance and safety had trumped desire.

Not now.

Now these waves of heat prickling her skin were pure sexual desire, and she felt as if she'd die if she didn't have him inside her as soon as physically possible.

Now now now! was the drumbeat in her head, the only words she was capable of thinking.

Dan was standing there, naked, a beautiful male in his prime, fully aroused and watching her, awaiting his cue. She pushed at his chest again and he fell back onto the bed with a groaning laugh.

Claire could never have budged him if he hadn't wanted to move. That was abundantly clear. He wouldn't even have registered her push if he didn't want to be on that bed as badly as she wanted him on it.

He was on his back, watching her. "Claire?" he whispered.

"Right here." Claire took off her T-shirt. Instead of dumping it on the floor like he had, she folded it neatly and put it on the chair that doubled as a bedside table.

In under a minute she was naked, crawling on top of him, nearly delirious at the feel of him under her. Hot. Strong. Hers.

She sat up on his chest, as if he were some magnificent thoroughbred she was riding. His hands rose to her but she caught his wrists in her hands, lifting his arms above his head, back onto the mattress. Her hands couldn't encompass his wrists but she pressed on them, holding them down. "Stay."

There was no way in the world she could force him to do anything, let alone keep his arms restrained, but he nodded and lay still under her, arms outstretched over his head, wrists together as if manacled. She knew, without a shadow of a doubt, that he would stay that way until she signaled he was free.

She had all the power here, completely and totally.

Claire looked down at him, at this strong man who had put himself in her hands. His chest was so broad, her legs were stretched to their maximum extension. His skin was naturally dark, slightly paler on the underside of his arms. The hair on his forearms and chest was thick and curly, but long and straight under his arms.

Every single feature, every detail fascinated her. The heavy muscles, the feeling of immense power between her thighs like some superb racing engine, the dark heated look in his eyes.

She reached out her left hand and ran the backs of her fingers from his jaw, over the strong, corded muscles of his neck, down over his pectorals and the thick mat of chest hair. Her fingers found scar tissue, circular scar tissue.

"Is that what I think it is?" she whispered.

He nodded.

He was strong but he wasn't indestructible. He'd been shot, he'd been to battle, and he was willing to go into battle again, for her. Under her hand, his heart beat strong and steady.

Claire felt so many things she couldn't even articulate them. She couldn't speak anyway, her throat was too tight with emotions, the full range of them except for one: fear. She had no fear at all. The past year had been full of fear—of her nightmares, of the future, of what was in her head. But now she felt completely liberated from her fears.

She and Dan were walking into danger. Something big and ferocious was after them and there was no guarantee they would find out what it was before it killed them. But they were going to face that danger together and if they went down, they would go down fighting.

Dan had lent her a little of his strength and courage and now she was back to her old self and she would die before she let herself be consumed by fear again.

He was watching her carefully. "Can I use my hands now?" he asked quietly.

She nodded, unable to speak. The feelings in her were so intense she felt as if she could hardly contain them.

Dan's arms came down slowly, wrapped themselves around her back and pulled her down to him.

"Dan, I—"

"Sh." He put a finger over her mouth. "I know."

Kissing her deeply, he turned them over and entered her, a long, slow, tender penetration.

He lifted his head and looked down at her, wiping the tear that had escaped with a rough finger. "You're mine now," he whispered.

SIXTEEN

"SO which is it gonna be?" Wizard asked, sitting back in Bowen's Louis XV chair that had cost the better part of six thousand dollars. Bowen tried not to wince at the thought of the Doritos crumbs clinging to Wizard's skinny ass being ground into the original green damask silk.

Wizard had asked for the one-on-one meeting, saying he'd been trolling the "darkweb" and had something of interest.

Wizard was crazy but no one else could search the underbelly of the web and come up with such big game. The biggest—a sitting US senator.

They both studied the stills laid out on the long table in his study. The stills were taken from videocams that had obviously been placed in various upscale hotel rooms. He had no idea how Wizard had found them and he had no intention of asking. It was enough that they were there.

This went way beyond accepting skyboxes from corporate lobbyists. This was Major League Scandal. The kind where voters spat on your grave.

He studied the photographs with deep pleasure, feeling

again that strong wind of destiny blowing over him. He'd needed for Senator Neff to disappear and had even been contemplating calling in Heston because the corruption scandal was going fairly slowly. But no need—like the hooked end of a cane yanking a bad comic offstage, these would more than do the trick.

The stills were almost an extravaganza of riches, an orgy of ruin. Any one of them was a career-stopper, guaranteed to get the senator resigning and beating a trail back to his hometown with his tail between his legs. Wizard had turned over his darkweb rocks and found at least a hundred of them, plus the videos.

Ah, the videos. Better than the stills, of course. More convincing. But in the delicate art of blackmail and ruin, you start slow and then escalate.

He ran his fingers over the table, walking up and down, studying the photographs. This one—too grainy. That one—a back view of the senator, could be any horny man in a corset, wielding a whip.

Finally he decided, tapping four of the twenty photographs, marvels of lighting and form, almost as if they had been staged for his benefit. The better to ruin the senator with.

And, in a way, they had been staged, only not for a voyeuristic public. *You do like your drama, don't you Senator?* he thought, looking at one notable composition.

The senator, in bra, panties and garters holding up black fishnet stockings, and with killer size fourteen stiletto heels, on hands and knees, face turned completely to the hidden camera.

Such an unmistakable face, too. Handsome, ruddy, with a shock of thick white hair. A face that had graced hundreds of front pages of the *WaPo* and the *Times*. A face that was a regular on *Hardball* and *Larry King Live*. A face that was the very epitome of strong and successful American manhood.

Except, of course, for the outsized Victoria's Secret underwear the senator was wearing and the lines of white powder on a coffee table in the foreground of the picture. There were photographs of the senator hoovering the white powder up his nose with a hundred-dollar bill, too.

But the kicker was the senator's sex partner, standing in front of the senator, who was crouching like a dog at her feet.

Only it wasn't a her.

It took a second to get the full import of the photo because the person wielding the riding crop looked so much like a woman—and a beautiful one, at that. Long, black hair that brushed smooth shoulders, beautiful breasts barely contained by a black lace bra and black garters holding up black silk stockings. No panties.

An image to goose any man into instant horniness except for the prominent Adam's apple on that long, smooth throat and the big, erect penis jutting out from between the legs.

Christ, this photo was going to become a classic, and would stay up on the net till the end of time.

He tapped that photo and turned to Wizard. "We'll start with this one. Sent in jpeg of course, a thumbnail. Say that more is forthcoming. Caption—An American Senator. Send it to Sarkos and Richards." The two top bloggers on politics, both of whom hated the senator, both of them fully willing to release the photos. The dailies would pick up the news soon enough. They wouldn't publish the photos, oh no. But in a few days, this still, together with the others Wizard would leak in a slow and devastating sequence, would be all over the internet.

Wizard shrugged his skinny shoulders. "Okay, man, but it'll cost you."

He smiled. Wizard was such an easy man to read, for someone so smart. "Check your bank account," he suggested gently.

Wizard pulled out his iPhone and his eyes rounded when he checked his account in Aruba. The amount was guaranteed to make him work especially well.

Bowen didn't care. Money was now the least of his concerns. The Africa business was sending money to him in torrents, and that was before two new diamond mines were slated to come online.

He went to his liquor cabinet, which was a converted Florentine Renaissance *madia*, pulled out a crystal glass and poured himself a sixty-year-old Macallan that had made the *Forbes* list of most expensive whiskies. He handed Wizard a can of Red Bull without a glass.

They were both happy.

Ah, give people what they want. Such a simple rule, with such spectacular results.

"I'd say we send a video on day three. By that time the mainstream media will be in full howl. We send it to Sarkos again and he can decide what parts he wants to black out. The original will be leaked a couple of hours after Sarkos puts it up on his site. We'll choose the one that shows the senator at his . . . best."

Oh yeah, there were a couple showing the senator engaged in sex acts that were illegal in ten states. Not to mention the coke. "He won't last a week."

And during that week, there would be wild speculation about who would run for the seat. He already had plans for the two top runners. One would be discovered with an extra hundred thousand dollars in his bank account that would be eventually traced back to an Aryan Brotherhood faction and the other would have a tragic car accident.

The first one was Wizard's lookout, the second Heston's. He frowned as he looked at the last splash of Macallan's in the glass, a subtle shade of light bronze, catching the light of the Murano chandelier overhead.

Heston.

Heston, who *wasn't* doing his job. Who had let Claire Day slip through his fingers. Twice.

Heston, who had one more chance and that was it. Hit man baseball. Three strikes and you're out.

A plan a long time in the making was coming to fruition. Each step had been carefully plotted, even more carefully carried out. He was advancing, step by careful step, in his master plan.

Claire Day was, all in all, a minor irritant, even coupled with that jarhead, who was probably fucking her. But he didn't like even minor irritants spoiling the smooth progression of his plans.

Heston was supposed to take care of this small problem. If he couldn't, then Heston had to go and by God he'd take care of Claire Day himself.

It would be a pleasure.

EVENTEEN

THEY landed in the familiar muggy heat, so thick it was like a living presence. Walking out of the air-conditioned plane into the sultry Makongan afternoon had been like landing on another planet.

They'd flown on a tiny six-seater from Lungi. Claire swore she could smell alcohol on the pilot's breath when he came into the airport lounge to call the flight himself.

But there wasn't much choice, there weren't many flights from Lungi. Jesse, Frank and Dave were coming in from Cairo in a couple of hours, having flown out of New York.

Claire had had to fly under her own name from Montreal. It was simply a question of time before her nemesis found her and traced her. He couldn't, however, know four warriors had flown in, too.

Laka airport was busy, she thought, looking around as they descended the rusty roll-on steps down to the tarmac. Military planes filled with cargo were everywhere. Huge warehouses had been built since the last time she'd flown into what was now called General Mbutu International

Airport, and forklift trucks were ferrying crates and boxes to and fro like so many ants on an anthill.

"Busy place," Dan said, slipping on the sunglasses he'd bought at Lungi airport. She did the same. She'd forgotten how blinding the African sun could be.

They watched a stack of ten palettes trundle by, all donations of the New Day Foundation, stenciled in black and red on the sides in foot-high letters. She looked around. "My God, it's a huge operation."

As far as the eye could see, there were cargo planes being unloaded, and in the distance, planes lining up on the tarmac. One by one, they lifted up gracefully into the painfully blue sky and the next in line readied for takeoff. The takeoffs were staggered and precise, like clockwork.

The airport she knew had been lackadaisical, with bored security guards smoking and playing cards. This looked positively Prussian in its organization. "It's changed," she murmured.

"Yeah." Dan was pulling the single piece of hand luggage they'd flown with and took her elbow with his other hand. "Let's see whether the rest of the country's changed."

Passage through customs was quick, without any hassles. Dan had stood tensely by her side as she slipped her passport across to the border control officer. If their ultimate enemy was Bowen, this country was like his personal fiefdom. If he'd discovered her travel plans, if Claire was on some list, Bowen could mobilize the entire Makongan Army.

Dan had flown with sharply pointed ceramic knuckles and a ceramic knife in a sheath inside his jeans and she knew that he would use both in a heartbeat, though knuckles and a knife, no matter how deadly sharp, were no match against the AK-47s all the guards brandished.

She also knew beyond a shadow of a doubt that he would defend her to the death.

She looked at him somberly as they walked through the crowded airport and out toward the taxi stand.

She'd never really had any protection in her life. When her mother died, her father basically just gave up the ghost. He'd loved her, but he'd been a shell of a man and she'd known that she'd have to fight her own battles. Through high school, college and climbing the ranks in her career, she'd been alone. Boyfriends and lovers had come and gone. It wouldn't have even occurred to them to offer protection and, frankly, it hadn't occurred to her to ask.

The truth of the matter was that she was perfectly capable of taking care of herself under normal circumstances. Perfectly capable of studying well, getting good grades, getting scholarships, sitting for entrance exams and starting up in her new profession.

She'd been on her own and the men in her life had been fleeting presences, like comets across the sky, often more trouble than they were worth.

But now she really needed Dan, and he was right here, solidly by her side. Every single move he made drove that point home. He was with her and wouldn't leave her.

He'd saved her life twice and was continuing to look after her. Whatever mess she was in, it was hers, not his. And yet he had simply walked away from his old life, unquestioningly and uncomplainingly, to become her paladin.

As he walked with her through the airport, he checked every angle thoroughly, completely alert, eyes constantly moving. When he'd finished with the field of vision ahead of him, he'd stop to tie a shoelace or look at postcards and check the entire perimeter behind him. It was done very smoothly and unobtrusively. As was the way he angled to ensure that he covered her as much as possible from snipers. He all but danced around her to make sure that if there was a bullet, he'd catch it and not her.

Behind the dark glasses her eyes pricked with tears.

Outside, Dan flagged a taxi, then turned to her. He bent his face to hers, mouth against her ear, eyes moving behind his sunglasses.

"What is it, honey?" he murmured.

All of a sudden, Claire couldn't stay silent anymore. As

far as she knew, they hadn't been followed. But if they had, killers were after them right now. They could die at any moment in a hail of bullets, and Dan would never know.

"Thank you," she whispered. "For everything you're doing for me."

He'd been studying the tops of the buildings outside the airport, but at her words, he turned sharply to her.

His jaw muscles clenched and his hand tightened around her arm. "My pleasure."

There. For right now, it had all been said.

They were quiet on the short ride into the city center, Dan holding her tightly against him, bracing her against the huge potholes in the road. Their driver clearly enjoyed the bouncing. Claire could swear he aimed directly for the potholes, the bigger the better.

They'd booked into the Etoile Africaine, the only decent hotel in town. As the driver took them the long way around, angling for a more expensive fare, Claire observed the streets.

She'd loved Laka, loved its vibrancy, vivid colors, even its lunacy. The streets had been full of vendors, selling everything possible under the sun, mostly illegal. Music had drifted down from many of the second-floor apartments, some recorded, some live. Put three Makongans together and you had a musical group. And four political parties. People argued constantly. The din had been almost unbearable at times, and a lot of fun, as people quarreled, hawkers screamed lists of their wares, musicians played. It had all been chaotic and cheerful.

Now the streets were deserted. Even the shops seemed deserted. Every third or fourth shop was closed, its metal mesh barricade pulled down, though it was the middle of the day.

The few people on the streets were standing still, watching the taxi make its way through the empty streets with dull, incurious eyes.

And they were all men. Before, most of the street vendors had been women. Women dressed in garishly colored batik had been everywhere. Now it was as if they'd disappeared, which said a lot to Claire.

Women have a built-in radar for danger. If the women had abandoned the streets, something was wrong.

Even the smells were different. Laka had had a heady smell of diesel fumes, wood charcoal from the braziers of food stalls, overripe fruit, grilled meat, the bitter chocolaty smell of the coffee stalls on every street corner. Now, the deserted streets smelled of food gone bad and of the rank river flowing lazily through the city.

"God," Claire murmured. "It looks like East Berlin before the wall came down." She'd only been seven when the wall fell, but she remembered seeing the magazine pictures. And a professor of hers at Georgetown had escaped from East Germany in the seventies and had assigned research projects on East Berlin. "What happened?"

"President for Life Mbutu happened," Dan said grimly. He let out a relieved breath. "I guess our driver has finally decided to take us to the hotel."

The taxi pulled up in front of the ornate, stucco baroque façade of the Etoile Africaine. Dan leaned forward with a sheaf of dollars then walked around the cab to Claire. As soon as she was out of the cab, the driver took off with a squeal of tires.

They stood looking at what used to be the best—actually, the only—hotel in town.

The Etoile had been where cynical NGO officers, alcoholic foreign correspondents, jaded businessmen, hopeful prostitutes and unhappy UN personnel stayed. The food and alcohol had been excellent and hardly a week went by where you didn't stop by for a drink with a friend.

Now it looked like it belonged on the back side of the moon.

Where last year there had been a clerk with a uniform worthy of an Italian admiral, known for his smile and knowledge of the city, now the big revolving door was unattended. The huge front windows and the panels of the revolving door were filthy.

Strangest of all, it appeared deserted. The Etoile had been full of customers, the venue of the elite of the city and the international institutions night and day.

Dan was tense as he checked everything out. Finally, he looked at her and she nodded. Where else would they go? They had reservations and there really wasn't any other place in town that she knew of. If the Etoile had degraded so much, she didn't even want to think of the small boardinghouses and bed-and-breakfasts that had dotted the city.

Inside, the air was closed and stuffy, another huge change. If you got too hot shopping in town you could always nip into the Etoile and cool down in the air-conditioned bar, where drinks were served twenty-four seven.

Though the hotel looked abandoned, it wasn't closed. There was someone behind the desk and a few patrons could be seen.

Claire hung back while Dan checked them into a double room under his fake name. With a little luck, the clerk wouldn't ask for her documents and there wouldn't be any trace in the hotel records of her presence.

They were in luck.

Dan's fake passport was enough and Mr. and Mrs. Kenneth Doran rode up to the fifth floor, where Dan checked the fire escapes at both ends of the corridor. In the room, he checked out the windows, the bottom of the telephone and all the lamps, all the plugs. He got up on a chair and checked every inch of the wainscoting and every inch of the bathroom. It took him half an hour of silent work, but he was finally satisfied that there were no bugs and no cameras.

"Damn," he said, sitting down on the bed. Claire was horrified to note a faint cloud of dust rising when he sat down. "I've got a kit back home that would have done that in three minutes flat."

"Well," she offered, "you can't expect to run for your life with all your equipment, can you?"

She turned, startled, at the sound of a soft knock on the door. Her eyes rounded. "Oh my God. We didn't order room service, that might be—"

"Sh." Dan bent to kiss her briefly. "It's a friend, bringing some of that equipment I had to leave behind."

He opened the door and a Marine walked in carrying two big briefcases. He was wearing fatigues and combat boots and a boonie cover. *Sgt. Lee* was stitched onto the shirt pocket. His high and tight was so short she couldn't tell what color his hair was.

"Gunny," Sergeant Lee said quietly. "Good to see you."

"Yeah, good to see you, too, Sarge. What have you got for me?"

Sergeant Lee placed the briefcases on the bed, raising another small cloud of dust, and opened them. Four sniper rifles, components broken down and nestled in foam cut-outs, four Glocks with shoulder holsters and several dozen magazines. "Exactly what you asked for, Gunny, except the number of magazines. I wanted to get you more ammo, but it wasn't possible."

Dan looked up at his friend with a sharp look. "You sure you're not going to get in trouble with this? Because I'm telling you, if I need to shoot I will. And to kill."

"Well, what the fuck do you want a rifle and a gun for if you're not intending to use them?" the sergeant asked in a reasonable voice. "And don't worry, I won't get any flak. It's not our stuff. I got it off a fucking arms dealer here. Place is fucking lousy with them. Could have got you a fucking RPG or a fifty cal, easy." He rolled his eyes. "Hell, coulda prolly got you a fucking nuclear bomb." He laughed, then his grin froze as he remembered they weren't alone in the room. His eyes as they stole to Claire were so wide he looked like a startled pony. "Oops. Begging your pardon, ma'am."

Claire waved that away. They were up against people trying to kill them. A little healthy profanity wouldn't hurt them any.

Dan was busy fitting the shoulder holster, checking the mirror to see if his jacket hid it. Then he put the rifles together, checked them, then broke them down again, hands steady and practiced and fast. It was true what they said about a Marine and his rifle.

"So . . . what's the deal here? It's changed a lot since my last post." Dan closed the cases and put them in the closet.

"Yeah. President for Life keeps a pretty tight rein on things. We hear a lot of stories about political opponents getting tortured or offed, but we can't do anything about it. Guy's untouchable—he's now officially Our Guy. He's also become the go-to guy for distributing food and medicine throughout the region. It goes through this big-shot foundation. We're called in sometimes to escort a shipment, but mostly Makongan soldiers and a few 'security experts' take care of it. The security experts are mercs, some American, some South African." Sergeant Lee shrugged. "That's about it. Makongo's become a real calm posting now. Nobody does anything that might piss off the president. If you do, you're disappeared."

"Does Bowen McKenzie come often?" Claire asked.

Sergeant Lee shrugged. "Not that often, no, ma'am. As far as I know, he's only come twice this year. He sleeps in the Presidential Palace and we're called in for protection detail. Easiest detail ever, cause no one wants him dead. He's Saint Bowen around here." This last was said in a heavily sarcastic tone.

"Yeah." She shook her head. "It's hard to think of him as Saint Bowen. He's made a real leap from being CIA Creep of the Year to sainthood."

Sergeant Lee's mouth firmed as if repressing a smile. "Yes, ma'am." He turned to Dan. "You need backup? Because Flynn and me, we can take some personal leave, catch your six, know what I mean?"

Dan shook his head. "For now, I've got men coming in. We're on recon. I'll call you if I need you."

Lee fixed him with a hard stare. "You do that. Flynn says he still owes you one. A big one. And I do, too." He turned his hand into a gun and cocked it at Dan. "So you call if you need us, you hear me?"

Dan nodded.

When Lee walked out, Dan went out and watched him walk down the corridor, standing there for two or three minutes. In that time the elevator remained silent and no one came. The hotel seemed almost empty of guests.

Finally, satisfied, Dan closed the door and looked at her. Unwittingly, as if the young sergeant had released some Marine hormones in the air, he stood at modified parade rest, broad shoulders back, hands over crotch.

"So . . . we're here, we're armed and we're pissed. What do we do now?"

Well, for starters, Claire wanted to kiss him. A big fat smackeroo right on the mouth. Not for sex—for one thing that dusty bed was unappealing—but because he turned to her for leadership. They were a team. He was providing physical security and she was supposed to provide guidance and direction.

Claire Day, who had spent three months in a coma, and the next three months learning to walk again, who'd had nightmares every night and had had trouble distinguishing up from down, was now the team strategist. No question.

Dan stood quietly, waiting to hear what she had to say. He was, as he'd said, armed and pissed and now he was ready to strike in the direction Claire indicated.

And she was up for it, oh yeah.

Her constant dizziness was gone, as if it had never been. Though she'd twice escaped attempted murder, though the trip up through to Canada, then on to Paris, Lungi Airport and then Laka had been long and wearying, she wasn't tired. She felt . . . strong. Energized. Clearheaded.

She was back.

Claire saw clearly what had to be done, and the steps to be taken. It was as if someone had given her her mind back, her ability to reason things through, to analyze situations and decide on the next step.

"First off," she said, "I want to talk to Marie Diur's mother and sister."

Dan didn't hesitate a second. "Then let's go."

$\mathcal{E}$IGHTEEN

THE one thing about walking around a city that looked like the set of the *Night of the Living Dead* was that it was easy to check whether you were being followed.

Dan was really good at countersurveillance and he'd have bet that they weren't being followed. He *was* betting, with the most precious currency he had—Claire's life.

If he had had any feeling that they were being tagged, he'd have aborted the mission, no question.

And Claire would have followed his lead, instantly, no question. She was good with strategy, he was good with tactics. Being with Claire on a mission felt like . . . like dancing with a superb partner. Their movements meshed, each willing to give the other primacy where their talents were strongest.

It was teamwork at its finest, and he hadn't had that since he'd retired from the Marines.

Except in the Corps, though his fellow soldiers had been good men in a fight, they were also smelly and with skin like leather. They were called Leathernecks for a reason.

Man, being on an op with a partner who was the most

beautiful woman in the world, with eyes that could make you drown in them and a mouth that made you whimper . . . that was the best.

Dan didn't know what the future would hold. He didn't even know if they had a future. Something powerful was arrayed against them and there was no knowing if they would come out on top. But he knew, like he knew right from wrong, that whatever time was allotted to him on this earth, he wanted it to be with Claire by his side. As his partner in all ways.

She tugged on his arm. "In here."

They'd been walking through the Cité Administrative, built by the French in the nineteenth century for the managers of the companies running the gold and diamond mines. Though the stucco mansions were dilapidated and were often home to multiple families, they still held a residual grace and beauty.

Claire led them through a rusted but graceful wrought-iron gate that was unlatched and down a brick path that was almost completely overgrown with banana trees and huge palm trees at least a century old. The fronds overhead were so thick they blotted out the sun. Claire followed the path around the back and stopped before a solid door painted bright blue.

It looked completely deserted. Nothing moved in the hot, still air except for the buzzing of insects in the lushly overgrown garden.

There were no signs of human habitation, no sounds of people, no kids running around. Dan remembered that a year ago, the streets had been knee-deep in lively, chocolate-colored kids getting into all kinds of trouble. But right now, there was only the buzz of insects and underneath that, silence.

If the Diur family had moved, he and Claire were in the deepest shit. This was the only part of town that actually had streets, and street addresses. If the Diur family had uprooted and gone to the center of Laka, with its twisting streets and dense population, they'd never find them.

Or if they'd moved out of Laka or, worse, been killed, then he and Claire had traveled halfway around the world only to butt up against a dead end.

Claire walked up to the bright blue door, with peeling paint and splits in the wood, and knocked loudly. "Hello?" she called out. Only the bees answered.

After five minutes of knocking, Claire went farther along the back of the house, feeling for something with her fingers. She gave a little hum of pleasure and held up a key.

"Claire . . ." he said, putting a warning in his voice.

She smiled angelically. "What?" Just as she was fitting the key to the door, it opened. A very beautiful middle-aged African woman stood on the doorstep.

"You. What do you want?" she asked, her voice cold and abrupt.

But Claire had already put her arms around the woman's slender waist and was hugging her, murmuring something soft in French. The woman frowned, features drawn in pain. At first she stood stiffly in Claire's embrace. Then she broke down and hugged Claire back, dropping her face to Claire's shoulder.

When they broke apart, both women had wet eyes. Mrs. Diur looked around carefully and tugged Claire inside. Dan followed, eyes sharp.

Inside, the house was dark and clean, but looked empty, as if nobody lived there. Mrs. Diur led them down a dark, narrow corridor running through the entire house to a living room that gave out on to the street. The curtains were drawn and there was a hush in the air.

They sat down, the two women together on a small sofa, Dan in an armchair at right angles. He kept his right hand free, ready to draw. There was a feeling here he didn't like. He didn't know if it was the generally eerie vibe Laka was giving off or this empty house. Whatever. If there was going to be trouble, he was going to be ready for it.

Claire kept her voice low, starting to speak French. Then, with a quick glance at Dan, she switched to English. Ordinarily he would have been happy to have her speak whatever language she wanted to put the woman at ease, but he had to understand what was being said.

Mrs. Diur spoke English with a heavy French accent. "What are you doing here, Claire? I was told you were badly injured."

"Yes, I was," Claire said softly. "I don't remember anything about that day, *Maman*. I wasn't even capable of talking on the phone until last February. I called here and left a message. Aba called my father's home while I was in a coma." Claire closed her eyes briefly. She was pale again, almost as pale as when Dan had seen her in his office. Man, he didn't ever want to see her that color again, and yet here it was. Whatever it was she was remembering, it was painful. "Aba was . . . angry, *Maman*. And I don't know why. She said . . . she said Marie was killed because of *me*. Because of something I'd done." The tears were back in her eyes and her face was drawn. The pale, slender hands holding on to Mrs. Diur's black ones were white-knuckled with tension. Her voice dropped to a whisper. "I would never have hurt Marie, never. I loved her like a sister. I miss her."

"I miss her, too," the woman said simply. "Is that why you have come back to Makongo, *ma chére*? To discover why Marie died? To make—how would you say it?—to make amends?"

Claire released a hand to swipe at her eyes. "I don't know how to make amends for something I don't remember doing. I'm here"—she looked swiftly at Dan, then back at the woman—"*we're* here because someone is after me and I have a feeling in my gut that the answer lies here, in Laka. In what happened a year ago."

The woman reared back. "After you? What do you mean?"

"There have been two attempts on my life," Claire said simply. "We have no idea why."

Mrs. Diur frowned. Her dark features were refined, with high cheekbones and a full mouth. She had to be nearing fifty but she was still a beautiful woman. Dan remembered that her daughter, Marie, had been beautiful, too.

"What makes you think the answer lies here?" Mrs. Diur looked around at her darkened living room, with its empty, deserted air and Dan knew she was also talking about the city outside, just as empty and deserted.

Claire blew out a frustrated breath. "A feeling. I can't explain it much better than that. But it's a strong feeling. And the fact that the bombing in Laka is a huge hole in my head, in my life. I don't remember any of it. Maybe if I filled in the blanks, I could understand what is happening. So I ask you, *Maman*. What happened that day? Do you remember? All I know is that Marie came back to the embassy and called me to come with her. I was with this man." Claire pointed at him. "He was the head of the embassy guards. He said Marie came to get me and that we both disappeared and then there was the blast. Why? Why did Marie come back to the embassy when there was practically a war outside? It must have taken her at least an hour to get to the embassy, trying to avoid the soldiers shooting in the streets."

"We begged her not to go." Mrs. Diur's eyes welled. A tear tracked down over a high cheekbone and dropped to her lap. She didn't wipe it away. "Aba fought with her, tried to physically restrain her. But Marie was convinced that you were in danger and she wanted to get you out of the embassy. She knew you were working that day." Her huge dark eyes burned with emotion. "Marie loved you almost as much as she loved Aba. There was nothing we could say. In the end, she simply ran out the door."

Claire was crying too, now.

"Oh God. She should have just waited for the Red Army's troops to wear themselves out. I was safe there in the embassy. Or at least we thought we were. Who would have thought the Red Army would blow the embassy up?"

Mrs. Diur sat up straight, wiping her eyes. "But *ma chère*. That's the point. That's why Marie wanted you out of there. Those weren't Red Army soldiers shooting in the streets."

"What?" Dan spoke for the first time. "If it wasn't the Red Army, then who was it?"

"Mbutu's men. We recognized them. Their plan all along was to bomb the embassy and blame the Red Army. It worked, too. Mbutu was able to portray himself as the enemy of terrorists, the friend of America. And anyone who knew, or who said anything, they had them killed. My husband published an article on the Red Army, on how they weren't capable of trying to take over Laka and certainly weren't capable of bombing the embassy. He was obsessed with trying to find out who had killed Marie." Her voice turned harsh, bitter. "A month after the bombing, masked gunmen came to our house and dragged him away. I never saw him again."

"*Maman*," Claire murmured, and placed her hand on her arm. "I'm so sorry. And Aba? What happened to her?"

The woman swiped at her eyes again, but the tears were rolling down her face now. "Aba's husband was killed, too. She shut up. What else could she do? She works at a hospital, the Hôpital Générale de la Charité. She's very agitated about something but she won't tell me. But there's something going on that is tearing her in two."

Suddenly she turned her head, staring blindly out the window, tears shiny against her dark skin. "Go away," she said dully, without turning her head. "Please, Claire, if you ever felt something for us, go away now and never come back."

CLAIRE was shaken when she left *Maman* Diur's house.

So much had changed, so very much had been lost. When she'd frequented the house as Marie's friend, it had been filled with music and laughter and superb food.

Mr. Diur had been a university lecturer and there had always been students and other professors hanging around. And Aba's doctor friends, cynical and dedicated. And Marie's friends, who loved music and art.

There'd been good-natured arguing, teasing, friendliness, a sense of family. Claire had been considered a third daughter and she'd simply lapped it up. An only child growing up in a household grieving for her lost mother, she'd been used to the quiet of loneliness.

Though her father had never forbidden her to bring her friends home, she could tell he didn't enjoy noise and confusion, so she just grew into the habit of stopping friendships at the door.

Not that there had been that many. Claire had been a studious girl, from a sad home. It had turned out to be easier to just close herself away with her books and her computer.

Marie's home had been an eye-opener and she dove in happily, soaking up the chaotic and cultured atmosphere, full of noise and laughter and arguments and delightful food and unquestioning friendship.

All lost, forever gone. The Diur home now was even sadder than her own in Safety Harbor, because its walls had once held happiness and companionship. Hers never had, and now never would

They were walking along the street, Dan helping her to navigate around the cracked pavement of the sidewalk because she was lost in space. Last year, it had been a well-maintained street, full of traffic, people strolling in the evenings on the smooth asphalt. Now it looked like it had survived a war.

Maybe it had.

Dan was not only helping her navigate the cracks and holes, he was watching the street and the houses, vigilant and prepared. He had his left arm around her, right loose, ready to reach for a weapon. Just like a Marine. Trusting in God and firepower.

Claire wasn't any help at all, she was still stunned by what she'd heard, and she stumbled along, impervious to the outside world.

She stopped and Dan stopped, too, eyes roaming expertly along the tops of the buildings.

She wasn't doing any good here, dazed and sad. She had to regroup.

"Let's go back to the hotel," she said.
Dan nodded.

RICHMOND, VIRGINIA

It was on the op-ed page of the *Richmond Times Dispatch*.
An eloquent plea for a new morality in politics, decrying
the decadent spectacle of Senator Neff's insalubrious private life, calling upon men and women of goodwill outside
the usual sphere of politics to come to the aid of democracy
in the grand old state of Virginia.

The long article was signed by Concerned Citizens for
Democracy and mentioned a number of prestigious men
and women who might be drafted in to serve out Senator Neff's term. Judges, doctors, a famous journalist. But
it mentioned his name twice. In two days' time a similar
article would be published, mentioning only his name.

The three hundred thousand dollars to set up the Concerned Citizens had been money well spent. It was starting
to create an air of inevitability around his candidacy.

It was perfect. Just absolutely perfect. It was working
out even better than he'd hoped.

The photo on the more tabloid-y political blogs had
raised a firestorm. The blogosphere was going wild,
inflamed postings raging in a viral whirlwind. The time-
line was even tighter than he had anticipated.

Things were moving fast and he calculated that the full-
blown scandal—spread out on the front pages of the press
from coast to coast—could break in less than twenty-four
hours.

The first photograph, the face artfully pixelated, was
moving its way fast up the food chain, in an explosive
upward spiral. Already he could read in the latest postings
from the three most respected political bloggers a breaking news alert, announcing the upcoming resignation of
Senator Neff. One of the bloggers used to work for *Time*
and the other for The *Washington Post*, and they still had

low friends in high places. Once the blogosphere was talking openly about it, the ball would be passed to the online magazines, then the print magazines and newspapers.

That's when the second and third photos would go out. And the only pixelated thing on the photos would be the tranny's woodie, though anyone over twelve would understand what it was. Old Neff's face with its unmistakable shock of thick white hair and spa ruddiness was instantly recognizable.

Those photos wouldn't make it to the mainstream press, but verbal descriptions of them would. And there would be at least ten million hits on the photos.

Allow a day for another media feeding frenzy and the videos would be released. The howls for Neff's resignation would become deafening.

And there Bowen was, an independent who could lean either way, with fabulous Washington connections and a reputation for philanthropy. Ready and willing to be drafted.

He could feel the power of it tingling through his body from fingertips to toes. It was always this way, always had been, since he was a boy. He'd felt fate tugging him in its wake. He'd planned things out, he'd *seen* the way things had to go and by God, they did. Every single damned time.

He never told anyone—certainly not his whey-faced idiot wife who was a mistake he was going to have to correct very soon. But he knew—*knew*—that he was destined for greatness. He'd known all his life. He'd had a sense of destiny since he'd been a boy and nothing in his life had ever contradicted that.

It was as if he could see more, see better than others. Perceive the movements of destiny and move in the direction of history rather than crosscurrent to it, as so many did. Destiny was like a raging river that trammeled most people, dragging them under. But not him. He rode the crest, always had, always would.

He could see his destiny, feel it, taste it, even smell it. It smelled of lemon polish and expensive cologne and brand-new cashmere and crisp hundred-dollar bills.

It wasn't just the money, though, it was the power. Power should be in the hands of men like him. Men who bestrode the world, men who understood its ways, men who saw the future and made it happen.

First the Senate, sponsoring a few big bills, known for being a man who got along but also known as a man who could make things happen. He was an expert on foreign affairs. He had the CIA and NSA and the top elements of Homeland Security behind him. He had a shitload of money behind him, a pipeline of money pumping from Africa straight to him.

He'd make a perfect vice presidential candidate for 2016. And while he was vice president, well . . . accidents could happen.

Because the world was a terrible, treacherous place. No one knew that better than him. No one knew what hidden dangers there were. No one knew better than him how utterly ignorant and clueless the current class of leaders was. Three times in the past year, disaster had been averted thanks only to some behind-the-scenes maneuvering by the CIA. The chairman of the Senate Foreign Relations Committee had nearly created an international incident last year, endangering American interests abroad, and he'd done so out of sheer, bone-deep ignorance.

The chairman had deserved the heart attack he'd been given and America had dodged a bullet.

It was time for the pros to take charge and he was ready and able. There were a lot of men in the top echelons of spookdom who knew what he knew—America was teetering on the edge of the abyss. One tiny push and she'd go over. America needed him and by God, he was ready.

The second half of the campaign was in the wings, waiting. And here money really smoothed the way. Bloggers earned very little and were very susceptible to . . . let's call them inducements. Those who wouldn't accept payment outright were more than happy to accept advertising money or perks that wouldn't go on the books. Club memberships, plane tickets, skyboxes. A lot of bloggers were for sale, and cheaply, too.

The drums would start beating very soon. Today, in fact. A couple of political commentators would all make the point that there was a stalwart, patriotic and scandal-free American waiting in the wings, ready to take over from randy, depraved Neff.

That, too, would go viral fast. In a week, it would be an unstoppable tide, the skids greased with money. The bloggers and then the journalists would find a lot of consent in the upper echelons of power. The "unnamed sources"— basically, a handful of men—would echo the drumbeat, because they knew that he was one of them.

Neff had been an asshole. A mildly useful idiot. He, on the other hand, was one of them and he'd be quietly welcomed into their ranks.

And he'd have huge support from them in his presidential run.

He hummed happily as he cruised the internet, watching the blogs popping up, Senator Neff's face appearing in a little thumbnail photo at the top. The thumbnail was a studio portrait, Senator Neff beaming like the idiot he was.

Soon everyone would be baying for his blood. Assassination by blog.

The world changed, and he changed with it. He was riding the crest of the wave, moving as one with the tide of history. Nothing could stop him now.

NINETEEN

LAKA

BACK at the hotel, Claire attacked the computer the way you attack an enemy fortress.

Dan sat quietly by her side. He was good with computers but Claire was in another league entirely. She seemed to have a sixth sense for intel, how to dig for it, how to put it together.

That was fine. Dan was the muscle here and he was good with it. No one was going to touch Claire while she did her thing. Or even afterward.

She was scrolling through websites and files at an astonishing pace. If it had been any other woman, he'd have said she wasn't reading, only skimming. But he was sure she was reading and absorbing. DIA analysts had to absorb tons of intel.

Claire sat back. "Okay, this is what our boy's been doing this past year. He quit the CIA, which surprised me because the one thing I know about Bowen—besides the fact that he's a jerk—is that he's also ambitious as hell. But I've got about ten interviews with him to the effect that he felt the bombing was a 'wake-up call' for the West to do better and so he quit to dedicate himself to improving conditions in Africa."

"Which is total bullshit," Dan said.

"Of course." Claire raised her eyebrows. "However, the fact of the matter is that he quit a very promising career that might have led him all the way to the top echelons of the CIA to become the manager of the New Day Foundation. That's historic fact."

"Are they secretly funneling in drugs? Arms?"

"You'd think so, wouldn't you? That would make some sort of sense here." Claire drummed her fingers on the table next to the mouse. "But, alas, apparently not. The Foundation looks utterly legit. Last year it delivered something like a hundred million dollars of medicine into Makongo and throughout sub-Saharan Africa. That's a lot of money. Bowen would doubtless want to put his hands on some of it, but how?"

"Maybe the Foundation should be audited? Figure out if some of that money is making its way into Bowen's pants pocket?"

"It *was* audited." Claire brought up a spreadsheet that hurt Dan's head just to look at it. "By one of the top six auditing companies in the world. All aboveboard. No one seems to be siphoning off funds. And so Bowen sprouts a halo."

"That doesn't sound like him."

"No, it doesn't." She curved her fingers over the keyboard again. "So, Bowen—what else have you been up to, eh?" News aggregate sites flew by. "Well . . . there's sort of a pattern here. He's set up shop in Virginia and it looks like he's joined a bunch of power clubs and is edging his way toward politics. Maybe 'sidling' would be a better term. But he's definitely got ambitions there and—whoa."

Dan had been carefully checking the street outside but turned his head at her tone. "What?"

"Wow. It looks like a real shitstorm is about ready to hit the honorable senator from Virginia."

"That idiot Neff?"

She peered at the screen. "Yes. Jeffrey Neff. Senior senator from Old Dominion, been senator since Reconstruction. At first it was a corruption scandal. But now it looks like a big sex scandal is hitting. The blogosphere is going wild."

Dan was apolitical. Fuck 'em all, was his opinion. He shrugged. "So?"

"Well . . . I don't know. It's just sort of interesting, what he's done. Bowen set up headquarters in Richmond, he's made a name for himself in philanthropy, he's sort of dipping his toe into politics and then—pow! It looks like maybe a senate seat is coming up for grabs and he just might be interested. There's this organization called Concerned Citizens for Democracy and they're putting forward Bowen's name. I'm not too sure how that fits in with Makongo, though." She quivered with frustration in her seat and if Dan weren't worried about security, he'd have jumped her bones right there.

Jesus, what man could resist her? She was in profile and with her pale skin and long, slender neck she looked like something that belonged on a cameo. But then she turned her head and flashed those silvery blue eyes at him, that stunning beauty almost drowned in the fierce intelligence and—right now—fierce frustration on her face and she nearly brought him to his knees.

She was everything he could ever want in a woman, and much, much more than he ever thought he could have. She had a beauty that was off the charts, was amazingly intelligent, took no nonsense but wasn't hard or calculating. A woman in a million, classy and gorgeous and smart as a whip.

His woman.

Not bad for a jarhead who'd started out life with absolutely nothing and a whole world just standing back, tapping its feet, waiting for him to fall on his face. God knows his father had. His father, high, drunk or sober, had told him over and over again what a fuckup he was and that he would never amount to anything.

Son of a bitch had been wrong. Dan had done very well in the Marines, was doing really well as the head of his own company and now, by God, he had the most desirable woman in the world, right here, not a few feet from him.

It just didn't get any better.

He'd had to work his butt off in the Marines and in his company, but Claire? She'd been a gift from the gods. Everyone said you had to "work" at relationships and for all he knew, that was true. What the fuck did he know? He hadn't grown up seeing any relationships that weren't crazy dysfunctional and he hadn't had any of his own.

But being with Claire . . . man, it was as easy as drinking water. Whatever she wanted, it felt like the most natural thing in the world to get it for her, or do his damnedest trying. All that romantic shit he'd never been good at? With her, it just came naturally. He wanted to take her arm when they were out walking. Particularly when she'd been a little unsteady on her feet. Not just to help her, but to touch her, because touching her was like plugging into something magnificent, something he didn't even know existed up until now.

This past year he'd fed his obsession with the little sensory input he'd had at the embassy. The feel of her long French braid running through his hands like silk, the smell of her, fresh and clean even in the sweat-soaked Post One, where he'd smelled like a goat, the taste of her mouth, minty and enticing, a little honey trap.

It had been intel to plug into his Claire jones but it hadn't been much to go on. Man, now he had the whole deal.

Now he knew how delicate she felt in his arms lying down, chest to breasts, sex to sex. The taste of that soft spot of skin behind her ear. The way she jumped when he nipped along her jaw.

And oh, God, how her nipples tasted, like salty cherries, and how she clenched tightly around him as she came . . .

He rested his forehead against the window frame and breathed out slowly.

Keep your head in the game, he told himself sternly. A

woodie in the middle of the day, in an African city where enemies could be around the next corner, while Claire was as focused as a laser beam on her computer screen and the things it was telling her—well, it was a bad idea.

But fuck, there it was. And a huge distraction.

This had never happened to him before, ever. Dan had decided at seventeen that he was heading for either an early grave or ten to twenty hard time, and so he'd thrown himself at the Corps. The Corps had taken over. If he thought he'd been tough before, he didn't have a clue as to what toughness was.

The Corps had taken him apart and put him back together again, cell by cell, muscle by muscle, sinew by sinew. Even his thoughts had changed.

Dan had learned how to single-mindedly focus on a mission with almost frightening ferocity, until it became second nature. Focusing had never been a problem since his seventeenth year, when he'd decided to save his own life.

Focus was a problem now and it scared the shit out of him.

They didn't know who was after them—after *Claire*. It could be one man, it could be two, it could be a dozen. He or they had enormous resources and, worst case scenario, they weren't going to quit, ever.

All those shitheads had to do was be lucky once and Claire's life would be snuffed out like a candle. Gone in a flash. Man, he'd seen plenty of young lives snuffed out. One fucking bullet. That's all it took. He knew what her head would look like with a bullet through it. How long it would take her to die, gut-shot. Maybe they had orders to kidnap her, torture her for whatever it was they thought was in that beautiful head of hers.

Dan had seen men who'd been tortured for what was in their heads. Oh, yeah. They went crazy long before their bodies died.

He clutched the wooden frame of the window so hard it was a miracle he didn't dig holes into it.

The only thing that stood between those nightmare scenarios of a dead or dying or tortured Claire was him. He'd saved her twice because he was good with weapons, could combat drive and had been trained to think like a soldier, tactically.

She was smart as a whip, no question. Way smarter than he was. But he'd felt every inch of her body and she was no warrior, had no way to defend herself. She was small and soft and tender and oh, Christ, just the idea of someone hurting her . . .

He swallowed hard against the ball of bile that was rising in his throat.

This wasn't doing her any good. It did do him some good, though, since his hard-on went down. Nothing like picturing the woman you wanted to have sex with dead or dying to get it down and keep it down.

"Ah!"

Dan turned his head at the soft exclamation, glad to get away from the images of a dead or hurt Claire in his head. "What?"

"One of the big recipients of New Day Foundation's donations is the Hôpital Générale de la Charité."

Dan came away from the window to look over her shoulder. She was checking the website of a hospital. He couldn't make out much because it was in French. "So?"

Claire clicked and pulled up another page, of names this time. She pointed at a name halfway down, with an office phone number. Dr. Aba Diur.

Dan frowned. "Marie's sister?"

Claire was punching out a long number on her satphone. "Oh yeah. She's an oncologist and as luck would have it, she's also second in command at the hospital. If anyone knows anything about what's going on, it's her. She's mad at me for getting Marie killed, but she'll talk to me." Her mouth firmed. "She has to. *Allo?* Aba? Claire, Claire Day *ici.*"

The rest of the conversation was in French. Dan couldn't follow the words but he could follow the gist. This Aba didn't want to talk to Claire, that was clear, but whatever Claire was saying was convincing her.

Atta girl.

Claire closed the connection, punched her fist in the air with a sharply hissed *Yes!* and grabbed her bag. "Let's go, Dan."

Okay. He'd follow her into hell itself, let alone to some hospital. He checked his weapon for perhaps the hundredth time, made sure he had spare mags with him and with a last, longing look at the rifle he had to leave behind, he followed Claire out the door.

WENTY

RICHMOND, VIRGINIA

THE dialog box in the corner of his screen popped up. Wizard. What the hell did he want?

Hey man. U there?

Yes

Found her. Took a while. Thought she'd just gone up in smoke, possibly offed. But no. CD made it out of the country. Flew from Montreal to Paris, Air France flight AF467 on Dec 1. Then Paris to Lungi, Pan African Airways flight number PA529 December 2. Lost track of her there, people there don't keep computer records, WTF do they do? Scratch names on bark? Anyway, she paid cash and flew alone, both flights. No jarhead.

That's worth another 100K. Waiting . . .

The cursor pulsed, patiently.
"Goddammit!" The glass of whiskey he'd been happily

sipping exploded against the wall, the amber liquid running like teardrops to the floor. The smell of whiskey blossomed in the room, together with the smell of his own sweat pouring out, instantaneous, uncontrollable.

His entire body went into overdrive. He'd been tasting success, a taste as fine as any caviar or champagne. Refined and heady. And now he had the taste of ashes in his mouth.

The bitch should have died back in Laka! He'd had no fucking idea she was out there in the compound, none, otherwise he'd have had her shot through the head just like that other bitch, Diur.

He was just too good, that was it. When he'd heard, months later, that Claire Day had been found badly wounded in the embassy compound, he'd contemplated sending one of his men down. Easiest thing in the world to slip into a hospital room dressed in scrubs and inject 20 ccs of air or press the carotid arteries gently enough to stop blood flow without leaving a mark.

Christ, he'd been tempted.

But his man said she was in a coma, and she was half crazy when she came out of it. Couldn't even walk for fuck's sake. So he'd weighed the slight risk of sending a man down against the almost zero risk Claire Day represented and had made a strategic decision.

The wrong one.

Fuck!

There was no doubt whatsoever why Claire had flown to Lungi. She was making her way to Laka. He checked his watch. She was there now, had been for almost a day. What was she doing? Who was she seeing? Had she gone to the embassy?

He was tempted to give Mbutu a call and have some of his men take care of this. But Mbutu's men were not efficient. They were clumsy, their violence a club, not a scalpel. There could be a real stink if a US citizen showed up dead in Makongo, bludgeoned to death by the trademark beating of Mbutu's goons.

At least she didn't have the fucking jarhead with her. He'd probably dumped her. Smart man. Claire Day was trouble on a stick, not worth it, no matter how beautiful she was.

The jarhead had fucked her and left her. Good for him.

He sat in his chair, gently swiveling back and forth, thinking it through. Finally he leaned forward to his computer, sent Wizard another two hundred thousand dollars and typed him a message, encrypted it and sent it.

Ck yr account. Ck list of guests Etoile Africaine, hotel in Laka, for name Claire Day.

This required immediate action.

He picked up his phone and punched the button that would connect him with his secretary.

"Sir?"

"Have the Lear brought around. I want to fly to Laka. Now."

LAKA

"Claire."

Oh God. This was going to be bad.

Dr. Aba Gawey née Diur had come out from the bowels of the hospital into the lobby and walked briskly across the great marble expanse to stand in front of her. She crossed her arms, standing erect, torso slightly back.

Her body language couldn't be clearer. She wasn't happy to see Claire and couldn't wait to get rid of her.

And yet Claire eyed her hungrily. She was still the beautiful Aba she remembered and had had so many happy meals with at the Diur household. She and Marie had been invited several times to eat with Aba and her husband. The husband who was now dead.

Claire had liked Aba a lot. She'd loved Marie, but she'd felt Aba was her friend, too.

It was so hard to stand here, wanting to throw her arms around the friend she hadn't seen in a year, only to have Aba show such steely resistance, almost repugnance.

This was going to be so hard.

"Aba." Claire sketched a smile and touched Dan's arm. "This is former Gunnery Sergeant Daniel Weston, the detachment commander at the embassy at the time of the bombing. He's accompanied me here. It's really good to see you. You're looking good."

It was true, though it was as impossible for Aba as it had been for Marie to look bad. The last year had taken its toll on Aba, though. There were lines bracketing her beautiful mouth and her deep brown eyes, always so expressive, were now so cold and bloodshot.

But she was still as erect as an arrow, still impressive in her hospital whites, still filled with the light of intelligence.

Aba didn't follow Claire's gentle opening. "*Maman* told me you'd be coming." Her eyes flicked to Dan, standing straight and impassive by Claire's side. "Together with your friend."

Claire threaded her arm through Dan's. He had picked up on Aba's hostility and was stiff and disapproving. He clearly didn't like Aba's attitude to Claire. Surreptitiously, Claire patted his hand.

It's okay.

It wasn't, really. This past year had taken so much away from Claire, including, apparently, Aba's friendship. Tight bands of emotion wrapped around her chest.

"What are you doing here in Laka?" Aba checked her wristwatch, which she wore with the dial on the inside of her wrist. The message was clear. *What are you doing wasting my time?*

"Aba—" Claire began, then looked around at the busy lobby. It was also the A & E entrance, and it was filled with men and women patiently waiting to be seen by a doctor.

Everyone was talking at once. A number of men were sitting on the floor playing what looked like a variation on jacks, only with bones. It was more like a village fair than a waiting room. Several babies were wailing and every couple of minutes the loudspeakers came on to make service announcements. The noise level was as loud as a rock concert.

"Can we go somewhere to talk?"

Aba's beautiful mouth tightened. She was clearly struggling with "no."

"Please?" Claire asked quietly.

The doctor turned on her heel and Claire followed her, Dan right behind them. Dan was in warrior mode. Unsmiling, grim, alert.

The hospital was a shocker. Claire had, thank God, never had occasion to enter the old Charité hospital but the embassy had called it the Roach Motel—you checked in but you never checked out. It had been a dank, unwelcoming building along the banks of the Makongo River and Claire had often thought, driving by it, that Dante's warning "Abandon Hope All Ye Who Enter Here" should have been chiseled on the stone portico.

The old building had been torn down and in its place was this one—light, airy, scrupulously clean, gleaming even.

The staff, doctors and nurses, bustled by just like in any urban hospital, looking busy and competent.

Aba led them down several corridors and finally opened a lacquered white door with a key. Inside was a modern office, neat and tidy. One wall was filled with medical textbooks, another with Aba's various diplomas and certificates.

And on another wall . . .

Claire walked over, mesmerized. It was a wall of framed photographs, mostly of Aba—in lycée, in medical school, graduating, with a white coat and stethoscope in a small clinic in the jungle, arms over the shoulders of her colleagues.

And then Aba with her parents, with her husband and . . . oh God. Claire's heart gave a huge thump in her chest. She touched the largest photograph of Marie. It must have been taken several years ago; her hair had been long then. Claire traced the outlines of Marie's face and it was as if she had somehow sprung back to life and was right here in the room with them.

Marie was smiling in the photograph and that was as it

should be because Marie was always smiling. It was her default expression. Sometimes the smile was ironic because she'd been an intelligent woman and there was much in life that didn't bear thinking of. She'd been so funny, so incredibly cutting and smart in her take on things, at times devastatingly witty. Claire remembered her imitations of Crock-of-Shit and Danielle Crocker that had had her in stitches. And God, when she walked like Bowen, with that stiff, pompous gait of his, Claire had laughed until she was gasping.

Marie. The best friend she'd ever had. Devastatingly funny. Fiercely loyal. Always there.

"Not a day goes by that I don't think of her," Claire whispered. "I miss her . . . so . . . *much*."

A long, slender black hand rested on her shoulder and Claire turned into Aba's arms, clutching her desperately. They were both crying and that felt so right because Marie not being in the world left this aching black hole that nothing could ever fill.

They cried their loss and their sorrow and their outrage, until no tears were left and Claire's arms dropped from Aba's waist.

A strong male fist clutching a bloom of tissues appeared and they both accepted them gratefully.

Claire glanced at Dan, wavering through the prism of her tears as if he were a mirage in a hot desert. For a moment, she'd completely forgotten about him. What did he think of this, two women weeping their hearts out?

But he didn't look embarrassed or disdainful or exasperated. He simply stood, handing out tissues to the two women, face sober and sad.

He was a soldier. He understood loss.

Something in Aba had broken, certainly her anger at Claire. Before, anger had swirled in the room, so intense Claire thought she could see it. Now there was an ease, an acknowledgment of their shared loss.

"Sit down." Aba pulled two chairs out in front of her desk and sat behind it in a swivel chair. She looked at them both once they'd been seated. "Would you like some coffee?"

"No, thank you." Claire leaned forward, wanting to dive in right away and talk about Marie's actions that day. But there had been a tentative peace made with Aba and she didn't want to break it. So she looked around and sketched a smile. "La Charité has certainly changed in this past year. It seems completely new."

Something flickered in Aba's face, gone before Claire could decipher it. "Yes, it is completely new. The old building was razed to the ground a month after the bombing and this new building was erected in record time. We have the New Day Foundation to thank for it. Another hospital is being built two hundred miles upriver where it will provide health care to over a million people who have no health care at all at the moment."

Claire nodded. "So . . . maybe something good came of that day?"

Again, that look. A flash, then gone. Anger. No, rage.

"Are you writing an article?" Aba asked.

"Good God, no!"

"Then what are you doing here?"

Good question. Claire was finding it a hard one to answer. Maybe it was the crying jag, maybe the long trip was finally catching up with her. All of a sudden she was seized with a deep weariness. The words simply wouldn't come.

Dan took over, leaning forward a little, looking Aba straight in the eye. "Claire doesn't remember anything about that day. She suffers from amnesia, which is not surprising given the level of damage she sustained. But I was there and I remember. The two of us were the only ones in the embassy on the twenty-fifth. We were in Post One, which is a secure area behind bulletproof glass, while the Red Army flooded the streets." He held his hand up when Aba opened her mouth. "Now, your mother told us that in her belief, it wasn't the Red Army at all that invaded Laka. Is that correct, in your opinion?"

Aba nodded. "Absolutely. Marie and I recognized a number of officers of Mbutu's army, all dressed up in red rags. We didn't understand what was going on, but one thing was clear. The Red Army wasn't involved. I'm not saying they aren't crazy, because they are. But my information from colleagues working in the bush was that they were at least five hundred miles away, intent on controlling the diamond mines in the hinterland, and certainly weren't planning on taking over the central government. They simply didn't have the strength."

"And why do you think Mbutu's men pretended to be members of the Red Army?"

Aba gave a cynical smile. "I went to a Catholic school, Gunnery Sergeant."

"Dan will do, doctor."

"Dan." She bowed her head, eyes never leaving his. "Well, Dan, in this Catholic school we were taught Latin and Roman history. The Latins had a saying when something unusual happened and no one could figure out why. *Cui bono?* Who gains? Who benefits? And, well, who gained in the end from the bombing?"

"Mbutu," Dan answered. "Mbutu gained. The US poured money into Makongo, buckets of it. The Red Army was destroyed. The central government became the new flavor of the month." He waved his hand around the new hospital room. "New hospitals, new schools."

There it was again. That cloud crossing Aba's face.

"Aba," Claire said, reaching across the desk to hold her hand. "What did Marie tell you? Why did she go back to the embassy for me?"

Aba looked away, but her hand tightened on Claire's. "She'd understood, too, that it wasn't the Red Army. And she'd seen something. Someone. Someone she didn't trust. It wasn't clear to me why she felt it was important but for her you were in terrible danger. She went back for you." Aba swiveled her head back to Claire. "She loved you," Aba said simply. "She went back to save you. And she lost her own life."

"Oh, God." Tears swam in Claire's eyes. Her heart was simply breaking. "*Why?* Who did she see?"

Aba shrugged and pulled her hand from Claire's. She stood, the interview at an end. "Now, if you'll excuse me—"

A bolt of electricity ran through Claire. Marie had given her life to make sure Claire lived. And now she had a duty to find out why.

"There's something wrong, isn't there? Here. At the hospital."

Aba's voice dripped sarcasm. "Here? This hospital? So shiny and new? What could be wrong?"

Claire looked at her steadily. "And yet there is."

Aba was still for a long time, then nodded jerkily. Her voice was bitter. "Hard to believe, isn't it? Okay. Let me show you something." She sat back down, reached in a drawer under her desk and brought out two packages. She threw them on the desk.

Claire picked them up and examined them carefully. Inside each package were two blisters with ten capsules each. Twenty capsules. The two packages were identical. Medicine by a famous international pharmaceutical company, but she had no idea what kind of medicine.

"Do you know what that is?" Aba asked.

Claire shook her head.

Aba picked up one. "This is a latest generation antiretroviral drug, to combat AIDS. The very latest drug, proprietary, not generic, and cutting-edge. The very best modern medicine has to offer. Taken properly, it extends the life span of an AIDS sufferer by at least twenty years. Makongo currently has an AIDS epidemic. One in five adults is infected, one in six children. This is literally a miracle drug, which will keep children alive until we finally find a cure. This kind of medicine doesn't come cheap. Look at the price on the box."

Claire turned it around in her hand until she saw the price printed in the back lower left-hand corner. Her eyes widened.

"Indeed," Aba said dryly. "This costs eight hundred euros a box. That's about a thousand dollars. And it's not being doled out sparingly, either. Our pharmacopoeia has plenty and there's a warehouse full of this drug and other very expensive miracle drugs out at the airport, ready to be airlifted into the hinterland. No expense has been spared."

She stopped. There was silence in her study, broken only by a distant loudspeaker calling for a doctor to come to the emergency ward.

Aba picked up the other box of medicine between her thumb and forefinger and wagged it. "And this?" She threw it back down on the desk. "This is about a dollar's worth of paper and talcum powder pressed into capsules and put into blisters." She laid them side by side on the desktop and looked at Claire and Dan.

"So. Which is which?"

"I can't tell," Claire whispered.

"Neither can I," Aba said. "And I live with that, daily. I've had ten boxes of this drug, ten boxes of our most powerful antibiotics and ten doses of chemotherapy secretly tested in a lab in Paris. I paid for it myself. About two-thirds are fakes. And so every time I have a child dying of cancer or a mother dying of AIDS and I administer medicine to them, I'm either saving their lives or condemning them to death, and I don't know which." She slapped the desktop with her open hand, her voice suddenly harsh. *"I don't know which!"*

"Can you have them all tested?" Dan asked.

She shook her head angrily. "Absolutely not. It's out of the question. The tests cost about a thousand dollars. I paid for them myself because I couldn't figure out what was going on. I was getting incredibly erratic results from the drugs. Testing all our medicine would cost millions of dollars. And if I were crazy enough to come out into the open about this, you can rest assured that only the real drugs would be tested. I would immediately lose my job and I would be arrested for slander. Not to mention earning the enmity of my countrymen. Doubting the New Day

Foundation, which gave us all this." She waved her hand at her modern office, encompassing the efficient hospital outside. "It doesn't bear thinking about. I would be put in an insane asylum. Or, considering the way Mbutu is going, taken out to the river and shot, my body left for the crocodiles." Her lips pressed together and a lone tear ran down an ebony cheekbone. "My husband was almost ready to write an article about it when he disappeared. They found his body ten days later. I identified it only by his wedding band."

"These are perfectly identical." Claire held the two packages side by side and could detect no difference at all, not even a minute one.

"Yes, they are. The Foundation shipped about a hundred million dollars' worth of medicine last year. If two-thirds are fakes, that's almost seventy million dollars in profit. Tax free. I'm sure some of it goes to Mbutu, but you can bet a good chunk would go to the man who is the great benefactor of Makongo." She leaned forward to Claire and Dan. "To the man Marie went back to the embassy to warn you about. And the man who probably killed her."

"Bowen McKenzie," Claire breathed and Aba nodded grimly.

TWENTY-ONE

IT was time to tell him.

"Marie was killed," Claire said quietly as they walked out of the hospital. "They never even found her body, but she was killed before she was blown up."

Dan checked their surroundings, then honed in on her face. "How do you know that, honey?"

She took a deep breath and watched his eyes. "When I came out of the coma, I couldn't move very well. It took me another month to sit up and many more weeks to start walking down the hospital corridor. And at first I was really confused. I had trouble"—here she mimicked Dr. Fallows, her neurologist—" 'orienting myself in space and time.' I'd lose track of the time completely. Sometimes I forgot whether it was day or night. And I forgot I was in the hospital, I thought I was back in Laka. A few times I thought I was in Durban and a couple of times I thought I was a student again, in Georgetown." She huffed out a breath. "Did any of that happen to you?"

"No," he answered. "But I didn't sustain any head injuries at all. I lost my spleen and my knee and blew an eardrum, that's it. But I've seen plenty of cases of head injuries and PTSD and they're not fun."

"No, they're not," she agreed. She looked down at the ground, at the weeds growing out of a crack in the pavement and tried to flatten them with her toe.

"Claire?"

She drew in a deep breath, blew it back out again in a controlled stream.

"I had nightmares. Like the one you saw. Every night. Sometimes several times a night. It got so bad I was terrified to fall asleep. I think I was half crazy for a while there. The only thing that would work was sedation so strong I lost my REM sleep and that was even worse."

"Jesus," Dan breathed. "That must have been hell."

She nodded jerkily. "Oh yeah." Hell was almost a mild term for it. "And though I didn't remember during the day what had happened, I think there was information in my subconscious that just kept geysering up, horribly. It's as if the images simply wouldn't let me alone. The nightmares varied but a lot was the same. In the most frequent one, I am crouching in some bushes and things are going on. Things I don't understand. There are flashlights, men—Africans—moving around, shifting things. And then a big truck drives out and another big truck, looking exactly the same, drives in. And then—" Her throat went dry and she licked her lips. "And then a woman beckons to me. And in doing that, she has to stand up a little and a man sees her. A white man. And this is when it gets truly horrible. The sky is always red and the men are more devils than men. Red-skinned, scampering, like some scene out of Hieronymus Bosch. And the white man is the head devil. I can't see his face, but somehow I know him. I know I know him but I don't know how. He points to the woman and turns to one of the other devils, who grins and brings a rifle to his shoulder and fires. There's like this red mist around the woman's head and she crumbles. Then the white man turns to me and opens his mouth. It's bloodred inside and he cocks his finger at me and . . . I wake up." She couldn't suppress a shudder and Dan put his arm around her shoulders. "That's the one I had nightly, for months."

That terrible chill had come over her again, though the temperature was in the mid-eighties, hot and humid. The cold penetrated to her core

"There was a shrink in the neurology ward. We had a lot of sessions, while he was assessing my neurological responses. He'd listen to me, then ask me totally unrelated questions. I told him about the dream and that I had it over and over again. That had never happened to me before, either with dreams or nightmares, not that I'd had that many nightmares before the bombing. The doctor said it was an anxiety dream and a guilt dream. I felt guilty that I had survived and Marie hadn't. And that I was anxious that I was never going to recover fully. The white man represented weakness, loss." She shook her head. "He never really convinced me, but in those days, I didn't have the energy to argue."

Claire looked at Dan. His face was tight, eyes hard.

"Dan, I think I witnessed a murder," she whispered. "I think that's what it's about."

His jaw muscles clenched. "I think you did, too. And maybe someone isn't too hot on you getting your memory back. Where are your medical records?"

"My what?"

"Your medical records. Do you know what they say?"

"I guess. Traumatic amnesia, functional loss, hallucinations. Or at least the Latinate terms for those. I hacked into my records one afternoon. It wasn't in any way hard to do. There were reams of documents and a lot of assessments but the bottom line was that I was crazy from the trauma. That scared me. And I think I understood that day that I was never going to get my job back. DIA could never afford to have an analyst who'd had that kind of psych evaluation."

Dan looked around sharply at the sound of a car coming up behind them. It was a taxi, one of the few cruising the streets. He hailed it, bundled her inside and gave the name of the hotel.

In the backseat, he rested his arm along the back of the seat and brought his mouth to her ear.

"I think those records saved your life. I think you saw that mysterious white man kill your friend and if he had had any inkling that you were a witness he'd have had you killed down in Florida. And you would never have seen it coming."

God no, she'd never have seen it coming. She'd barely escaped with Dan by her side. For most of this spring and summer, she'd have been as vulnerable as a newborn kitten.

It had to be said. Horrible as it was to think, it had to be said.

"It all boils down to Bowen, doesn't it?" she said slowly. "My troubles started when I did a search for his name. And he was in Laka that day, instead of in Algiers. And the deputy prime minister isn't around anymore to give him an alibi." She swallowed against a dry throat. "If Aba is right, the Red Army didn't invade that day. And if my dreams are right, then Bowen McKenzie is—"

"A murderer," Dan said harshly. "And guilty of high treason."

ATLANTIC OCEAN
FIFTY MILES BEYOND US TERRITORIAL WATERS

The scandal was coming to a peak, some blogs registering ten million hits a day. He read them on his laptop as the Lear arrowed its way east.

All in all, Bowen thought, it was a good thing that he wasn't immediately available for comment. He checked his email. Ah, yes. Hundreds of messages, requests for callbacks.

Well, he was heading for Africa, doing God's work, wasn't he? He would be back on US soil just as the frenzy reached its apogee, having overseen the distribution of life-saving drugs and having gotten rid of that bitch Claire Day, who was a danger at exactly the wrong moment.

He relaxed in the soft, buttery ergonomic chair in the luxurious aft section of the cabin and poured himself a celebratory finger of cognac. Hennessy, 1974, an excellent year. By the time the plane landed in Laka, it would have worked its way through his system and out again. He could afford it.

He pressed a button. "Heston."

A moment later, the door at the end of the cabin opened. The back of the plane was outfitted with ten regular coach seats and a roomy area for weaponry.

Heston stood at attention. "Sir."

Bowen looked up lazily at his soldier. His war-dog. Who lately had not been a good dog at all. He got one more chance. If he fucked this up, he'd have to go.

The next stage of his life was going to be high-stakes, with no margin for error. He couldn't afford having a fuckup in his life.

"Men all squared away, Heston?"

They were traveling with three other soldiers, Heston's men. Heston hadn't wanted any more, because in the new Makongo, four white men traveling in a group already attracted enough attention. Heston had insisted on the men, though. Which was absurd. Four trained soldiers against an untrained woman. Overkill.

So if anything went wrong this time, he'd shoot Heston himself.

He speared Heston with a hard look. "This time we do it right. As soon as we find her, I want a snatch and grab, I need to know what she's got. We'll pump her for any information she might have. See if she's passed anything on. I don't care if you get the info the hard way. She's costing me time and money so she has to pay before we get rid of her." He gave a wintry smile. "She's a looker. You'll like that part, won't you, Heston?"

"Yessir." Heston tried to keep a soldierly demeanor, but his cheekbones turned red. This was what turned Heston on. Violence made him horny and it was the reason Heston had been kicked out of the army on a dishonorable discharge. One rape charge too many.

It was massively stupid. Heston had sacrificed a military career because he couldn't keep it in his pants.

Once again, he questioned his reliance on Heston, who was proving to be an inadequate and inefficient tool.

Sooner or later dull tools got discarded.

LAKA
DECEMBER 3

"Fuck no, no fucking way!" The next day, Dan stood in the hotel room, clenching his jaws against saying anything else, because what he wanted to do was order Claire to stay far away from this. The thing was, though, she didn't take orders well.

He felt the hot flush of frustration rise up through his body. He was normally like ice when planning an op, but this one . . .

Jesus.

In frustration he thrust his hands in his hair and pulled.

Last night he'd somehow sensed that this was coming. He'd made love for hours to Claire, as if joining his body to hers could create a magical aura of protection, as if the more time he spent inside her, the safer she'd be. If he could have, he'd have tucked her right into his own body and kept her there.

He'd felt danger approaching and he'd been right. Claire had just proposed setting herself up as bait.

"Yes, way," Claire said calmly. She turned in her chair. "Jesse, you tell him."

Dan rounded on Jesse, willing him to be the rational one here and tell Claire it was a crazy plan. Jesse scratched his head because he didn't have enough hair to pull and sighed.

"Well, I've looked at it upside down and right-side up, Dan. It makes a lot of sense. Right guys?"

Frank Rizzo and Dave Lee looked up from checking their weapons and nodded. But they wouldn't look him in the eyes. They wouldn't look him in the eyes because the whole fucking plan was *insane*.

The Etoile was mostly empty of guests. On the off chance that someone was checking, and somehow knew his fake name, Dan had relocated them to an empty room that he'd slipped fifty bucks to the clerk to keep empty. If the guy at the front desk thought it was strange to pay for a room and then pay to use another room instead, he kept it to himself.

The Makongans thought all white men were crazy anyway.

Jesse, Frank and Dave had arrived last night at nine on the seven p.m. flight, which had only been two hours late. Dan didn't know Frank and Dave well but he knew *of* them and knew they were good men to have at your back. Right now, together with Jesse, they were his absolute new best friends, because they'd come to protect Claire.

And now Claire was planning on throwing herself straight into the line of fire.

No. No way.

She wasn't trying to wheedle, either. That was what had Dan so scared. She wasn't asking permission or sounding him out. She was planning this, full speed ahead.

Five minutes after arriving, Frank and Dave had already fallen half in love with her, so there was no use turning to them. He'd hoped Jesse would at least see his point of view, but no. He was just as infatuated as the other two.

All three were sitting on the edge of the bed like idiots, watching her pace back and forth, eyes glued to her, their heads swiveling as if at some championship tennis match.

"We don't have proof, that's the thing," Claire said, her beautiful face scrunched in ferocious concentration. "The best thing—the *only* thing—we can do is trick out a confession. And the only way Bowen would do that is if he is convinced I'm alone. I know him, he'd love for a chance to gloat, to show me how smart he is."

"And he'll do it knowing he's going to have you killed!" Dan was gritting his teeth so hard the grinding sound filled the room. "Of course he'll gloat. Because you'll never live to tell anyone and he knows that."

Claire turned to him, looking surprised. She waved at her little fan club sitting on the edge of the bed. "Well, what do I have you guys for? You're there as backup. Bowen will think I'm alone and he'll have his guard down. It's a classic ambush."

Dan tried to sound reasonable even though his head was ready to explode. "We're fast and we're good, honey. But what if he comes armed? We're not Superman. We can't outrun a bullet."

She was shaking her head before he finished. "No. The one thing about Bowen everyone knows is that he was all intel, he wasn't an operative at all. I know for a fact he doesn't know how to use a gun. He used to boast about it, and the security types used to snigger behind his back. He's not going to be carrying a gun, trust me."

"He'll have backup," Dan warned.

"Yes, he will. And that's where you come in. I expect you four to neutralize the backup and be ready. Now—I need to check equipment. I know you guys have checked your weapons. Jesse—did you bring what I asked?"

"Oh yeah." Jesse stood up and pulled a tiny piece of plastic from his jeans pocket. It was shaped like a comma and he fit it behind Claire's ear. When he pulled a lock of hair over her ear it was invisible. "Perfect. A bud is always visible but this conducts through bone. No one could possibly know it's there. One of my buddies in the detachment command is a nut for this stuff. He's going to want it back."

Dan ground his teeth even harder. It was going to be hard to give the jarhead back his earpiece if a sniper put a round through Claire's head. It would be all covered with blood.

He opened his mouth to say something when Claire held up a hand.

"Let's test this. Talk to me."

Jesse went into the bathroom. Dan could barely hear a low male murmur.

When Jesse came out, Claire's eyes were shining. "Wow. It was like you were talking directly into my ear. What about video, now? What did your friend have that we can use?"

Jesse brought out a small, thin panel of plastic with a circle on top. "Top of the line miniaturization," he said, tapping the button. "This turns it on. It's very lightweight. You slide this button through a buttonhole of a shirt. I brought you a size small shirt in case you didn't have one. One of Dan's would never fit you." He held up a plain white cotton shirt that was too big for Claire but not outrageously so. Most people wore loose clothing in the tropical heat. He held the shirt up, with the button threaded through it. Then he placed a small video screen on the table and switched it on. The screen showed Jesse, and Dan behind him wearing a ferocious scowl.

"See how it works?" Jesse said, and the speakers on the video screen repeated *See how it works?*

The sound was excellent, the image was sharp.

"Good to go," Claire murmured.

"Let me talk to Bowen," Dan pleaded. "And you stay out of it." Let Bowen come after *him*, not Claire.

Claire put her hand against his face and smiled at him. "No," she said gently. "It wouldn't work. You know that, Dan. It has to be me and he has to think I'm working alone. That I'm this idiot who will just walk unaware into a trap. He'd never believe you don't have backup and he'd never talk to you." She sighed. "I'm not entirely sure even I can trip him up but I'm the only one who can try."

"Claire—" Dan began in a reasonable tone, though he felt anything but reasonable. He felt like beating his head against the hotel room's stuccoed wall.

"No, Dan. You listen to me." Claire's voice was sharper now. "Did you hear what Aba said? People are dying. Bowen's going to continue these criminal acts unless someone stops him. It has to be done."

"You want to avenge Marie, that's what you want," Dan grumbled.

"Absolutely. That, too. But this is bigger than us. And you know that." She didn't even wait for him to respond, just went to her computer. "Now that that's settled I'm going to send a clear message to Mr. Bowen McKenzie, wherever he is."

She went into Computer Mode, hunched over the keyboard, nose an inch from the monitor, hands flying.

Jesse looked at him. *What's she doing?*

Dan shrugged. How should he know? Claire was a law unto herself.

She was mumbling to herself under her breath. "Come on, Bowen," she whispered, "where are you?"

Jesse, Frank and Dave simply sat on the bed, unmoving, letting Claire do her thing.

Finally, Dan couldn't stand it anymore. He put a hand on her shoulder, controlling the wince at the feel of her fragile bones. Right now, Claire looked capable of taking on the world. She was infused with fury and righteousness, a woman on a mission of revenge.

But she was small and not back to full strength. Dan had seen big strong men, trained to kill, tough as nails, fall. All it took was one bullet. With Claire, it was entirely possible that Bowen could fell her with one strong blow, if it was true he wouldn't draw a weapon.

Dan was terrified of losing her. The line between life and death was so very fine and could be crossed at any moment . . .

"What are you doing, honey?"

Claire blew out a big breath and sat back, frowning.

"Looking for Bowen. I figured he'd have someone tracking me and that they'd have found out by now that I'd flown to Laka. I thought Bowen would be the kind of man to come after me, damn it. But there are no reservations from the continental United States in the name of Bowen McKenzie. His face has been plastered all over the newspapers lately. He wouldn't dare fly under an assumed name. But I simply can't find . . ."

She stopped suddenly.

"What? What, honey?"

But she was lost to him again, back communing with the computer. Another five minutes went by. The only sound in the hotel room was the clacking of the keyboard at twice the speed he'd ever heard.

Claire smiled and narrowed her eyes. "Gotcha," she said softly. "Look."

She angled the netbook so he could see the monitor better. A flight manifest.

"He's flying on a private plane, the Foundation corporate jet. The pilot filed a flight plan to Laka. And he's flying with four men." Dan's hand tightened on her shoulder. "We've got him now, oh yeah."

Claire pounded the keyboard for another minute. "The plane is scheduled to land in Laka at two thirty p.m. this afternoon. I need to send him a message. I'll text him."

"You have his cell phone number?" Dan asked, startled.

She smiled again and for a moment looked positively wicked. "Darling Dan, the day I can't find a cell phone number is the day I hang up my computer."

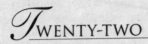WENTY-TWO

OVER THE AZORES
ATLANTIC OCEAN

HE tried to relax during the flight. It made him feel a little better to think about the photos of Neff bouncing around the internet.

He controlled his breathing, smoothed out his thoughts.

Claire Day could do some mischief, but he was tracking her down now and she'd be neutralized soon.

She was isolated, sick, a little crazy. Even if she contacted people with some wild story, who was going to believe her? She had no official standing at all, and even a cursory check of her medical records would show how unreliable she was. When she was dead, things would return to normal. No one would even remember her name.

It was all okay, all on track, all as it should be. This was a glitch, nothing more.

Wizard's signal sounded.

No trace of Day at hotel but computer records not updated since October 14. Who r these people? How do they run a business?

Shit! She might or might not be in Laka. For a second, he was tempted to just forget about it, tell the pilot to turn around. Who knew what Claire thought she was doing? Maybe she was just spinning her wheels. Maybe she wasn't even in Laka at all, but had stayed in Freetown.

Should he be leaving the country right now to head her off? Would it be wise? The next few days were going to be really interesting as Neff clung uselessly to power while a grassroots movement to recruit *him* was gathering force.

On the other hand, if Neff started drowning in new scandalous photos popping up every six hours and videos being released daily, no one could suspect *him* if he were overseeing the delivery of lifesaving drugs to poor Africans.

Lot of good photo ops there.

He could come back at the very height of the scandal, to witness Neff's shame.

Hmmm. He could be photographed stepping off the plane from Makongo, tanned, vigorous, a patriot, a philanthropist, just the man to step into a pervert's shoes.

He could see it very clearly. Above all he could see the headlines, clamoring for a new morality, journalists pressing around him as he got off the plane, shouting questions about his plans. Would he be willing to be drafted to replace reviled Senator Neff, caught in the mother of all scandals?

Why yes, yes he would. And in fact, on the tarmac of Richmond International Airport would be the perfect backdrop to answer the call of the people.

He was mentally drafting a catchy reply to the press that would be on the tarmac to greet him when his cell phone gave its distinctive incoming text buzz.

Frowning, he checked the display, annoyed at the interruption.

Unidentified caller.

He was tempted to just leave it, but these were days in which a lot of stuff was happening. He had to be on top of it all.

He clicked open the message and his blood froze. He

was sure his heart stopped for a second or two in his chest, then thundered to life again in a frantic tattoo of panic.

Hi Bowen, long time no see. I've found out some very interesting information about you here in Laka. I hear you're looking for me and you're on your way to Makongo. I'll be in the lobby of the Etoile Africaine this afternoon at 4 p.m. local time. You want me? Come and get me, you son of a bitch. Claire

LAKA

"Hello, Bowen." Claire stood up, making sure her hands were visible. "I can't say it's nice to see you again."

Bowen McKenzie's easy charm was gone. He was tense, nostrils white with stress. Dressed elegantly, as always, in a tailored white linen shirt that screamed Armani, chocolate linen trousers, kidskin Gucci loafers without socks.

"Claire." He showed his teeth. "You were supposed to be dead."

"Sorry to disappoint you, Bowen. Now, it's not that I don't trust you or anything, but I'll have to ask you to turn in a circle."

He bent his head and slowly turned on his heel.

Nothing about Bowen was accidental. The clothes were fairly tight and lightweight. Nothing weighed down his trouser pockets, front or back. There was no way he could be carrying a gun.

He could have a knife in a sheath along his back, or a garrotting wire in his belt, but neither could be easily accessed. And it wasn't Bowen's style. He had other people get their hands dirty for him.

"Fair is fair." His blue eyes blazed. "Now you turn around."

Claire hated turning her back to him, but she did it, slowly, sure that the loose white shirt hid the miniaturized vidcam. She was boiling with emotions—fear and anxiety, of course. But the top layer was rage, white-hot and fierce, though nothing showed on her face.

This man had killed Marie, was killing sick people every day. None of it meant anything to him. Marie and the patients in the New Day Foundation's hospitals and clinics were merely pawns to be moved about on a chessboard so he could get what he wanted.

Money and power.

It always came down to that.

But pitted against him were four men and one woman who weren't in the iron grip of lust for power and money and they were going to bring him down. Oh, yes. Particularly since she also had two aces up her sleeve.

Her earpiece had clicked four times. Dan and his men had found Bowen's men, taken them out and were now in position.

She'd fought with Dan for hours over this. Dan didn't want a showdown in Makongo, where Bowen could call on Mbutu.

She knew Bowen. He wouldn't want Mbutu anywhere near this. But he *would* have his guard down, knowing he was on friendly territory and knowing Claire was alone, in a country that was essentially his.

She looked around. Dan and his men were nowhere to be seen. She didn't know where they were hiding, but she had no doubt they were there, weapons at the ready.

The ancient lobby was deserted. Claire had had a quiet talk with the manager, saying that she was to meet with Mr. Bowen McKenzie himself and that Mr. McKenzie wanted privacy.

The manager had nearly tripped over his own feet to get out of her way. There were no guests, no one at the front desk, no bellhops.

The lobby looked like a hotel would after the end of the world. Beaten down, abandoned. It had once had lush palms in huge enameled vases, so thick they had mimicked the jungle outside.

Now the palms were desiccated, thin brown leaves pointing to the ground, making a chittering noise whenever anyone walked by.

"Open your purse," Bowen said and she did. She even emptied it for him on the marble-topped table, her effects making a light clatter as they fell out.

He poked a long finger through them—leather cosmetics bag, satphone, pocket diary he thumbed through, keys. He picked the keys up with a lazy smile.

"Yes, I know," Claire said in a low voice. "It doesn't open up anything now except for a heap of ashes."

He checked her satphone, weighing it in his palm.

"It's off," she assured him.

"Okay. Let's sit down."

They sat, by unspoken mutual agreement keeping their hands on the table.

He was checking her over and she knew he wasn't seeing the Claire he thought he would. The Claire of her medical reports—crushed, grieving, unstable.

She kept her eyes steady on his and he finally blinked.

No, not the old Claire.

She watched him digest that.

Finally, Bowen looked away a second, then brought his gaze back to hers. He leaned back in his chair, body language clear. He was communicating that he was relaxed, that he didn't have anything to fear.

Boy, was he wrong.

"Where's your jarhead boyfriend?"

She turned her face utterly blank. "Who?"

"The Marine. Weston."

She gave a small frown then smoothed her face out. "Oh, him. I wanted some information about the bombing, but he was in the embassy building the whole time. He didn't have any information at all."

Bowen's mouth lifted in a cruel smile. "Got scared off by my men, did he?"

Claire bowed her head, scrutinizing the marble tabletop. "Yes," she whispered. "It was too much for him."

"You should choose who you fuck better, my dear. You should have chosen me."

She kept staring at the tabletop so he wouldn't see the revulsion that went through her at the thought of touching Bowen.

"He just couldn't take it." She talked to her clasped hands, voice low and sad. "I had some questions to ask him. You attacked twice and he decided that answering my questions wasn't too good for his health."

Dan was listening in on every word. She hoped he wasn't having a stroke right about now.

She lifted her head to look at Bowen, putting weariness and vulnerability on her face. They stared at each other in silence.

"I want you to know," he said finally, when it was clear that she wasn't going to speak first, "that I'm in Laka for business. I was planning on coming anyway when I got your ridiculous SMS. I don't know what you're talking about, but out of a sense of duty, because you were injured in the line of duty and we were, after all, colleagues, I agreed to meet you here." He ostentatiously checked his ultra-thin Patek Philippe watch. "And I can give you about ten minutes, so shoot."

Unfortunate terminology, because that was precisely what Claire wanted to do. Shoot him right through his black, treacherous heart. It surprised her how much she wanted that.

She wanted payback. For Marie. For Dan. For the thousands of cancer-striken Makongans who died with tap water in their veins instead of chemotherapy. For her father. For her lost year.

"Then I'll be quick," she answered. "It's taken me a year to go after you, but I want you to know that I know exactly what you did on the twenty-fifth of November last year."

He leaned forward aggressively. "I don't have the faintest idea what you're talking about. On the twenty-fifth I was in Algiers, having talks. And anyway, you don't remember anything. Everyone knows you have amnesia."

Nobody except her doctors knew she had amnesia. Only someone who'd checked her medical files would know that.

Claire leaned forward slightly, too, as if to echo him, but actually to center his image in the vidcam. "You most definitely were not in Algiers, you were in Laka. You took advantage of the Thanksgiving holiday and the cover of a supposed rebel uprising to bomb your own embassy. You thought the embassy was deserted, but I was *there*, Bowen. Marie Diur came to get me to show me what you were doing. And what I saw was—you directing the theft of a truck from the compound—"

Bowen slapped the table with his hand. "That's the most ridiculous thing I've ever heard of! Why would I rob a *truck* for God's sake?"

"Because it had at least ten million dollars' worth of medicine and medical equipment in it," Claire answered quietly. "You stole the truck and replaced it with a truck full of explosives so powerful the explosion dug a crater twelve feet deep. Recognize these?"

She threw the two packets of medicine she'd taken from Aba onto the table.

Bowen looked, but didn't touch them.

"I don't know if this was your original plan or if you decided that stealing ten million dollars wasn't enough, but you've been raking in money all year off counterfeit drugs. And that's going to stop. Right now, right this minute, two hundred randomly chosen specimens of every drug distributed by the New Day Foundation is being tested by labs in England. And you know what? I'll bet they'll find that two out of three is a fake. So what is the New Day Foundation going to say to that, hmm? Do your rich guy sponsors know you're raking off two-thirds of the money?"

He'd turned beet red then white with rage. He reached out and grabbed her wrist, holding her tightly, digging hard with his fingers.

A red dot appeared on his right shoulder. Claire shook her head. *Not yet.*

"You little bitch!" His voice was low, enraged. Spittle flew when he talked. "You have no idea what you're dealing with here. I have money behind me, money and power like you can't dream of. And I'm going to crush you. Who's going to believe you? Poor Claire. Poor, addled Claire, who was so messed up by the explosion. Who lost her memory. Who's going to believe you instead of me?"

He let go of her with a harsh laugh. Poor Claire against Bowen McKenzie. In his mind, there was no contest there. He'd been shaken for a second, but now he was back in control.

Time for him to lose it.

"Do you want to know what I saw, Bowen? That afternoon? And I'm willing to swear to in court? I saw you direct the truck full of medicine and equipment out of the embassy compound and I saw you direct a truck full of explosives in. Do you know what that makes you, Bowen? A terrorist, that's what. And guilty of treason. The needle isn't good enough for you. But you know what else?" She leaned forward again, tactics forgotten. She was white-hot with fury now and wasn't measuring her words. "That's not the worst thing you did, horrible as that was. The most horrible thing was you seeing Marie and directing one of your soldiers to shoot her through the head. You didn't even hesitate, you son of a bitch. You saw her and you ordered her put down like you'd put down a dog."

"I don't know what you're talking about," he said with a smirk.

Claire balled her fists to keep from hitting him. As far as she was concerned, there was no difference between Bowen and any murderous third-world tyrant. Both were willing to kill, as casually as you'd swat a fly, to get what they wanted. The evil loose in the world wasn't abstract. It was sitting right across from her in an Armani linen shirt.

He was shaking his head. "And anyway, you could never prove anything in a court of law. You're whistling in the wind, Claire." He was smiling at her. How could anyone have thought Bowen was handsome? His regular features no longer hid his essence, the monster that was inside.

She was going to bring him down if it was the last thing she ever did.

"You were caught on tape, Bowen. Every second of it. The switch with the trucks, killing Marie, all of it. And you're going to spend the rest of your life in solitary in federal prison. Unless they go for the death penalty."

His cheekbones turned red but he still had that smirk. She wanted to slap it off his face so badly her hands itched.

"There you're wrong, my dear. Poor, delusional Claire, making up stories. The security cameras were down." He gave a truly reptilian smile. "Everything you're saying is only in your head. Your sick head."

Oh, Bowen, she thought. *You're going down.*

"Most of the cameras were down, yes. Because someone had cut the wires. The Marines found signs of sabotage, the wires cut, not broken. But you know what, Bowen?" Claire leaned forward just a little more. His face would fill the image she was recording. "The security camera over the motor pool wasn't down. There'd been problems with it the day before and instead of repairing the wires, the maintenance guys just spliced the feed into the backup generator. So when you cut the wires of the security cameras, you overlooked that one. The tape was archived and forgotten about, until the Marines checked it this morning. And there you are, Bowen, in all your glory . . ."

Bowen jolted in his seat and reached out again, grabbing her wrist, twisting it. "You *bitch*! You *lie*, you fucking bitch! All the cameras were out that day. I made sure of it myself. And as for your fucking friend, she just stuck her nose where it didn't belong. Just like you have. And you're going to end up just as dead as she did."

"You didn't need to kill Marie," she said steadily. "It wasn't necessary."

"Of course it was necessary, you bitch. She would have—"

His mouth closed with a snap and Claire felt a surge of triumph. His words came out slurred, as if he were drunk. He twisted her wrist harder.

"Okay, you fucking asked for this. You're going to walk out right now with me. My men will be right behind us—"

"Your men aren't here, Bowen."

His eyes went wide. She could see the whites all around the pupils. "What the fuck does that mean?"

"Look down," she said softly. "Look at yourself."

He stared at her, jaws bunching, trying to guess what her bluff was. Finally, he looked down at himself.

"That little dot, Bowen? That's a laser sight. Attached to a Remington sniper rifle. And behind that is a Marine sniper. None better." Another dot appeared on his chest. "*Two* Marine snipers. And your men have been taken out. You're all on your own, Bowen." She unbuttoned the first two buttons of her shirt, tapping at the plastic. "And by the way, everything you said is on tape and has just been loaded onto YouTube. Life as you know it is over."

Bowen screamed, his muscles bunched to deliver a blow and . . . he fell backward out of his chair, a red hole in his shoulder, the rifle's report echoing in the hotel lobby.

Claire slumped in relief and realized that she was sweating like a pig. And shaking.

"Guys," she murmured, knowing they could pick up the feed. "You can come out now."

Dan, Jesse, Frank and Dave appeared from the shadows, hard-eyed men, cradling their rifles, prodding Bowen's men in front of them. Bowen's men had their hands handcuffed behind their backs.

Bowen was screaming obscenities, so enraged Claire wondered whether he even felt the gunshot wound. Adrenaline must have been flooding his body because he rose to his knees, then he stood up, slipping a little in the pool of his own blood on the white marble floor.

Two more men appeared, a tall, grizzled African American and a short, broad man. The short man was armed, a Glock in a well-used shoulder holster.

"Well done, Claire," the tall African American said and smiled at her.

"Ambassador." Claire sketched a tremulous smile. She knew she should offer her hand to the new US ambassador to Makongo, Calvin Cooley, the man she most admired and respected in the Foreign Service, but her hands were shaking.

The respect was mutual. When she'd asked him to come and witness the exchange with Bowen, he'd agreed without question.

The short man, Leo Kellerman, the new FBI legat, turned to Bowen. "On behalf of the US government, I hereby arrest you on charges of murder, treason, terrorism and massive fraud."

Bowen swayed on his feet, eyes wild.

"Oh God, Boss." The man Dan had prodded turned a teary face to Bowen. "I'm so sorry." He sniffled, unable to wipe his nose. "They got the drop on us, I'm so sorry—"

"You fucking son of a bitch, this is all your fault. If you'd killed the bitch the first time this would never have happened!"

Bowen was screaming, spittle flying, every cell of his body enraged. His hand snaked out, grabbed the legat's gun out of its holster and before anyone could stop him, drilled a bullet through the man's head.

Half a second later four shots rang out and Bowen crumpled, lifeless, to the floor.

Claire was rooted to the spot, unable to move, unable to breathe. The noise of the shots filled her head, deafening her. Bowen's body on the floor was riddled with bullets, a small lake of blood already appearing under him, half his face and chest shot away.

She swayed and was caught in two strong arms. She finally was able to pull in a breath and smelled him. Dan. Gunshot and musk and . . . Dan.

Safety. Strength.

She gave a mewling sound and buried her head in his chest, gasping, trembling. He tightened his arms, covered the back of her head with a large hand, and simply absorbed her trembling into himself.

A weight on her shoulder, a large, gentle black hand.

"You did good, Blondie," a deep voice rumbled way over her head. "Was any of that true? About the drugs being tested and the security camera that recorded everything?"

Claire shook her head against Dan's chest and the ambassador laughed. It sounded like thunder rumbling in the distance.

"Gunny, you've got yourself a remarkable woman, there. You keep her safe, you hear?"

"Yessir," Dan answered and oh, God, just hearing his voice made her feel better.

"She's scary brave, Gunny. And wily. You're going to want to watch your step in the future."

She felt more than heard Dan's laugh in his chest.

"Yessir. I know that, sir. But I'm willing to take the risk."

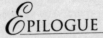

EPILOGUE

DAN stepped quietly into his new, luxurious office. Claire was focused on her computer monitor and when she was working like this, man, it was like she and the computer were one. Claire concentrating was a sight to see.

Uh-oh.

She was *smiling*.

A smiling Claire and computers was not a happy combo. That smile, in particular, spelled trouble. Wicked and knowing, which usually meant that she was doing something she shouldn't. Something probably illegal.

Dan sighed and she turned around, her face lighting up when she saw him.

Oh man.

He rubbed his chest. When she smiled at him like that, his heart just gave this enormous thwack inside his chest, even after a year of marriage. He should maybe see a cardiologist.

Claire held out her hand and he took it. "So," she said. "How did it go?"

He'd just come back from talks with the CEO of a small, but very rich private bank.

"Really well. We've got the contract. 100K a year, for five years, plus expenses."

She threw her arms around his neck and gave him a smacking kiss on the cheek. "Well done! You've got the golden touch."

They were doing really well. They'd moved into new premises, in this swank high-rise near Crystal City with three times the space he'd had before. Roxanne now oversaw an office with two receptionists and four secretaries. Dan had six men on retainer, all ex-Marines, all excellent, for jobs that required physical security. More were in the pipeline.

Though Claire never took credit for bringing Bowen down, letting journalists think it was an FBI sting, the top echelons of government knew. They were grateful and threw work their way whenever they could.

Even the New Day Foundation's backers showed their gratitude by offering a very lucrative contract.

They were starting to get feelers for jobs abroad, mainly in Latin America, though Dan was ambivalent about that. The thought of leaving Claire for even a couple of days was painful. But they were growing fast and soon travel would be routine.

His men were top-of-the-line when it came to planning and executing a security program in a dangerous world and word had gotten around. Dan was going to have to expand the company once again in a couple of months.

Weston and Weston Security was a runaway success.

But what W and W was *really* good at was computer security, and that was all Claire. Nobody could beat her. Nobody could even touch her. She was the rainmaker of the company.

Dan had landed the contract because the computer security program he had outlined for the bank was a dealmaker. But actually, it was Claire's program. By all rights, it was Claire who should have gone to the incredibly plush office of the CEO on the forty-first floor to hear praise and then sign on the dotted line. But that way lay disaster. They'd tried it a couple of times, but the instant Claire opened her mouth, she lost the client.

The client would try to follow the first sentence or two, then his brain popped, whirred, shorted, then just shut down. Claire danced rings around the men at the top and they didn't like it, so she stayed in the office, where she was happiest.

It was what she'd done as a DIA analyst and it was what she did in her own company and she loved it like that.

It all worked out just fine.

Everything had worked out fine. The New Day Foundation now randomly analyzed the medicine it sent, and the Bowen McKenzie scandal toppled the general. He was replaced with a young, energetic, Harvard-trained economist who was bringing the country back to life, according to Claire's friend Aba. Claire and Aba spoke on the phone often and there were plans for a visit stateside.

They'd been married a year and Dan had no idea that happiness on this scale was even possible. He loved her and she scared the shit out of him.

Particularly when she smiled like that.

He dropped a kiss on her perfect little nose. But before he could get tempted to kiss her mouth—once he did that, he was a goner—he pulled away and looked sternly at her. Or tried to.

"What were you doing when I walked in?"

She batted her eyes at him and reached up to kiss him, knowing that would be the end of the interrogation.

But Dan was tough. He was a Marine, after all. He held her off.

"Come on . . . tell the truth. You were cracking some site, weren't you?" He rolled his eyes at her innocent expression. "You know, honey, you're going to end up in jail if you don't watch out. I'll spend the rest of my days bringing you cake and books in the brig."

"Well, I did get some interesting info."

"Interesting enough to go to jail?" he asked glumly and she laughed.

"And here I thought you were so brave. Tough guy, my ass."

"Okay, I'm a wuss. Particularly when it comes to the thought of you being incarcerated. So . . . spill it. Who were you cracking?"

Claire twined her arms around his neck and kissed him, pulling away before he could take control of the kiss.

"I was . . . um . . . visiting the records of a lab in Baltimore. You know which one."

Oh, God, he did. His heart started thudding. His mouth went dry. "Yeah? And what did you find out?"

She kissed him again. "Congratulations, Gunny. It's a boy."

Enter the rich world of historical romance with Berkley Books.

Lynn Kurland

Patricia Potter

Betina Krahn

Jodi Thomas

Anne Gracie

Love is timeless.

penguin.com